PENGUIN BOOKS

PRISON WRITING IN 20TH-CENTURY AMERICA

One of America's preeminent cultural historians, H. Bruce Franklin is generally acknowledged to be the world's leading authority on American prison literature. He is currently the John Cotton Dana Professor of English and American Studies at Rutgers University in Newark.

OTHER BOOKS BY H. BRUCE FRANKLIN

The Wake of the Gods: Melville's Mythology
Future Perfect: American Science Fiction of the 19th Century
Who Should Run the Universities (with John A. Howard)
From the Movement: Toward Revolution
Herman Melville's Mardi *(editor)*
Herman Melville's The Confidence Man *(editor)*
Back Where You Came From
The Scarlet Letter *and Hawthorne's Critical Writings (editor)*
Prison Literature in America: The Victim as Criminal and Artist
Countdown to Midnight
American Prisoners and Ex-Prisoners: An Annotated Bibliography
Robert A. Heinlein: America as Science Fiction
Vietnam and America: A Documented History (with Marvin
Gettleman, Jane Franklin, and Marilyn Young)
War Stars: The Superweapon and the American Imagination
M.I.A. or Mythmaking in America
The Vietnam War in American Stories, Songs, and Poems

Prison Writing

in 20th-Century America

EDITED BY
H. BRUCE FRANKLIN

WITH A FOREWORD
BY TOM WICKER

PENGUIN BOOKS

FOR MY GRANDCHILDREN

Emma Lourdes Amelia Dunning Franklin
Gregory Saboya Franklin
Samantha Michelle Franklin
James Bruce Franklin

PENGUIN BOOKS

Published by the Penguin Group
Penguin Group (USA) Inc., 375 Hudson Street, New York, New York 10014, U.S.A.
Penguin Group (Canada), 10 Alcorn Avenue, Toronto,
Ontario, Canada M4V 3B2 (a division of Pearson Penguin Canada Inc.)
Penguin Books Ltd, 80 Strand, London WC2R 0RL, England
Penguin Ireland, 25 St Stephen's Green, Dublin 2, Ireland (a division of Penguin Books Ltd)
Penguin Group (Australia), 250 Camberwell Road, Camberwell,
Victoria 3124, Australia (a division of Pearson Australia Group Pty Ltd)
Penguin Books India Pvt Ltd, 11 Community Centre,
Panchsheel Park, New Delhi – 110 017, India
Penguin Group (NZ), cnr Airborne and Rosedale Roads,
Albany, Auckland, New Zealand (a division of Pearson New Zealand Ltd)
Penguin Books (South Africa) (Pty) Ltd, 24 Sturdee Avenue,
Rosebank, Johannesburg 2196, South Africa

Penguin Books Ltd, Registered Offices: 80 Strand, London WC2R 0RL, England

First published in Penguin Books 1998

20 19 18 17 16 15 14 13 12

LIBRARY OF CONGRESS CATALOGING-IN-PUBLICATION DATA
Prison writing in 20th-century America / edited by H. Bruce Franklin.
p.   cm.
Includes bibliographical references.
ISBN 0 14 02.7305 0 (pbk.)
1. Prisoner's writings, American. 2. Prisoners—United States—
Literary collections. 3. Prisons—United States—Literary
collections. 4. American literature—20th century. I. Franklin,
H. Bruce (Howard Bruce), 1934– .
PS508.P7P68 1998
810.8'09206927—dc21   97-42354

Printed in the United States of America
Set in Stempel Garamond
Designed by Sabrina Bowers

CONTENTS

THE AMERICAN GULAG TODAY

ACKNOWLEDGMENTS

My research on the lives, works, and whereabouts of various authors owes a considerable debt to Dr. Karen Franklin of Franklin Investigations, Folsom Librarian Dennis McCargar, Shirley Cloyes, Peter Sussman, Judith Scheffler, Joseph Bruchac, Karlene Faith, Ada Coddington, Jack W. Fleming, Bruce Jackson, John A. Pyros, Janine Pommy Vega, and Director Jane Moriarty of the American Poetry Archives at San Francisco State University.

My greatest debts are, as always, to Jane Morgan Franklin, my lifetime companion, who participated in every stage of composition, read the manuscript, and contributed more than I can possibly acknowledge.

FOREWORD

American prisons, with their stone walls and barbed wire fences, metal gates and gun towers, have a dual function: to keep *us* out as well as *them* in.

That is why this anthology is so important and so riveting, and why prison authorities frown on and do their best to put a stop to the kind of inmate writing sampled here. Writers scribbling away in their cells or in limited prison libraries tell us most of what we know about these dark fortresses of gloom and terror. They disclose the nasty, brutish details of the life within—a life the authorities would rather we not know about, a life so far from conventional existence that the accounts of those who experience it exert the fascination of the unknown, sometimes the unbelievable.

Can these things really happen in prosperous, freedom-loving America? Can Patricia McConnel be writing from experience when in her novel *Sing Soft, Sing Loud* she describes the blank, dead-eyed look she calls "jailface" and observes that it "ain't necessarily a bad thing to have, 'cause the minute a screw knows you're scared or weak she's got the upper hand, and she jumps on you with both feet and don't let up 'til she's had her satisfaction, which in most cases is to see your spirit dead. But if you're walking around with jailface she can't tell if something is still stirring in there or not. Most likely she thinks by your look that you're already dead. . . ."

Could it ever have been true in democratic America that—not in the benighted Deep South but in Niagara Falls, New York—so-called vagrants got "fifteen seconds [in court] and thirty days [in prison]" with no chance to defend themselves or even plead to the charge? Yes, testifies Jack London, one of the greatest American writers, who suffered conviction and imprisonment in just that fashion in 1894. And as a reporter in modern times, I've seen defendants hustled as impersonally through, and sentenced as automatically in, municipal, particularly night, courts.

Typically enough, in self-preservation, Jack London learned in his thirty days in the Erie County Penitentiary to scam, cheat, and coerce other inmates. "A broom-handle, end-on, in the face, had a very sobering effect," he writes in "The Pen," quoted here. And of his fellow "trustys" ("hall-men" at Erie): "Oh, we were wolves, believe me—just like the fellows who do business in Wall Street."

That suggests another theme of this anthology, one that some readers may resist: what happens inside the walls inevitably reflects the society outside.

In 1971 during the Attica prison uprising, American society was torn by protest—against the oppression of blacks, the war in Vietnam, unresponsive government, fossilized society, predatory capitalism. It was not surprising, therefore, that the rhetoric of prison orators was heavily Marxist: "Oppressed peoples of the world, throw off your chains!" Most inmates, however, actually were rebelling against the usual harsh prison conditions (overcrowding, poor food, one shower a week, etc.). At about the same time, prison writers such as Iceberg Slim, Mshaka, and Piri Thomas—whose work is found in this anthology—were being radicalized by events in the outside society.

That what happens outside recurs inside is obviously true of prison violence, in what is statistically the world's most violent nation. Here's what happened in one of Jerome Washington's (only semifictional) prison stories to Bo Green, a convict who tried to fight back against a guard who told him "you're my hoss and I'm your boss":

> Years later when Bo Green was let out of solitary, he was blind in one eye and walked with a limp. His brace of beautiful white teeth had been broken from the gums, and nerve damage caused his right hand to twitch. . . . Now he just wanders sort of aimlessly around the yard and sometimes he sits in the sun. Once in a while he mutters, "I ain't nobody's hoss. . . ."

Jerome Washington was writing of contemporary American prisons, Jack London of those a century ago. But things have not changed much and the reason is not hard to discern: law and order are harder to maintain in a prison than in any town or city anywhere. Guards are too few, too fearful, too ignorant, too often corrupt; the "population" is largely unskilled and unlearned, hopeless, self-loathing, resentful of society, and inured to violence —outside as well as in. Where the only rule is what the powerful (whether guards or guarded) say it is, and the only appeal is to violence, the result is bound to be what prisons are: citadels of lawlessness and violence.

By what logic, moreover, does society hope to make men better, more productive citizens by locking them in cages? Particularly now that most efforts at what once was known hopefully as "rehabilitation" have been abandoned under the pressures of public fear of crime and political reaction to that fear?

In 1995, for only one example, New York State abolished its twenty-year-old program of financial support for twenty-three colleges that had offered opportunities for higher education to inmates in forty-five state prisons. The approximately 3,500 "criminals" who had annually taken advantage of these opportunities later composed a recidivism rate of 26 percent against 48 percent for inmates in general. Bear this in mind when studying Malcolm X's moving account, excerpted here, of his intellectual awakening through reading and studying while doing prison time.

H. Bruce Franklin's scheme in this harrowing book—to which he contributes illuminating notes and brief sketches of the prison writers included—is to trace the "development" of the prison from the leasing of convicts and the use of chain gangs in the South after the Civil War to today's costly, crowded, ineffective (as I believe) institutions. The system began—as do so many American mistakes—in a reform impulse, the idea that if offenders were isolated, shielded from the public mockery that had accompanied hangings and the stocks, given time to repent, and worked hard, they could be turned away from crime and transformed into useful citizens. Philadelphia's Walnut Street prison was constructed in 1790 for that purpose.

This basically humanitarian idea, like most well-intended reforms, hasn't worked out as expected—in earlier times, Franklin tells us, because it "turned into a convenient rationale for using prisons as a source of extremely cheap labor"; in our era because incarceration is seen primarily as deserved punishment, the harsher the better, for "murderers, rapists and thieves," rather than as an opportunity to redeem the offender.

The Thirteenth Amendment, which abolished slavery—another reform impulse—actually encouraged some forms of incarceration by providing that "neither slavery nor involuntary servitude, except as a punishment for crime whereof the party shall have been duly convicted" could exist in the United States. Using the "punishment" clause as a legal basis, southern states in the latter half of the nineteenth century developed ingenious ways to sentence blacks who once had been slaves—and who often were innocent of any crime save having no job or address—to new forms of involuntary servitude as convicts (in effect, slave laborers) in work gangs on farms, in mines and factories, and on the railroads.

Nathaniel Hawthorne's son, Julian, who did a stretch in Atlanta Federal Penitentiary (for mail fraud, at age sixty-seven), wrote in 1914 that his jail experience had convinced him that by such methods "we are creating some five hundred thousand slaves, white and black, each year."

Ancient history? As late as 1936, Franklin reminds us, *The New York Times* reported on a black youth sentenced to life imprisonment in Alabama for the theft of $1.50. Blacks today get longer sentences for smoking cheap crack than do whites for sniffing expensive powdered cocaine—a discrimination for which President Clinton sees no need to seek redress. And blacks are the most incarcerated Americans (1,947 per 100,000, as opposed to 306 per 100,000 whites), though they are only about 12 percent of the population.

Franklin takes due note of one salutary result—the development in the old work-gang days of black music of "the blues," arguably the most significant contribution of the United States to world culture. Not many readers may know, for instance, what Franklin relates: that the popular country music ballad "Midnight Special" was first sung by blacks in southern prison gangs, where "its everlovin' light" was a longed-for pardon.

In the main, however, American prisons have had and still have few redeeming features, as this book makes all too clear. This is not the place to repeat in detail the argument I and others have made elsewhere, that prisons cost too much and are too ineffective in the prevention of crime to justify the reliance placed on them by the public and the criminal justice system, or to warrant their indifference to alternative treatments of offenders. But those who read the writings culled by H. Bruce Franklin from the vast and impressive library of prison literature will be left with little doubt that prisons and the violence and despair they symbolize have been and are still a blot on American life and history.

Nevertheless, as Franklin points out, some states now spend more on incarceration of offenders than they do on higher education, and the percentage of Americans imprisoned since 1980 has tripled—though there has been no commensurate decline in the incidence of crime and violence. He details the vengeful, fearful attitudes, exemplified in the popular slogan "lock 'em up and throw away the key," that have led to what he calls "the American Gulag."

Above all, however, this anthology provides unforgettable testimony to the human spirit: from its existence even in the least of these, our brothers and sisters, to its survival in the most unforgiving and uncharitable conditions.

—TOM WICKER

INTRODUCTION

One of the most extraordinary achievements of twentieth-century American culture is the literature that has come out of the nation's prisons. True, there have been many eminent individual prison writers from other countries, such as Boethius, Cervantes, Campanella, Thomas More, Walter Raleigh, John Donne, Richard Lovelace, John Bunyan, Daniel Defoe, Leigh Hunt, Oscar Wilde, Maxim Gorky, Chernyeshevsky, Dostoyevsky, Solzhenitsyn, François Villon, Voltaire, Diderot, the Marquis de Sade, and Jean Genet. But unlike the works of these individuals, modern American prison writings constitute a coherent body of literature with a unique historical significance and cultural influence.

This book offers a representative sample of that literature. It consists of writings by twentieth-century American prisoners. Some of the authors are prominent figures in American letters, while others are virtually unknown. The works have been chosen for what they reveal both about prison, specifically the modern American prison, and about human beings in the most difficult circumstances.

Each selection in this volume is about prison experience. Imposing this limitation eliminated the majority of works by American convicts and actually excluded those convict authors who chose not to write about prison. The most obvious example of the latter is O. Henry, arguably the most widely read of all, who acquired his nom de plume and his characteristic style while incarcerated for three years in the Ohio State Penitentiary.

But this limitation also focuses the collection into a vision of America from the bottom, an anatomy of the American prison, and an exploration of the meanings of imprisonment. To comprehend what this literature offers, we need to understand the special role of the American prison system.

THE PRISON SYSTEM: MADE IN AMERICA

We in America have become so used to the prison as a major institution of our society that we tend to forget that the prison system is a recent—and especially American—innovation. Prior to the American Revolution, imprisonment was seldom used as a punishment for crime in England and was rarer still in its American colonies. Even in London, between 1770 and 1774 only 2.3 percent of convicted criminals were sentenced to prison.[1] What then was done with convicts?

Tens of thousands were transported to the American colonies, especially Virginia, Maryland, and Pennsylvania, with smaller numbers going to New Jersey, Delaware, Georgia, New York, the Carolinas, and Massachusetts. These men and women were eagerly bought to be used mainly as plantation laborers and house servants (George Washington as a child was tutored by a transported felon and then later owned convicts).[2] But resentment toward Britain using the colonies as a dumping ground helped lead to the American Revolution (which in turn led Britain to open convict colonies in Australia as a replacement). A more provocative impetus to the revolution was England's main penal system: the notorious "Bloody Code," which provided the death penalty for over two hundred offenses. Executions were carried out before huge throngs of curiosity seekers, who also witnessed various forms of public torture, especially whipping, branding, mutilation, the stocks, and the pillory (which also led to death whenever the crowd hurled enough stones at the offender).

These capital and corporal punishments were designed as public spectacles. In stark contrast, the prison system institutionalized isolation and secrecy. Whereas the earlier modes of punishment were supposed to be witnessed by the public, the walls of the prison exclude the public from all direct knowledge of what is taking place behind them. The public is not supposed to know of or be concerned with any degradation or abuse going on inside the prison nor with the prisoners' responses to their punishment (unlike the confessions often expected on the scaffold or in the pillory, or the ballads sometimes attributed to the condemned). Hence, there has always been a contradiction between the prison and whatever literature is able to reach out from within its walls to those outside.

The modern prison was instituted by reformers who were appalled by the horrors of pre-industrial punishment, and who believed that criminals could be "reformed" by incarcerating them, forcing them to work, and preventing them from communicating with each other. The vanguard of penal reform emerged from the American Revolution, and the single most influential institution, often called "the cradle of the penitentiary," was the Quaker-inspired Walnut Street prison, constructed in Philadelphia in 1790. Two other American "penitentiaries" completed in the 1820s served as models for prison construction throughout Europe and the northern United States: Pennsylvania's Cherry Hill, prototype of the "separate system," where convicts were kept in perpetual solitary confinement; and New York's Auburn, prototype of the "silent system," where convicts marched in lockstep from their cells to labor together in factory-like settings and were whipped if they spoke.

The modern prison was part of the revolutionary transformation of industry and society that took place between the application of steam power in the 1760s and the American Civil War a century later. As industrial capitalism became dominant, the reformers' principle that prisoners should work as a means to achieve "reformation" turned into a convenient rationale for using prisons as a source of extremely cheap labor. The Civil War itself hastened this process, as prisoners in the North were forced to produce massive amounts of goods for the Union army.

One of the earliest books by an American convict, *An Autobiography of Gerald Toole*, published in 1862, is also one of the very first American literary narratives set inside an industrial workshop—along with Herman Melville's "The Tartarus of Maids" (1855) and Rebecca Harding Davis's "Life in the Iron Mills" (1861). Toole tells how the convicts' "pale, emaciated looks showed that the very life blood was being worked out of them" as they labor "from dawn to dark" to produce boots for the army and profits for the contractors who are using this Connecticut prison as their factory. Toole is brutally flogged for failing to produce twelve pairs of boots in one workday, and the next day, while his back is still oozing blood, he uses a shoe knife to kill the warden who is forcing him back to the flogging dungeon. Before being executed at the age of twenty-four, Toole managed to write his exposé of industrial slavery.

FROM PLANTATION TO PENITENTIARY

Meanwhile the United States was in the midst of a war against a breakaway confederation openly based on another form of imprisonment: African-American chattel slavery. Of course, prior to the Civil War this slavery was not legitimized or rationalized by any claim that the slaves were being punished for crimes. That was to come next.

Slavery in the United States did not end after the Civil War; it merely changed forms. The necessary legal transformation was effected in 1865 by the very amendment to the Constitution—Amendment 13—that abolished the old form of slavery:

> Neither slavery nor involuntary servitude, except as a punishment for crime whereof the party shall have been duly convicted, shall exist within the United States, or any place subject to their jurisdiction.

Amendment 13 actually wrote slavery *into* the Constitution of the United States, but only for those people legally defined as criminals.

The former slave states, led by Mississippi in late 1865, immediately devised legislation defining virtually every former slave as a criminal. Known as the Black Codes, these laws specified that many vaguely defined acts—such as "mischief" and "insulting gestures" —were crimes, but only if committed by a "free negro." Intermarriage was a crime to be punished by "confinement in the State penitentiary for life." Mississippi's Vagrancy Act defined "all free negroes and mulattoes over the age of eighteen" as criminals unless they could furnish written proof of a job at the beginning of every year.[3] In other states, "having no visible means of support" was a crime being committed by almost all the freed slaves. So was "loitering" (staying in the same place) and "vagrancy" (wandering). "Disturbing the peace," "creating a public nuisance," "lewd and lascivious conduct," "using profane language," "drunkenness"— all provided highly subjective and convenient definitions of crime.[4]

Criminalization of the former slaves was expedited by the fee system. Many local deputy sheriffs and police received no regular salary, but were paid a fee for each person arrested. The judge who tried the accused then drew his pay from the court costs he levied against those he found guilty. Whenever former slave owners, construction companies, labor contractors, or the state itself needed a supply of cheap labor, local sheriffs, police, and judges operating on the fee system obliged with alacrity. Black men and women would be rounded up, thrown in jail, convicted, and given fines they were of course unable to pay.

In many cases, the former slave owners or private contractors would pay their fines, and the "criminals" were then bound over to their creditors. Most of the southern states had laws making it a crime for persons in debt to leave the employ of their creditors; hence they became imprisoned slaves surrounded by armed guards and bloodhounds.

Those whose fines were not paid were openly enslaved. Some became leased convicts, an arrangement that had been emerging in the South even before the end of the Civil War to supplement the older form of slavery. The private lessee guarded, disciplined, fed, housed, and worked the convicts as he saw fit. The convict lease system had a big advantage for the enslavers: since they did not own the convicts, they lost nothing by working them to death. (For example, the death rate among leased Alabama black convicts during the year 1869 was 41 percent.[5])

Convicts were leased to railroad companies, coal mines, canal companies, plantation owners, brickyards, and sawmills in Tennessee, Alabama, Mississippi, Georgia, and the Carolinas. Florida leased most of its convicts to turpentine farms, others to phosphate mines. Much of the railroad system throughout the South was built by leased convicts, often packed in rolling iron cages moved from job to job, working and living in such hellish conditions that their life expectancy rarely exceeded two years. But their usefulness did not end with death. For example, the bodies of convicts leased to the mines and railroads of Tennessee were sold to the Medical School at Nashville.[6]

Convict leasing was gradually supplanted by other forms of prison slavery. Under "state use," the state uses prison products (such as license plates or office furniture manufactured in prison factories) or services (such as building public roads). The infrastructure of many southern states was built and maintained by convicts. For example, aged African-American women overseen by armed guards dug the campus of Georgia State College, and prisoners as young as twelve worked in chain gangs to maintain the streets of

Atlanta.[7] In the "state account" method, the state goes into business, selling products of convict labor on the market. The most monstrous examples of state account were the vast state prison plantations established in Arkansas, Tennessee, Mississippi, and Texas, where the cotton picked by the prisoners was manufactured into cloth by other prisoners in the state's prison cotton mills. These plantations dwarfed the largest cotton plantations of the slave South in size, brutality, and profitability.

Out of the prison experience of the African-American people came an astonishing contribution to American and world culture. The songs of slavery metamorphosed into the songs of prison, and scores of African-American convict artists then transmuted those collective prison songs into individual works that shaped the blues tradition at the heart of much twentieth-century American music.

The prison experience is explicit in many of the formative blues songs such as "Penal Farm Blues," "Prison Bound," " 'Lectric Chair Blues," "Chain Gang Trouble," "Back in Jail Again," "Mississippi Jail House Groan," "Shelby County Workhouse Blues," "The Escaped Convict," "My Home Is a Prison," "Jailhouse Fire Blues," "High Sheriff Blues," "Heah I Am in Dis Low-Down Jail," and the many different songs entitled "Prison Blues," "Jailhouse Blues," and "Chain Gang Blues." Many of the finest artists were prisoners and ex-prisoners: Bukka White, Leroy Carr, Charley Patton, Charles "Cow Cow" Davenport, Robert Pete Williams, Texas Alexander, Son House, Willie Newbern, and of course Leadbelly, Lightnin' Hopkins, whose ankles bore the scars of chain gang shackles, and Billie Holiday, who was first jailed at the age of ten for resisting a sexual assault.

The long-standing practice of rounding up black people for chain gang labor was so commonplace that it gave rise to a host of songs such as "Standin' On the Corner." In the dozens of variants of this song collected all over the South prior to World War II, the singer usually describes how he was "Standin' on the corner, doin' no harm," when "Up come a policeman and grab me by the arm." He is taken to a judge, who winks at the policeman, says "Nigger, you get some work to do," and sends him "shackle bound" for six months on the chain gang. The song typically ends with the lament:

> Miserin' for my honey, she miserin' for me
> But, Lawd, white folks won't let go holdin' me.[8]

In one of the many songs entitled "Chain Gang Blues," the singer starts off "Standin' on the road side, / Waitin' for the ball and chain" and ends up reassuring his woman, who "cried the whole night long" when he was sentenced, that he is only "goin' on the chain gang" until the fall (when presumably there will be less need for slave labor on the roads).

This forcible separation of men and women by the prison outdoes slavery. In the pre–Civil War South, even when individuals were removed from their wives or husbands or lovers they at least were allowed to live with other people of both sexes. In the modern prison system, people are usually removed from all members of the opposite sex, often for decades or even the rest of their lives.

One way to deal with unemployed young black men was—and is—to keep them from either competing on the labor market or from having children by sending them up for long terms, no matter what the crime. As *The New York Times* reported in the midst of the Depression, on October 1, 1936:

> Alabama's new Burglary Law was applied here for the first time today when a jury found James Thomas, Negro, guilty of burglary in which $1.50 was the loot and fixed his punishment at life imprisonment. The jurors had heard a strong plea from the prosecutor for the death penalty.

The great convict blues artist Bukka White sings about the separation from "my wife and home" in "Parchman Farm Blues," a song about the 16,000-acre prison farm that was Mississippi's single main source of revenue, where White was sent to toil on a life sentence. When White hears his sentence of toiling there for the rest of his life, he says "good-bye wife," "I hope some day, you will hear my lonesome song."

Sometimes it was the woman who was put in penal servitude:

> . . . On Nov. 15, 1909, Mary Jackson, for using abusive language, was fined $10 plus $25.10 costs and hired out as a farm hand for eight months and eleven days at $4 per month.[9]

> Milly Lee was a Negro woman convicted of using "abusive language" and fined one dollar and costs. She worked out the fine in two days, but it required nearly a year of labor to satisfy the "costs" consisting of fees to judge, sheriff, clerks and witnesses, totaling $132.[10]

African-American women were frequently given a sentence of "11.29"—one year on a chain gang. Leroy Carr, another great ex-convict blues artist, sings in "Eleven Twenty-Nine Blues" of how "my heart struck sorrow" when his "good gal" became a "long-chain woman that got 11.29"; because he's "got the blues so bad," he wants to ask the judge and the jailer, "Can I do my good gal's time myself?"[11]

Between the Civil War and World War II, many African Americans were held in bondage even without being convicted of a crime. Well into the 1930s, vast numbers of black people were still being forced to sign contracts in which they agreed to work under armed guards, to be locked up at night for "safe keeping," and to pay for any expenses incurred in recapturing them should they run away.[12] A remarkable narrative originally published in 1904 under the title "The New Slavery in the South—An Autobiography, by a Georgia Negro Peon," reprinted in the present volume, shows how "free" African-Americans were forced into prison slavery alongside convicts.

The evolution from plantation to penitentiary is perhaps best expressed in the work songs of African-American convicts, such as the three included here. For the cultural corollary of this evolution was the metamorphosis of slave songs into prison work songs and blues, which then became the tap root of later blues, jazz, and rock, as well as a prime source of modern prison literature.

THE EARLY MODERN AMERICAN PRISON

The systematic use of prisoners as slave laborers in the South was hardly a secret. The scale was massive, chain gangs were every-where, the prisoners were overwhelmingly black, and this new form of slave labor played a central role in the economy. In the North, prison slavery was on a smaller scale, was mostly concealed within the walls of the penitentiaries, was predominantly white, and played a somewhat different role in the political economy, mainly serving as a weapon to be used against the burgeoning union movement.

Moreover, while imprisoned black people in the South expressed their reenslavement in music that was a major component of African-American and eventually American culture, the northern prisoners at first left only a slim cultural record of their slavery, mostly in the form of writing by the few who had the necessary skills. Two examples in this volume come from the pens of Jack London and Kate Richards O'Hare.

Writing about what he saw as a key formative experience in his life, Jack London describes how he and other men were arrested as vagrants, incarcerated in New York State's Erie County Penitentiary, and put to work unloading barges on the Erie Canal. Kate Richards O'Hare, imprisoned for speaking out against conscription during World War I, was already a socialist and had keen insights into the labor she and other prisoners were forced to do by the U.S. government for the profits of private manufacturers.

In the first two decades of the twentieth century, most books by American convicts were authored by political prisoners such as Emma Goldman, Alexander Berkman, and Carlo de Fornaro. There were also some works by other literate convicts, typically convicted of white-collar crimes. One of these was Nathaniel Hawthorne's son, Julian, a popular and prolific author (he published close to forty books), who at the height of his career and at the age of sixty-seven served a year for mail fraud in the Atlanta Federal Penitentiary.

After his release, Julian Hawthorne worked nonstop on *The Subterranean Brotherhood*. In this 1914 prison narrative he directly confronted the ugly reality of prison slavery:

> Before the Civil War there were some millions of negro slaves in the South, whom to set free we spent some billions of dollars and several hundred thousand lives. It was held that the result was worth the cost. But to-day we are creating some five hundred thousand slaves, white and black, each year.

Hawthorne's horrific prison experience led him to this conclusion:

> Let every judge, attorney general, district attorney, and juryman at a trial spend a bona fide term in jail, and there would be no more convictions—prisons would end. Every convict and ex-convict knows that.[13]

One of the most popular pre–World War I works by a convict author was Donald Lowrie's first book, *My Life in Prison*. Published in 1912, this autobiography of a man driven to crime by poverty told of the prison slavery and torture endemic to San Quentin, but also gave a favorable account of the efforts of a new warden to make the system more humane. The book inspired Thomas Mott Osborne to embark on his career of prison reform; when he became warden of Sing Sing he brought Lowrie in as his adviser.

After World War I, a number of talented convict authors began to emerge on the American literary scene, and prison literature gained an important patron when H. L. Mencken became editor of *American Mercury* magazine in 1924. During the ten years of his editorship, among the notable convict authors who contributed regularly to the *Mercury* were Jim Tully and Ernest Booth, both represented in this collection. Though now obscure figures, Tully and Booth had a significant impact on popular culture, especially through Hollywood.

In the economic boom times of the 1920s, prison writing hardly posed any subversive threat. But then came the Crash of 1929, and immediately a wave of suppression swept over the convicts trying to write from inside the prison to the people outside. According to Herman K. Spector, the senior librarian at San Quentin, the crackdown on prison writers was a direct response to their attainments: "Ironically enough, their flurry of success set off a counterflow of reaction and prohibition, during which California adopted the policy that convicts were in prison 'to be punished, not to make money.' "[14] For a while, the suppression had devastating effects on prison writing, as Miriam Allen De Ford attested to in a 1930 article: "cells were searched all through *San Quentin*—not for narcotics or knives, but for manuscripts" to be confiscated and destroyed.[15]

The suppression of prison writers was broken dramatically by Robert E. Burns's best-seller, *I Am a Fugitive from a Georgia Chain Gang*, which became a national sensation when it was published in 1932, the same year that scores of coal miners striking in Harlan County, Kentucky, were imprisoned for "criminal syndicalism," a year in which over a quarter-million acres of land in the United States were under cultivation by convicts.[16] A World War I veteran suffering from what was then known as "shell shock," Burns had been sentenced to six to ten years on a Georgia chain gang for a minor robbery. He managed to escape when a black convict used a sledgehammer to help him slip out of the shackles around his emaciated ankles in 1922. Burns fled to Chicago and by 1929 was a prominent editor and businessman when he was be-

trayed as a fugitive, extradited, and sent back to become the thirty-
third white man among the 102 convicts in Georgia's most brutal
chain gang camp. Escaping again, Burns was living a furtive existence under false names in New Jersey when he published his
shocking exposé of the living hell of prison slavery. Later in 1932,
a powerful movie version of Burns's prison experience, starring
Paul Muni as Burns, exposed millions more Americans to some of
the facts of American prison life.

As the Depression made poverty and crime intrude more and
more into everyday life, prison literature continued to gain a wider
and more appreciative audience. With overwhelming unemployment and a bottomless supply of cheap labor, prison slavery in the
North and West became more marginal. But the convict authors of
the 1930s—like the African-American creators of prison songs—
could now speak to an audience that shared much of their own
experience.

Two important American authors who emerged in the 1930s,
Chester Himes and Nelson Algren, both saw prison as integral to
the larger society. Himes's potent imagination was actually forged
in the matrix of prison, as shown in his very early tale, written
during his years of incarceration, "To What Red Hell?" Algren's
short story "El Presidente de Méjico" comes directly from his experience in a Texas prison (for stealing a typewriter).

THE MOVEMENT AND THE PRISON

During World War II and the postwar period extending into the
early 1960s, a diminished but steady stream of writing flowed rather
quietly from convicts and ex-convicts into American literature.
Then in 1965 came one of the most influential books in late-
twentieth-century American culture, *The Autobiography of Malcolm X*, the first published full-length autobiography of an
African-American common criminal and convict. Malcolm X's
seminal work marked the beginning of a new epoch in American
prison literature.

The Autobiography of Malcolm X appeared at a crucial moment
in American history. In 1965, the civil rights movement metamorphosed into the black liberation movement. The Mississippi Freedom Summer Project of 1964, during which civil rights workers

Michael Schwerner, Andrew Goodman, and James Chaney were murdered, occurred simultaneously with the first of the "long, hot summers," the urban rebellions that would climax in April 1968, the week after the murder of Martin Luther King, Jr., with simultaneous uprisings in 125 U.S. cities. And 1965 was the year when the covert U.S. war in Vietnam transformed into the open full-scale war that would end in U.S. defeat a decade later.

As the streams of rebellion and protest against social inequality and the Vietnam War began to merge in the late 1960s and early 1970s, they were fed in complex ways by the nation's prisons. Unlike earlier periods when reformers and even revolutionaries viewed prisoners mainly as victims to be rescued by progressive social movements, some of the radicals of the late sixties and beyond viewed prisoners as a potential revolutionary vanguard. The Black Panther Party, for example, deeply influenced by Malcolm X and Martinique revolutionary theorist Frantz Fanon, saw what they called the lumpenproletariat, not the traditional proletariat, as the true revolutionary class, and their main theoretical leaders included ex-convicts such as Eldridge Cleaver as well as George Jackson, the main spokesman of the movement inside the prison itself. At the same time, many members of what was called "the movement" were imprisoned because of their political or revolutionary activity. For example, Huey Newton and Assata Shakur were major leaders of the Panthers before they became prisoners. Meanwhile, many convicts and ex-convicts were becoming radicalized, as exemplified by four authors included in this collection: Iceberg Slim, Mshaka, Piri Thomas, and Jack Henry Abbott.

THE LITERARY RENAISSANCE

The political movement of the 1960s and 1970s generated an unprecedented surge of prison literature and also created an audience for it. Looking back to the Depression era, one can see a similar dialectic between the consciousness emerging inside the prison and the forces at work in the larger society. But the scale and significance of these interrelations in the earlier period are dwarfed by those in the later.

The political forces energized during the Vietnam War epoch

were also cultural forces. The movements for peace, the liberation of peoples of color, women's equality, gay rights, and economic democracy were all on one side of the culture wars of late-twentieth-century America. A major front in these wars was and is literature.

The battles about literature swirl around these questions: Are the works worthy of serious reading limited to a canon produced almost exclusively by a handful of "great" male white Europeans, Britons, and Americans? Is "great" literature distinguished by its timelessness and aesthetic excellence, or is the value of literature largely determined by its social content? Are aesthetic standards themselves expressions of class, gender, and ethnic values? Are complexity and ambiguity the hallmarks of literary excellence, or are simplicity and accessibility literary virtues? Does the meaning of a work reside inside its text or does its context shape its meaning? The social and political significance of these cultural questions is dramatized starkly by prison literature.

Indeed, it is no mere coincidence that prison literature exploded along with the political and social movements of the late 1960s and afterward. All the authors included in the final two sections of this book were profoundly influenced by those movements, and some were actually participants. But the significance of their literature in the culture wars goes much deeper than questions of influence and participation.

Most of these authors came from the very bottom of American society. Some were functionally illiterate, even at the point when they decided to become writers. For these—and thousands of other American convicts—Malcolm X, who taught himself to write by reading an entire dictionary (violating prison rules by continuing after cell lights were extinguished), remains an inspiration. The power of their writings comes from their lives as dropouts, rejects, criminals, and rebels in American society and as inhabitants of America's prisons.

Few of these authors are known outside the circles of those who explore and support prison writing, including the dozens of dedicated writers who have taught prison workshops, some small presses, and organizations like the Fortune Society and PEN, which sponsors annual contests for incarcerated writers. If these unknown writers, most with little formal schooling, can produce eloquent and invaluable works of literature, their achievements raise fundamental challenges to the very concept of a literary canon and its supporting framework of elitist values.

Late-twentieth-century American prison literature also offers an unusually revealing perspective on sexual relations. The American prison, where typically all sexual activity is forbidden—and the only available sex is homosexuality and masturbation—invokes troubling questions about sexual identity. As one convict explained to a prison psychiatrist who was grilling him about his sexual relationships with other men, "I do not know if I am a homosexual or not, because being locked up all of my life, I've never had the opportunity to have a heterosexual relationship."[17]

Gay and lesbian prison writers, including the prominent gay poet Paul Mariah, express the poignancy of relationships threatened by guards and officials, while other writers reveal the threats to the sexuality defined as "normal." Another arena of sexual activities spotlighted by prison is the exploitative relationships between pimps and prostitutes. Juxtaposed with a selection from the sensational and confessional writings about pimping by Iceberg Slim (Robert Beck) are poems and fiction based on the experience of prostitutes who discover feminist consciousness during their incarceration.

By the late 1970s, the river of prison literature was overflowing its banks, pouring out to the American public in mass-market paperbacks, newspapers, magazines, and major motion pictures. Then came the repression that was to build during the 1980s and 1990s. Creative writing courses in prison were defunded. By 1984, every literary journal devoted to publishing poetry and stories by prisoners was wiped out. New York State led the way in mounting a legislative attack on prison writings with its 1977 "Son of Sam" law. Almost every state soon followed in passing similar laws making it illegal for convict authors to collect money from their writings.[18] Although ostensibly designed to "protect the victim" and to keep criminals from profiting from their crimes, the real purpose of these laws was identical to the purpose of the repression of prison literature in the 1930s: to keep the American people in the dark about the American prison.

Some of these laws so blatantly attacked free speech that even Justices William Rehnquist and Antonin Scalia joined a unanimous 1991 U.S. Supreme Court decision that struck down New York's

"Son of Sam" law as an attack on the First Amendment to the Constitution. Most states responded by passing even more repressive legislation and prison regulations designed to skirt the Supreme Court decision. Meanwhile, Title 28 of the Code of Federal Regulations, Section 540.20(b) still stands on the books: "The inmate may not receive compensation or anything of value for correspondence with the news media. The inmate may not act as reporter or publish under a byline." When this U.S. regulation was challenged in court by the *San Francisco Chronicle*, testimony revealed that it had been drafted in the 1970s specifically to ensure that federal prisoners with "anti-establishment" views would "not have access to the media."[19]

THE AMERICAN GULAG TODAY

One response to the political and social upheaval of the 1960s and 1970s has been an immense political and social reaction in the 1980s and 1990s. Central to this countermovement has been unrestrained growth of the prison system, harsh mandatory sentences, a "lock 'em up and throw away the key" media campaign, "three strikes and you're out" laws, a stampede toward capital punishment, the creation of "supermax" penitentiaries, and abandonment of all pretense that prison should be designed for rehabilitation.

Between 1980 and 1995, the percentage of imprisoned Americans tripled. California alone gained the distinction of having the world's third largest prison population, as its spending on prisons began to surpass its spending on higher education. By 1994, the incarceration rate for African-American males had soared to seven times that for white males, and for the first time the number of African-American prisoners exceeded the number of white prisoners. During the 1990s, the United States and Russia (where the rate of incarceration doubled within three years of the collapse of the Soviet Union) have seesawed in their rivalry for the world's highest rate of incarceration.

The table on the following page gives some sense of comparison between the United States and other countries and also suggests the blatantly racist nature of the U.S. penal system. In this 1992–93 period, there were more prisoners in the United States than there were in all these thirty-six nations, which have a combined population well over five times the population of the United States.

RATES OF INCARCERATION,
1992–1993[20]

NATION	NUMBER OF INMATES	RATE PER 100,000 PEOPLE
Australia	15,895	91
Austria	6,913	88
Bangladesh	39,539	37
Belgium	7,116	71
Brazil	124,000	84
Bulgaria	8,688	102
Canada	30,659	116
Czech Republic	16,368	158
Denmark	3,406	66
Egypt	35,392	62
England/Wales	53,518	93
Finland	3,295	65
France	51,457	84
Germany	64,029	80
Greece	6,252	60
India	196,221	23
Indonesia	41,121	22
Irish Republic	2,155	62
Italy	46,152	80
Japan	45,183	36
Korea, South	62,711	144
Malaysia	22,473	122
Mexico	86,334	97
Netherlands	7,935	49
New Zealand	4,694	135
Philippines	16,122	30
Poland	62,139	160
Portugal	9,183	93
Singapore	6,420	229
South Africa	114,047	368
Spain	35,246	90
Sri Lanka	10,470	60
Swaziland	760	88
Sweden	5,668	69
Switzerland	5,751	85
Thailand	90,864	159
TOTAL	1,338,176	AVERAGE: 96
United States	1,339,695	519
U.S. whites	658,233	306
U.S. blacks	626,207	1,947
U.S. black males	583,024	3,822

African Americans were imprisoned at a rate (1,947 per 100,000) six times greater than whites (306 per 100,000) and more than twenty times the international rate of imprisonment (96 per 100,000), bringing the number of imprisoned African Americans (626,207) to almost half the total number of prisoners in all thirty-six of these nations combined (1,338,176). And in the four years after these statistics were compiled, the U.S. rate of incarceration increased almost twenty percent while the rate of incarceration of African-American males increased by eighty percent.

In the twilight of the twentieth century, the United States, birthplace of the modern prison two centuries earlier, has transformed the prison into a central institution of society, unprecedented in scale and influence. Out of this transformation has come another kind of writing, far more bleak and desperate than the prison literature of any earlier period. And yet even these works, rising like their forerunners from the depths of degradation, reveal the creativity and strength of humanity.

NOTES TO THE INTRODUCTION

1. Michael Ignatieff, *A Just Measure of Pain: The Penitentiary in the Industrial Revolution, 1750–1850* (New York: Pantheon Books, 1978), 15.

2. A. Roger Ekirch, *Bound for America: The Transportation of British Convicts to the Colonies, 1718–1775* (Oxford: Clarendon Press, 1987), 127, 130, 144, 148.

3. David M. Oshinsky, *"Worse Than Slavery": Parchman Farm and the Ordeal of Jim Crow Justice* (New York: Free Press Paperbacks, 1997), 21. This book provides a marvelous history of how the penal system was used to re-enslave African-American people.

4. An excellent overall account of this, including a history of how the Thirteenth Amendment was consciously designed to legalize slavery, is given in Barbara Esposito and Lee Wood, *Prison Slavery* (Washington, D.C.: Committee to Abolish Prison Slavery, 1982).

5. Report of the Board of Inspectors of Convicts for the State of Alabama, cited in John G. Van Deusen, *The Black Man in White America* (Washington, D.C.: Associated Publishers, 1938), 124.

6. Oshinsky, 58–59.

7. Paul Oliver, *The Meaning of the Blues* (New York: Collier Books, 1963), 240; W. E. B. DuBois, *The Souls of Black Folk* (New York: Fawcett, 1961), 134.

8. For a mid-Depression version, see Lawrence Gellert, *Negro Songs of Protest* (New York: American Music League, 1936), 21.

9. Pete Daniel, *The Shadow of Slavery: Peonage in the South, 1901–1969* (Urbana: University of Illinois Press, 1972), 26.

10. Van Deusen, 131.

11. Oliver, 240.

12. Daniel, 26; Richard Barry, "Slavery in the South To-Day," *Cosmopolitan Magazine* 42 (March 1907), 481–96; for extensive documentation see Walter Wilson, *Forced Labor in the United States* (New York, 1933).

13. Julian Hawthorne, *The Subterranean Brotherhood* (New York: McBride, Nast & Co., 1914), 149, 320.

14. Herman K. Spector, "What Men Write in Prison," *Tomorrow* 5 (December 1945), 53.

15. Miriam Allen De Ford, "Shall Convicts Write Books?" *Nation* 131 (November 5, 1930), 496.

16. Walter Wilson, *Forced Labor in the United States* (New York: International Publishers, 1933), 37.

17. Letter from "Sherman J. Warner" (pseudonym) in *Maximum Security: Letters from Prison*, edited by Eve Pell (New York: Bantam Books, 1973), 105.

18. Joseph Bruchac, "The Decline and Fall of Prison Literature," *Small Press* (January/February 1987): 28–32; Scott Christianson, "Corrections Law Developments: Barring the Convict from the Proceeds of His Story," *Criminal Law Bulletin* 16 (May–June 1980): 279–87.

19. Dannie M. Martin and Peter Y. Sussman, *Committing Journalism: The Prison Writings of Red Hog* (New York: W. W. Norton, 1993), 127, 212.

20. Marc Mauer, *Americans Behind Bars: The International Use of Incarceration, 1992–1993* (Washington, D.C.: The Sentencing Project, 1994), 3.

FROM PLANTATION
TO PENITENTIARY

PLANTATION PRISON

After the old form of chattel slavery was abolished by the Thirteenth Amendment in 1865, the former slaves had to do one of three things to be legally returned to servitude: (1) "voluntarily" sign a contract they could not read; (2) become indebted to the people who owned all the land and commodities; or (3) commit a crime as defined by an all-white criminal justice system. The contracts that illiterate ex-slaves signed with their previous owners bound them to servitude and often stipulated that they required the plantation owner's permission to set foot off the plantation. Any person leaving this servitude would be, under the law, a criminal.

As the following oral autobiography makes clear, there were often few distinctions made between contracted workers, debt peons, and convicts. The narrative, transcribed in South Carolina by a reporter "who took the liberty to correct the narrator's errors of grammar and put it in form suitable for publication," was originally published on February 25, 1904, in the Independent *under the title "The New Slavery in the South—An Autobiography, by a Georgia Negro Peon." The narrator, who was born during the Civil War, lucidly describes not only his own incarceration but also how the plantation was turned into an actual prison.*

Autobiography of an Imprisoned Peon

I AM A NEGRO and was born some time during the war in Elbert County, Georgia, and I reckon by this time I must be a little over forty years old. My mother was not married when I was born and I never knew who my father was or anything about him.

Shortly after the war my mother died, and I was left to the care of my uncle. All this happened before I was eight years old, and so I can't remember very much about it. When I was about ten years old my uncle hired me out to Captain ———. I had already learned how to plow, and was also a good hand at picking cotton. I was told that the Captain wanted me for his house-boy, and that later on he was going to train me to be his coachman. To be a coachman in those days was considered a post of honor, and, young as I was, I was glad of the chance. But I had not been at the Captain's a month before I was put to work on the farm, with some twenty or thirty other negroes—men, women and children. From the beginning the boys had the same tasks as the men and women. There was no difference. We all worked hard during the week, and would frolic on Saturday nights and often on Sundays. And everybody was happy. The men got $3 a week and the women $2. I don't know what the children got. Every week my uncle collected my money for me, but it was very little of it that I ever saw. My uncle fed and clothed me, gave me a place to sleep, and allowed me ten or fifteen cents a week for "spending change," as he called it. I must have been seventeen or eighteen years old before I got tired of that arrangement; and felt that I was man enough to be working for myself and handling my own things. The other boys about my age and size were "drawing" their own pay, and they used to laugh at me and call me "Baby" because my old uncle was always on hand to "draw" my pay. Worked up by these things, I made a break for liberty. Unknown to my uncle or the Captain I went off to a neighboring plantation and hired myself out to another man. The new landlord agreed to give me forty cents a day and furnish me one meal. I thought that was doing fine. Bright and early one Monday morning I started to work, still not letting the others know anything about it. But they found out before sundown. The Captain came over to the new place and brought some kind of officer of the law. The officer pulled out a long piece of paper from his pocket and read it to my new employer. When this was done I heard my new boss say:

"I beg your pardon, Captain. I didn't know this nigger was bound out to you, or I wouldn't have hired him."

"He certainly is bound out to me," said the Captain. "He belongs to me until he is twenty-one, and I'm going to make him know his place."

So I was carried back to the Captain's. That night he made me strip off my clothing down to my waist, had me tied to a tree in his backyard, ordered his foreman to give me thirty lashes with a buggy whip across my bare back, and stood by until it was done. After that experience the Captain made me stay on his place night and day,—but my uncle still continued to "draw" my money.

I was a man nearly grown before I knew how to count from one to one hundred. I was a man nearly grown before I ever saw a colored school teacher. I never went to school a day in my life. To-day I can't write my own name, tho I can read a little. I was a man nearly grown before I ever rode on a railroad train, and then I went on an excursion from Elberton to Athens. What was true of me was true of hundreds of other negroes around me—'way off there in the country, fifteen or twenty miles from the nearest town.

When I reached twenty-one the Captain told me I was a free man, but he urged me to stay with him. He said he would treat me right, and pay me as much as anybody else would. The Captain's son and I were about the same age, and the Captain said that, as he had owned my mother and uncle during slavery, and as his son didn't want me to leave them (since I had been with them so long), he wanted me to stay with the old family. And I stayed. I signed a contract—that is, I made my mark—for one year. The Captain was to give me $3.50 a week, and furnish me a little house on the plantation—a one-room log cabin similar to those used by his other laborers.

During that year I married Mandy. For several years Mandy had been the house-servant for the Captain, his wife, his son and his three daughters, and they all seemed to think a good deal of her. As an evidence of their regard they gave us a suit of furniture, which cost about $25, and we set up housekeeping in one of the Captain's two-room shanties. I thought I was the biggest man in Georgia. Mandy still kept her place in the "Big House" after our marriage. We did so well for the first year that I renewed my contract for the second year, and for the third, fourth and fifth year I did the same thing. Before the end of the fifth year the Captain had died, and his son, who had married some two or three years before, took charge of the plantation. Also, for two or three years, this son had been serving at Atlanta in some big office to which he had been elected. I think it was in the Legislature or something of that sort —anyhow, all the people called him Senator. At the end of the fifth year the Senator suggested that I sign up a contract for ten years; then, he said, we wouldn't have to fix up papers every year. I asked my wife about it; she consented; and so I made a ten-year contract.

Not long afterward the Senator had a long, low shanty built on his place. A great big chimney, with a wide, open fireplace, was built at one end of it, and on each side of the house, running lengthwise, there was a row of frames of stalls just large enough to hold a single mattress. The places for these mattresses were fixed one above the other; so that there was a double row of these stalls or pens on each side. They looked for all the world like stalls for horses. Since then I have seen cabooses similarly arranged as sleeping quarters for railroad laborers. Nobody seemed to know what the Senator was fixing for. All doubts were put aside one bright day in April when about forty able-bodied negroes bound in iron chains, and some of them handcuffed, were brought out to the Senator's farm in three big wagons. They were quartered in the long, low shanty, and it was afterward called the stockade. This was the beginning of the Senator's convict camp. These men were prisoners who had been leased to the Senator from the State of Georgia at about $200 each per year, the State agreeing to pay for guards and physicians, for necessary inspection, for inquests, all rewards for escaped convicts, the costs of litigation and all other incidental camp expenses. When I saw these men in shackles, and the guards with their guns, I was scared nearly to death. I felt like running away, but I didn't know where to go. And if there had been any place to go to, I would have had to leave my wife and child behind. We free laborers held a meeting. We all wanted to quit. We sent a man to tell the Senator about it. Word came back that we were all under contract for ten years and that the Senator would hold us to the letter of the contract, or put us in chains and lock us up—the same as the other prisoners. It was made plain to us by some white people we talked to that in the contracts we had signed we had all agreed to be locked up in a stockade at night or at any other time that our employer saw fit; further, we learned that we could not lawfully break our contract for any reason and go and hire ourselves to somebody else without the consent of our employer; and, more than that, if we got mad and ran away, we could be run down by bloodhounds, arrested without process of law, and be returned to our employer, who according to the contract, might beat us brutally or administer any other kind of punishment that he thought proper. In other words, we had sold ourselves into slavery—and what could we do about it? The white folks had all the courts, all the guns, all the hounds, all the railroads, all the telegraph wires, all the newspapers, all the money, and nearly all the land—and we had only our ignorance, our poverty and our empty hands. We decided that the best thing to do was to shut our mouths, say nothing, and go back to work. And most of us worked side by side with those convicts during the remainder of the ten years.

But this first batch of convicts was only the beginning. Within six months another stockade was built, and twenty or thirty other convicts were brought to the plantation, among them six or eight women! The Senator had bought an additional thousand acres of land, and to his already large cotton plantation he added two great big saw-mills and went into the lumber business. Within two years the Senator had in all nearly 200 negroes working on his plantation—about half of them free laborers, so-called, and about half of them convicts. The only difference between the free laborers and the others was that the free laborers could come and go as they pleased, at night—that is, they were not locked up at night, and were not, as a general thing, whipped for slight offenses. The troubles of the free laborers began at the close of the ten-year period. To a man, they all wanted to quit when the time was up. To a man, they all refused to sign new contracts—even for one year, not to say anything of ten years. And just when we thought that our bondage was at an end we found that it had really just begun. Two or three years before, or about a year and a half after the Senator had started his camp, he had established a large store, which was called the commissary. All of us free laborers were compelled to buy our supplies—food, clothing, etc.—from that store. We never used any money in our dealings with the commissary, only tickets or orders, and we had a general settlement once each year, in October. In this store we were charged all sorts of high prices for goods, because every year we would come out in debt to our employer. If not that, we seldom had more than $5 or $10 coming to us—and that for a whole year's work. Well, at the close of the tenth year, when we kicked and meant to leave the Senator, he said to some of us with a smile (and I never will forget that smile—I can see it now):

"Boys, I'm sorry you're going to leave me. I hope you will do well in your new places—so well that you will be able to pay me the little balances which most of you owe me."

Word was sent out for all of us to meet him at the commissary at 2 o'clock. There he told us that, after we had signed what he called a written acknowledgment of our debts, we might go and look for new places. The storekeeper took us one by one and read to us statements of our accounts. According to the books there was no man of us who owed the Senator less than $100; some of us were put down for as much as $200. I owed $165, according to the bookkeeper. These debts were not accumulated during one year, but ran back for three and four years, so we were told—in spite of the fact that we understood that we had had a full settlement at the end of each year. But no one of us would have dared to dispute a white man's word—oh, no; not in those days. Besides, we fellows didn't care anything about the amounts—we were after getting away; and we had been told that we might go, if we signed the acknowledgments. We would have signed anything, just to get away. So we stepped up, we did, and made our marks. That same night we were rounded up by a constable and ten or twelve white men, who aided him, and we were locked up, every one of us, in one of the Senator's stockades. The next morning it was explained to us by the two guards appointed to watch us that, in the papers we had signed the day before, we had not only made acknowledgment of our indebtedness, but that we had also agreed to work for the Senator until the debts were paid by hard labor. And from that day forward we were treated just like convicts. Really we had made ourselves lifetime slaves, or peons, as the laws called us. But, call it slavery, peonage, or what not, the truth is we lived in a hell on earth what time we spent in the Senator's peon camp.

I lived in that camp, as a peon, for nearly three years. My wife fared better than I did, as did the wives of some of the other negroes, because the white men about the camp used these unfortunate creatures as their mistresses. When I was first put in the stockade my wife was still kept for a while in the "Big House," but my little boy, who was only nine years old, was given away to a negro family across the river in South Carolina, and I never saw or heard of him after that. When I left the camp my wife had had two children for some one of the white bosses, and she was living in fairly good shape in a little house off to herself. But the poor negro women who were not in the class with my wife fared about as bad as the helpless negro men. Most of the time the women who were peons or convicts were compelled to wear men's clothes. Sometimes, when I have seen them dressed like men, and plowing or hoeing or hauling logs or working at the blacksmith's trade, just the same as men, my heart would bleed and my blood would boil, but I was powerless to raise a hand. It would have meant death on the spot to have said a word. Of the first six women brought to the camp, two of them gave birth to children after they had been there more than twelve months—and the babies had white men for their fathers!

The stockades in which we slept were, I believe, the filthiest places in the world. They were cesspools of nastiness. During the thirteen years that I was there I am willing to swear that a mattress was never moved after it had been brought there, except to turn it over once or twice a month. No sheets were used, only dark-colored blankets. Most of the men slept every night in the clothing that they had worked in all day. Some of the worst characters were made to sleep in chains. The doors were locked and barred each night, and tallow candles were the only lights allowed. Really the stockades were but little more than cow lots, horse stables or hog pens. Strange to say, not a great number of these people died while I was there, tho a great many came away maimed and bruised and, in some cases, disabled for life. As far as I remember only about ten died during the last ten years that I was there, two of these being killed outright by the guards for trivial offenses.

It was a hard school that peon camp was, but I learned more there in a few short months by contact with those poor fellows from the outside world than ever I had known before. Most of what I learned was evil, and I now know that I should have been better off without the knowledge, but much of what I learned was helpful to me. Barring two or three severe and brutal whippings which I received, I got along very well, all things considered; but the system is damnable. A favorite way of whipping a man was to strap him down to a log, flat on his back, and spank him fifty or sixty times on his bare feet with a shingle or a huge piece of plank. When the man would get up with sore and blistered feet and an aching body, if he could not then keep up with the other men at work he would be strapped to the log again, this time face downward, and would be lashed with a buggy trace on his bare back. When a woman had to be whipped it was usually done in private,

tho they would be compelled to fall down across a barrel or something of the kind and receive the licks on their backsides. . . .

One of the usual ways of securing laborers for a large peonage
camp is for the proprietor to send out an agent to the little courts
in the towns and villages, and where a man charged with some petty
offenses has no friends or money the agent will urge him to plead
guilty, with the understanding that the agent will pay his fine, and
in that way save him from the disgrace of being sent to jail or the
chain-gang! For this high favor the man must sign beforehand a
paper signifying his willingness to go to the farm and work out the
amount of the fine imposed. When he reaches the farm he has to
be fed and clothed, to be sure, and these things are charged up to
his account. . . . [E]very year many convicts were brought to the
Senator's camp from a certain county in South Georgia, 'way down
in the turpentine district. The majority of these men were charged
with adultery, which is an offense against the law of the great and
sovereign State of Georgia! Upon inquiry I learned that down in
that county a number of negro lewd women were employed by
certain white men to entice negro men into their houses; and then
on certain nights, at a given signal, when all was in readiness, raids
would be made by the officers upon these houses, and the men
would be arrested and charged with living in adultery. Nine out of
ten of these men, so arrested and so charged, would find their way
ultimately to some convict camp, and, as I said, many of them
found their way every year to the Senator's camp while I was there.
The low-down women were never punished in any way. On the
contrary, I was told that they always seemed to stand in high favor
with the sheriffs, constables and other officers. There can be no
room to doubt that they assisted very materially in furnishing laborers for the prison pens of Georgia, and the belief was general
among the men that they were regularly paid for their work. I could
tell more, but I've said enough to make anybody's heart sick. . . .

But I didn't tell you how I got out. I didn't get out—they put
me out. When I had served as a peon for nearly three years—and
you remember that they claimed that I owed them only $165—
when I had served for nearly three years one of the bosses came to
me and said that my time was up. He happened to be the one who
was said to be living with my wife. He gave me a new suit of
overalls, which cost about seventy-five cents, took me in a buggy

and carried me across the Broad River into South Carolina, set me down and told me to "git." I didn't have a cent of money, and I wasn't feeling well, but somehow I managed to get a move on me. I begged my way to Columbia. In two or three days I ran across a man looking for laborers to carry to Birmingham, and I joined his gang. I have been here in the Birmingham district since they released me, and I reckon I'll die either in a coal mine or an iron furnace. It don't make much difference which. Either is better than a Georgia peon camp. And a Georgia peon camp is hell itself!

SONGS OF THE
PRISON PLANTATION

The work songs of African-American convicts constitute the most poignant evidence of the continuity from pre–Civil War chattel slavery to the twentieth-century prison. These songs have served much the same function for modern prison slaves as the work songs of their slave ancestors. They pace collective labor such as picking cotton under a broiling sun on prison plantations, precisely time dangerous joint activities like chopping down trees, and provide an assertion of people's creativity and a defense of their humanity. The songs thus make it possible to survive under the most brutal and degrading conditions, conditions designed to reduce them to work animals.

Some of the old slave songs actually persisted well into the second half of the twentieth century. For example, these lines were sung by modern convicts picking cotton on a Texas prison plantation:

> Well old marster told old mistress I could pick a bale
> a cotton.
> Old marster told old mistress I could pick a bale a
> day.
> You big enough and black enough to pick a bale a
> cotton.
> You big enough and black enough to pick a bale a
> day.

Chorus
But never will I pick a bale a cotton,
How in the world can I pick a bale a day.

Like the three complete songs reprinted here, those lines were recorded in the Texas prison system between 1964 and 1966 by Bruce Jackson and reproduced in his marvelous book, Wake Up Dead Man: Afro-American Worksongs from Texas Prisons.

Besides amassing a rich and deep book-length collection of songs from one prison system, Jackson also gathered from the prisoners themselves descriptions of the functions served by this poetry and music. In addition to timing the work so they could endure from sunup to sundown, the prisoners also used the songs to prevent any individual from being singled out for punishment for working too slowly, since they are all working to the same beat. One "long-time" man told him:

You get worked to death or beat to death. That's why we sang so many of these songs. We would work together and help ourselves as well as help out our fellow man. Try to keep the officials we was workin' under pacified and we'd make it possible to make a day.*

No verbal description of these convict work songs can do more than hint of their beauty and enormous power. Fortunately, many of them have now been preserved on records; each of the following gives a sample of their range and scope: Negro Prison Camp Work Songs *(Folkways FE-4475),* Negro Prison Songs from the Mississippi State Penitentiary *(Tradition TLP-1020),* Prison Worksongs *(Folk-Lyric LFS A-5),* Negro Work Songs and Calls *(Library of Congress Archive of American Folk Song L-8). A more immediate experience of the songs comes through in a 1966 film,* Afro-American Worksongs in a Texas Prison *(Folklore Research Films), by Dan and Toshi Seeger, with audio work by Pete Seeger and Bruce Jackson.*

Though some of the slave songs migrated into prison while others were metamorphosed as they were modified by the particulars of penal imprisonment, still other songs seem to have originated directly in the prison experience. "Go Down Old

---

* Bruce Jackson, *Wake Up Dead Man: Afro-American Worksongs from Texas Prisons* (Cambridge, Mass.: Harvard University Press, 1972), 2.

Hannah," the first song reprinted here, is almost certainly the special creation of African-American convicts, as attested to by Leadbelly, who does a magnificent version on his Last Sessions *(Folkways FA 1941):*

> They called the sun Old Hannah because it was hot and they just give it a name. That's what the boys called it when I was in prison. I didn't hear it before I went down there. The boys were talking about Old Hannah —I kept looking and I didn't see no Hannah, but they looked up and said, "That's the sun."*

Dozens of versions of "Go Down Old Hannah" have been recorded in prison or by ex-convict singers, and the song has picked up stanzas referring to historical events as early as 1910.

"Midnight Special"—the title is an old convict term for a pardon—also seems to have had its genesis in prison. Although "Easy Rider" may possibly have originated outside prison, it transmuted into a widely diffused prison work song, as shown in the version reprinted here, which is all about the problem of survival on the prison plantation (a "rider" is a guard on horseback). Both these songs later took on other identities as they were commodified.

Prisoner work songs recapitulate and expand the historic cultural role of the slave song. Like their enslaved forebears, the prisoners are allowed to own only one thing of any importance: the collective property embodied in their poetry and music. But that property, ironically enough, eventually transforms into a major commodity of American culture.

Go Down Old Hannah

Well you ought to been down on this old river, WELL, WELL, WELL,
Nineteen forty-four, NINETEEN FORTY-FOUR,

---

* *The Leadbelly Songbook*, ed. Moses Asch and Alan Lomax (New York: Oak Publications, 1962), 50.

Oughta been down on this old river,
Nineteen forty-FOUR.
Well you could find a dead man, WELL, WELL, WELL,
On every turn row, ON EVERY TURN ROW,
You could find a DEAD MAN,
On every TURN ROW.

I say get up dead man, WELL, WELL, WELL,
Help me carry my row, HELP ME CARRY MY ROW,
I say get up DEAD MAN
Help me carry MY ROW.
Well my row so grassy, WELL, WELL, WELL,
I can't hardly go, CAN'T HARDLY GO.
Well my row SO GRASSY,
I can't HARDLY GO.

I say go down old Hannah . . . (*burden and repetition continue
   as above*)
Don't rise no more . . .
If you rise in the mornin' . . .
Bring judgment sure . . .

SOLO SINGER:
Well I ain't tired a livin' . . .
Man, but I got so long . . .
Well they got some on the highway . . .
Little boy, they got some goin' home . . .

Well I looked at old Hannah . . .
And old Hannah looked red . . .
Well I looked at my poor partner . . .
Little boy was half mos' dead . . .

Well my partner said, "Help me, . . .
Help me if you can" . . .
I said, "Partner who fooled you . . .
Down on this long old line" . . . (*repeat is* "on this river line")

"Who told you you could make it . . .
On this river line?" . . .

He say, "I'm not tired a workin' . . .
Pardner I got so long" . . .

I said, "Write your mama . . .
Tell her the shape you in . . .
Tell her I say write the governor . . .
That your time has come" . . .

"Ask the governor for a pardon . . .
And he may grant you a reprieve" . . .

SOLO SINGER:
Well I see Bud Russell . . .
Little boy, with his ball and chain . . .
Little boys he gonna take you . . .
Back to Sugarland . . .

Little boys you get worried . . .
Little boy, don't try to run away . . .
Little boy you'll get to see your mama . . .
On some lonesome day . . .

And who fooled you on the river . . .
With the great long time . . .

Midnight Special

Let the Midnight Special shine her light on me,
Let the Midnight Special shine her ever-lovin' light on me.

"Here come Bud Russel." "How in the world do you know?"
Well he know him by his wagon and the chains he wo'.

Big pistol on his shoulder, big knife in his hand:
He's comin' to carry you back to Sugarland.

Let the Midnight Special shine her light on me,
Let the Midnight Special shine her ever-lovin' light on me.

———

Oh, yonder come Rosie. "How'n the world do you know?"
I know her by her apron and the dress she wore.

Umbrella on her shoulder, piece a paper in her hand,
She hollerin' and cryin', "Won't you free my man?"

Well she cause me to worry, whoopin', hollerin', and a-cryin',
Well she cause me to worry, 'bout my great long time.

Well let the Midnight Special shine her light on me,
Oh let the Midnight Special shine her ever-lovin' light on me.

If you ever go to Paris, man, you better walk right,
And you better not stumble, and you better not fight.

Po-lice he'll 'rest you, and 'll drag you down,
The judge he'll find you, you'll be penitentiary bound.

Let the Midnight Special shine the light on me,
Let the Midnight Special shine her ever-lovin' light on me.

Easy Rider

Oh, easy rider, what make you so mean,
You not the meanest man in the world, but the meanest one I've
    seen.

Say, oh, easy rider, what make you so mean,
I yell for water, partner, give me gasoline.

Waterboy, won't you bring the water 'round,
If you don't like your job, boy, set your bucket down.

I hate to see the rider, when he rides so near,
He so cruel and cold-hearted, boy, these twenty year.

I ask him for mercy, he don't give me none,
He ask me my trouble, and I didn't have none.

THE EARLY MODERN
AMERICAN PRISON

JACK LONDON
1876–1916

Before he died in 1916 at the age of forty, Jack London had published fifty books and become the highest paid writer in the United States. He remains one of America's most characteristic and most extensively translated writers.

Growing up in poverty and hardship, London in his early teens worked ten hours a day for ten cents an hour at an Oakland, California, cannery. He quit school at the age of fourteen, bought a boat with borrowed money and began raiding oyster fishermen in the bay. During the next seven years, he was a sailor, a factory worker, a hobo, a Klondike gold rusher. But in his own opinion, the most formative event of his early life was the month he spent in 1894 as a prisoner. In "How I Became a Socialist," first published in the Comrade *in 1903 and reprinted in* War of the Classes *(1905), London says that "no economic argument, no lucid demonstration of the logic and inevitableness of Socialism affects me as profoundly and convincingly as I was affected on the day when I first saw the walls of the Social Pit rise around me and felt myself slipping down, down, into the shambles at the bottom." This metamorphosis came when he "strayed into Niagara Falls, was nabbed by a fee-hunting constable, denied the right to plead guilty or not guilty, sentenced out of hand to thirty days' imprisonment for having no fixed abode and no visible means of support, handcuffed and chained to a bunch of men similarly circumstanced, carted down country to Buffalo, registered at the Erie County Penitentiary, had my head clipped and my budding mustache shaved, was dressed in convict stripes, compulsorily vaccinated by a medical student who practised on such as we, made to march the lock-step, and put to work under the eyes of guards armed with Winchester rifles." He described this experience most fully in the two selections included here: " 'Pinched': A Prison Experience" and*

"The Pen: Long Days in a County Penitentiary," published in Cosmopolitan *magazine in 1907 and reprinted later that year in* The Road.

" 'Pinched' " and "The Pen" provide extraordinary inside views of the American prison system near the beginning of the twentieth century. They also reveal crucial contradictions in London's character and display the prime sources of his 1915 prison novel The Star Rover *and his astonishing 1908 prevision of fascism,* The Iron Heel.

"Pinched": A Prison Experience

THE TOWN WAS ASLEEP when I entered it. As I came along . . . the quiet street, I saw three men coming toward me along the sidewalk. They were walking abreast. Hoboes, I decided, like myself, who had got up early. In this surmise I was not quite correct. I was only sixty-six and two-thirds per cent correct. The men on each side were hoboes all right, but the man in the middle wasn't. I directed my steps to the edge of the sidewalk in order to let the trio go by. But it didn't go by. At some word from the man in the centre, all three halted, and he of the centre addressed me.

I piped the lay on the instant. He was a "fly-cop" and the two hoboes were his prisoners. John Law was up and out after the early worm. I was a worm. Had I been richer by the experiences that were to befall me in the next several months, I should have turned and run like the very devil. He might have shot at me, but he'd have had to hit me to get me. He'd have never run after me, for two hoboes in the hand are worth more than one on the get-away. But like a dummy I stood still when he halted me. Our conversation was brief.

"What hotel are you stopping at?" he queried.

He had me. I wasn't stopping at any hotel, and, since I did not know the name of a hotel in the place, I could not claim residence in any of them. Also, I was up too early in the morning. Everything was against me.

"I just arrived," I said.

"Well, you turn around and walk in front of me, and not too far in front. There's somebody wants to see you."

I was "pinched." I knew who wanted to see me. With that "fly-cop" and the two hoboes at my heels, and under the direction of the former, I led the way to the city jail. There we were searched and our names registered. I have forgotten, now, under which name I was registered. I gave the name of Jack Drake, but when they searched me, they found letters addressed to Jack London. This caused trouble and required explanation, all of which has passed from my mind, and to this day I do not know whether I was pinched as Jack Drake or Jack London. But one or the other, it should be there today in the prison register of Niagara Falls. Reference can bring it to light. The time was somewhere in the latter part of June, 1894. It was only a few days after my arrest that the great railroad strike began.

From the office we were led to the "Hobo" and locked in. The "Hobo" is that part of a prison where the minor offenders are confined together in a large iron cage. Since hoboes constitute the principal division of the minor offenders, the aforesaid iron cage is called the Hobo. Here we met several hoboes who had already been pinched that morning, and every little while the door was unlocked and two or three more were thrust in on us. At last, when we totalled sixteen, we were led upstairs into the court-room. And now I shall faithfully describe what took place in that court-room, for know that my patriotic American citizenship there received a shock from which it has never fully recovered.

In the court-room were the sixteen prisoners, the judge, and two bailiffs. The judge seemed to act as his own clerk. There were no witnesses. There were no citizens of Niagara Falls present to look on and see how justice was administered in their community. The judge glanced at the list of cases before him and called out a name. A hobo stood up. The judge glanced at a bailiff. "Vagrancy, your Honor," said the bailiff. "Thirty days," said his Honor. The hobo sat down, and the judge was calling another name and another hobo was rising to his feet.

The trial of that hobo had taken just about fifteen seconds. The trial of the next hobo came off with equal celerity. The bailiff said, "Vagrancy, your Honor," and his Honor said, "Thirty days." Thus it went like clockwork, fifteen seconds to a hobo—and thirty days.

They are poor dumb cattle, I thought to myself. But wait till my turn comes; I'll give his Honor a "spiel." Part way along in the performance, his Honor, moved by some whim, gave one of us an opportunity to speak. As chance would have it, this man was not a genuine hobo. He bore none of the ear-marks of the professional "stiff." Had he approached the rest of us, while waiting at a water-tank for a freight, we should have unhesitatingly classified him as a "gay-cat." Gay-cat is the synonym for tenderfoot in Hobo Land. This gay-cat was well along in years—somewhere around forty-five, I should judge. His shoulders were humped a trifle, and his face was seamed by weather-beat.

For many years, according to his story, he had driven team for some firm in (if I remember rightly) Lockport, New York. The firm had ceased to prosper, and finally, in the hard times of 1893, had gone out of business. He had been kept on to the last, though toward the last his work had been very irregular. He went on and explained at length his difficulties in getting work (when so many were out of work) during the succeeding months. In the end, de-ciding that he would find better opportunities for work on the Lakes, he had started for Buffalo. Of course he was "broke," and there he was. That was all.

"Thirty days," said his Honor, and called another hobo's name.

Said hobo got up. "Vagrancy, your Honor," said the bailiff, and his Honor said, "Thirty days."

And so it went, fifteen seconds and thirty days to each hobo. The machine of justice was grinding smoothly. Most likely, con-sidering how early it was in the morning, his Honor had not yet had his breakfast and was in a hurry.

But my American blood was up. Behind me were the many gen-erations of my American ancestry. One of the kinds of liberty those ancestors of mine had fought and died for was the right of trial by jury. This was my heritage, stained sacred by their blood, and it devolved upon me to stand up for it. All right, I threatened to myself; just wait till he gets to me.

He got to me. My name, whatever it was, was called, and I stood up. The bailiff said, "Vagrancy, your Honor," and I began to talk. But the judge began talking at the same time, and he said, "Thirty days." I started to protest, but at that moment his Honor was call-ing the name of the next hobo on the list. His Honor paused long enough to say to me, "Shut up!" The bailiff forced me to sit down.

And the next moment that next hobo had received thirty days and the succeeding hobo was just in process of getting his.

When we had all been disposed of, thirty days to each stiff, his Honor, just as he was about to dismiss us, suddenly turned to the teamster from Lockport—the one man he had allowed to talk.

"Why did you quit your job?" his Honor asked.

Now the teamster had already explained how his job had quit him, and the question took him aback.

"Your Honor," he began confusedly, "isn't that a funny question to ask?"

"Thirty days more for quitting your job," said his Honor, and the court was closed. That was the outcome. The teamster got sixty days all together, while the rest of us got thirty days.

We were taken down below, locked up, and given breakfast. It was a pretty good breakfast, as prison breakfasts go, and it was the best I was to get for a month to come.

As for me, I was dazed. Here was I, under sentence, after a farce of a trial wherein I was denied not only my right of trial by jury, but my right to plead guilty or not guilty. Another thing my fathers had fought for flashed through my brain—habeas corpus. I'd show them. But when I asked for a lawyer, I was laughed at. Habeas corpus was all right, but of what good was it to me when I could communicate with no one outside the jail? But I'd show them. They couldn't keep me in jail forever. Just wait till I got out, that was all. I'd make them sit up. I knew something about the law and my own rights, and I'd expose their maladministration of justice. Visions of damage suits and sensational newspaper headlines were dancing before my eyes when the jailers came in and began hustling us out into the main office.

A policeman snapped a handcuff on my right wrist. (Ah, ha, thought I, a new indignity. Just wait till I get out.) On the left wrist of a negro he snapped the other handcuff of that pair. He was a very tall negro, well past six feet—so tall was he that when we stood side by side his hand lifted mine up a trifle in the manacles. Also, he was the happiest and the raggedest negro I have ever seen.

We were all handcuffed similarly, in pairs. This accomplished, a bright nickel-steel chain was brought forth, run down through the links of all the handcuffs, and locked at front and rear of the double-line. We were now a chain-gang. The command to march was given, and out we went upon the street, guarded by two officers. The tall negro and I had the place of honor. We led the procession.

After the tomb-like gloom of the jail, the outside sunshine was dazzling. I had never known it to be so sweet as now, a prisoner with clanking chains, I knew that I was soon to see the last of it for thirty days. Down through the streets of Niagara Falls we marched to the railroad station, stared at by curious passers-by, and especially by a group of tourists on the veranda of a hotel that we marched past.

There was plenty of slack in the chain, and with much rattling and clanking we sat down, two and two, in the seats of the smoking-car. Afire with indignation as I was at the outrage that had been perpetrated on me and my forefathers, I was nevertheless too prosaically practical to lose my head over it. This was all new to me. Thirty days of mystery were before me, and I looked about me to find somebody who knew the ropes. For I had already learned that I was not bound for a petty jail with a hundred or so prisoners in it, but for a full-grown penitentiary with a couple of thousand prisoners in it, doing anywhere from ten days to ten years.

In the seat behind me, attached to the chain by his wrist, was a squat, heavily-built, powerfully-muscled man. He was somewhere between thirty-five and forty years of age. I sized him up. In the corners of his eyes I saw humor and laughter and kindliness. As for the rest of him, he was a brute-beast, wholly unmoral, and with all the passion and turgid violence of the brute-beast. What saved him, what made him possible for me, were those corners of his eyes—the humor and laughter and kindliness of the beast when unaroused.

He was my "meat." I "cottoned" to him. While my cuff-mate, the tall negro, mourned with chucklings and laughter over some laundry he was sure to lose through his arrest, and while the train rolled on toward Buffalo, I talked with the man in the seat behind me. He had an empty pipe. I filled it for him with my precious tobacco—enough in a single filling to make a dozen cigarettes. Nay, the more we talked the surer I was that he was my meat, and I divided all my tobacco with him.

Now it happens that I am a fluid sort of an organism, with sufficient kinship with life to fit myself in 'most anywhere. I laid myself out to fit in with that man, though little did I dream to what extraordinary good purpose I was succeeding. He had never been in the particular penitentiary to which we were going, but he had done "one-," "two-," and "five-spots" in various other penitentiaries (a "spot" is a year), and he was filled with wisdom. We became pretty chummy, and my heart bounded when he cautioned me to follow his lead. He called me "Jack," and I called him "Jack."

The train stopped at a station about five miles from Buffalo, and we, the chain-gang, got off. I do not remember the name of this station, but I am confident that it is some one of the following: Rocklyn, Rockwood, Black Rock, Rockcastle, or Newcastle. But whatever the name of the place, we were walked a short distance and then put on a street-car. It was an old-fashioned car, with a seat, running the full length, on each side. All the passengers who sat on one side were asked to move over to the other side, and we, with a great clanking of chain, took their places. We sat facing them, I remember, and I remember, too, the awed expression on the faces of the women, who took us, undoubtedly, for convicted murderers and bank-robbers. I tried to look my fiercest, but that cuff-mate of mine, the too happy negro, insisted on rolling his eyes, laughing, and reiterating, "O Lawdy! Lawdy!"

We left the car, walked some more, and were led into the office of the Erie County Penitentiary. Here we were to register, and on that register one or the other of my names will be found. Also, we were informed that we must leave in the office all our valuables: money, tobacco, matches, pocket-knives, and so forth.

My new pal shook his head at me.

"If you do not leave your things here, they will be confiscated inside," warned the official.

Still my pal shook his head. He was busy with his hands, hiding his movements behind the other fellows. (Our hand-cuffs had been removed.) I watched him, and followed suit, wrapping up in a bundle in my handkerchief all the things I wanted to take in. These bundles the two of us thrust into our shirts. I noticed that our fellow-prisoners, with the exception of one or two who had watches, did not turn over their belongings to the man in the office. They were determined to smuggle them in somehow, trusting to luck; but they were not so wise as my pal, for they did not wrap their things in bundles.

Our erstwhile guardians gathered up the handcuffs and chain and departed for Niagara Falls, while we, under new guardians, were led away into the prison. While we were in the office, our number had been added to by other squads of newly arrived prisoners, so that we were now a procession forty or fifty strong.

Know, ye unimprisoned, that traffic is as restricted inside a large prison as commerce was in the Middle Ages. Once inside a penitentiary, one cannot move about at will. Every few steps are encountered great steel doors or gates which are always kept locked. We were bound for the barber-shop, but we encountered delays in the unlocking of doors for us. We were thus delayed in the first "hall" we entered. A "hall" is not a corridor. Imagine an oblong cube, built out of bricks and rising six stories high, each story a row of cells, say fifty cells in a row—in short, imagine a cube of colossal honey-comb. Place this cube on the ground and enclose it in a building with a roof overhead and walls all around. Such a cube and encompassing building constitute a "hall" in the Erie County Penitentiary. Also, to complete the picture, see a narrow gallery, with steel railing, running the full length of each tier of cells and at the ends of the oblong cube see all these galleries, from both sides, connected by a fire-escape system of narrow steel stairways.

We were halted in the first hall, waiting for some guard to unlock a door. Here and there, moving about, were convicts, with close-cropped heads and shaven faces, and garbed in prison stripes. One such convict I noticed above us on the gallery of the third tier of cells. He was standing on the gallery and leaning forward, his arms resting on the railing, himself apparently oblivious of our presence. He seemed staring into vacancy. My pal made a slight hissing noise. The convict glanced down. Motioned signals passed between them. Then through the air soared the handkerchief bundle of my pal. The convict caught it, and like a flash it was out of sight in his shirt and he was staring into vacancy. My pal had told me to follow his lead. I watched my chance when the guard's back was turned, and my bundle followed the other one into the shirt of the convict.

A minute later the door was unlocked, and we filed into the barber-shop. Here were more men in convict stripes. They were the prison barbers. Also, there were bath-tubs, hot water, soap, and scrubbing-brushes. We were ordered to strip and bathe, each man to scrub his neighbor's back—a needless precaution, this compulsory bath, for the prison swarmed with vermin. After the bath, we were each given a canvas clothes-bag.

"Put all your clothes in the bags," said the guard. "It's no good trying to smuggle anything in. You've got to line up naked for inspection. Men for thirty days or less keep their shoes and suspenders. Men for more than thirty days keep nothing."

This announcement was received with consternation. How could naked men smuggle anything past an inspection? Only my pal and I were safe. But it was right here that the convict barbers got in their work. They passed among the poor newcomers, kindly volunteering to take charge of their precious little belongings, and promising to return them later in the day. Those barbers were philanthropists—to hear them talk. As in the case of Fra Lippo Lippi, never was there such prompt disemburdening. Matches, tobacco, rice-paper, pipes, knives, money, everything, flowed into the capacious shirts of the barbers. They fairly bulged with the spoil, and the guards made believe not to see. To cut the story short, nothing was ever returned. The barbers never had any intention of returning what they had taken. They considered it legitimately theirs. It was the barber-shop graft. There were many grafts in that prison, as I was to learn; and I, too, was destined to become a grafter—thanks to my new pal.

There were several chairs, and the barbers worked rapidly. The quickest shaves and hair-cuts I have ever seen were given in that shop. The men lathered themselves, and the barbers shaved them at the rate of a minute to a man. A hair-cut took a trifle longer. In three minutes the down of eighteen was scraped from my face, and my head was as smooth as a billiard-ball just sprouting a crop of bristles. Beards, mustaches, like our clothes and everything, came off. Take my word for it, we were a villainous-looking gang when they got through with us. I had not realized before how really altogether bad we were.

Then came the line-up, forty or fifty of us, naked as Kipling's heroes who stormed Lungtungpen. To search us was easy. There were only our shoes and ourselves. Two or three rash spirits, who had doubted the barbers, had the goods found on them—which goods, namely, tobacco, pipes, matches, and small change, were quickly confiscated. This over, our new clothes were brought to us—stout prison shirts, and coats and trousers conspicuously striped. I had always lingered under the impression that the convict stripes were put on a man only after he had been convicted of a felony. I lingered no longer, but put on the insignia of shame and got my first taste of marching the lock-step.

In single file, close together, each man's hands on the shoulders of the man in front, we marched on into another large hall. Here we were ranged up against the wall in a long line and ordered to strip our left arms. A youth, a medical student who was getting in his practice on cattle such as we, came down the line. He vaccinated just about four times as rapidly as the barbers shaved. With a final caution to avoid rubbing our arms against anything, and to let the blood dry so as to form the scab, we were led away to our cells. Here my pal and I parted, but not before he had time to whisper to me, "Suck it out."

As soon as I was locked in, I sucked my arm clean. And afterward I saw men who had not sucked and who had horrible holes in their arms into which I could have thrust my fist. It was their own fault. They could have sucked.

In my cell was another man. We were to be cell-mates. He was a young, manly fellow, not talkative, but very capable, indeed as splendid a fellow as one could meet with in a day's ride, and this in spite of the fact that he had just recently finished a two-year term in some Ohio penitentiary.

Hardly had we been in our cell half an hour, when a convict sauntered down the gallery and looked in. It was my pal. He had the freedom of the hall, he explained. He was unlocked at six in the morning and not locked up again till nine at night. He was in with the "push" in that hall, and had been promptly appointed a trusty of the kind technically known as "hall-man." The man who had appointed him was also a prisoner and a trusty, and was known as "First Hall-man." There were thirteen hall-men in that hall. Ten of them had charge each of a gallery of cells, and over them were the First, Second, and Third Hall-men.

We newcomers were to stay in our cells for the rest of the day, my pal informed me, so that the vaccine would have a chance to take. Then next morning we would be put to hard labor in the prison-yard.

"But I'll get you out of the work as soon as I can," he promised. "I'll get one of the hall-men fired and have you put in his place."

He put his hand into his shirt, drew out the handkerchief containing my precious belongings, passed it in to me through the bars, and went on down the gallery.

I opened the bundle. Everything was there. Not even a match was missing. I shared the makings of a cigarette with my cell-mate.

When I started to strike a match for a light, he stopped me. A flimsy, dirty comforter lay in each of our bunks for bedding. He tore off a narrow strip of the thin cloth and rolled it tightly and telescopically into a long and slender cylinder. This he lighted with a precious match. The cylinder of tight-rolled cotton cloth did not flame. On the end a coal of fire slowly smouldered. It would last for hours, and my cell-mate called it a "punk." And when it burned short, all that was necessary was to make a new punk, put the end of it against the old, blow on them, and so transfer the glowing coal. Why, we could have given Prometheus pointers on the conserving of fire.

At twelve o'clock dinner was served. At the bottom of our cage door was a small opening like the entrance of a runway in a chicken-yard. Through this were thrust two hunks of dry bread and two pannikins of "soup." A portion of soup consisted of about a quart of hot water with floating on its surface a lonely drop of grease. Also, there was some salt in that water.

We drank the soup, but we did not eat the bread. Not that we were not hungry, and not that the bread was uneatable. It was fairly good bread. But we had reasons. My cell-mate had discovered that our cell was alive with bed-bugs. In all the cracks and interstices between the bricks where the mortar had fallen out flourished great colonies. The natives even ventured out in the broad daylight and swarmed over the walls and ceiling by hundreds. My cell-mate was wise in the ways of the beasts. Like Childe Roland, dauntless the slug-horn to his lips he bore. Never was there such a battle. It lasted for hours. It was shambles. And when the last survivors fled to their brick-and-mortar fastnesses, our work was only half done. We chewed mouthfuls of our bread until it was reduced to the consistency of putty. When a fleeing belligerent escaped into a crevice between the bricks, we promptly walled him in with a daub of the chewed bread. We toiled on until the light grew dim and until every hole, nook, and cranny was closed. I shudder to think of the tragedies of starvation and cannibalism that must have ensued behind those bread-plastered ramparts.

We threw ourselves on our bunks, tired out and hungry, to wait for supper. It was a good day's work well done. In the weeks to come we at least should not suffer from the hosts of vermin. We had foregone our dinner, saved our hides at the expense of our stomachs; but we were content. Alas for the futility of human effort! Scarcely was our long task completed when a guard unlocked our door. A redistribution of prisoners was being made, and we were taken to another cell and locked in two galleries higher up.

Early next morning our cells were unlocked, and down in the hall the several hundred prisoners of us formed the lock-step and marched out into the prison-yard to go to work. The Erie Canal runs right by the back yard of the Erie County Penitentiary. Our task was to unload canal-boats, carrying huge stay-bolts on our shoulders, like railroad ties, into the prison. As I worked I sized up the situation and studied the chances for a get-away. There wasn't the ghost of a show. Along the tops of the walls marched guards armed with repeating rifles, and I was told, furthermore, that there were machine-guns in the sentry-towers.

I did not worry. Thirty days were not so long. I'd stay those thirty days, and add to the store of material I intended to use, when I got out, against the harpies of justice. I'd show what an American boy could do when his rights and privileges had been trampled on the way mine had. I had been denied my right of trial by jury; I had been denied my right to plead guilty or not guilty; I had been denied a trial even (for I couldn't consider that what I had received at Niagara Falls was a trial); I had not been allowed to communicate with a lawyer nor any one, and hence had been denied my right of suing for a writ of habeas corpus; my face had been shaved, my hair cropped close, convict stripes had been put upon my body; I was forced to toil hard on a diet of bread and water and to march the shameful lock-step with armed guards over me—and all for what? What had I done? What crime had I committed against the good citizens of Niagara Falls that all this vengeance should be wreaked upon me? I had not even violated their "sleeping-out" ordinance. I had slept outside their jurisdiction, in the country, that night. I had not even begged for a meal, or battered for a "light piece" on their streets. All that I had done was to walk along their sidewalk and gaze at their picayune waterfall. And what crime was there in that? Technically I was guilty of no misdemeanor. All right, I'd show them when I got out.

The next day I talked with a guard. I wanted to send for a lawyer. The guard laughed at me. So did the other guards. I really was *incommunicado* so far as the outside world was concerned. I tried to write a letter out, but I learned that all letters were read, and censured or confiscated, by the prison authorities, and that "short-timers" were not allowed to write letters anyway. A little later I tried smuggling letters out by men who were released, but I learned that they were searched and the letters found and destroyed. Never mind. It all helped to make it a blacker case when I did get out.

But as the prison days went by (which I shall describe in the next chapter), I "learned a few." I heard tales of the police, and police-courts, and lawyers, that were unbelievable and monstrous. Men, prisoners, told me of personal experiences with the police of great cities that were awful. And more awful were the hearsay tales they told me concerning men who had died at the hands of the police and who therefore could not testify for themselves. Years afterward, in the report of the Lexow Committee, I was to read tales true and more awful than those told to me. But in the meantime, during the first days of my imprisonment, I scoffed at what I heard.

As the days went by, however, I began to grow convinced. I saw with my own eyes, there in that prison, things unbelievable and monstrous. And the more convinced I became, the profounder grew the respect in me for the sleuth-hounds of the law and for the whole institution of criminal justice.

My indignation ebbed away, and into my being rushed the tides of fear. I saw at last, clear-eyed, what I was up against. I grew meek and lowly. Each day I resolved more emphatically to make no rumpus when I got out. All I asked, when I got out, was a chance to fade away from the landscape. And that was just what I did do when I was released. I kept my tongue between my teeth, walked softly, and sneaked for Pennsylvania, a wiser and a humbler man.

The Pen:
Long Days in a County Penitentiary

FOR TWO DAYS I toiled in the prison-yard. It was heavy work, and, in spite of the fact that I malingered at every opportunity, I was played out. This was because of the food. No man could work hard on such food. Bread and water, that was all that was given us. Once a week we were supposed to get meat; but this meat did not always go around, and since all nutriment had first been boiled out of it in the making of soup, it didn't matter whether one got a taste of it once a week or not.

Furthermore, there was one vital defect in the bread-and-water diet. While we got plenty of water, we did not get enough of the bread. A ration of bread was about the size of one's two fists, and three rations a day were given to each prisoner. There was one good thing, I must say, about the water—it was hot. In the morning it was called "coffee," at noon it was dignified as "soup," and at night it masqueraded as "tea." But it was the same old water all the time. The prisoners called it "water bewitched." In the morning it was black water, the color being due to boiling it with burnt bread-crusts. At noon it was served minus the color, with salt and a drop of grease added. At night it was served with a purplish-auburn hue that defied all speculation; it was darn poor tea, but it was dandy hot water.

We were a hungry lot in the Erie County Pen. Only the "long-timers" knew what it was to have enough to eat. The reason for this was that they would have died after a time on the fare we "short-timers" received. I know that the long-timers got more substantial grub, because there was a whole row of them on the ground floor in our hall, and when I was a trusty, I used to steal from their grub while serving them. Man cannot live on bread alone and not enough of it.

My pal delivered the goods. After two days of work in the yard I was taken out of my cell and made a trusty, a "hall-man." At morning and night we served the bread to the prisoners in their cells; but at twelve o'clock a different method was used. The convicts marched in from work in a long line. As they entered the door of our hall, they broke the lock-step and took their hands down from the shoulders of their line-mates. Just inside the door were piled trays of bread, and here also stood the First Hall-man and two ordinary hall-men. I was one of the two. Our task was to hold the trays of bread as the line of convicts filed past. As soon as the tray, say, that I was holding was emptied, the other hall-man took my place with a full tray. And when his was emptied, I took his place with a full tray. Thus the line tramped steadily by, each man reaching with his right hand and taking one ration of bread from the extended tray.

The task of the First Hall-man was different. He used a club.

He stood beside the tray and watched. The hungry wretches could never get over the delusion that sometime they could manage to get two rations of bread out of the tray. But in my experience that sometime never came. The club of the First Hall-man had a way of flashing out—quick as the stroke of a tiger's claw—to the hand that dared ambitiously. The First Hall-man was a good judge of distance, and he had smashed so many hands with that club that he had become infallible. He never missed, and he usually punished the offending convict by taking his one ration away from him and sending him to his cell to make his meal off of hot water.

And at times, while all these men lay hungry in their cells, I have seen a hundred or so extra rations of bread hidden away in the cells of the hall-men. It would seem absurd, our retaining this bread. But it was one of our grafts. We were economic masters inside our hall, turning the trick in ways quite similar to the economic masters of civilization. We controlled the food-supply of the population, and, just like our brother bandits outside, we made the people pay through the nose for it. We peddled the bread. Once a week, the men who worked in the yard received a five-cent plug of chewing tobacco. This chewing tobacco was the coin of the realm. Two or three rations of bread for a plug was the way we exchanged, and they traded, not because they loved tobacco less, but because they loved bread more. Oh, I know, it was like taking candy from a baby, but what would you? We had to live. And certainly there should be some reward for initiative and enterprise. Besides, we but patterned ourselves after our betters outside the walls, who, on a larger scale, and under the respectable disguise of merchants, bankers, and captains of industry, did precisely what we were doing. What awful things would have happened to those poor wretches if it hadn't been for us, I can't imagine. Heaven knows we put bread into circulation in the Erie County Pen. Ay, and we encouraged frugality and thrift . . . in the poor devils who forewent their tobacco. And then there was our example. In the breast of every convict there we implanted the ambition to become even as we and run a graft. Saviours of society—I guess yes.

Here was a hungry man without any tobacco. Maybe he was a profligate and had used it all up on himself. Very good; he had a pair of suspenders. I exchanged half a dozen rations of bread for it—or a dozen rations if the suspenders were very good. Now I never wore suspenders, but that didn't matter. Around the corner lodged a long-timer, doing ten years for manslaughter. He wore suspenders, and he wanted a pair. I could trade them to him for some of his meat. Meat was what I wanted. Or perhaps he had a tattered, paper-covered novel. That was treasure-trove. I could read it and then trade it off to the bakers for cake, or to the cooks for meat and vegetables, or to the firemen for decent coffee, or to some one or other for the newspaper that occasionally filtered in, heaven alone knows how. The cooks, bakers, and firemen were prisoners like myself, and they lodged in our hall in the first row of cells over us.

In short, a full-grown system of barter obtained in the Erie County Pen. There was even money in circulation. This money was sometimes smuggled in by the short-timers, more frequently came from the barber-shop graft, where the newcomers were mulcted, but most of all flowed from the cells of the long-timers—though how they got it I don't know.

What of his preëminent position, the First Hall-man was reputed to be quite wealthy. In addition to his miscellaneous grafts, he grafted on us. We farmed the general wretchedness, and the First Hall-man was Farmer-General over all of us. We held our particular grafts by his permission, and we had to pay for that permission. As I say, he was reputed to be wealthy; but we never saw his money, and he lived in a cell all to himself in solitary grandeur.

But that money was made in the Pen I had direct evidence, for I was cell-mate quite a time with the Third Hall-man. He had over sixteen dollars. He used to count his money every night after nine o'clock, when we were locked in. Also, he used to tell me each night what he would do to me if I gave away on him to the other hall-men. You see, he was afraid of being robbed, and danger threatened him from three different directions. There were the guards. A couple of them might jump upon him, give him a good beating for alleged insubordination, and throw him into the "solitaire" (the dungeon); and in the mix-up that sixteen dollars of his would take wings. Then again, the First Hall-man could have taken it all away from him by threatening to dismiss him and fire him back to hard labor in the prison-yard. And yet again, there were the ten of us who were ordinary hall-men. If we got an inkling of his wealth, there was a large liability, some quiet day, of the whole bunch of us getting him into a corner and dragging him down. Oh, we were wolves, believe me—just like the fellows who do business in Wall Street.

He had good reason to be afraid of us, and so had I to be afraid of him. He was a huge, illiterate brute, an ex-Chesapeake-Bay-oyster-pirate, an "ex-con" who had done five years in Sing Sing, and a general all-around stupidly carnivorous beast. He used to trap sparrows that flew into our hall through the open bars. When he made a capture, he hurried away with it into his cell, where I have seen him crunching bones and spitting out feathers as he bolted it raw. Oh, no, I never gave away on him to the other hall-men. This is the first time I have mentioned his sixteen dollars.

But I grafted on him just the same. He was in love with a woman prisoner who was confined in the "female department." He could neither read nor write, and I used to read her letters to him and write his replies. And I made him pay for it, too. But they were good letters. I laid myself out on them, put in my best licks, and furthermore, I won her for him; though I shrewdly guess that she was in love, not with him, but with the humble scribe. I repeat, those letters were great.

Another one of our grafts was "passing the punk." We were the celestial messengers, the fire-bringers, in that iron world of bolt and bar. When the men came in from work at night and were locked in their cells, they wanted to smoke. Then it was that we restored the divine spark, running the galleries, from cell to cell, with our smouldering punks. Those who were wise, or with whom we did business, had their punks all ready to light. Not every one got divine sparks, however. The guy who refused to dig up, went sparkless and smokeless to bed. But what did we care? We had the immortal cinch on him, and if he got fresh, two or three of us would pitch on him and give him "what-for."

You see, this was the working-theory of the hall-men. There were thirteen of us. We had something like half a thousand prisoners in our hall. We were supposed to do the work, and to keep order. The latter was the function of the guards, which they turned over to us. It was up to us to keep order; if we didn't, we'd be fired back to hard labor, most probably with a taste of the dungeon thrown in. But so long as we maintained order, that long could we work our own particular grafts.

Bear with me a moment and look at the problem. Here were

thirteen beasts of us over half a thousand other beasts. It was a living hell, that prison, and it was up to us thirteen there to rule. It was impossible, considering the nature of the beasts, for us to rule by kindness. We ruled by fear. Of course, behind us, backing us up, were the guards. In extremity we called upon them for help; but it would bother them if we called upon them too often, in which event we could depend upon it that they would get more efficient trusties to take our places. But we did not call upon them often, except in a quiet sort of way, when we wanted a cell unlocked in order to get at a refractory prisoner inside. In such cases all the guard did was to unlock the door and walk away so as not to be a witness of what happened when half a dozen hall-men went inside and did a bit of man-handling.

As regards the details of this man-handling I shall say nothing. And after all, man-handling was merely one of the very minor unprintable horrors of the Erie County Pen. I say "unprintable"; and in justice I must also say "unthinkable." They were unthinkable to me until I saw them, and I was no spring chicken in the ways of the world and the awful abysses of human degradation. It would take a deep plummet to reach bottom in the Erie County Pen, and I do but skim lightly and facetiously the surface of things as I there saw them.

At times, say in the morning when the prisoners came down to wash, the thirteen of us would be practically alone in the midst of them, and every last one of them had it in for us. Thirteen against five hundred, and we ruled by fear. We could not permit the slightest infraction of rules, the slightest insolence. If we did, we were lost. Our own rule was to hit a man as soon as he opened his mouth—hit him hard, hit him with anything. A broom-handle, end-on, in the face, had a very sobering effect. But that was not all. Such a man must be made an example of; so the next rule was to wade right in and follow him up. Of course, one was sure that every hall-man in sight would come on the run to join in the chastisement; for this also was a rule. Whenever any hall-man was in trouble with a prisoner, the duty of any other hall-man who happened to be around was to lend a fist. Never mind the merits of the case—wade in and hit, and hit with anything; in short, lay the man out.

I remember a handsome young mulatto of about twenty who got the insane idea into his head that he should stand for his rights.

And he did have the right of it, too; but that didn't help him any. He lived on the topmost gallery. Eight hall-men took the conceit out of him in just about a minute and a half—for that was the length of time required to travel along his gallery to the end and down five flights of steel stairs. He travelled the whole distance on every portion of his anatomy except his feet, and the eight hall-men were not idle. The mulatto struck the pavement where I was standing watching it all. He regained his feet and stood upright for a moment. In that moment he threw his arms wide apart and omitted an awful scream of terror and pain and heartbreak. At the same instant, as in a transformation scene, the shreds of his stout prison clothes fell from him, leaving him wholly naked and streaming blood from every portion of the surface of his body. Then he collapsed in a heap, unconscious. He had learned his lesson, and every convict within those walls who heard him scream had learned a lesson. So had I learned mine. It is not a nice thing to see a man's heart broken in a minute and a half. . . .

Sometimes, however, a newcomer arrives, upon whom no grafts are to be worked. The mysterious word is passed along that he is to be treated decently. Where this word originated I could never learn. The one thing patent is that the man has a "pull." It may be with one of the superior hall-men; it may be with one of the guards in some other part of the prison; it may be that good treatment has been purchased from grafters higher up; but be it as it may, we know that it is up to us to treat him decently if we want to avoid trouble.

We hall-men were middle-men and common carriers. We arranged trades between convicts confined in different parts of the prison, and we put through the exchange. Also, we took our commissions coming and going. Sometimes the objects traded had to go through the hands of half a dozen middle-men, each of whom took his whack, or in some way or another was paid for his service. . . .

Often we conveyed letters, the chain of communication of which was so complex that we knew neither sender nor sendee. We were but links in the chain. Somewhere, somehow, a convict would thrust a letter into my hand with the instruction to pass it on to the next link. All such acts were favors to be reciprocated later on, when I should be acting directly with a principal in transmitting letters, and from whom I should be receiving my pay. The whole prison was covered by a network of lines of communication. And we who were in control of the system of communication, naturally, since we were modelled after capitalistic society, exacted heavy tolls from our customers. It was service for profit with a vengeance, though we were at times not above giving service for love.

And all the time I was in the Pen I was making myself solid with my pal. He had done much for me, and in return he expected me to do as much for him. When we got out, we were to travel together, and, it goes without saying, pull off "jobs" together. For my pal was a criminal—oh, not a jewel of the first water, merely a petty criminal who would steal and rob, commit burglary, and, if cornered, not stop short of murder. Many a quiet hour we sat and talked together. He had two or three jobs in view for the immediate future, in which my work was cut out for me, and in which I joined in planning the details. I had been with and seen much of criminals, and my pal never dreamed that I was only fooling him, giving him a string thirty days long. He thought I was the real goods, liked me because I was not stupid, and liked me a bit, too, I think, for myself. Of course I had not the slightest intention of joining him in a life of sordid, petty crime; but I'd have been an idiot to throw away all the good things his friendship made possible. When one is on the hot lava of hell, he cannot pick and choose his path, and so it was with me in the Erie County Pen. I had to stay in with the "push," or do hard labor on bread and water; and to stay in with the push I had to make good with my pal. . . .

At last came the day of days, my release. It was the day of release for the Third Hall-man as well, and the short-timer girl I had won for him was waiting for him outside the wall. They went away blissfully together. My pal and I went out together, and together we walked down into Buffalo. Were we not to be together always? We begged together on the "main-drag" that day for pennies, and what we received was spent for "shupers" of beer—I don't know how they are spelled, but they are pronounced the way I have spelled them, and they cost three cents. I was watching my chance all the time for a get-away. From some bo on the drag I managed to learn what time a certain freight pulled out. I calculated my time accordingly. When the moment came, my pal and I were in a saloon. Two foaming shupers were before us. I'd have liked to say good-by. He had been good to me. But I did not dare. I went out through the rear of the saloon and jumped the fence. It was a swift sneak, and a few minutes later I was on board a freight and heading south on the Western New York and Pennsylvania Railroad.

DONALD LOWRIE
1875–1925

Destitute and desperate, Donald Lowrie in 1901 flipped his last coin to decide whether to kill himself or commit his first burglary. The toss led to a valuable watch, a bungled pawnshop transaction, a fifteen-year sentence to San Quentin, and an influential career as a writer.

Lowrie's first book, My Life in Prison, *serialized in 1911 in the San Francisco Bulletin, won a wide audience when it was published the following year in New York and London. Although he exposed to public view San Quentin's prison slavery, its use of the straitjacket as punishment, and its abominable physical conditions, Lowrie attempted to give a very balanced view of the prison and took pains to praise a number of prison administrators. This book engendered major efforts at prison reform. In 1926, the convict author Jack Black wrote that Lowrie's "writings did for American prisons what John Howard's did for those of England."*

The most tangible impact was on Thomas Mott Osborne, the former mayor of Auburn, New York. Inspired by his reading of My Life in Prison *in 1912, Osborne embarked on his career as the most eminent of all American prison reformers. To find out what prison was really like, Osborne in 1913 spent a week as a convict in the infamous Auburn penitentiary and then accepted the chairmanship of the New York State Prison Reform Commission. As the warden of Sing Sing from 1914 to 1916, Osborne brought Lowrie in to serve as his secretary and adviser in instituting his program of radical reform under which the prisoners were allowed to establish a form of democratic self-government.*

During Osborne's great experiment, Lowrie in 1915

published his second book, My Life out of Prison. *A much
sadder narrative was serialized in the* San Francisco Call and
Post *and then published in 1925 as* Donald Lowrie's Story:
Back in Prison—Why? *Lowrie died that June, two weeks after his parole from the Arizona State Penitentiary.*

The selection from My Life in Prison *reprinted here may
have been the most direct influence on Osborne, for it describes how John E. Hoyle, a new warden at San Quentin,
wrought one remarkable transformation in the prisoners by
treating them like human beings.*

from *My Life in Prison*

IT IS THE DEAD OF NIGHT, and save for the subdued whir of the
lights in the electric tower all is still as the grave. The drab cellhouses, checkered with the apertures of numerous counter-sunk
steel doors, resemble four huge tombs. Not even the drone of the
waves against the rugged coast a few yards distant penetrates the
vast walls that rise on every side and hem in this colony of crime
from the world of righteousness, out of which it has been wrested
by the strong arm of the law.

"Twelve o'clock, and all-l-l-l's well!"

The blatant voice of the guard in No. 1 post suddenly breaks
upon the midnight calm. The cry is caught up and repeated by
No. 2, and then, in varying intonations, in voices deep and reso-
nant, in voices harsh and cracked, in squeaky, in shrill, in twanging
voices it is tossed and bandied and passed from post to post until
every nook and cranny of the great prison reverberates with the
multisonous discords.

"Twelve o'clock, and all-l-l-l's well!"

Hundreds of fitful sleepers turn uneasily on their hard, narrow
cots in the ill-ventilated cells. Resignedly they recognize the call of
the law—their hourly nocturnal nemesis—reminding them that,
even in sleep, they are convicts, convicts, convicts—outcasts and
pariahs.

And this is midnight of the 31st of December—the call has ush-
ered them into a new year. To some this means nothing, for time

has lost its relation to life—they are "doing it all." To others—to that row of cells where the lights burn all night so that a suicide in the dark may not cheat the gallows—it means the dawn of eternity, their last new year—a day nearer the "rope." To a few it signalizes the approach of freedom, the beginning of the year which has been so patiently awaited, perchance for five, ten or fifteen years. To still others it brings hazy recollections of boyhood, of the gala times spent in celebrating the dawn of the new years long since dead and gone.

"Twelve o'clock, and all-l-l-l's well!"

The echoes finally die away, and all is again still. Once more the men and the boys in the bare, cheerless cells fall into troubled sleep. Not a sound save the shuffling feet of the second night watch, who come in to relieve the first watch, and a few gruff "good nights," as the relieved men turn over their arms, breaks the stillness.

But hark! What is that noise, faint and far away? At first it sounds like the moaning of the wind, but presently resolves itself into the blasts of remote whistles. They are so far away that individuality is lost, and it sounds like a wail; the element of rejoicing is absent. A drizzling rain begins to fall as the last guard passes out of the front gate to his sleep. It has come to baptize the infant year.

"They're having a great old time in 'Frisco town tonight," he remarks, as the gatekeeper softly closes the steel door behind him. Over on the porch of the office a lone figure is standing. It is the figure of a tall, broad-shouldered man in dark clothes and derby hat. It is the Warden of San Quentin prison. He has been Warden for six months. What is he doing inside the prison at that hour of the night? Why isn't he at home and asleep? The guards are all at their posts, and the prisoners are all securely locked in the black cells across the quadrangle. The explanation is contained in the remark that he makes as he passes the guard at No. 1 post on his way out of the prison a few minutes later:

"Well, it worked. They responded to the call on their honor. Good-night."

What did the Warden mean by that remark, and who are "they"?

For years and years the prisoners at San Quentin had looked upon New Year's Eve as a time when they might take matters into their own hands. For years and years they had remained awake on the night of December 31, waiting for the midnight call; waiting with wash basins, heavy brogans, stools and bed slats in their hands.

And no sooner did the guard in No. 1 post begin the midnight call than pandemonium broke loose. Iron doors were beaten with stool and cans and shoes. Curses were shrieked from the wickets out into the night. Band instruments were blown in horrible discord. The bass drum in the bandroom was usually beaten into a pulp.

All the repression, all the hate, all the despair of the year was suddenly released and poured forth in a torrent that made fear clutch at the heart. The thing was contagious. Men of quiet dispositions, opposed to the lawless outbreak, would find themselves shrieking and pounding with the others. For three hours the noise would continue. Sometimes it would die down and almost cease when one or two spirits more untamed, more bitter, more lawless than the others, would shriek afresh, and then the outburst would follow with redoubled vigor. Many men took advantage of the occasion to bellow the most horrible curses at the guards or officers whom they disliked. The residents of San Quentin village used to assemble on the little hill just beyond the prison wall to the north and listen to the outburst. The next morning the yard would be strewn with broken stools and demolished buckets.

Many Wardens had tried to stop this New Year's demonstration. Some had placed guards on the tiers with orders to take the numbers of the cells where any noise occurred. Others had posted notices in the yard that any noise at midnight would be followed by a deprivation of all privileges during the new year. Still others had stretched the fire hose with instructions to the guards to play streams of water into the cells and dormitories if an outburst occurred. But all these measures failed of their purpose. They were like waving a red flag before an angry bull.

On one occasion when there was sickness in the Warden's house he had sent a request to the prisoners asking them to keep quiet. Most of them did so, but a few did not. That particular Warden was not liked.

And yet on New Year's Eve of 1907 midnight came and went without a sound save the regulation call. There were no guards posted on the tiers; there were no lines of fire hose stretched from the stand-pipes; there had been no threat of loss of privileges. Old-time prison officials had frequently expressed the opinion that it would never be possible to stop the demonstration on New Year's Eve. Wardens with eight years' experience had been unable to stop it. Surely a young man who had been Warden for only six months could not hope to accomplish it. But the young man did, and by doing so placed a period at the end of decades of misunderstanding between prisoners and their keepers.

What had he done to bring about such an attitude of respect. Had he threatened the men with punishment? Had he doped them with sedatives at the evening meal the night before? No; he had done neither of these things. He had simply had notices distributed in the cells and dormitories asking each prisoner to refrain from making any noise at midnight, and stating that he hoped they would feel that the request was made in good faith, and that he felt confident each one would respond to it.

Why had the men responded? Well, a week before, on Christmas Eve, the Warden had come inside the prison and had been much surprised to see socks hanging from nearly every wicket. It had been an amusement for the old-time prison officers to see socks hung out on Christmas Eve, but to Warden Hoyle it was something more than amusing. He promptly sent an officer to San Quentin Point and bought every bit of confection and fruit in the town; and when the officer got back with his load it was distributed in the socks at midnight.

Next morning when the prisoners awoke and found that they had at last been remembered it struck deeply. It was not the first instance of the new Warden's humanitarianism, but it made a deeper impression than anything else he had done. Some may call it sentiment—perhaps it was—but it did not prove so a week later on New Year's Eve. And at each New Year's Eve since that time the whistles and bells at San Francisco, San Rafael and from the Contra Costa shore have merely served to lull the inmates of San Quentin into deeper sleep.

AGNES SMEDLEY

1892–1950

Born in rural Missouri and raised in poverty that kept her from finishing grade school, Agnes Smedley was—as her friend Margaret Sanger wrote—"consistently for the under dog." During World War I, she was an active supporter of socialism, legalizing birth control, and freeing India from British rule. Denounced by British intelligence agents as a German spy because of her association with Indian anticolonialists, Smedley was arrested in 1918 by U.S. government agents who brutally interrogated her for several days. A search of her personal belongings uncovered several copies of Sanger's birth-control pamphlet Family Limitation. *Because advocating birth control was then a federal crime, this gave federal authorities another legal basis for imprisoning Smedley in the Tombs, New York City's notorious jail. There she served six months, mainly in solitary confinement. She was never brought to trial but charges against her were dropped after the Armistice.*

In 1929, Smedley published her stunning autobiographical novel Daughter of Earth, *which was rediscovered in the early 1970s and is now widely taught as a distinguished achievement of twentieth-century American literature. The long section of the novel based on Smedley's arrest, interrogation, and imprisonment draws heavily on the sketches reprinted here of the women she encountered in jail, sketches originally published in the Sunday supplement to the New York socialist magazine the* Call *(February 15, 22, 29, and March 14, 1920).*

After the end of World War I, Smedley spent several years in Germany and the Soviet Union. In 1928 she went to China, then in the early stages of its protracted revolution. There she found her main calling in life as one of the most informed and influential chroniclers of that revolution. Her books on China include Chinese Destinies: Sketches of Present-Day China *(1933);* China's Red Army Marches *(1934);* China Fights Back: An American Woman with the Eighth Route Army *(1938);* Stories of the Wounded *(1941);* Battle Hymn of China *(1943), which also contains an important autobiography; and the posthumous* The Great Road: The Life and Times of Chu Teh *(1956).*

Cell Mates

From the Call Magazine, *Sunday supplement to the New York* Call, *15, 22, 29 February, 14 March 1920.*

Nellie

M Y FIRST IMPRESSION of Nellie was gained when I looked up from my lukewarm breakfast coffee to listen to an avalanche of profanity in an Irish brogue. Nellie was swearing at the food, and was showering blessings of wrath upon the wardens and matrons of the Tombs prison, who she swore by all the angels and the Blessed Virgin had built the jail and ran it for their own pleasure and profit.

The matron spoke: "Shut your mouth, Nellie, or I'll lock you in your cell."

Nellie looked up, took up the matron's words, and set them to music. She sang hilariously and, finishing her coffee, two-stepped down past the matron and looked her in the eye, still singing. She two-stepped down the corridor and around behind the iron gate into the "run," in which old offenders are locked during the day.

Nellie was short, blocky, square in build. Fifty-three summers had come and gone without leaving their touches in her hair. She had grown ugly and scarred, knotted, twisted and gnarled like an old oak. But her vitality had never waned. Her figure had been permitted to develop, unhampered by corsets—and it had developed, particularly her stomach and hips. The expression on her square, scarred Irish face was good-natured and happy-go-lucky, with a touch of sadness which gripped your heart at times.

From the North of Ireland, Nellie had come to America while still a girl under 20. And, being pretty and very ignorant, with no means of support, she had, in due course of time, become a prostitute. Since that time she had served innumerable short terms in all the jails in Jersey and New York City. Her offenses generally consisted of intoxication, fighting, or "hustling."

In her day, according to her story, she had been much sought after by "gentlemen," and her "clients" included pillars of the law—all the local judges and such. She told me that once she had been brought by a policeman before one of these estimable personages, and after he had rebuked her and sentenced her to pay a nominal fine, she had made some interesting disclosures in the court room and insisted upon his paying the fine for her.

Nellie had never lost her Irish brogue in all these years, and she greeted those whom she liked with "Top o' the mornin' to ye," and those whom she disliked with a "Well, damn ye, ye're able to git up this mornin' and raise hell, ain't ye?"

The girls at the long bare breakfast table had laughed as Nellie gaily responded to the matron's rebuke. From back of the iron gates Nellie's voice came like a fog-horn from a distance. She was feeling fine this morning, and the girls finished breakfast quickly.

"Come on, give us a jig, Nellie," one called.

Nellie pulled her old dirty blue skirt half way to her knees, exposing dirty white stockings, and started to jig. It was an Irish jig, and her old run-down shoes made a sound like fire-crackers on the cement floor. She sang as she danced—Irish songs and songs indigenous to the soil of America and to Nellie's peculiar mode of life. Some of them are unprintable. One of them began:

> "Oh-h-h-h!
> Did you ever have a fight
> In the middle of the night
> With the gur-r-rl you love?"

And so throughout the day Nellie kept the girls at attention, vile in talk, always profane, dipping snuff and brow-beating the matrons. When visitors appeared at the gate and gazed back with round eyes at the strange creatures in the cage, Nellie would call "Oh-h-h! Where did you get that hat!" or "Top o' the mornin' to ye, lady; are ye plannin' to break in?"

No one could be depressed for long, with Nellie present. One morning I came in from my gray cell into the dull gray corridor. Life seemed quite as dull and gray as my surroundings. Nellie was sitting on a bench near my door, baking her feet against the radiator. She looked up, and her voice scattered the gloom into a thousand fragments:

"Oh-h-h!
Good mornin', O Missus O'Grady,
Why are you so blue today?"

I sat down by her.

"Ye're a nice thing," she said; "and why are ye in this place?"

"I don't think you'd understand if I told you, Nellie," I replied.

Nellie fixed her eyes on space for a few moments. That expression of sadness crept about her mouth.

"I guess ye're right," she said. "I mighta once. I was a purty gir-rl once"—

I felt that I had inadvertently recalled long-dead summers of a tragic life. But before I had time to rebuke myself, she kicked the radiator and brightly asked:

"And how do ye like this hotel?"

I asked why she was there. She reflected for a moment.

"By the holy mother uv Jesus," she started, "I'm as innicent as a baby."

"What is the charge?"

"Hittin' a man on the head with a hammer," she replied.

"I didn't do it," she reiterated, to my back.

"Why didn't you?" I asked.

She chuckled and took some snuff.

"Jest ye wait till I git out."

Then she told me how it happened. It took a long time, and she went into the family history and her personal relations with all the neighbors. She had been out all night, it seems, and in the early morning had gone home. She stopped at a saloon beneath her flat and reinforced herself with liquor before facing her husband, Mike.

Tim, the bartender, had warned her.

"Nellie," he cautioned, "ye'd better not go home now. Ye'll sure git in a tussel with Mike if ye do."

But Nellie, according to her own statement, was "feelin' like a bur-r-d"; so she "ups and flits up the stairs jist as airy as ye please."

Mike was indignant, as husbands sometimes are. He questioned his erring and reinforced wife. The forewarned struggle ensued. The kitchen suffered somewhat, and Mike retreated down the stairs to the first landing. There a friend opened the door, grasped his predicament, and came to his assistance. Somewhat pressed, Nellie picked up a hammer which was lying on a trunk and laid low the intruder.

When Mike's would-be assistant came to consciousness he got a bandage and a policeman, the former for himself and the latter for Nellie.

Nellie concluded her tale. "They arristed me—an', would ye believe me, it wuz Holy Thursday!"

She had been in the Tombs for a number of months. Once Mike came to see her, and she had asked him for a dollar to buy a little extra food. What he replied I don't know, but when she returned to us she sat down in a corner and cried piteously.

The next morning she came in as usual, to see if I wished to get up for breakfast. I asked her to order some extra food from the restaurant.

"And, Nellie," I said, "order yourself a good breakfast."

She grinned and thanked me. And about an hour later her breakfast bill was sent in to me. Nellie had done as I had asked, and had ordered a *good* breakfast! It included, among a dozen other things, four or five pieces of pie. It seems she had stocked up for the winter. And I paid the bill gladly.

When I saw Nellie last she came around to the iron gate to tell us goodby. She had on a clean white waist, and her hair was combed. She was being released, without going to trial.

"What are you going to do now?" I asked.

Her old face assumed that peculiar expression of goodness and sadness—and of helplessness. I knew she didn't know, and that it didn't matter much what she did. She was turned loose on the streets again. No one met her; no one was waiting to welcome her. She turned and left us, a little stooped, and I heard her old shoes click as she went down the cement corridor.

May

May sat near the barred gate smoking a cigarette and resting her fat hands on her fatter knees. If convicted of forgery this time it meant eight fingerprints—one for each year she had been in the business. She was no amateur; one isn't an amateur at 45, after passing from the factory and the stage into private business.

May's complaint wasn't so much that she had been caught, but that she had been caught on such a trifle. She had sent cigars to a fictitious son in Camp Upton and given a check to the cigar store, receiving only $10 in change.

Her bail was $500, but her man, Vic, was too cowardly to furnish it. It meant trouble for him if he did. He had managed to keep out of the law's grip for eight years, just as she had managed to keep in it; but as years went by the danger seemed to creep closer. Even when May had been arrested this time he had been with her. But she had explained to the detective that he was a strange man who had kindly offered to carry her packages. So he had escaped the law again.

Of course, she realized that Vic couldn't risk arrest; but it seemed unfair at times; she had always shouldered the blame, and always served time, often for him. Even now he wrote letters declaring that had it not been for rheumatism he would have been down to leave money for her personal expenses; but it never occurred to him to send money by mail. Yet again she would forgive him, as women often do. She had his picture in her purse; it was dim and worn from much handling, and she looked at it with mingled anger and compassion. When any one agreed with her that Vic was a worthless scoundrel, she launched into a long defense which would have wrung tears from any jury who didn't happen to know the facts.

"How you worry about a $500 bail!" I exclaimed. "Mine is $10,000."

"Well," May retorted, "*I* didn't try to swing the world by the tail. All I wanted was a little change."

"Tell me," I asked her, "why did you stop working in a factory?"

"Go work in a factory and find out," was her reply.

"Well, why did you leave the stage?"

"Look at me," she challenged sarcastically, "and look at my figger!" I looked. It *was* rather discouraging; about five feet high and five feet wide, yellow hair and an accordion pleated chin. Eight years ago she had been thirty-seven. One can't be a successful chorus girl at thirty-seven, after your renowned cuteness becomes buried beneath a bed of fat.

"Couldn't you do something else besides—this?" I inquired, hesitatingly.

"Yes," she grimly retorted, "I could scrub floors or take in washin', or 'hustle,' or do a few little things like that."

May warned me that a "stool pigeon" would undoubtedly be put in to watch me and try to get information from me, that perhaps one was there already; that maybe she, herself, was one. She was scornful of my "greenness."

"Gawd!" she exclaimed once, "I guess if some bull came in here dressed up like a priest, you'd believe him. Now, listen to me, never trust a man dressed like a priest."

May constituted herself my guardian and carefully kept the other girls out of my cell. "Get out, you hussey, you low-down thief," she yelled at them when they wandered into my cell. And if they didn't get out, she would put them out.

"Don't give them any money," she cautioned me time and again. But when she left, she carried some of my money with her. My "greenness" was very profound.

When taken to court, she wore a hat over which flowed a long black veil.

"Some veil," she laughed. "It ought to be a mask!" But even her jokes were told in a tremulous voice, as if she were telling them to keep from thinking of other things.

When the women returned from court, they told me that a very ugly man had appeared against May and that she, when asked if what he said were true, had replied that "any man with a face like that ought to have a check passed on him." She and the other women had been compelled to walk between the long row of masked detectives, veils thrown back; two of the detectives recognized May. She was given the "Indefinite," which means anything from three months to three years in the penitentiary.

Mollie

For circulating leaflets opposing intervention in Russia, Mollie Steimer, with three men comrades, had been sentenced to 15 years in prison, a $500 fine and deportation to Russia. A good start for a little Russian girl less than five feet in height who had not yet reached the age of 21.

Mollie had come from the Ukraine five years before, and since that time had worked in a waist factory for $10 a week. A few months preceding her arrest she had received $15. She was the eldest of five children. A sister, aged 17, and a brother, aged 14, as well as her father, were all factory workers.

Mollie was sitting in her cell writing when I was put into jail. Her greeting was characteristic of her cast of mind.

"I am glad to see you here!" she said. "I wish the prisons to be filled with the workers. They soon will be. Then we will wake up."

Before her, pasted on the wall, were newspaper photographs of Karl Liebknecht, Eugene V. Debs and John Reed, and, printed in red letters high up on the stone wall, were the words, "Long live the Social Revolution!"

Mollie wore a red Russian smock. Her short hair was glossy black and curled up at the ends. Her face belonged to Russia, and the expression of seriousness and silent determination had first been cast in that country many years before. Her carefully chosen words were expressed with a slight foreign accent. Seldom did she speak of anything save Russia, the revolution in Germany and Austria and the future of the workers in America. She was always looking toward that world which she had described on the witness stand to a judge from Alabama:

"It will be a new social order," she had said, "of which no group of people shall be in the power of any other group. Every person shall have an equal opportunity to develop himself. None shall live by the product of another. Every one shall produce what he can and enjoy what he needs. He shall have time to gain knowledge and culture. At present humanity is divided into groups called nations. We workers of the world will unite in one human brotherhood. To bring about this I have pledged myself to work all my life."

"Is there any such place as you tell about?" the prosecuting attorney had sneered. Mollie replied:

"I believe those who represent Russia have been elected by the workers only. The parasites are not represented in the Bolshevik administration."

The girls in prison loved Mollie. She talked with them at great length, disagreeing with them and frankly criticizing them if she thought best. At night she would talk gently to some girl who was trying to smother her sobs in the rough prison blankets. After the cell doors clanged behind us in the late afternoon, Mollie would stand grasping the steel bars. In simple, slow words she would talk to the girls. She used English which the most humble could understand, and as she spoke the three tiers would become silent and only an occasional question would interrupt her talk.

Mollie's philosophy of life had not been gleaned from books. A child of the soil, the finely-worded sentiments of the *intelligencia* did not impress her as being sincere. The *intelligencia* had deserted the workers of Russia when the great crisis came, when the workers of that country had challenged. "Peace to the huts, war to the palaces, hail to the Third International!"

With her own hands Mollie had labored for many years, had longed for, but never enjoyed, the beautiful things of life, and little, save the most sordid, bare necessities. Even the possibility of school had been closed to her. About her in the factory she had seen thousands like herself, pouring out their lives for crumbs, suffering, and then dying, poor and wretched. The class struggle to her became a grim reality.

Mollie championed the cause of the prisoners—the one with venereal disease, the mother with diseased babies, the prostitute, the feeble-minded, the burglar, the murderer. To her they were but products of a diseased social system. She did not complain that even the most vicious of them were sentenced to no more than five or seven years, while she herself was facing 15 years in prison. She asked that the girl with venereal disease be taken to a hospital; the prison physician accused her of believing in free love and in Bolshevism. She asked that the vermin be cleaned from the cells of one of the girls; the matron ordered her to attend to her own affairs—that it was not *her* cell. To quiet her they would lock her in her cell. "Lock me in," she replied to the matron; "I have nothing to lose but my chains."

Then the news of the German revolution and of the armistice came. Outside the whistles shrieked and people yelled. In the prison yard outside some of the men prisoners were herded together as a special favor to join in the rejoicing. The keepers moved about among them, waving their arms and telling the men to be glad. The men stood with limp arms and dull faces, looking into the sky and at each other. A few endeavored to show signs of happiness when the warden came their way.

"Peace has come," Mollie said, standing at my side, "but not for us. Our struggle will be all the more bitter now."

The time came when Mollie's old mother, arising from the sick bed, came with a bandaged ear to the prison to tell her of the death of her father and of her 14-year-old brother. Mollie did not cry. She returned to the cell and quietly sat down on the bed beside me.

But once I felt the convulsive trembling of her body. Her words came slowly at last:

"You should have seen my father," she said, "so thin, so worked out! Since he was but 10 years old he had worked 14 to 15 hours each day. He was so worked out, so thin! I knew he did not have the strength to live if he ever became ill."

Then, later: "Our dreams," she said; "how fragile! I have dreamed for years—oh, such dreams! Of my brother and sister in school, of studying, of a new order of society. In one minute my dreams are shattered!"

Through the bars of the cell door, through the dirty windows across the corridor could be seen the tops of unbeautiful, dingy buildings. Outside the windows the great stone wall surrounding the prison obstructed all view of the street. The roar of the elevated train, the rattle of drays on cobblestone pavement, and the shouts of men disturbed but slightly the misery of the jail. From the tiers below came the shouts and the curses of the old offenders.

"Our dreams—how fragile!" mingled with the curses of the women, and before long it seemed that the women, too, were saying, "Our dreams—how fragile; our dreams—how fragile." At times they laughed it, and at times they cursed and sneered as they said it.

Yet the thought: Can that which is so fragile endure so much? And the doors of the past swung back and revealed dreams which have endured for thousands of years, suffering defeat only to rise again; braving prisons, torture, death, and at last wrecking empires.

Mollie was released under $10,000 bail to await her appeal to the Supreme Court. I watched her pass through the prison yard. A marshal walked beside her, talking out of the corner of his mouth. He did not offer to carry her suitcase, heavy with books. His neck bulged with fat, his chest was high and his shoulders primitive. Mollie did not listen to him. Her eyes were looking straight ahead into the distance.

Weeks passed, and in the world outside I met Mollie once more. She was on strike with the 40,000 clothing workers, and was among the many pickets arrested. A few weeks afterward she came to see me. Her shoulders had grown sharp and thin and she cynical. She had been arrested a number of times upon suspicion; secret service men seemed to follow her and arrest her as a matter of general principle. At last she was arrested for alleged distribution of radical leaflets and held at Ellis Island for deportation. There she went on hunger strike to protest segregation from her fellow political prisoners. A friend, holding her thin, cold hand, asked if she thought it worth while. Mollie replied:

"Every protest against the present system is worth while. Some one must start."

Mollie did not object to deportation—provided it was done at once, and to Soviet Russia instead of to the region under Czarist generals. The city authorities evidently conferred with Federal agents, and decided to try her in the city courts instead. She was sentenced to serve six months in Blackwells Island jail, a place notorious for its filth and barbarity.

A short time has now elapsed since the Supreme Court upheld the decision of the lower court on the first indictment against Mollie. And she, frail, childlike, with the spirit which made the Russian revolution possible, will be taken after her jail term is finished to Jefferson City prison, where she is sentenced to spend 15 years of her life at hard labor.

Mollie's reasoning is something like this: Under the Czar we knew there was no hope; we did not delude ourselves into believing that he would release those who worked against the system which he represented and upheld. In America we have been carefully taught that we live in a democracy, and we are still waiting for some one to feed us democracy. While waiting, we starve to death or are sent to prison, where we get free food for 15 or 20 years.

Kitty

Kitty Marion was serving thirty days for giving a pamphlet on birth control to a Mr. Bamberg, who had come to her office and told her with much feeling of his large family, his low salary and the fear of adding more children to his household. Bamberg turned out to be a "stool pigeon" for the notorious Association for the Suppression of Vice. He justified his existence by making people break the law and then having them arrested. Kitty Marion was one of his victims.

Kitty came clattering down the stone corridors every morning with her scrub pail in her hand. "Three cheers for birth control," she greeted the prisoners and matrons. And, "Three cheers for birth control," the prisoners answered back.

Her marked English accent recalled to mind that she had been one of Mrs. Pankhurst's militants in London, had been imprisoned time without number and had had her throat ruined by forcible feeding. She holds the record; she was forcibly fed 233 times in Halloway prison.

"Dirty work," I remarked one morning, as she came in to scrub the Tombs corridors.

"Not half so dirty as cleaning up the man-made laws in this country," she replied. Then we continued our discussion of peace and change.

The prison physician came in to examine two infants.

"Three cheers for birth control," Kitty called to him from her kneeling position. She held her mop rag in mid air. He turned, and she, scrubbing away, remarked:

"Some way or other every time I see a man the more I believe in birth control."

When visitors or keepers came into the prison Kitty was always heard cheering for birth control. When peace was declared she expressed the hope, in a voice that those who run might hear, that now America would apply a little freedom to her own people and grant women the right of personal liberty. So taken up by the injustice of her imprisonment was she that when her room was infested with vermin she remarked that they reminded her of a mass-meeting of Bamberg's vice society; and when she had been forced to put on a striped dress of the convicted women, she looked at it and remarked, "Ah! blue and white stripes! Now, if there were only a few red stripes and some white stars!"

The matrons were glad when her term was finished. When she left she announced that she had come in a spark but was going out a living flame.

KATE RICHARDS O'HARE
1876–1948

In the tiny, remote town of Bowman, North Dakota, a small crowd gathered on a hot summer day in 1917 to listen to a woman from the Socialist Party speaking out against America's participation in World War I. Although she never urged young men to avoid the draft or suggested any violation of law, she was accused of saying that the women of the United States were being turned into "brood sows, to raise children to get into the army and be made into fertilizer." For this speech, the U.S. government convicted Kate Richards O'Hare of violating the Espionage Act of 1917 and sentenced her to five years in prison.

After all appeals were exhausted and despite considerable public protest, O'Hare, the mother of four children, began serving her sentence in April 1919, five months after the Armistice had ended World War I. Because there were then no federal prisons for women, O'Hare was incarcerated in the women's section of the Missouri State Penitentiary in Jefferson City, where she was to dwell until May 1920, when President Woodrow Wilson commuted her sentence because of her deteriorating health.

The atrocious conditions that she encountered led O'Hare to send In Prison; Being a Report by Kate Richards O'Hare to the President of the United States as to the Conditions under Which Women Federal Prisoners Are Confined in the Missouri State Penitentiary . . . *to Wilson in 1920. Three years later she published an expanded version, entitled* In Prison, *a book that was to become a major text in the prison reform movement of succeeding decades. In 1938, O'Hare became the assistant director of the California Department of Penology, a position she used to help reform the barbarous California prison system.*

from *Crime and Criminals*

I.

NEWSPAPERS AND MAGAZINES have been busy for the past few months discussing a disturbing social phenomenon which they call the "crime wave." Judging from the reports of the press, crime has increased in the United States in an alarming manner during the last year. The jails are full, the criminal court dockets are overburdened and penitentiaries are crowded to capacity. Rare indeed is the newspaper that has not demanded more effective policing, more stringent laws and more drastic penalties for the detection and punishment of crime. . . .

In all the noise and shouting of the discussion of crime and criminals I feel inclined to take part. You see, I know considerable about these great social problems from the inside. Most people who study crime and criminals study from the outside peering in, but I studied on the inside peeping out—through prison bars. . . .

I had the task of making a study of criminals and crime thrust upon me. It was not a pleasant school; I have enjoyed certain periods of my life much better than the fourteen months I spent in Jefferson City; but it was an extremely valuable schooling. It was the opportunity that comes to few to study a great social problem at its source, and I have no regret and feel not one particle of bitterness for the men who thrust my big job upon me.

My Prison Mates.

Among my prison mates I found women were sent to prison for three kinds of crime. Crimes against property, crimes against person and crimes against the government. Crimes against property and person are common, but the sort of crimes against the government that I and my prison mates were charged with having committed are new, they have only existed since 1917; they were created by the "Espionage Act." A law penalizing treason has been upon our statute books ever since the foundation of the government, but to be guilty of treason one must commit some definite overt act, injuring or endangering the government. The "Espionage Act" penalizes not acts of injury or menace, but the expression of opinion. One need not commit an overt act to be guilty of a felony under this law; one need only say or write or print an opinion that differs, not with the fundamental laws of the country, but differs from the opinions held by the political party in power.

I know quite well, I think, every woman who served prison sentences for alleged violations of the "Espionage Act." There were women of spotless character, of more than average intelligence, and all useful workers. Most of them were of middle age and had received their education some time ago, before it had become a "crime" to read the Declaration of Independence and "disloyal" to quote the Constitution of the United States. They were for the most part women who had been raised in the religious faith of yesterday. The women who could not conceive of it being a crime to quote the commands of God, given through Moses the great lawgiver—"Thou shalt not steal" and "Thou shalt not kill." They were the sort of women whose anchorage to spiritual life was that command of Jesus, "Love thy neighbor as thyself and do unto others as ye would that they should do unto you."

Of the women who had committed crimes against person and property, I found that they were for the most part tragic misfits of life. They were very poorly educated, few having reached the sixth grade in school. A large percentage were feeble-minded, or on the borderline of mental subnormality. They were practically all diseased in body, brain and soul. Ninety per cent or more of them had been convicted of some minor offense against property. A small percentage had committed offenses against person, and a few had taken human life. And they were all poor; all from the most poverty-pinched section of the working class. The net of criminal law that gathered in the catch at Jefferson City had held only the little criminals and let the big ones escape. My prison experience did not give me the advantage of association with "malefactors of great wealth." So in discussing crime and criminals from my own personal experiences, I shall be compelled to deal with that small section of the criminal class who land in prison—the poor and humble.

And this is not a criticism of law; it is merely a statement of the facts, for which there are perfectly logical reasons. Lawyers and judges, and for the most part juries, are drawn almost entirely from the "upper classes," the property-owning classes. Their birth, education, moral and political training, as well as their economic interests, are all those of the property-owning class. Their entire psychology is that of the "haves," and it is inevitable that all of their legal decisions should express their fear and dislike for the "have nots."

It is perfectly logical that when a poor, ill-dressed, uncouth, ignorant person is brought before the court charged with a minor crime against person or property, that those who administer law should do it from their own psychological bias. This human misfit has been proven a failure. His station in life proclaims his "unfitness;" he looks like a criminal, and is no doubt dangerous, and society will be safer with him behind prison bars. He has no money to pay for an expensive defense. Laws may not have human weaknesses, but the men who interpret them and execute them have, and all legal decisions are the expression of the human bias of the court.

It is also perfectly logical that courts should feel differently towards the educated, well bred, well groomed, correctly tailored man who comes into court with a group of expensive and eminent legal advisors to represent him. And men of this type are not usually charged with such sordid, ugly crimes that offend the sensibilities of a cultured judge. Naturally he feels differently, and the procedure is different for a dirty bum charged with stealing from a freight car than for a respectable and wealthy business man charged with the violation of some vague law like the "Lever Act." The man charged with petty stealing "looks like" a criminal, and the man charged with "profiteering" looks like a business man, and the judge unconsciously shades the law accordingly. The dirty bum goes to prison and the respectable business man goes back to his business affairs. . . .

In the punishment of crimes against the person the same thing is true. The person who looks like a criminal is presumed to look, and is therefor offensive to the court, goes to prison; the person who looks like a pillar of society, and behaves like one in the presence of the court goes free. Mamie F. was a "hasher" in a cheap restaurant in St. Louis. Another "hasher tried to cop her steady," according to Mamie, so she "just carved her, to spoil her map." Mamie served two years in Jefferson City for inflicting a slight gash on a woman's face. The Fulton Bag Co. used presses in their factory that were dangerous and unlawful to use. One of these presses cut off both of Marie Montemann's arms at the shoulder, making her a helpless cripple for life. But neither the owners nor the manager of the Fulton Bag Co., responsible for the use of dangerous machinery, served time in prison.

Laura was a poor love-starved "old maid" whom life had denied love or wifehood or motherhood, and given the lot of a housemaid drudging in more fortunate folks' kitchens. Laura was charged with being the mother of an illegitimate baby. The baby died. Laura was convicted for having permitted it to die for want of food. And Laura served a five-year term in prison. Five great dairy companies in St. Louis raised the price of milk to a point where the wages of poor men cannot buy milk and hundreds of babies die as a result.

But no dairy owners ever serve time in Jefferson City for starving babies to death. . . .

In the case of Schwartz & Jaffe vs. The Amalgamated Clothing Workers, Judge Vansiclin makes the position and the perfectly natural bias of the court plain. He said:

"They (the courts) must stand at all times as the representatives of capital, of captains of industry, devoted to the principle of individual initiative, protect property from violence and destruction, strongly opposed to the nationalization of industry." And this honest judge states the case very neatly and explains why there are no captains of industry in prison, and why I missed the advantage of making a study of "malefactors of great wealth." Not because there are no "malefactors of great wealth;" they are plentiful as fleas on a mangy pup; but because the "courts must stand at all times as the representatives of capital, of captains of industry."

II.

When we go to prison and study the people whom society has definitely set aside, branded and caged as criminals, we find strange and puzzling things. We seem to have decided pretty definitely that most criminals who go to prison are poor people, but I doubt if we are willing to agree that poverty in itself is a crime. We know that rich people don't go to prison, as a rule; but I doubt if we are willing to agree that wealth in itself is a virtue. . . .

In the studies that I was able to make of that small section of our criminal population which lands in prison, I found prison management quite as interesting a study as prison inmates. I found that under the guise of punishment for crime, and in the name of reformation of criminals a tremendously profitable form of chattel slavery is carried on.

When I reached prison I found that I had been sold by the United States Department of Justice to a prison Board made of three men, one a backwoods editor, one a livery stable keeper, another a mule buyer and all of them of the most sordid type of professional politicians.

The process whereby the United States Department of Justice becomes a dealer in slaves is very simple. It does not maintain sufficient prisons to care for nearly all of its male prisoners and has no facilities whatever for caring for female prisoners. Here at stated times the Department of Justice sends out letters to the various prison boards announcing that they have prisoners to dispose of and asking for bids. One prison which feeds its prisoners decently, works them with some degree of humanity and cares for them in something approaching a civilized manner, bids, say, twenty-five dollars a month. That is, this prison will board and guard the prisoner, the Department of Justice pays twenty-five dollars a month, and the prison board has the right to make all the profit possible out of the labor of the prisoner. The prison board securing the contract is paid by the Department of Justice for caring for the prisoner and the labor is what thieves call "velvet." A prison less humane and decent will bid twenty dollars a month. The Missouri State Prison bids eighteen dollars per month.

So I know from actual experience what the auction block means, I have tried it. I know from actual experience that the only difference between Cassie and me was that Cassie was sold to the highest bidder and I was sold to the lowest. Cassie also had a market value that made Simon Legree give the sort of a life that would not lower her market value. I had no market value and the prison board who bought me had but one incentive, and that to transform every particle of my life in the few years they were to own me.

I found that the prison board to whom the women convicts had been sold in turn sold them for nine hours per day to the Oberman Mfg. Co., who manufactures overalls. The state of Missouri is forbidden by law to sell its convicts to contractors of convict labor. I do not know how this law is evaded. I only know that it is evaded. I also know that the Oberman Mfg. Co. made garments that bore the labels of reputable firms all over the country.

And God knows that the profits of these chattel slaves are enormous! Every day I worked in the prison slave pen I earned, at scab wages, paid in the worst of scab shops, from $4.80 to $5.20 each day. I was paid 50¢ a month the first three months, 75¢ a month the next three months and $1 a month after that. I made about $2,000 worth of unionalls, I was paid $10.50 for making them. And all of the difference between what I made and what I received went, not into the treasury of the United States, but into the pockets of the prison contractors as profits. Figure what the profit on the labor of 2,800 convicts amounts to in a year!

The Task.

The black woman on the plantation was given a cottonsack and she must do her "task" of picking a certain number of pounds of cotton each day. If she failed to do the "task" she was punished by the slave driver, hired for that purpose. I was given a power sewing machine in an overall factory, and worked under the "task" system. My "task" was to make eighty-eight unionall jackets each day, regardless of my physical condition, previous training or the size or weight of the garments. If I failed to make the "task" I too was punished by a slave driver hired for that purpose.

I don't know whether it is the deliberate plan, or merely a condition that has grown up, but the "task" consumes a woman's life in about the average length of a prison sentence, and the women usually go out fit only for the human scrapheap.

The lightest punishment for failure to make the "task" was to be sent to the punishment cell without supper, be denied mail and all communication with other inmates, and sent back to the shop the next morning without breakfast. The second time the convict failed to "pull the task" she went to the punishment cell at noon on Saturday, stayed there until Monday morning, then went back to the shop. From Saturday morning until Monday noon she received no food except two very small slices of bread and half a teacup of water.

The third time a woman failed to make the "task" she went to the "black hole" or the "blind cell" as it is sometimes called. This cell is built in the solid stone wall; it is without light, heat or ventilation, and is without furniture or toilet facilities. The floor is concrete, and regardless of the physical condition of the women, or the temperature, they must stand continually, or lie upon the stone floor. In cold weather the women would pull the buttons from their clothing, flip them up, then crawl about on the stone floor to find them; then do it all over again to keep themselves awake for days at a time, to avoid contracting pneumonia from the ice cold stones.

While in the "black hole" the women were given two tiny slices of bread each day and half teacup of water. After I went to Jefferson City and became to some extent a public eye, the women were not often kept in the "black hole" more than fifteen days. Before I arrived, there seemed to be no limit, except the slave driver's brutality.

There is a tragic story of a young woman by the name of Minnie Eddy, which can be verified by living witnesses, who was sent to Jefferson City for some minor crime. She was mentally and physically incapable of making the task, so she went to the "black hole" again and again. Finally she was kept there twenty-one days, taken out in a dying state with pneumonia, fed on coarse prison food, and the next day Minnie Eddy died.

The most revolting punishments I saw inflicted had to do with sex perversions, and I cannot discuss them because there is no language available. If I used the prison argot, you would not understand, and if I tried to translate it into what you could grasp, I would be arrested for using vulgar and obscene language.

And the most terrible thing of all is that in one instance and one only, did I see a convict punished for bad behavior, for misconduct, for the sort of things you would naturally imagine convicts would do. Every punishment but one that I saw inflicted, was not administered for correction, or discipline, or reconstruction. Punishments were not given with any idea that they would make "bad" women "good." They were administered for one purpose only—to wring a little more profit out of the unpaid labor of these modern galley slaves—for failure to do the task.

Loathsome Diseases.

My more horrible experience in prison had to do with the lack of civilized sanitation. I was called to take my bath two days after entering. I found that there were two old dilapidated bathtubs and more than a hundred women forced to use them, and no attempt to separate the clean from the unclean.

As I waited my turn a woman by the name of Alice Cox stepped out of the bathroom and I was ordered to follow her. Alice was an Alaskan Indian, and her story is both old and common. The ancestors of Alice Cox lived in Alaska. Then gold was discovered in the Klondyke, the great onrush of gold seekers came, and the old, old story of the white man's invasion of the Indian's home was re-enacted.

Alice told her story, not once but many times, and it is so common that I have no reason to doubt it. She said when she was a young girl of seventeen, a white goldseeker hired her to take him out to a distant claim in her canoe. On the trip she was overpowered and violated by this white man, and in the process infected with the most terrible disease we know.

Alice was just an Indian; she had reached about the same stage of civilization as the white gentlemen down South who "lynch niggers." Alice was not fortunate enough to have any Southern gentlemen to avenge her, so she took vengeance in her own hands, and killed the man who violated her. She was arrested and held in a federal jail for seventeen months awaiting trial. During this time she insisted that she received no medical attention, though it was well known that she had been infected by the man she killed. Alice was found guilty of murder and sentenced to twenty-five years in prison. She had served at Lansing, Kan., and Jefferson City, Mo., about nine years. She had been in the custody of the United States Department of Justice about eleven years. She insisted that until the time Emma Goldman was sent to Jefferson City as a political prisoner she had never received any treatment for venereal disease. But she said that after Miss Goldman raised a row about it, she did have some sort of treatment.

As Alice stepped out of the bathroom she was one of the most appalling creatures I have ever seen. From her throat to her feet she was one mass of open syphilitic sores dripping with pus. I have seen her clothing so stiff with pus that it rattled when she walked and the live maggots working out of the filthy bandages about her throat. Alice had the cell directly under me and the flies that swarmed the cellhouse attracted by the stench from her sores would walk over them, and then come up to my cell and walk over me.

Alice had used the bathtub, and I was ordered to follow her. I asked the matron if it was necessary that I use the same tub as she and she said it was. I then asked her who cleaned the tub and she said that Alice was ill and that I should do it. I then asked what disinfectants were used. "Disinfectants, whaddaya mean?" she snarled. "I mean what prophylactic measures do you use to keep the clean women from becoming infected," I replied. She said: "Hell, we ain't got none of them things here. This ain't no swell boardin' school; this is the pen."

I protested: "Miss Smith you know what disease Alice has, you know how communicable it is, you know if I have a scratch on my body I may be infected too. You know that I am a married woman with a husband and four beautiful children outside. You know I must travel a great deal, sleep in Pullman cars and hotels, use public lavatories and hotel bathrooms. Surely the United States Department of Justice does not expect me to become infected with this frightful disease and then go back to civilized life and infect others who are innocent of committing crime."

Sputtering and snarling with rage the matron said: "I don't know anything about that and I don't care. You are a convict, this is what is provided for you. Now get ter hell out of here and take yer bath."

But I flatly refused; "to do so would be a crime," I replied. Shrieking and cursing the matron told me that I would either bathe in the infected bathtub or she would send me to the "black hole" and "break me." I knew she had the power to do it—she had "broken" Minnie Eddy in the "black hole" a few weeks before and Minnie had been carried out in a pine box. I was not ready to die, so I stepped into the bathroom, turned on the taps and splashed the water—but I DID NOT BATHE.

That night I got a letter out to my husband. He reproduced the letter and sent it to a thousand influential people. It was published in newspapers and magazines. A perfect storm of protest arose all over the country. In less than three weeks we had shower baths installed in that prison and that disgrace was abated.

I was able to rout the common bathtub, but I was never able to rout the diseased from handling the food. The women who were too ill to work in the shop were used in the dining room. Practically all of them were tubercular and syphilitic. I have seen women ladling out the food we were compelled to eat with syphilitic pus oozing out of their bodies and the germs of consumption being sprayed over our food by coughing convicts. The most loathsome and frightful of my prison experiences had to do with filthy diseases and disgraceful methods of dealing with them.

It is quite natural that a prison managed by a livery stable keeper and a mule buyer, with no other objective except to make profits for a prison contractor, would give its inmates about the same conditions that a mule would have in a livery stable. These men were blissfully ignorant of any knowledge of penology, criminology or psychology. I said to one of them that the young brute "overseer" should be replaced by a more mature man who knew something of human psychology. He stared at me blankly and said: "Huh! I don't reckon we need any of them new-fangled things. A good hickory club and the 'black hole' will fix 'em." This brilliant specimen of public servant had not the slightest idea of the meaning of the word psychology. He did not know whether it was a breakfast food or a religion.

There was no hospital for the women at Jefferson City, no attempt to segregate the clean women from the venerally diseased, no fever thermometer, no disinfectants, and no provisions for caring for the women, one overworked physician for 2600 inmates, the majority of whom were physically, mentally and spiritually ill. . . .

The Overseers.

There are many gruesome tales that one might repeat of the tortures incident to the convict labor system, but my time is too limited. Suffice to say I saw women slugged, beaten, starved, gagged, and handcuffed to the steel bars of "blind cell" doors. I have seen every manner of punishment you can imagine, and many that you can't imagine, for normal minds can not conceive of the punishments bred in the diseased brains of subnormal perverts. And a very large percentage of all guards and under prison officials are sadistic perverts.

The foreman in charge of the shop, called by the women the "overseer" was a brutal, vulgar, obscene, ignorant, degenerate youth of about twenty-one years of age. He had gone to work in the prison as an errand boy at fifteen and spent all the formative period of his life in the brutal, vicious, degrading atmosphere of the prison regime. He was cruel and intolerant beyond words, and we were always at the mercy of his adolescent brutality and his undisciplined passions. His vocabulary was rich in unspeakably vile epithets and disgusting profanity. His favorite pastime was subjecting the women to his lewd vulgarity and filthy obscenity. But vile language was the least of his brutalities. He counted our jackets and gave us credit for our work as he saw fit and any woman who asked for a verification of the count was terribly punished. He was the judge of our work, and if for any reason his vile temper was ruffled he would go down the line of sewing machines ripping and slashing the work without mercy or reason. We would be forced to remake the spoiled work in addition to the task, and be punished for "bad work" in addition.

I found that this young pervert practically had the power of life and death over all of us, practically sentenced women to death at his will.

The matron in charge of the women was ignorant, illiterate, coarse, brutal and sadistic to a marked degree. She was neither mentally, physically or educationally fitted to handle subnormal and helpless human beings. The salary paid for this work is not sufficient to command the services of any but very inferior persons.

The assistant matron was less coarse and cruel, but not superior in education or fitness for her position. She had been a house maid until approaching age made her physically unable to do this sort of work, then a politician in whose home she had served secured her the position of assistant prison matron.

For twelve hours each night both matrons left the cellhouse in the absolute charge of a brutal, perverted negro murderess, a stool pigeon, whose power over us at night was as absolute and despotic as that of the young foreman during the day. This stool pigeon's "graft" came from pandering to and encouraging sex perversions, and it was during the night when she was in sole charge that the horrible abuses of this phase of prison life occurred.

IV.

There is much time for meditation in prison, and much to meditate upon. One is presumed to meditate upon their sins and repent the evil of their ways, but I was never able to regret that I had taken, and steadfastly maintained, the position that had landed me in prison and my conscience refused to smite me. So I spent most of the weary, monotonous hours that we were locked like wild beasts in fetid, disease reeking cells, trying to fathom the dark mysteries of the application of law and morals.

I knew that prisons were social institutions, presumably founded and maintained by society to cure the criminal of his criminal ways, and to return him to society fit to mingle and share community life. Yet when I arrived in prison I found that by the workings of the prison system society commits every crime against the criminal that the criminal is charged with having committed against society.

We send our criminals to prison to teach them not to lie and defraud, and the prisoner is forced to live one long lie, and can exist only by becoming party to fraud. In Jefferson City the "silence" system is used. This means that only for one hour during the twenty-four any conversation among the inmates is permitted. For the convict who is "on punishment" for failure to "pull the task," even this hour is withheld. No normal human being can live day after day, week after week and month after month surrounded by human beings and cut off from communication. Deceit and fraud and petty lying are forced upon the inmates as a matter of self-preservation. . . .

The first work I ever did in the prison slave pen was a lie, that foisted a fraud upon the citizens who bought the product of my labor. There is a deep-seated repugnance in the heart of every really normal and decent person against wearing prison-made goods; there is a feel and smell of blood about them discernible to the souls if not to the physical senses of men. So prison-made goods are fraudulently labeled and the convict is forced to be party to the fraud. Into the first jacket I ever made in prison I was forced to stitch the label of the Sibley-Hesse Co., of Sioux City, Ia. Into the next lot I stitched the label of the Smith, Follet and Crowl Co., of Fargo, N. Dakota, and so on for the fourteen months. I stitched labels in all the way from Buffalo, N. Y., to Los Angeles, Cal., and I never left the prison slave pen to do it, and each jacket was a fraud and a lie.

We send thieves to prison to teach them not to steal and rob and all prison life is thievery and robbing. The fundamental theory of prison management, as I found it at Jefferson City, is that the first thing to be done to convicts is to "break" them. And "breaking" them means to rob them of every shred of self-respect, initiative, will, intelligence and common decency. Laughter, love and kindness are stolen also for nothing in prison is punished more brutally than these. And all human sympathy is stolen away. In all the months I lived with convicts I never heard one addressed by their keepers with common courtesy, and I never heard a kind, helpful or encouraging word given them. I never heard normal words spoken to an inmate; our keepers either snarled, cursed or screeched at us, and the echo of those snarling, rasping, hateful voices steals my rest and sleep even to this day.

The cream was stolen from our milk, every particle of sugar was stolen from our diet, the wholesome food the taxpayers paid for was grafted from us and we were fed on food filled with bugs and worms and weevils, because it could be bought cheaply. The supply of food was kept so low that in order to live and make the task the women were compelled to beg money from outside sources and buy food for existence at thievish prices. Graft stole the clothing provided by the state, and the women were compelled to depend on their friends and relatives outside for underwear, stockings, soap and the decencies that make life bearable.

We send people to prison to punish them for murder, yet the prison system murders more human beings in one year than individuals murder in a century. For the prison system murders not only the bodies of men, but the minds and souls of them as well.

One vivid memory of my prison experience is Pearl Hall. Pearl was a "dope" sent up from Little Rock, Arkansas, charged with a violation of the Harrison Drug Act. She was too far gone to be of any value in the shop; there was no profit in her poor old body, so she was eliminated. Pearl had been a drug addict for years, and naturally when drugs were taken away from her instantly and completely she was frantic with agony. Insane with misery, craving for "dope," she moaned and cried and begged for it all the time. There was no hospital and no facilities for caring for her and she kept the women who could work from their rest. One night I saw the negro stool pigeon and a demented white convict dragging a great cake of ice down the corridor from the dining room ice box to the bathroom. A few moments later I heard Pearl Hall's cell door open, heard her dragged out, sobbing and pleading, and then I heard her ducked again and again in the ice water until insensibility mercifully ended her agony. She was dragged back and thrown in her cell in her wet clothing and left without attention, so the women whose cells adjoined hers told me.

I was released two days later, but all of those two days and nights I heard Pearl Hall raving in delirium. A letter was sent out underground to me a few days later saying Pearl Hall had died of pneumonia.

But Pearl Hall was one of the more fortunate victims of our prison system. Her murder was swift enough to be merciful. There were many more in Jefferson City whose murder was long drawn out, whose bodies, brains and souls were murdered bit by bit. Aggie Myers is the most tragic example of the effect of our prison system that I have ever known. And there is Hattie Shrum and Willie Wilkenson, and Cecil Tillman and Mattie Lowe and many others of my prison mates who are being murdered in body, brain and soul by the processes of slow torture.

You shudder at these things and console yourselves with the thought that these are "bad" women who have broken the law. Well, they may be "bad." I won't argue that point. But I did not find them all "bad." They were as kind and gentle and loving to me as was the harlot who washed the feet of Jesus with her tears and wiped them on her hair. The only difference I found in these women and the common mass of women outside, was that they were a little more kindly and sympathetic because they had suffered more. But you may call them "bad" if you like, and I will agree that they have broken laws, and that they are being punished for crimes. "What have we to do with these degraded creatures? What are they to us?" you ask.

You have this to do with them: They are human beings, they are a part of society, they are what society has made them. They are flesh of our flesh, bone of our bone, soul of our soul! We cannot separate ourselves from them. Their lives in prison are what we in our ignorance and smugness have permitted prison officials to force on them. . . .

It has always been the history of crime that crime increased in "hard times," and abated in "good times." It is gradually dawning upon us that crime increases and decreases, as it is harder, or more easy, for the individual to secure the means of life. If the World War had been followed by "prosperity" for the masses instead of poverty and unemployment, in all possibility the "crime wave" would not have reached its present danger. The whole world is seething with crime, not alone because of the evil effects of the World War upon the souls of men, but because of the famine and poverty and exhaustion that always follows the false prosperity of war industry. And to lessen the "crime wave" requires not more police, and sawed off shotguns and machine guns, not more courts and judges and prisons, not more inhuman punishments, but less poverty for the masses and more morality for the state. If organized governments would curb crime among its individual citizens, they must establish for their own discipline the same standard of morals and righteousness that they demand from individual citizens. If governments would reform criminals, they must first reform themselves. If existing governments would reduce individual crime, they must take more heed for the welfare of the masses, they must take from private hands the unlimited power that now exists to do the world harm, and make state morality the pattern for individual morality.

If there is to be any abatement of the "crime wave" in the United States, our government must show as much efficiency in making peace as in making war. It must recognize the fact that if a nation has the right to demand a human life in war, it has the duty to protect that life in peace. If it can take men from the jobs and send them out to kill, it must see that they are provided with jobs when the killing is done. If it can send men out to be maimed and gassed and shell shocked and unfitted for ordinary work, it must see that these incapacitated men have decent hospital treatment, reeducation and a comprehensive system of vocational training that will lift them from the ranks of beggars and criminals. If the government has the right to spend billions making war, it must also have the right, and use it, to spend millions making peace for the masses.

JIM TULLY
1888–1947

Born into a poverty-stricken Irish immigrant family in 1888, Jim Tully became a "road-kid" at the age of eleven, and his adventures in the ensuing twelve years as a hobo, circus roustabout, prisoner, and professional prizefighter provided the material for most of his twenty-six books. During this time, he spent a total of about five years in jail, almost all on vagrancy and similar charges. Tully gained national reputation in 1924 with his second book, Beggars of Life, *which describes his initiation into the life of a hobo, his first arrests, and the lives of people on the fringes of society—tramps, jailbirds, and prostitutes. His characteristic style was both cynical and sentimental, hardboiled on the outside but filled with compassion for the underdog, always aligned with the victims and misfits against organized society. In 1943 Damon Runyon ranked Jim Tully at least "among the first five" of living writers, and*

H. L. Mencken wrote: "If Jim Tully were a Russian, read in translation, all the professors would be hymning him."

Convict authors were regular contributors to American Mercury magazine between 1924 and 1934, when Mencken was co-editor. The most frequent and popular writer was Tully, who published fourteen stories and sketches in the Mercury during that decade, including "A California Holiday," a 1928 piece written on assignment from the magazine. Tully used "A California Holiday" as the grand finale of his 1930 collection, Shadows of Men, about those victims of law-abiding society defined as "criminals," living and dying under the perpetual threat of prison.

A California Holiday

SAN QUENTIN STRETCHES, drab and sun-scorched, along the blue waters of San Francisco Bay. Majestic clouds seem always to be riding the heavens on the watery horizon. Boats glide, far out on the bay, as if fearful of drawing too near the crowded castle of the doomed.

Originally built for less than two thousand prisoners, it now houses thirty-six hundred, about one hundred of whom are women. The roads are gravelled. There is a detour sign two miles from the prison upon which is printed in large black letters, beneath a hand pointing prisonward:

THIS IS THE RIGHT ROAD

The front of the prison is grass and flower bedecked. A horseshoe, token of good luck, is over the main gate. In spite of its beautiful setting, it is, to me, the dreariest of American prisons—a place where the music of the spheres is ragtime.

About twenty miles from San Francisco, the most charming of American cities, San Quentin is often bathed in fogs and lacerated with cold winds. The very sea-gulls seem to fly over it with the monotony of despair. The guards live and bring up their children in the fear of God and the law within a few hundred yards of where men are hanged with sanctimonious gesture.

I had called to visit several prisoners. A reporter for the San Francisco *Examiner* accompanied me. The city editor had telephoned the warden of our arrival. Less than a month on the job, the new warden, a man-hunter all his life, was unusual in that he had none of the illiterate man's blind acceptance of life.

A very quiet man, between fifty and sixty, slightly stooped, with most of his upper teeth missing, he might have been the leader of a Salvation Army band, instead of one who had long been known as quick on the trigger. A Hindoo had once run amuck in a crowded court-room. The new warden had drilled him dead with a bullet. That was his claim to fame in California.

He took us to the office of the captain of the guard. We walked through three iron gates before reaching the interior yard. Save for the small walks, this yard was literally covered with blooming flowers of many sizes and colors. After the drab cement and iron bars, and the stern dull faces of the guards, the contrast was startling.

We waited in this room until my friends arrived. They were Kid McCoy, Robert Joyce Tasker, Joe Mackin and Paul Kelly.

Mackin, a shriveled little ex-jockey, perhaps with the seeds of a writer about to germinate in his head, doing a fifteen year jolt for highway robbery. Tasker, twenty-four, tall, good looking, a sheik type for society girls and stenographers, with black hair carefully combed, doing five to twenty-five years for holding up a crowded dance-hall. He is now the associate editor of the San Quentin *Bulletin* and a contributor to The American Mercury.

As gruff old Carlyle might have said, "By such incontrovertible ways do men find themselves."

Kelly, accidentally caught up with bootleg gin and a woman, spasmodically married, was now working a loom in the jute-mill, that modern California inferno which drives even dull men mad.

It is a place where a yell subsides to a whisper, so great is the whirring noise. Particles of hemp dust fly all about the mill. Wheels, pulleys and machines roar with deafening noise. A convict must do his task each day—so many sacks, so much twine, or be penalized if he fails.

I had known Kelly in happier days. Generous, a square dealer, with the pride and the laughter of the Gael, life had always been to him a Lambs Club frolic.

And now the crows of trouble were walking around his eyes. The smile on his face was hard pushed to keep back the tears. An actor, Thomas Meighan, had contributed ten thousand dollars for his defense. Other friends had rallied to him.

Sensational newspapers, a corporation lawyer untrained in mob psychology, a shallow judge, and middle-class hatred of Hollywood had done for Kelly.

It was no time now for the imbecilities by which more fortunate men try to placate others in trouble.

The conversation lagged. There was a pause. Kelly's body trembled in its ill-fitting grey and hemp dusty suit.

"Well, Paul—all you can do is take your jolt," I finally said.

"But I didn't kill him—I didn't kill him," and then, "God!—but it's great to get away from that jute-mill—you've got to live it, Jim—to know it—there's no other way."

"I know, Paul—you're right—I'd rather read one page by a man who had been in Hell—than all of Dante."

I watched his face. The deep lines running down from the eyes were those of an emotional man forced by the exigencies of circumstance and environment into a withering restraint. We walked toward Kid McCoy and the warden. The once great pugilist was saying—"I'll tell you, Warden,—Tunney hasn't got a chance—no man has with Dempsey when he's right. There's too many big words in Tunney's head."

Not wishing to rob McCoy of a moment's pleasure, I turned my head.

Through the flowers, followed by a guard, walked a young girl, slim and beautiful. In white blouse and dark skirt, her hair carefully combed, and with blue laughing eyes, she seemed a pretty high-school girl on her way to an easy lesson.

"Who's that?" I asked Paul Kelly.

"It's the jazz murderess," he replied. "The kid who killed her mother." It was as if McCoy had smashed me under the heart. Another prisoner, perhaps seeing my expression, said, "There's all kinds in here, Jim."

II

Tasker and the reporter joined us. Soon we bade the four men goodbye and walked into the garden.

The warden went to his lunch. We walked toward the hospital. The reporter wished to ask the prison physician, Dr. L. L. Stanley, a question. There was a rumor that certain other prisoners had lately tried to kill the Rev. Herbert Wilson, arch-bandit, murderer, informer and one-time Baptist minister, with a poisoned arrow.

We accompanied Dr. Stanley to the dining-room. The man who waited upon our table was Tom Mooney, whose conviction as a dynamiter stirred the nations of the world. Still in middle life, the years are nevertheless crawling heavily across Mooney. Though even the intercession of Woodrow Wilson failed to get him a new trial, he still hopes for a pardon. A naïve man, he dreams of justice.

Allowed to languish in prison the past dozen years, he is neglected by the parlor radicals, now grazing in more luscious publicity fields. Men high in financial power have said of Mooney, "Well, if he's not guilty of the Preparedness Day bombing, he's guilty of something else. He belongs in San Quentin." Mooney's enemies are unlike his friends: they know exactly what they want.

Mooney, now phonographic, talked for an hour, detailing his acquittals and convictions. If he is innocent, it seems incomprehensible that semi-civilized men should be guilty of such a crime. But even Sinclair Lewis suppressed the hardness of a Babbitt to gain his end.

"Well, Tom," said the reporter, "if they let you out tomorrow, what would you do?"

Mooney stood erect, the picture of subdued virility, "I'll tell you what I'd do—I'd look after my health right away."

All of us glanced at the physician. No man spoke for a minute.

"What's the matter with your health, Tom?" the doctor finally asked.

"No reflections on you, Doctor," returned Mooney, "but you know how it is," and then further explanations, which wended back to the injustice of twelve years' imprisonment.

Those years have eaten at the mind of Mooney, stooping his shoulders. They have carved hollow places beneath his eyes.

As he went to the kitchen the doctor said, "It's the first time I've ever heard his story—you know there's thirty-six hundred of them here."

The reporter asked if the newspaper report of Clara Phillips' attempted suicide were true. "No, it wasn't," he replied, "but it's a wonder all the women don't go mad—cooped up the way they are." The corners of his mouth twitched with pity.

Dr. Stanley listens to the last heartbeats of gallows-hung men.

He remains kindly, even sentimental over the most atrocious of his charges.

He talked of Bluebeard Watson, said to be a hermaphrodite, convicted of having married and killed many women.

"It will be centuries before anyone is able to give Watson's case justice. He's my head nurse over in the hospital. He makes pets out of birds. There's nothing he won't do for a sick man. He nurses them as tenderly as a woman. I wish you'd say something about him. He's in here forever—he'll never get out—so all you can get him is a little understanding."

Eager to change the subject, I said, "You've been here a great many years, haven't you, Doctor?"

"Yes, yes," he half drawled, "a good many years. I went into private practice a short time but I gave it up and came back. Got homesick, I guess."

Someone told the story of a ball-throwing contest in which a condemned young dope fiend had participated. He was soon to dangle in a noose.

Three thousand prisoners cheered the lad who was soon to leave for another country. Strangely enough, no contestant was in good form that day. Even the champion ball-thrower, a giant Negro, was off. The youth won, amid cheers.

He died in the belief that he could throw a ball further than any man in prison. Ego attends us all.

As we talked to the doctor there appeared James McNamara, the labor agitator, convicted of blowing up the Los Angeles *Times* Building and killing twenty-one people, and now serving his fifteenth year of a life sentence.

Steel grey eyes, perfect features, about forty-five years of age. McNamara smiled when asked if he were on the Los Angeles *Times* mailing list. Five years before, I had said to him, "You'll soon get out."

His reply was, "What an optimist you are, Jim! Did you make four-minute speeches during the war? Tom Mooney's innocent and *he* can't get out. How long do you think they'll keep *me?*" Then with emphasis, "I'm supposed to have killed twenty-one men."

McNamara was then in charge of the condemned row. I had told him the outline of a novel in which a youthful radical was to be hanged. He was much interested in the plan.

He was eager to help me get the correct details and atmosphere.

He talked of my embryonic leading character as though he were a reality.

"You want to get it right," he then said, "it'll help the cause."

He had followed my career and always asked me, "Are you still going to do the story of the boy?"

And now, in leaving me, he said, "You ought to come over Friday, Jim, they'll top a guy here then. It'll be what you want for your book."

Topping is the prison term for hanging.

III

On Friday morning at six o'clock I started again for San Quentin with Raymond Griffith, the actor, and Malcolm Waldron, a reporter for the San Francisco *Call*. Fremont Older, that most humane of editors, had asked me to write a description of the execution.

The man was to mount the thirteen steps which lead to the gallows at ten o'clock. The newspapers wanted a preliminary story. A morbid public was interested in how he had passed the night, and even what he had eaten for breakfast. Hence the early start.

As we huddled back from the foggy wind on the bay, Griffith said, "They talk of Nietzsche and all that gang—why, those birds were soft! The real hard people are the Baptists, the Methodists, the Puritans. Nietzsche couldn't hang a man like this."

"Cromwell, for instance," I suggested.

"Yes—that's the guy—now, he *was* hard."

Said Waldron: "I covered a hanging in the East, and we were all given black coffee before we went to the death-room. I wonder if they'll do that here?"

While Griffith tried to see Paul Kelly, I went with Waldron. At the door of the warden's office was a plaster bust of Senator Hiram Johnson. Spectacles were upon it to accentuate the likeness. The artist seemed to have difficulty in adjusting the Senator's scarf. He compromised by allowing it to hang under his collar.

We met two other reporters in the office.

"Now listen, fellows," said Waldron, "we'll make a gentleman's agreement. There's only two 'phones here—so let's all 'phone our stories in together."

"All right," they agreed.

That weighty matter settled, we greeted the warden's clerk. He was frozen indifference. The clerk of the Prison Board, a two-hundred-pound porpoise of a man, with a neck bulging over his collar, entered the room.

"Meet the newspaper boys here," suggested the warden's clerk.

"I'll meet 'em later," was the terse reply.

"It's mutual," returned a reporter, as the clerk of the board passed into another room. From another reporter:

"That guy hates us—God, I'm glad! You know it's funny about these hangings. I knew a fellow who covered thirty of them. He fainted at the last one."

It was not eight thirty.

"Damn this waiting around," blurted a reporter whose eyes were swollen from a night's debauch. "The time sure drags."

"It may for us," put in Waldron, "but I'll bet it flies for *him*."

We remained silent for some time. "That's right—the poor devil," at last came from the reporter with the swollen eyes—then, smiling, "It won't be long now."

"Is it true they give them a shot of booze or dope before they bump them?" The remark was delivered to the warden's clerk.

He answered, "This guy says, 'A glass o' whisky.' Send up a barrel of it!" The clerk left.

"Well, it won't be long now," said the blear-eyed reporter for a second time, in the midst of a news competitor's words:

"I think it was here that they used to grant a fellow's dying request before they strung him up." He smiled. "A Negro asked the warden if he couldn't dance a jig on the gallows. That was a hard one for the warden, but he finally consented. The chaplain objected strenuously, though, in the name of dignity and religion, so the poor shine had to keep his feet still."

I watched a pelican sailing beautifully toward the sun. Waldron touched my arm. "A miserable business for 1927—eh?"

"You've just got the fidgets, Waldron," I bantered as the warden entered the room.

His face sagged as if weights were on his chin. The warden of a California prison is forced to see all executions. His raised hand sends the doomed man downward. It was this warden's first.

"How do you feel?" a reporter asked.

"All right," he answered slowly, removing the pipe from his half toothless mouth, "It's not pleasant to jerk a man into the great beyond."

We agreed with silence and said no more while the warden remained in the room.

Waldron, looking toward the Bay, said nervously, "Gee—the grass is nice and green—the sun's warm—even the sea-gulls are more beautiful than I've ever seen them before."

We all knew his drift. Our minds were with him.

"Be a realist, Waldron," I jerked at him. "You mean it's hell to die on a morning like this."

He murmured weakly, "Yes."

"Well, it surely is hell," I half laughed, with the hope of lifting Waldron's mood, when my own was no higher. "But this fellow, Earl Clark, certainly got a tough break. If a fellow read about it in a book he wouldn't believe it. He escaped from the county jail in Los Angeles after he was convicted, and he beat it to this little town in South Dakota—married a girl who didn't know a thing about his record and went into the painting business. He was getting along fine when a young kid who'd taken a mail-order course to become a detective turned him in. He was really making good, you know. Clark was supposed to have carried poison to bump himself off if they caught him, but he was too slow. I see where Frank Dewar, the jailer down in Los Angeles, wired the Governor that there was even a chance that he wasn't guilty."

"He was guilty all right," from a voice behind a desk.

"You'd think they'd give a fellow at least a life term after that," said Waldron.

"But there's six feet of grass over the other guy—remember that," threw in the warden's clerk. No man answered.

"The guy was sentimental, that's all," said the reporter with the bleared eyes. "He killed a sailor because he brought a red rose to his girl every night. Why didn't he wait a while—the sailor would have gone to sea—they all do—don't they?" looking at me as if I knew.

"Yes—I guess so—I think that's their job."

"But who was the dame?" the reporter asked.

"Just a broad," was the reply from somewhere.

"Just a broad," two voices took up.

"A million dollar price for a ten cent woman," said the reporter with the swollen eyes, as we walked toward the main entrance.

IV

At least seventy men in citizens' clothes stood in groups. I could tell by their faces that many were guards and detectives.

It was now twenty minutes of ten.

We marched one by one through the flower garden. A guard, laughing outright, pointed his club at a marching gentleman, and said, "He's turnin' pale already." Several of the marchers laughed.

Prisoners looked out of the hospital windows at life marching to see death. The subserviency of iron bars could not obliterate their contempt of us from their faces.

This section of the prison had the appearance of an abandoned saw-mill. The accumulated débris of generations was about us.

To the left of the hospital was the condemned row where other cattle, in prison vernacular, awaited their chance to meet the Christians' God. Down a little hill we walked, passing on our left a heavy iron door with a large padlock upon it. It was the entrance to the cooler, where all was pitch darkness—eighteen stone cages of icy torture and Zolaesque despair.

The authorities often place men there for infractions of prison rules. They are given a diet of bread and water and their own thoughts, if any, on the mercy of mankind.

Further on was the butcher shop—the morgue. Above us was a herder with a loaded rifle. I noted that the guards did not carry guns inside the prison. The reason seemed obvious. In a wild scramble of mutiny or for freedom, the convicts might disarm them.

We reached the rear of the prison and walked down a less pretentious alley. We stopped at the foot of aged stairs which projected about five feet from the wall. They reached three flights. Fearful of the rickety steps, about twenty men were allowed upon them at a time. We now went two by two. Waldron walked with me.

A fat man grumbled at the long flight of steps. "They do hangin's better in Folsom," he panted.

A guard near the railing commanded, "Step lively there!" I recognized his face. He was the Irish gentleman who had long before commented, "It used to be a good graft—sellin' the rope—a dollar an inch—now the board makes us burn it."

And then—at the foot of the gallows, in showing me a leather contraption, he elucidated, "We put 'em in here if they wriggle." My mind on the Irish boy I was to hang in a book, I remembered.

As I counted the seventy-five decrepit steps, I had the diabolical wish that they would crumple beneath us. "Wouldn't it be funny," I said to Waldron, "if all of us croaked before Clark?"

He made no answer. His mouth was tight shut. His eyes betrayed the life hurt dreamer.

The debonair Griffith walked behind me. His face was more impassive than a Chinaman's at a lottery. I stumbled as I watched it. "Careful," he said, as we turned in on the third floor.

We passed through the print-shop. Four prisoners sat at desks, editing the prison paper. Tacked to the walls were the pictures of actresses of a long ago period. They looked smilingly grotesque in the abominable costumes and hats which were then in style.

"Convicts, forever free, must have tacked them there," I thought. Musing on the sex agonies of men in prison, I became more tolerant of the fatuous faces which stared from the lithographs.

Inside a small room were three prisoners. Thin, with suppressed leers, and furtive eyes, they lolled about in the manner of laborers before the day's work begins. They were the scavenger crew. It was their job to take the dead man from the rope, place him in a pine coffin made by other convicts, and hurry him to the little cemetery on the hill where rest the men with broken necks.

We now halted in front of a large door opening into a room which contained the gallows.

It was ten minutes of ten.

I stood within a half dozen feet of the coffin. A guard with a hard, flat face, not over thirty, leaned upon it. Another guard approached. "Here's his overcoat," smiled the first guard.

I touched Waldron's arm. His body trembled.

The shuffling of feet stopped. One could literally hear hearts beat. A sinuous three-quarter length picture of Lillian Russell smiled above the coffin at the nonchalant legality of murder. I started to say some words to Griffith. They rattled in my throat.

The door opened. We marched into the room of death.

It must have been sixty feet long and thirty wide. Save for the gallows, it was bare. It was painted a sickly blue, like a Kansas sky after a tornado. The death-cell was about thirty feet from the gallows. It was also painted blue. It was quite large, the ceiling very high. A gas-jet, about three feet long, hung from the center.

One rope, already knotted, hung from the gallows. Above were three small ropes, one of which held the trap. In seven minutes they were to be cut by three guards. In this way, no man knew which one had sent the body to dangling in the air. There was a small platform at the bottom. Thirteen steps led to the gallows. They were worn with the feet of many men who never came down alive.

Other lines of rope stretched from the ceiling. They were in different stages of the testing process through which each rope must pass before its last service. The ropes were all new; they are used but once. To each was attached a tag bearing the name and execution date of the next man to die.

After a man is hanged his picture is placed, along with many others, behind a large glass in an adjustable frame. It stands in the Bertillon room. No face seems natural. By, perhaps, some thought transformation which takes place in each brain at the time the picture is taken, each mouth seems puckered as though the rope were quicker than the lens.

It was two minutes to ten.

The room was closed tightly. Not a rift of air entered. We were aware that a man must be pronounced dead before any of us could leave the room. Each one of us looked toward the raised gallows.

The warden and two doctors faced the gallows.

An oppressive silence rolled in waves through the room. The hinges of a door creaked.

The doomed man entered. The chaplain preceded him.

V

His neck was bare. His eyes were wide open, glassy. His mouth sagged, as if too tired to appeal to ears that could not hear. His knees bent. All power of locomotion had gone from his legs. The eyes seemed to see nothing. His arms were strapped to his sides. Under each armpit was the hand of a heavy guard. Their iron arms did not bend. The man was literally carried to the trap. His legs were strapped together. The hood was pulled over his head. He turned slightly, as if to say a word. The rope was adjusted. The chaplain read from his book in a dreadful monotone. I recall the words, "Confide his soul to the mercy of God." The warden's hand raised. The trap sprang with an awful noise. The man's body dropped ten feet. It did not move.

A small step-ladder was placed in front of the body. The some-time sentimental doctor stood upon it, ripped the dying man's shirt down to his heart, and applied a stethoscope. A convict, in the rear, held the body firm. An assistant physician held the victim's hand. Every now and then he would feel the pulse. I watched the hand become stiff and turn blue.

Griffith, the comedy actor, had turned his face to the wall. There were tears in his eyes. Waldron gulped. The warden stood, eyeing the fast becoming corpse. He might have been posing for the trag-edy of mankind. He swallowed often. His hands opened and closed.

The minutes dragged, like horrible wounded soldiers, into eter-nity. A man held a watch near me.

A crash came at six minutes after ten. A two-hundred-pound railroad detective fainted to the floor. Men scrambled to carry him away. "It had to be a fellow that size," murmured someone. I thought it was Griffith. I smiled grimly. Suddenly, in a far corner, another form crashed to the floor. It was a very large policeman. "Another two-hundred-pounder," whispered the same voice. It was now eight minutes after ten.

The doctor listened patiently, even tenderly, with his stetho-scope. The warden still watched. Vengeance seemed to have fled temporarily from the hearts of all in the room.

Life was pumped from the powerful chest slowly. It was thirteen minutes after ten before the man was pronounced dead. The rope was cut. The scavenger crew came.

I hurried with Waldron to get a statement from the warden. As if fearful of comment, he eluded the writing craft.

The other reporters had vanished. "Gosh, I hope they don't double-cross me," was Waldron's comment, as we rushed down the rickety stairs.

A guard yelled, "Hey there, you paddocks." We stopped. "You guys wait for the rest of the gang." When the other men joined us, we marched out.

Once released from the curiosity brigade, we dashed into a telephone-booth in the front office of the penitentiary. Waldron telephoned his story and my impressions to the *Call*. Mistrusting our fellow writers, we scooped them by accident.

We found them in the warden's office, busily telephoning their papers. Something else had happened. The doomed man, who, in bidding farewell to the warden in the death-cell had said to him, "I'll see you again if I'm lucky," had also left him a letter.

The reporters scrambled over the letter. Then two men copied it as another reporter read it aloud over the telephone.

The Governor had refused to commute the dead man's sentence on account of his prison record. The letter, scribbled on coarse paper with a soft lead pencil read:

> DEAR WARDEN: Many thanks for the kind treatment. I know how you feel, Sir, and believe me, I can sympathize with you—it's your first and I hope your last. I have only a few minutes and I want to say now with my last breath that I had no more to do with de Silve's death than you did.
>
> I don't blame the jury—how can I when the State's witness lied?—yes, two of them. The rest told the truth. But with a poor lawyer and a record the verdict would have been the same had I been charged with the death of Abe Lincoln.
>
> Yes, I have one prison record and two $50 fines against me. The rest is just arrests—no charge, or just "vag"—not even a jail term. My prison term was for a $14 check—for which I was pardoned.
>
> Thank you again. Goodbye, Warden.
>
> *Sincerely yours,*
> E. J. CLARK

On the margin was scrawled,

> *This is true, so help me God. Just a few minutes to go.*

ERNEST BOOTH
1898–1959

In "Two-Time Losers," a 1928 article on the California prison system published in American Mercury, *Jim Tully describes a remarkable prison interview he had with Ernest Booth. Booth, then twenty-nine years old, had achieved prominence through three articles published the previous year in the* Mercury: *"We*

Rob a Bank," "A Texas Chain-Gang," and "Ladies of the
Mob." Tully had sought him out because these articles made
him regard Booth as "potentially the greatest prison writer to
emerge from the iron wilderness of America." What he found
was a living swarm of contradictions. Born into a prominent
family—one brother had been a California assemblyman—
Booth had "read widely and well" and was the most "charming conversationalist" Tully had ever met. Yet he had also
become a legendary prison rebel who had escaped six times
and who had fallen fifty feet in a daring but foiled armed
escape attempt from San Quentin.

Two more pieces by Booth appeared in the Mercury in
1928, and the following year his autobiography Stealing
Through Life was published in New York and London by
Alfred Knopf. In 1931 came "Ladies in Durance Vile," the
American Mercury article reprinted here, which was the basis
for his play Ladies of the Big House, made into the 1931
Paramount movie of the same name. In 1945 Doubleday published Booth's With Sirens Screaming, at once a prison protest
novel and a surprisingly early expression of a theme that
would become commonplace in 1960s America, the oppression
of youth by straight society.

Although Booth had told Tully "I'm through with crime"
and was paroled in 1937, he was convicted in 1947 on California and federal robbery charges, spent the next nine years
in the California state prisons of San Quentin, Folsom, Terminal Island, and Vacaville, and died in 1959 in McNeil Island Penitentiary, Washington.

Ladies in Durance Vile

A HAPHAZARD, emergency building scheme had placed the
women's department in one corner of the main prison yard.
It was a low, two-storied, U-shaped building. The lower floor, facing the men's yard, was occupied by the captain's office and the
runners' desks, and at the corner, by the turnkey's office, the mail
office, and the Bertillon room. The quarters of the incarcerated la-

dies were on the second floor, and over the captain's office was their work room. At one corner was their recreation room.

The results of this delightfully stupid arrangement were, for the prisoners, a constant titillation of excitement, and for the officials, the labor of constant surveillance. Such enticements, alas, know no barriers. The captain had a favorite moan: "Some of my most trusted men have betrayed my confidence because of them broads up stairs."

To go to the hospital, the women, with a matron accompanying them, came out through the turnkey's office, walked the length of a porch on which a dozen male prisoners were invariably awaiting the daily grief on the mourner's bench, and then, with their heads turning and their faces smiling, crossed the flower beds to the hospital, where another group of male prisoners were always "accidentally" lounging. Often it was necessary for them to walk through a veritable gauntlet of men, and often the men knew them, and often the notes exchanged contained morphine—although that was a risky connection.

I worked in the photograph gallery, a small building close to the side of the women's department. Every incoming woman was brought to the gallery, a number was pinned on her breast, and she was mugged: front and profile. A large slate, hung on her by the matron, showed her name, age, crime, sentence and nativity, and the county in which her crime was committed. That was indeed a hard-boiled bobbed- or straight-haired bandit who passed through the ordeal without shedding at least a couple of tears.

In the courtyard of the women's quarters, on the outer wall of which an armed guard patroled, there was an almost constant sound of voices. Probably the chatter of the ladies was no louder than that in the men's yards, but at any rate it *seemed* louder. If one girl called from the courtyard to another girl in the cells or work room, her voice always seemed to carry a note close to hysteria. The slightest excitement in the offices was immediately reflected by the rising of the women's voices. When in the early evenings they were in the recreation room, a small place about twelve by fourteen, they banged the piano lustily, and their singing was both a treat and a torment to the men working beneath them.

The magnetism passing between the two departments was so powerful that the walls ceased to exist. The office men visualized all of the girls, and discussed the probable place of each one as indicated by the sound of her voice. In short, they lived on our side of the division, and we lived over there with them. Many of us had, under one pretext or another, been in the women's department. Myself and an assistant had gone in to photograph the rooms, newly decorated for the matron; Jack from the bakery, to carry a basket of bread into their kitchen each day; several of the plumbers, to repair the bathroom; and carpenters, upholsterers, runners, shoe-makers, painters, chaplain's men from the library, tinners, cooks, stone masons—all of these found work in the women's department. One day the matron said: "With all the attention we receive from the repair men, our department should be as strong as a fortress. But it seems to be always needing further repairs."

What the matron was either blind to, or philosophically accepted, was the fact that no matter how many men worked there, an army corps could not repair the calculated but surreptitious vandalism of the girls. Whenever one of the small wooden tables in the cells was broken, it went to the carpenter shop. It was repaired, painted and returned—with the legs hollowed out and filled with generous quantities of smoking tobacco, notes, matches, or narcotics. Meanwhile, the matron bemoaned the fact that the girls smoked! This vice seemed to worry the chaplain also. He wanted them to lead pure lives, free from all taint. He counted that day lost when he did not go to their quarters and pray with some girl struggling for the higher ecstasies. What he never discovered, apparently, was that some of the girls slipped notes into his coat pockets, and that these notes were later extracted by the prisoner librarians when he returned to his office.

The first girl that comes to mind, of the many I saw pass through, is one Blanche. An attractive hula-hula dancer, she had worked with a carnival, displaying her charms in the sideshow for which her lover sold tickets. Following the performance he would usually have to listen to the importunings of some yokel who had, that night, become enamoured of Blanche. It was hard to arrange a meeting with her, her lover would protest. Just because a girl was with a carnival, that didn't mean that she was easy. She was a nice girl . . . She was supporting an aged mother, two shell-shocked brothers, etc. . . . . But still—

The yokel would become insistent, and the argument continued until the lover ascertained the size of the yokel's purse. Well . . . If he would stick around after the show closed, perhaps the beautiful hula dancer would speak to him . . . but there was nothing certain . . . He would have to see her himself.

Invariably he did. Often, because of his position in the town, he preferred to talk where the lights were not bright. He could, and did, walk with Blanche, guiding her down streets which insured safety from prying eyes. The lovely climate of California was a boon. For on those mild, scented evenings, what lovelier scene of love than the star-sprinkled night?

Blanche's lover was an expert at selling tickets, but his real specialty was collections. When the idyllic strollers had reached a sufficiently secluded spot, the yokel would suddenly experience an emotional thrill—a thrill compounded of the sight of a revolver and the command: "Get 'em up!"

Relieved of his money, he usually bade Blanche a hasty good night and departed swiftly. But there was, in the end, one staunch supporter of law and order who left the field and galloped straight to the constable's office. He may have been a gosh darn fool to go gallivantin' with that dancer, but, by God! right was right and wrong was wrong—he would have the law on 'em. And he did.

I first saw Blanche in the turnkey's office. She and her lover were being booked together. When the matron told her to come over to the photograph gallery, she whirled and threw her arms about her lover. She clung to him with a long drawn-out kiss that should have lasted a lifetime. The matron and turnkey smiled. Several prisoners working in the office grinned. One wit called: "Time!" And after Blanche had tightened her embrace in a last convulsive sob and then released her lover to stagger drunkenly after the matron, one of the office men exploded: "Boy, that's real love!"

While she was being photographed, Blanche smiled dreamily, happily. I got the impression that she had not yet come to a realization that she was in prison.

II

Grace, whose fourteen-years-served had bestowed on her the title and dignity of con-matron, was a large, dark-haired, generously built woman. She had disagreed with her husband years before, chopped him up, put him in a trunk, and shipped him to a country station, thereby earning a life sentence.

Although styles had changed, Grace clung to her heavy braids, to her long dresses, to her princess figure. She had a marvelous complexion: a creamy color, with a skin that looked as soft as peach fuzz. Her eyes, dark and bold, had no wrinkles about them; and, although she was forty or more when I first saw her, she looked half her age. Her movements were quick, she walked with a decisive stride, and her large rounded capable arms were usually bare to the shoulders. Although she covered her calves, she wore very low-cut dresses which her semi-official position allowed her the choice of designing.

Handling the women in the absence of the matron, Grace was like a section foreman. Her voice carried easily, and to me it always seemed to have a hard brown autumnal color in it. When she stood on the balcony in the women's courtyard, I could clearly hear her talking to the other girls. She was not always successful in handling them.

Just before noon the squads of men working in the vegetable gardens returned along the road that ran parallel to the rear wall of the women's department. Some of them called to the girls when the wall guard was napping. Sometimes it was possible to throw a note over the wall. During this hour Grace often stood on watch within the courtyard.

One day at noon the sounds of the returning squads reached me clearly. Then I heard Grace explode: "Don't pick that up, Blanche!"

"The hell I won't," Blanche replied in her off-key voice.

Sounds of Grace's heels on the iron stairs. Sudden silence. A flurry, then the rich angry voice of Pat (Patricia Geraldine Washton), a hard-boiled Negress: "Let 'at gal 'lone, Grace!"

Other voices joined in. There came the protestations of a reedy English girl doing time for issuing rubber checks. Then the excited chattering of Dot and Mae, two hypos, one in for shooting a narcotic agent after he had ditched her boy friend, and the other for the burglary of a hotel room. Then the staccato exclamations of an Italian woman, a gaunt angular vixen with the nose and eyes of a hawk. She and her husband were doing time together for possession of a still. Into the rising whirlpool of voices there came a new sound. It was the authoritative metallic voice of the matron:

"Stop! Stop! Blanche, Mae, Dot, Washton! I'll isolate you all for a month! Stop! Stop!"

The rising voices held steady a moment, then, like water running out of a tank, the noise subsided into uneasy gurgling. Over this came the disciplinary admonitions of the matron. Dot and Mae should go to their cells. Pat should return to the kitchen. Grace was to bring Blanche upstairs and the matron would attend to her. The rest of the girls, immediately, under threat of going without lunch, were to return to the dining-room . . .

Beside me, on the rail at the entrance to the photograph gallery, was the locksmith who had a corner in the gallery. He was a former railroad switchman. He grinned. With his large pop eyes in a sun-and-booze-reddened face, he lifted the grin until it puckered the corners of his eyes and he looked like an old house dog. "Them cats," he snickered, "is just naturally onery. They bust 'em locks on the cells on purpose, 'an when the cap'an sends me up to fix 'em, them cats cuss hell outa me."

I left him and walked toward the front porch. I wanted to see a friend who was coming in with one of the garden squads. At the edge of the building I stopped. There on the porch was Blanche's lover, trying to explain to the captain that the guard on the wall had erred in singling him out as the man who had thrown that note into the woman's courtyard. The matron's quarters were directly over where he stood, and doubtless Blanche could hear him. He was loud and vehement in his denial, but he lost the argument.

With a guard, he passed around the end of the building and down the sloping road to the dungeon cells. They were located directly beneath the place where on Sundays men knelt to pray.

The windows on this side of the women's department were barred and the glass was frosted, but into one of the panes had been let a metal circular vent which rotated. By removing one of the leaves, the girls had a sight of the gallery and the road to the dungeon. I glanced at the window and saw the leaf removed. I assumed that Blanche was watching her lover's departure to the dungeon. But just then her voice mounted in a scream that rose above the combined voices of the matron and Grace.

Out in the courtyard I heard Pat, too, expressing herself. The girls at the vent in the window shouted something unintelligible. Blanche's screaming was coming from the matron's quarters, but it grew louder as she fought through the sewing-room. Hastily the leaf was replaced. A moment later Blanche was in the room, fighting furiously. Grace was calling out loudly in that brown tone of hers, so heavily weighted with hatred. The matron seemed to have her hands full with Dot and Mae. Out of the yard came the hard-boiled declarations of Pat. Then she came upstairs and entered the corner room. By now probably twenty of the eighty women confined in that small building had joined in the free-for-all. The electric bell over the captain's office door insistently implored aid.

While the captain and several guards prepared to enter the courtyard, it was discovered that the key was with the turnkey, who was out to lunch at his home. With his short black mustache bristling, the captain came to the locksmith for help. While that worthy sought through his bag for a duplicate key to the lock, the riot increased in violence. Glass was broken from a window in the corner room. Some one hurled a chair at the other window, and the leg of the chair stuck out between the bars. Glass danced on the pavement.

Pat's activity in the corner room was marked by some of the highest pitched screaming I ever heard. The matron yelled in horror. Pat lunged with a knife, and the matron retreated until she was pressed against the bars of the glassless window. Grace appeared against the other window, and Pat's frenzied "I'll cut you loose from all you evah owned!" became a regular chant: "I'll cut you —LOOSE—from all—YOU evah owned!"

Then the matron was slugged. She turned imploring eyes to the window and to the captain, still waiting for the locksmith. Her hands clasped her stomach. "Oh, I'm *so* sick . . . Oh-o-o . . . Help, Captain, Pat is murdering me!"

She dropped from sight. In the window now appeared the tousled blonde head of Blanche. Seeing the captain, she loosed a stream of objurgation that would have done credit to an evangelist. She traced the genealogy of both the locksmith and the captain from the time when they were trembling movements in the primeval slime. And she returned them to that state with a thoroughness worthy of a scientist. Through it all the captain stood with his hands in his pockets, his eyes calm, his teeth chewing slowly on his mustache. In a whine he urged the locksmith: "Better hurry up a bit, Jim. They're needing us upstairs."

Eventually the captain, the locksmith, and three guards entered the courtyard. Behind them the large iron door closed. Some of the girls, having dropped the matron and Grace, hurried down to meet the captain. There was a swift clash of forces. Through the partition it was easy to follow the battle. Pat threatened the captain with her knife. He loudly invited her to do her worst, and then dropped her with a punch to the jaw. Suddenly the door opened. I saw the locksmith fighting with the Italian woman and a large Swedish girl. The captain was trying to shake off Mae, who had fastened her teeth in his hand. Two girls were prostrate beside Pat. Blanche scurried up the stairs with several other girls.

The guard who came out before the door was closed was a squat, broad-shouldered man with snow-white handle-bar mustaches. He always walked with a precision that provoked chuckles from the prisoners. He had gone in with the captain. The door had closed behind him. There had been the sound of that first furious encounter. The door had then opened. Out he walked: his carefully kept mustaches bent all out of shape, his cheek cut below the eye, and his coat ripped completely up the back. Like a little duck he walked, looking neither to the right nor to the left, directly through the office, across the porch, and along the path to the front gate. In his wake his torn coat-tails fluttered.

Gradually the turmoil lessened until only one girl's voice was raised. She had been down early in the fight, and she now started where she had left off. She was captured and forcibly escorted up the stairs. Suddenly her voice stopped with the abruptness of a radio turned off.

Presently, the captain came down, his hands bloody, his clothing torn. The guards followed, likewise disfigured. But it was the locksmith who attracted most attention. His heavy blue-grey pants and shirt had been ripped to shreds, and one of his eyes was swollen shut.

"What a beaut!" one of the men near me exclaimed.

"Think so?" the locksmith inquired, belligerently.

As the captain and guards went out the front gate we were alone.

"Yep, I think it's very appropriate. You sure lent the captain a lot of assistance—locking them broads into them cells. He ought to get you a parole."

"Uh, huh," the locksmith smirked, "I did good work—"

He was interrupted by the man who spat at him in loathing: "You lousy—! You ought to be wearing a badge!"

Later I learned that it was Blanche the hula dancer who had kicked the locksmith in the eye. And several years later, when prison was but a memory to Dot and Mae and Blanche, and several of us were together at a party in San Francisco, I congratulated her on the kick.

"That one wasn't so hot," she smiled mischievously. "You ought to have seen the darb I caught Grace—right in the nose!"

I asked her what started the row, and she said that nothing started it; it was just always there, waiting below the surface, ready to break out at any time.

Memory of the lover who had come to prison with her returned to me and I asked if she had seen him since his release.

"Him!" Blanche was contemptuous. "I should say *not!* He was nothing but a hoosier kid I picked up to work with. He beat it right back to the plow when he got out. I got a regular guy now."

III

One of the prisoners was a cultured woman serving time for so-called criminal syndicalism. She was wealthy, educated, and carried herself with a dignity that even the prison uniform could not efface. I admired the fine disdain with which she viewed the mugging process. I admired her reserve in answering the brutally embarrassing questions of the entrance clerk. I admired her friendliness with the girls, and it was to me small wonder that even the matron called her *Mrs.* Loring.

Although prison life was strange to her, for she had been on bail until after the highest court had affirmed her conviction, she had that easy adaptability which ever bespeaks tolerance, intelligence, and a broad understanding. Thanks to her influence, some of the ancient atrocities of the women's quarters were abolished. The girls were allowed increased privileges. When a situation became unbearable, and the tormented girl was frantically seeking any emotional release from the awful reality closing in upon her, it was to Mrs. Loring that she always turned. Even Mae, ruthless, rowdy little gun-moll that she was, respected her.

"What did she do in the way of work?" I asked Mae.

"Same as the rest of us. She could have been boss of the sewing-room anytime she wanted. Or she could have had the ace job of taking care of the matron's rooms. But she just stuck with the bunch, and sewed that baggy old underwear same as the rest of us."

"How long did she do after I left the joint?"

"About a year or so. They wanted to parole her. But she had the notion that by taking parole she was somehow pleading guilty, and she always said there was no guilt attached to her." Mae wrinkled her forehead. "It's hard to figure out, sometimes." Again she frowned heavily. "I don't give a damn myself—I'm a thief, and nothing they can ever do will hurt me. But Mrs. Loring, now, she was different. That jolt did hurt her bad. But she wouldn't let it show, and all the time she was helping other girls, getting them jobs to go to on parole, or writing letters to judges and D. A.'s getting them to lay off some girl who was trying to get out. She had her friends outside see a lot of people in my case. I'd probably done my time solid if she didn't get the explanation to my judge that I only killed that narcotic snitch because I was hooked at the time, and that in prison I got off my habit and was ready to take my place in society and all that balony. And all the time Mrs. Loring knew that I was getting junk through those religious books that the psalm-singers used to bring me from a friend who loaded them up outside. But it didn't make any difference to her. She knew that it didn't do no one any good to stick too long in that madhouse . . . She was one hundred per cent!"

Mae blew out a long breath. "Geez, I get all mushy thinking about her. Give me a drink."

IV

Facing the women's department, but separated from it by seventy yards of flower garden ("The Garden Beautiful"), was the first building of the men's cell blocks. On the second tier were ten or twelve double cells in which condemned men were stored. In the afternoon these men exercised on the pavement in front of the cell block. There they could see the girls going to the hospital, or going out to receive visits (ironically called "receptions"). There, also, they could hear the voices of the girls, and, in the evenings, listen to their music and see their forms, dimly, against the frosted glass of the windows.

I have often watched the eyes of the condemned men follow the girls as they crossed the garden. Since they had nothing to lose by an infraction of the rules, they frequently waved or called to the girls. By adroitly hiding notes along the edge of the pavement in the evening, when the condemned men were locked up, several of us prisoners were able to supply them with a certain sad entertainment. Just why a "guy waiting to be topped" should develop a passion for a distant girl whom he could never hope to see nearer than seventy yards is one of the mysteries of the human mind.

In the corner room of the women's department was a window with another vent through which the girls could watch the condemned men playing catch or walking. Notes dropped through the gallery side of the room were easy to collect in the evening. The large Swede girl, who had been in the middle of the battle with the captain and guards, became infatuated with a tiny killer in Condemned Row. I learned of it when I opened a roll of camera film which the matron had sent to the gallery for development. One of the girls had inserted a note from the Swede in the film roll, asking me if I would get it to "that little guy in the next to the end cell that's waiting to be topped for killing that 'Frisco copper."

I agreed readily and after that got notes regularly from both parties. The Swede's notes were dropped out of the vent in the window, and the killer dropped his where a friend of mine in the bandroom could recover them. These replies were got to the Swede by inserting them in the daily bread from the bake-shop and marking the loaf so that Pat could detect it. The notes were terse and elemental, and proclaimed deathless passion. During the swift development of the affair, for each feared the approach of the day which would mark the end of their love on this earth, I followed their meteoric passions with as keen an interest as though I had been one of the principals.

The killer was without funds. His appeal to the State Supreme Court had been decided against him. A new date for his execution had been set. He had less than fifty days to live, and love. The Swede was serving a five-year term for larceny. She had stolen a flock of jewelry while employed as a maid. When arrested, she dumbly refused to answer questions after her initial explanation that some man had taken the jewelry from her and vanished.

When the killer had less than two weeks of life left to him, I noticed the Swede going out for a visit. During the walk to the front office, her eyes remained on the killer, who was leaning against the cell block smiling at her. At first she looked at him dumbly. Then she appeared to realize that he wanted her to smile back. A broad tender grin broke through her usually placid face, and for that instant, with the sun burnishing to golden yellow her magnificent hair, and her ample arms half raised toward him, she looked like a Norse goddess. She missed a step, lagged behind the matron's vision, and swiftly threw a kiss to the killer.

The condemned men were in their cells when she returned from her visit. That night I got a note from her for the killer. She told him that she had arranged to surrender to an attorney all her hidden stolen jewelry as a fee if the attorney would carry the killer's case to the United States Supreme Court.

He did, and for more than a year the killer remained in communication with the Swede.

Then one day he accused her of flirting. He had seen her, he asserted. When she was stepping off the porch she had smiled at one of the office men. In vain did the Swede aver her innocence. She declared that rather than have him think her untrue, she would remain immersed in the women's department. She would not even go for another trip to the hospital, where she went only because she could see him and he could see her. Those were tearful notes. The killer refused to write for more than two weeks. The rains began, and the condemned men did not come down for exercise. Several more days passed while I accumulated that many notes from the Swede which I could not pass on until a clear day.

But the killer would write no longer. His appeal had been dismissed and again he was sentenced to be hanged. On his last Wednesday evening, when he was taken from the condemned cell and walked across the yard in full view of the Swede at that small vent in the window, he did not look up.

It was Mae who explained the other side of the affair. "That Swede could have been paroled any time after she had served a year if she would kick back with the slum she stole. But she refused parole, gave that shyster the slum, and did her whole jolt solid."

V

Some of the women had husbands serving time in the prison. On visiting day there came out of the women's department a line of twenty girls. At that time there were a hundred women in quarters built to contain thirty. In the visiting room the women entered at the end usually reserved for free visitors, and the men came in on the other side. I was visiting with a friend one afternoon when in trooped the men. Quickly they angled for seats at the long narrow table. In the middle of the table was an upright twelve-inch board which prevented visitors holding hands and passing forbidden articles. When the women came in on the other side, the husbands leaned across that board, disdaining the chairs, and there, locked in embrace across a two-foot table, was a solid wall of delighted couples.

It was impossible to hold any conversation with my friend unless I shouted. Listening to the chatter, my mind ran back over the passionately worded notes of the Swede. If only she could have known one such visit! . . .

"Listen honey, I got a lousy job now . . . Yep, right in the middle of all the dust in the jute mill—it's plain hell!"

"I told that con-matron that ifen she didn't lay offen me, I'd report her to the warden."

"Aw, don't do that! You know, its different here. You can't do like what you would outside . . ."

Then a complaining woman's voice: "Why don't you get a shave? Your whiskers are like wire."

A thin ascetic prisoner, who was book-keeper in the furniture factory: "Really, Ethlyn, I think there should be different places for the various—ahem, inmates, to visit their wives."

And his wife, a beefy woman with glasses pinched into her nose: "Oh, *this* is nothing to what *I* have to endure up there."

Her sigh mingled with the other voices. The room was filled with lamentations.

But there was one woman who did not visit with her husband in the outside room. Mary was about eighteen, a slender kid who looked as if she were not yet ready to graduate from high-school. When she was mugged, her tears flowed easily, and the resultant distortion of her features would not have been recognized by her mother. The slate hung on her by the matron announced that Mary was serving life for a murder committed in Los Angeles.

Her youthful husband was in the condemned cells. Theirs had been a hot, tempestuous marriage. She was in Los Angeles, alone; he was in Los Angeles, and possessed the cash of a recent robbery. Three days they knew each other. She believed him to be a bond salesman. She asked him nothing of his business. She had found and married a good-looking husband, one able to provide for her, and she was happy.

One day, shortly after noon, he returned to her. A friend helped him into the house, then drove away. Carl was shot through the shoulder. He and Mary were alone. She ministered to him, and despite his cautioning, telephoned for a doctor when he became unconscious. With the doctor came the police.

Carl was tried and sentenced for the killing of a pay-roll guard. Mary protested that she knew nothing of his operations. But the neighbors told of seeing another man bring Carl home, and Mary, even in the face of an indictment for murder, persisted in her story that he had come home alone. All this was commonly known when she came to prison. She had been called the Tiger Woman by the papers.

Her first trial had resulted in a disagreement. At the second the district attorney made it plain to the jury that under California law *all* accomplices, regardless of how far they were removed from the crime, are equally guilty with the principals. As soon as that fact had soaked into their minds the jurors found Mary guilty.

Carl's appeal having been decided adversely, he was due to be hanged in May. It was March when Mary arrived. Because one of the condemned men a few months previously had obtained poison and taken an easier death than the State had awaiting for him, Carl and Mary were permitted to visit in the captain's office but twice before he was moved up to the death cells near the scaffold. The first visit was a few days after Mary's arrival; the last was on the Wednesday evening before the Friday morning of execution.

The visits were both short. Mary came slowly from the captain's office on that Wednesday evening after lock-up. They had spent less than ten minutes together. Carl was already dressed in the new blue-grey clothing which he would wear until a few minutes before being hanged. He walked behind Mary a few steps along the porch, and his face was as radiant as though he beheld a vision. Above his collarless shirt his muscular neck and clean-cut features pulsed with vibrant life that seemed to defy any attempt to strangle him.

"Don't you worry, Mary," he called, while his guards paused on either side of him. "The lawyer said I'd get a commute, *sure.* They're only taking me upstairs now to throw a scare into me. It'll be all right." His voice held the high confidence of youth.

Mary stopped at the door of the women's department. The matron loomed large beside her as she smiled bravely; "All right,

Carl." There was a catch in her throat. "I know everything will come out . . . all . . . right."

The matron opened the door. Mary turned suddenly, with one hand pressed to her lips, and stepped quickly inside. The guards, Carl, and the captain following them, left the porch and went down the road past the dungeons into the alley between the hospital and the trades building. Up three long flights of iron stairs they climbed the last mile to the top of the building.

That night there was no music in the women's department. The voices drifting down from the form-shadowed windows were subdued. Over the place hung an atmosphere of hushed waiting.

Thursday passed in a drizzling rain. The girls in the rooms upstairs seemed to have lost the power of speech. There was no noise from the courtyard. Even the strident voice of the Italian vixen was silent. Late Thursday afternoon the rain broke, and overhead the clouds were shattered by the last shafts of the sun. Just after lockup time there appeared over the distant peak of Mt. Tamalpais a huge field of blue sky circled with golden-edged clouds. Through this came the last brightness of the day. It flooded the prison grounds until the darkness started creeping up out of the flagstones. The upper story of the women's department was bathed in a wash of sun, as though a large spotlight had been centered on the window with the vent. Gradually the darkness crept higher, and the wall was drawn into grey shadow. Lights were turned on and the windows appeared as yellow luminous glows. The shadows of the girls passed or stood silently before them.

Friday morning a ghostly grey fog drifted off the bay and shrouded the tops of the walls. The air was heavy with the salty tang of bitterness. Against my will I remained at the railing of the photograph gallery, watching the routine preparations for the execution. When the men from the trades building came straggling up to their cells, and the doors slammed behind them, and the visitors and witnesses came in through the main gate and passed down the road and climbed the long stairs to the execution chamber, and the yard was cleared of everyone except an office man or two, still I remained seated on that railing. There was about the whole scene an air of unreality. It was as though I watched the movements of dim figures in a horrible dream. Once or twice I caught the eye of an office man, then quickly averted my gaze. The fog drifted lower, poured, it seemed, from a huge invisible hand intent on obscuring for this hour all of the prison buildings. The men in the cells were unusually quiet.

Bolts released on the main gate sounded loud in that sepulchral quiet. The warden stepped into the yard. He was wearing a long black overcoat, and his dark hatbrim almost met his upturned collar. His face was a pale white wedge. He walked silently through the yard and disappeared in the grey swirls of fog.

Until that silent figure crossed the yard there was hope of a reprieve. But in his entrance, and with his passing, there came the thought: Before he comes *back* across that yard, a man will be strangled.

From my hunched-up position on the railing I glanced up at the lighted window with the vent. The leaf was out. The window showed two figures pressed against it. Mary, also, had seen the warden pass . . . Her form dissolved, left the window, and a single girl remained on watch . . . The seconds of the next few minutes crawled like ghoulish ants across my spine. And I visualized that girl up there in a room filled with silent women. She, too, was waiting.

The huge weight of the trap dropped with ponderous decisiveness. Through the heavy salt-bitter air that thud came with a sickening hard finality. More minutes dragged through my benumbed mind.

Again the warden appeared, now walking rapidly through the fog, as though he would lose in it a pursuing ghastliness . . . A gentle murmur rose in the cells. The prison stirred. Life moved again in the women's department. I heard the whirring of sewing-machines. At the window there was no shadow. The leaf had been replaced in the vent.

Down through the awakening life there came the brown autumnal voice of Grace: "Get to work girls! Get at your tasks!"

Suddenly her voice rose in harshness: "Mary, go on in and get to work! Go on! Go on! There's nothing more to wait for. It's all over!"

Then through that thin pane of glass, and out into the heavy fog, there came Mary's cry: "All over?" And all the bleakness of the endless years before her was in her final anguished scream: "Over? God, no! It's just *starting!*"

CHESTER HIMES
1909–1984

Recognized for decades in Europe as a major American author, Chester Himes has had a roller-coaster reputation in his native country. By 1934, while still a convict in the Ohio State Penitentiary, he reached the most prestigious market for short fiction as his stories appeared in Esquire *alongside those of Ernest Hemingway and William Faulkner. Paroled in 1936, he managed to publish three significant novels—*If He Hollers Let Him Go, Lonely Crusade, *and* Cast the First Stone—*before the indifference, racism, and sometimes downright hostility of America's critical establishment pushed him into a prolonged European exile in 1953. Amid the social upheavals of the late 1960s and early 1970s, his darkly comic Harlem detective novels, two of which were turned into major Hollywood films, won a considerable audience and critical acclaim in America. Yet by the time of his death in Spain in 1984, the marvelous achievement of his seventeen novels and dozens of stories was already lapsing back into obscurity.*

Prison was the most influential experience in the life and creative imagination of Chester Himes. As he put it in his two-volume autobiography: "I grew to manhood in the Ohio State Penitentiary. I was nineteen years old when I went in and twenty-six years old when I came out." But his most fully developed work about his prison experience was not published until 1998, fourteen years after his death. Entitled Yesterday Will Make You Cry, *it was the original manuscript from which the much sanitized and abbreviated* Cast the First Stone *was patched together in 1952 after sixteen years of publishers' rejections.*

Hints of his distinctive mature vision appear even in his earliest prison stories, published in the Chicago African-American magazine Abbott's Monthly. *"To What Red Hell?," first printed in the October 1934* Esquire, *is based on the catastrophic fire that swept through the Ohio State Penitentiary on April 21, 1930, killing 317 convicts. Here one sees*

*how Himes's characteristic absurdism emerges from the lurid
and grotesque details of the reality he lived, a reality he opts
to view from the perspective of a white convict named Blackie.*

To What Red Hell?

SMOKE ROLLED UP from the burning cell block in black, fire-
tinged waves. The wind caught it and pushed it down over the
prison yard like a thick, gray shroud, so low you could reach up
and touch it with your right hand. Flames, seen through the mist
of smoke, were devils' tongues stuck out at the black night. Buildings were shadows in the crazy pattern of yellow light that streaked
the black blanket of smoke.

The old cell block, stretching across the front of the prison, was
a big, gray face of stolid futility with grilled steel bars checker-
boarding the pale glow of the windows. Ghosts of forgotten sui-
cides lurked in the shadows of its eaves.

The new cell block to the West was an inferno of smoke and
flame, with the baking bodies of men trapped in its cells.

When Blackie turned left by the dining room he had an odd
feeling he could hear those men a hundred yards away crying: "Oh
God! Save me! Oh God! Save me!" over and over again. The words
spun a sudden fear in his mind.

The whole face of the yard was open to his view. Above him
the big, black water-tank was a dim blot through the smoke, like
a gigantic doodle-bug on stilts, looking down over a dung-hill of
confusion. Yellow light shining from the open door of the hospital
cut a kaleidoscopic picture in the confusion of the yard.

Blackie shifted his shoulders to a less irritating position in his
hickory-striped shirt, pulled his baggy, gray trousers higher up his
waist. He looked at the row of prone, gray figures on the bare
ground. The yard was spotted with them, and still more were coming . . . Figures of charred and smoke-blackened flesh wrapped
snugly in gray blankets, lying on the cold ground. He shuddered
slightly. They didn't need blankets now, he was thinking. They
didn't need a damn thing but a wooden box and six feet of ground
in the potter's field.

Suddenly a variegated color pattern formed behind his tense eyes—a black, smoke-mantled night, yellow light, red flames, gray death, crisscrossing each other into a maggotty confusion.

He ploughed through the confusion toward the hospital, feeling that each step he took was on a different color. Thoughts flashed like sheet lightning in the turmoil of his mind. He had a queer feeling that he could smell the odor of death in the smoke-thickened atmosphere.

He stumbled across a twisted body lying in the shadow of a large, concrete flowerpot. He looked down at the pinched, white face, streaked with soot; at the smoke clots still lingering in the half-opened lips. Stiffs everywhere! "Short hours ago we lived—heard voices—heard keys rattling in locks—saw walls of stone and barred windows and uniformed prison guards. Now we don't have to look at them any more." The words made him think of God and the Mission Houses on Clark Street in Chicago; made him think of "Killer" Burke with a jittery trigger finger; made him wonder what he'd be like when he got cut loose.

At the hospital door he paused and looked inside. White light was reflected from white walls. Gray bodies covered the floor, gasping for the breath that would keep them living the life of death. Convict nurses in white jackets were wiping away the black filth belched from the men's tortured lungs.

He saw a convict with creased trousers and a laundered shirt being pushed through the door by a burly policeman. "Come on get along," the cop was saying.

"But I tell you, I gotta see the doc," the fellow was protesting. "I gotta bad headache—I gotta get some of that whiskey or I'll have a nervous breakdown, I tell you . . ."

The cop pushed the fellow down the steps. A snarl coughed up in Blackie's throat. What the hell? A lousy John Law manhandling a con and men lying dead like blackbirds in the shooting season—men sent here by these blue-coated bastards . . .

But a headache! A *headache!* He laughed . . .

Confusion was a tangible thing about him. He could feel it pressing in on his clothes, feel it pumping excitement through his mind. Hundreds of men from "outside" were mingling shoulder to shoulder with the three thousand convicts until you couldn't tell them apart.

At the fringe of the light, where the shadow began, smoke was a thick, gray wall. He walked forward into the wall of smoke. For a moment he couldn't see. Someone bumped his shoulder hard, knocking him to his knees. He felt the side of his head strike the railing by the sidewalk. Then a heavy sound filled his ears like a roar. But it was only a voice yelling: "Gangway! Live one!" Four men swept by into the stream of light up the hospital stairs. They carried a writhing body—A live one! They were dumping the dead ones out in the yard.

He got up and walked over toward the door of the burning cell block. The acrid fumes were thick here. He began to cough. He stopped in front of the smoke-filled door. Water covered the ground. Fire hoses were everywhere. Water, bouncing from the hot brick, sprinkled his face.

A big Negro called Eastern Bill loomed suddenly in the door with a limp figure draped across his shoulder. The unconscious figure strangled suddenly and vomited.

Blackie looked at the slimy filth, felt his stomach turn over inside of him. He heard a voice say: "Get a blanket and give a hand here." His lips twitched slightly as a nausea swept over him. He said: "No can do," in a low choky whisper and walked over toward the chapel.

Didn't know what the hell was the matter with him, getting sick like a convent girl at a cess-pool. He really wanted to go up in that smoking inferno where heroes were being made and angels were being born. But he couldn't, just couldn't, that's all. It wasn't a case of being afraid . . . Hell, he'd been on the Marne—he'd seen liquid fire rolling across no man's land—he'd seen men carrying their guts in their hands . . . But he couldn't go up there on that sixth tier of hell and bring down a puking stiff on his shoulder for love nor money. He just couldn't do it!

He walked through the confusion with a slow, uncertain gait. His mind was in a gray daze. Blue-coated firemen were running all about him yelling instructions at each other . . . Prison guards were jumping about like chickens minus heads, bellowing at the cons. But the cons weren't listening.

He stood still a moment and looked at the men. Pedestrian traffic was as thick as a 42nd Street jam at noon . . . Men working overtime at their job of being heroes, moving through the smoke with reckless haste . . . White faces, gleaming with sweat, streaked with soot . . . White teeth flashing in sweaty black faces . . . Working like hell, seeming jolly about it . . . Men romping here and there without purpose . . . Men standing still . . . Men running in packs like wolves, bent on destruction . . . Men laughing, solemn, some a little hysterical . . . Drunk with their momentary freedom . . . All convicts, all clad in gray—the quick and the dead . . . To some it was just fun, excitement, something to do—a lurid break in the dull monotone of routine.

He walked on to the chapel, tried the door. It was open. He walked inside. A guy was standing in the vestibule just inside the door-way cursing God with a slow, deliberate monotony. Inside, some guys were shooting craps on the floor of the aisle down in front of the stage. He listened a moment to the snapping of their fingers, the rattle of dice. Then he heard a slow run on the bass keys of a piano.

He could hear the crackle of flame from the fire outside, see the red glare through the frosted glass.

He looked toward the stage. Somebody had rolled the cover from the grand piano over in the corner and a curly-headed youth was sitting on the stool, playing Saul's Death March with slow feeling. A pencil streak of light, coming through a cracked door, cut a white stripe down the boy's face. He saw that the boy's cheeks were wet with tears.

Then the slow, steady beat of the bass keys hammered on his mind like a cop's fist. He said: "Don't you know people are dying outside?"

The youth looked around and said: "Sure," without stopping. "I'm playing their parade march into some red hell."

He felt worms crawling in his stomach. He backed out of the chapel, got in the hospital-bound traffic, followed a convict ambulance as far as the deputy's office.

He saw two guys standing by the walk-rail looking over the bodies. He heard one of them say: "God damn! There's Yorky. He won dam' near five C's yesterday shootin' craps up in the idle house."

The fellow standing beside him said: "Yeah? Wonder if he's got any of it on him?"

They looked at each other and started moving casually through the rows of bodies.

Blackie turned away, walked over by the school. What the hell did he have to do with it? he asked himself.

A group of fellows stood in the darkness. A short, baldheaded fellow with a vibrant voice was talking. "Listen, fellows," the short guy was saying, "tomorrow's gonna be another day. There ain't gonna be no way in the world to get all these guys back in the cells. The guards ain't gonna be able to handle 'em and the John Laws is just gonna cause trouble. We don't want no trouble now, with our buddies laying out there dead. But we ain't gonna be ruled no more by bastards that burn us to death. Let's form a committee and rule ourselves—Passive Resistance—That's the way we'll work it."

Heads nodded.

Blackie said: "Uh huh, that's the way you'll work it—like hell!"

Faces turned toward him. A voice said: "Don't mind him, Wolf."

Blackie stepped inside a school-room, slammed the door behind him. Guys were sitting on the desk tops, smoking, laughing, talking. He walked across to the latrine. A guy was using a commode in one end. Another was washing his face in the basin. Over in the corner he saw a big, blonde guy kissing a nice-looking, brunette youth. Nobody seemed to notice him. He turned around and walked out.

He thought, I'd give fifty dollars and a diamond ring if somebody'd just say: "Hello, Blackie, how're *you* makin' it?" But everybody was in a hurry, either being a hero or a damned rogue. Nobody saw him.

He caught himself saying deep in his heart: Hell, if you weren't yellow you'd be helping like the rest of them . . . But that wasn't it, he argued with himself. He'd stand toe to toe and fight anybody in the world—with dukes, chivs or smoking heats. But he couldn't go up in that cell block—he just couldn't do it!

He got outside and started moving fast. A fellow by the personnel office stopped him and said: "Send a telegram home. Tell 'em you're living."

He looked at the yellow Western Union blanks in the guy's hand, said: "Gimme half a dozen."

The guy asked: "Who do you wanta send 'em to?"

He said: "My wife."

The guy said: "Hell, you must be a Mormon. You can't send but one."

Blackie laughed raggedly. "It was just a joke; don't nobody give a damn whether I'm living or not."

He sauntered over to the sidewalk, leaned against a post, looked out over the yard. The gray, prone bodies got into his eyes. Some were the bodies of old men with gray hair and weak eyes, some of young men, some of white men, some of black men—some used to be bankers, once upon a time, some used to be sneak thieves, some big shots, some chiselers . . . But now they were all just stiffs with a gray sameness. No more banquets and cocaine balls!

Doctors moving among the living were white angels. Black-robed priests flitting here and there among the dead were black ghouls. His lips twisted onesidedly with the thought.

He saw the dead face of a guy he had hated. He caught himself quoting: "Take off the paint, no need to longer clown." And then he caught himself wondering if he still hated the guy now that he was dead. He picked his way gingerly through the rows of corpses to see if he knew any more of them.

Somebody started crying loudly beside him. It sounded phony. He turned about searching for the source of the sound. A tall, black boy called Beautiful Slim was kneeling on the ground by the body of a little brown-skin fellow who was burned up around the mouth. When the black boy saw him, he blubbered: "Oh Lawd, ma man's dead."

But he had seen the boy slip a tobacco sack of money from its hiding place in the dead fellow's underwear.

The black boy snarled: "What the hell you got to do with it? I give 'im tha money. And now that he's croaked, do you think I'm gonna let some other nigger bitch get what I give 'im?"

Blackie swung a hard, wild haymaker at the shiny, black face. He missed and went sprawling across the corpse. He felt the soft, mushy form beneath him. He got up, started shaking his hands and feet with quick, jerky movements like a cat walking in molasses. He didn't see the black boy any more, but he saw other guys, white guys, stripping the shoes from the dead men's feet. "Dead Men's Shoes"—Hell, that was the name of a story he had read. Well, what did he have to do with it anyhow? he asked himself.

Suddenly he felt an insane desire to laugh. Something sticky was crawling about in his mind. He felt for a moment that he was going crazy. He started moving fast, trying to get away from the dense crop of corpses. His feet slipped on leg bones. The scalp rolled under his hair.

A second later he found himself standing in front of the entrance to the Catholic chapel. A guy standing there, had a potato sack full of Bull Durham, giving it away.

"What the hell is this, Xmas or donation day at the Y. M. C. A.?" he asked.

The guy said: "We're looting the joint; taking everything—*everything!*"

Blackie said: "Well, don't forget me when you start to taking time!" He went on up the stairs into the Catholic chapel, leaned against the wall beside the bronze basin of Holy Water just inside the door. Candles were burning on the white altar, their yellow flames tapering up toward the polished bronze crucifix . . . A well of peace amid chaos.

He noticed the curved backs of several fellows bent over the railing before the Images of the Saints. He caught himself reciting: "I believe in God, The Father Almighty, Maker of heaven and earth . . ." Then he thought of the prone, gray figures on the cold ground outside; of the smoke and flame and confusion. He felt a sneer form on the bottom side of his lips next to his teeth . . . "I believe in the power of the press, maker of laws, the almighty dollar, political pull, a Colt's .45 . . ."

He turned around and went back downstairs; turned to his left and walked through the darkness by the long wooden dormitory.

From where he stood he could see the death house, a low, red brick building at the end of the cell block. Just above it was a wall parapet. A guard stood on the cat-walk with a sub-machine gun cradled in his arm. Two searchlights shone in opposite directions down the sides of the gray, stone wall. The green door of the death house looked black in the vague light.

The end of the parade! The last mile! What a joke! The death house was on the other side of the yard tonight, he was thinking. It was quiet over here in the shadows with the scared ghosts of the executed men.

He heard a freight train puffing by outside; heard the scream of its whistle. "I wish to God I was riding you," he muttered.

He walked on down by the dormitory. Two guys were standing by the "hole," talking. One guy was saying: "Tuck clipped a screw, took the range key and went down to the end of the range through all that smoke to let those guys out. He just did make it. That's what I call love."

A heavy voice answered: "You goddam right, a sucker's got to love his fellow man a hell of a lot to risk his life like that."

The first guy said: "Hell, I wasn't talking about his fellow man. I was talking about his kid—he was in the last cell down."

He caught himself wondering what made heroes and what made cowards . . .

Then he heard the sound of running footsteps. He looked up the dark areaway between the "hole" and the dormitory. He saw the deputy and two firemen running toward the dormitory. He heard somebody inside yell: "We're burning down the joint!"

He thought: I got to get my box out before the shack goes up, I got my brand new tan shoes in it. He could feel the cinders roll under his feet as he ran toward the door. The deputy turned suddenly and snapped a flash dead in his face. He could feel his eyes getting big all up in his forehead.

Then he saw a guy step out of the dormitory door with an empty can in his hand. He caught the faint stench of gasoline. The deputy swung the light away from him, over on the man in the door-way. He stopped and stared, breathing hard.

Damn, my wind's short—heart's pumping like a trip-hammer. When I fought Kid Mack in the Garden . . . But hell, that was six years ago. A trey in stir . . .

He started suddenly as he saw the fireman draw a pistol and jam it into the guy's guts. He heard the guy's sudden oath, saw him back up a little from the gun and drop the can. He heard the can clanking on the pavement; heard the guy's loud laugh. He sensed the drama of the moment. It made him shaky clear down to his feet. Then he saw the flash; heard the roar of the gun; heard the laugh choke off . . .

He turned, started walking away fast. Let the tan shoes go to hell!

He turned left by the deputy's office. It was the center of the clock here, where the hands turned from. The confusion seemed more orderly.

He heard somebody say: "They're giving away clothes over at the commissary." A bunch of fellows started running over that way to get new clothes. He got in with the bunch and started running like the rest.

He passed the fire trucks bunched at the end of the burning cell block. Mud oozed under his feet. Hoses were writhing snakes in the darkness. The chrome steel and red paint of the fire trucks shone in the lurid glare of the fire. It made him think of a tenement fire he had seen as a kid in Augusta, Georgia.

He slipped between a Pump Truck and a Hook and Ladder; came out on the other side by the commissary door. A bunch of guys were lined up in their shirt-tails.

"What the hell is this, Paramount on Parade?" he asked.

"No, a strip act on Broadway," somebody cracked.

Another guy said: "You got to show your shape before you get new strides."

He said: "May as well," slipped his trousers off, threw them on the ground. He could feel the cool night air blowing through his underwear. Upstairs, men were hemmed together. Odor clogged his nostrils. He got a new coat, new pants—prison fit—and hurried out. He'd rather smell the smoke.

He heard somebody yell, "They're firing the woolen mill!" Sudden confusion sounded among the fire trucks. A motor roared. A truck backed, turned and sped toward the woolen mill. But it was all over before he got there.

He felt kind of chilly. Light shone invitingly from the dining room windows. He went over there.

A guy looked up from a steak and said: "Go on back in the kitchen and get something to eat. They're giving it away."

The steak looked good. He went back in the kitchen, heard a yell ring out. He looked up startled, saw a wide-mouthed Negro standing on the kitchen range with a six-inch dirk in his hand, yelling: "Bring Dangerous Blue some ham and eggs, you kitchen rats." Scars were shiny ridges in the guy's black face.

Blackie raised his hands and said, mockingly: "Don't shoot, Mr. Villa, I surrender."

The guy jumped from the range. Blackie backed from the kitchen, went over into the East dining room. He saw a guy he knew down near the front door, started over to speak to him.

Several sharp reports broke above the steady hum of sound like a staccato burst of gunfire. He ducked under one of the slate-topped tables. After a few seconds he heard somebody laugh; heard a voice saying: "Hell, that was just some damn fools throwing bricks through the windows."

He crawled out from under the table, stood up, brushed his knees off. He saw a score of other fellows coming out from under tables too. He began to laugh himself then. Hell, he thought, if somebody really starts shooting we'll all kill ourselves ducking.

He had forgotten about the guy he'd started to see. He went out the side door into the night. A guy coming around the corner of the tin shop almost bumped into him.

"What the hell you doin' here?" Blackie asked.

"I'm guarding the building," the guy answered. "They got cons guarding all the buildings since they tried to fire the woolen mill a few minutes ago."

Blackie said: "I think a con who'd guard a lousy building on a night like this is a goddam rat."

The guy laughed, said:

"That still don't make me a dam rat."

Blackie hawked, spat on the ground, turned away.

He moved on down the areaway between the tinshop and the dining room. Sound came through the night from behind him, but it was kind of quiet down here. Two guys passed him hurrying back to the confusion of the yard. He kept on walking through the shadows; away from the turmoil; away from the panicked figures racing to and fro like condemned souls jumping flame pots in the ante room of Hell.

He turned the corner by the store room and walked into the darkness . . .

NELSON ALGREN
1909–1981

Prison and writing are inextricably intertwined in the career of Nelson Algren, who has been called "the poet of the jail and the whorehouse." He was so intent on finishing his serious fiction, which he was writing on a typewriter at Sul Ross Teachers College in Alpine, Texas, that he stole the typewriter, packed it up for shipment to Chicago, and hopped a Chicago-bound freight car. Arrested on a tip by the Alpine freight master, he spent the next month in a Texas jail awaiting trial, an experience at the core of much of his fiction, including "El Presidente de Méjico," the story reprinted here.

Algren went on to become one of America's most celebrated novelists and short-story writers, winning the National Book Award for his 1949 best-seller The Man with the Golden Arm, *later made into the 1955 groundbreaking movie about drug addiction. Asked to name America's greatest writers, Ernest Hemingway replied: "Faulkner. (Pause.) Algren." Prison was still a central theme in Algren's final novel, published posthumously in 1983 as* The Devil's Stocking, *based on the murder trial and conviction of boxer Rubin "Hurricane" Carter as well as the Attica prison rebellion.*

El Presidente de Méjico

PORTILLO, a bridegroom of six weeks who looked like a youthful Wallace Beery, kept us informed of as much of the life of the town as he could see from the run-around; he had lived in the place all his life.

"There go pretty girl," he would observe, "walkin' with one ugly man."

All winter we had been waiting for court to convene. It opened any time in spring and closed as soon as the circuit judge disposed of cases accumulated during the winter; then he moved on to the next wide place in the road, usually reaching El Paso in time for the fall hunting.

Portillo didn't have to stand trial because there was no charge against him. The sheriff had simply picked him up to ask him the whereabouts of a certain still. Portillo didn't know. So the sheriff kept him in the run-around in the hope that he might remember. He kept him out of the cell block itself, as much as possible, because of Jesse Gleason.

Jesse was a wiry little man, about thirty, who had once killed a Mex over a game of dominoes, on the American side, and had gotten over the river in time to avoid arrest. He had lived in and around Juarez then, with a Mexican woman, until he had come another cropper and had gotten back across the river only half an

hour in front of the Mexican authorities. He had surrendered himself to the local sheriff with the explanation that his conscience had
at last brought him back. Everybody had liked good old Jesse for
that and the sheriff had shaken his hand and called him "Hair-
Trigger."

Yet the affair in Juarez had been simpler than any difficulty of
conscience could be: he had killed the Mexican woman over a game
of checkers. Here in Cactus County, however, he had more relatives than the sheriff, and was confident of beating the rap.

"There's more bad Mexicans in West Texas than good horses,"
good old Jesse was fond of saying.

The law apparently bore him out, for shooting a Mex was still
safer than stealing a horse. There were second-offender horse
thieves doing twenty to life at Huntsville, but nobody got that for
shooting two Mexicans. Jesse himself had said that Crying Tom,
whip boss of the Huntsville pea farm, was tougher on horse thieves
than anyone, having once lost a pair of army mules out of his own
corral. The whole thing was a legal hangover from a time when
stealing a horse meant leaving its rider helpless in the desert.

Jesse was the bad-man of the tank, and everyone soothed him.
"I'd trust my own sister with a man like that," his cell mate Wolfe
would vouch. And Portillo, watching for a sight of his wife from
the window, would agree absent-mindedly. "I trost sister too."
Portillo wasn't looking for trouble. He was fair stuck on his own
girl.

Jesse never exercised, but possessed a wiry prairie strength that
five months on two thin meals a day hadn't modified. He could
make the overgrown Wolfe howl with no more than the pressure
of two fingers on the shoulder.

Wolfe was voluble and timorous, chattering all day and after the
light was out, in a kind of snot-nosed New Jersey singsong. Until
Jesse said, "Naow shet up!" Wolfe wouldn't so much as finish what
he'd started to say.

There were days when Jesse said nothing, all day long, save this
good-night admonishment to Wolfe. While Wolfe sat cross-legged
in one corner of the cell like a tailor, Jesse squatted on his haunches
like an Indian in the other. Both pitied the other's posture and spent
hours trying to straighten each other out. Once, when Jesse managed to get his legs crossed beneath him, he was unable to disen-
tangle himself and regained his feet only with difficulty. He was

white with rage by then and made Wolfe squat "like a white man" for hours after. For Wolfe wished, more than anything in the world, to be a "white man," and suffered the agonies of the damned trying to achieve purity.

We all suspected, without saying so, that Jesse Gleason was insane.

Although he would have friends on the jury and already had a job waiting for him, we said we felt sorry for him because he had been arrested in the fall of the year. But we told the friendless, penniless, luckless, witless Wolfe he was altogether too lucky for one man, for he hadn't been picked up till spring. We pretended that any man who timed himself that closely to trial time must be a pretty slick customer. "Lucky as a dawg with two joints," was the way Jesse put it, "gittin' out of all thet jawbone time."

It must have been Wolfe's adulation for Jesse that made Jesse tolerate him. For when Jesse heckled the boy it was often good-naturedly. "Hey, Buckethead," he would ask seriously, "are all them Jews as crazy as you?" Wolfe was the only Jew Jesse had ever known, and he was quietly amused by Wolfe's peculiarities. "You got good sense though," he would assure Wolfe. "The only trouble is that, day by day, ever'thin' you do 'n say gets screwier 'n screwier."

Wolfe told us he had run off from a Passaic high school and insisted that, had he stayed only a week longer, he would have earned a letter in track. Although how anyone who had to breathe with his jaw hanging halfway to his navel could have run fifty yards was hard to understand. Yet he knew cowboy songs that Jesse had never heard, and could tell the circumstances of every Western outlaw's death from the Quantrells' to Billy the Kid's.

He was in for breaking into a hut somewhere along the river and stealing a rifle. He'd been wearing a CCC uniform at the time, but had since traded it off, piece by piece with the exception of the belt, to Jesse for corn bread. Thus Jesse wore oversized khaki trousers and CCC shoes, while Wolfe wore undersized county overalls and shoes so small he'd had to cut out the sides; and he still looked hungry enough to trade off his underwear to boot. His hunger would increase as the hours wore on toward night, till he looked most wondrously sad; toward evening he would sing in his adenoidal tenor:

Billy was a bad man
And carried a big gun
He was always after greasers
And kept 'em on the run.

He shot one every morning
For to make his morning meal
And let a greaser sass him
He was shore to feel his steel.

Jesse would never appear to be paying him any attention; but nevertheless he never ordered Wolfe to stop singing that particular song.

Every morning the sheriff came up with the breakfast tray. Jesse distributed the oatmeal and black coffee, calling the rightful owner of each as if a name were engraved on each tin plate. Alternately, either Portillo or Wolfe came up with a short piece of corn bread.

"My little ol' half-piece o' corn bread got cut wrong," Wolfe would complain as though getting ready to cry, but without daring to look accusingly at the piece and a half on Jesse's plate. He would whine until Jesse said, "Naow shet up!" Wolfe tried sulking, leaving a hunk of the stuff on the spoon holder above his blanket every day, as though too disappointed to bother with it. But by evening, after dark, he would put his head under his blanket and eat his undersized hunk all to himself: we heard his jaws moving softly in the dark, and wondered why he was always so secretive in such small things.

One afternoon, just after the courthouse chimes had tolled, Jesse reached up for the hoarded corn bread, bit it in two, and tossed the short half over to me. Wolfe leaped up wailing, thought better of it, and returned miserably to his blanket.

Late that night I wakened and heard him crying; he was mourning for corn bread, in his father's tongue, or for the letter in track he would have gotten in another week. It was hard to tell. There were still crumbs in my teeth that held the fine salty tang that corn bread takes after standing a day and I determined that, the next evening, I'd get his corn bread before Jesse; then Jesse would have to take the short half. As though dreaming of the same thing, Jesse said aloud in sleep, "Naow shet up!" And the wretched mourning ceased.

Wolfe never hoarded his corn bread again, however, and that convinced me that, as the others had suspected, he was a slippery devil all right.

After breakfast he always washed Jesse's plate, cup, and spoon, as a tribute to the fact that Jesse had once taken second prize in a local rodeo. But everyone else cleaned their own, and when the sheriff came up the utensils were always clean and lined up in front of Jesse's blanket as though Jesse himself had washed every piece of tin in the tank.

"I turned yer spoon toward the wall 'stead of 'way from it when I hung it this mornin', Judge," he would advise Jesse. "Was that all right?"

Jesse would deliberate, observing the spoon in the iron holder above his head as though it were the first time he had observed it hanging in precisely that position.

"There's always the right way to do a thing, Melonhead," he would say at last, affecting extreme patience. "An' then there's the wrong way. This time you picked out the wrong way. Now hang it like other people do."

Thus it was largely for Wolfe's benefit that Jesse added a rule or two to the regular rules of the kangaroo court. These were penciled, in Jesse's labored hand, on the wall below the unshaded night bulb:

These are the rules of the kangaroo court. Any man found gilty of braking into this jailhouse without consent of the inmates will be fined two dollars or elts spend forty days on the floor at the rate of five cents per day, or elts take fifty licks from a belt with a belt bukle on it. Every man entering this tank must keep clean and properly dressed. Each day of the week is washday but not Sunday. Every man must wash his face and hands before handling food. Any man found gilty of spitting in ash tub or through window will be given twenty licks. Each and every man using toilet must flush with buket immediately afters. Man found gilty of vilation gets twenty-five licks from the belt-bukle belt. Throw all paper in the coal tub. Don't draw pictures on your wall, somebody's sister might come visitin. When using dishrag keep it clean. Any man caught stealing from inmate of this tank gets 500 belt-bukle licks. Every man upon entering this tank with a ver'al disease, lice, buboes, crabs, or the yellow glanders must report same immedately. Any man found vilatin any of these rules will be punished according to the justice of the court. Anythin not covered here will be decided by the justice of this court. The judge of the court can search everywhere. He can search anybody. The judge could be treasurer too if he wanted. He is Judge Jesse Gleason.

And above the bowl some wag of another day had scratched a simpler legend:

> *A flush here is better than a full house.*

Before taking the breakfast tray back downstairs the sheriff always appointed either Portillo or Wolfe trusty for the day. This meant being allowed in the run-around until his return in the evening, and Wolfe vied slyly with Portillo for that honor. A trusty went through the motions of sweeping for an hour, emptied the ash tub, and then looked out of the small unbarred window until dark.

Wolfe wanted only the distinction involved, so as the day waned his enjoyment decreased as his hunger increased; he was always happy to hear the sheriff's military footstep on the stair when it was time for him to come back in the tank with us. To Portillo, however, the job was both a means of staying out of Jesse's way and a chance to wave at his wife on her way home from the Iglesia Metodista after vespers.

He seemed to suffer more from his separation from her than from hunger. It was for her sake he avoided Jesse: when Jesse shaved, Portillo's eyes never left Jesse's razor hand. He was usually up before any of us, his swart, high-cheekboned face washed, his Indian hair combed back to a black gloss, and his bridgeless nose pressed boyishly to the cold blue bars, waiting for the sheriff to let him into the run-around. He would take his breakfast out there, but it would stand until his wife had passed and waved. Then he would eat with relish.

She would stand in the middle of the rutted road, a slight girl in a bright Sears, Roebuck printed frock, pointing proudly to her belly. He would cup his hands, the broom beneath his armpit, and call down to her that he and the baby would be out the same day.

When she left he would feel so happy that he looked drunken. He would squeeze himself with both hands, wave his arms aimlessly, and would go through a little love dance, pretending the broom was his bride.

Once he paused in this routine, turned slowly, and looked at me searchingly through the bars, as though seeing someone he had never seen before. He put one hand on the back of my neck with a look so direct, and so questioning, that I laughed. Immediately he broke into a wide white grin, as though he, too, thought it funny to have a question for which there seemed to be no words in either Spanish or English. "I weel leeft you," he told me, like promising an award.

And sure enough, the first thing he did upon being let back in the cell block that evening was to walk up to me and, without warning as it was without apparent reason, "leefted" me.

"See, I leeft you."

And up I'd go by the elbows. Although I never divined what significance this odd ritual held for Portillo, he repeated it often; and always it seemed to him to be the same good joke.

"I'll bet your boy be *Presidente de Méjico* someday," I assured him. He looked at me as though startled, repeated the phrase to himself, then seemed to sadden and turned away.

"*El Presidente de Méjico,*" I heard him telling himself wistfully. "*Pequeño presidente infelíz.*" And stood looking out at the rutted place where his wife had stood that morning, rolling his head in a deep and Indian mood.

Although he never spoke to Jesse and Jesse never spoke to him, Portillo talked easily to Wolfe. Wolfe would lean through the bars, joking about the still which, we all knew, the sheriff claimed Portillo operated and of which Portillo had consistently denied all knowledge.

"I bet when your kid is born you'll put him to work out there in the bear grass before you name him," Wolfe ventured.

"No," Portillo answered seriously, "I name first."

What troubled me was why Jesse kept using Wolfe to pump the Mex about that still.

But there was the morning when Wolfe and Portillo were both, inexplicably, turned out into the run-around as trusties together. They took turns sweeping, though there wasn't enough work to keep one man busy. And then, from somewhere, Wolfe provided a bottle of tequila. He and Portillo finished the bottle between them, passing it back and forth as though no one else in the cell block existed. By noon Wolfe was sick and Portillo was huddled on his heels in a corner, singing loudly to the wall.

> *Una noche serena y oscura*
> *Cuando en silencio juramos los dos*
> *Cuando en silencio me detesto mano*
> *De testigos pucemos adiós*
> *Las estrellas, el sol y la luna——*

He broke off and consulted himself seriously. "*El Presidente de Méjico,*" he told himself. And sat laughing softly at the idea awhile.

Toward evening I heard Jesse laughing softly too. For several days thereafter I observed that Jesse split his corn bread with Wolfe, for some reason.

Portillo was released suddenly two days later, on a morning when the mountain rains came slantwise across the courthouse wall, and the courthouse chimes tolled evenly, as though tolling some long sea hours.

The night bulb, that usually faded each morning at six, burned that morning until almost nine. We knew it was nine by the courthouse chimes, a minute after the bulb dimmed slowly, leaving the cells still shadowed with night. By standing atop the bowl at the end of the cell block we could see the everlasting mountain mist crossing a line of Texas-Pacific boxcars, shrouding them to the roofs: we could see the car roofs being shunted across the arroyo for the noon run to El Paso.

After breakfast I crawled back into my blanket and considered how cold it would be riding one of those T-P boxcars into El Paso on the noon run. There'd be ice along the spine of the cars. I dozed off with my arms clasped under my knees and dreamed I was hunched up in a reefer. I wakened shivering, yet realizing I'd rather be riding than be where I was another hour. I was that dead sick for home.

"There goes the sheriff," Wolfe announced from the run-around. And I heard the muffled roar of the big car wheeling around the courthouse square and off toward the arroyo road. I fancied it swaying from side to side down a gravel road, its headlights cutting the fog like a train's through a tunnel. When it got off the gravel it would take the sand roads softly, and dust would follow into the mist. And there would be the smoky smell, through the fog and dust, that March brings to the chaparral and the long brown bear grass. The car thundered distantly across the arroyo and I was sick for the traffic of home.

Wolfe was making scratches on the wall with his fingernail again. He preferred such a tool because, he explained, a knife wouldn't be sanitary. He spoke as though his nose were clogged, and he was putting the final flourishes on a legend begun the day before, with his tongue caught between his teeth:

Me and Frank stayed overnight in this cell once—JESSE J.

He had scratched up a whole wall with similar myths.

Pretty Boy Floyd escaped from this cell.

And:

I got to be a copper-hater here myself—"Fox" WOLFE.

Of this outlawry of the West, almost to a man, all had effected escapes. Yet I never saw him use but the one fingernail. And never saw him blow his nose.

All that March afternoon the slant rain never ceased. We gathered together uneasily as dark came on, to read the rules of the kangaroo court to each other, like men reading Genesis, on a raft at sea, with a great wind rising. A couple minutes after the night bulb came on we heard heavy boots climbing with difficulty, as though burdened, and then the tank door being opened.

It always took the sheriff longer to open the tank door than the outer doors because the tank door was opened by an air brake locked in a box on the outer wall and the key to the box, smaller than his other keys, usually eluded him for a minute. We listened while we knew he was fumbling for it; and sensed he was not alone, as the door opened slowly.

There was the sheriff and the sheriff's grown son and between them Portillo, bent double, his face shadowed by his cheap straw sombrero and his toenails scraping the concrete as he was half dragged and half carried in.

The hat was the color of sotol cactus, and beneath it his face had been so drained of blood that it was ageless. He no longer looked like Wallace Beery; his face seemed smaller now, and held no expression at all. It looked like a plastic face; and he sagged in his middle. Behind the parade came the local doc, carrying the sheriff's bear gun. He handed it back to the sheriff as Jesse bundled a blanket through the bars.

Portillo's mouth gaped when he was stretched out upon the blanket. He placed his hands across his stomach, still clutching the gray sombrero, and said, "Oooo—*pobre mujer*—oooo—poor belly."

"Shouldn't run when the law hollers, boy," the sheriff advised him, looking down at the poor drained face; the fingers began searching feebly for the wound.

"When ah seen him vomitin' ah knowed ah had him," the sheriff explained earnestly to Jesse.

Jesse's interest was professional. "That's how ah got mah'n," he reminisced, "only a little higher 'n he were comin' *to'd* me."

I had never seen a man dying of such a simple thing as a gunshot wound through the stomach. His face was grayer than I had ever seen a living face and the eyes were dilating with shock. They stared, fixedly and without understanding, at the monstrous and ragged navel of his wound.

"Shouldn't have turned rabbit, boy," the sheriff repeated. The doc leaned over and swabbed the belly with cotton batting.

"He jumped out of the car comin' back across the arroyo," the sheriff was explaining as though he were already in court. "I hollered, but he just bent over 'n stahted zigzaggin'. They all try that. Zigged when he should of zagged."

Portillo's shirt was the color of the cactus-colored sombrero: the dead gray of his fumbling fingers, the gray of the cells we called home; the color of the concrete upon which he lay, and the color of the land upon which his eyes were fixed. His toes, still damp from the bear-grass rain, twitched occasionally and they too were gray.

"We'll have to op'rate, Poncho. Say 'Okay.' Say *'Sí.'* "

Portillo didn't answer. His fingers found the sombrero's rim and twisted it weakly, the dilated pupils never wavering from his stomach, still trying to understand something through the curtain of shock and horror and the nightmare grip of his weakness.

"Should've brought him to the hospital 'stead of up here," Jesse complained to no one in particular.

"Tell us we kin op'rate, Poncho," the doctor asked. "Ah got to sew you."

The sheriff inclined one ear downward in the hope of catching a whispered consent. The fingers forgot the sombrero and wandered, aimlessly as a madman's, about the wound's gray edge, tracing the torn tissue; the doctor laid the fingers back, and the sheriff confided in Jesse.

"First shot creased his laig. Second caught him four-squwar."

Outside the rain ceased a minute, as though listening with us for the whisper of consent. The doc looked up inquiringly at the sheriff and the sheriff looked down at the kneeling doc, his face a mask of impassivity. The odor of iodine began filling the tank.

"You tell yes, Poncho," the sheriff suggested softly. "You tell *sí . . .*"

"Ooo—*pobre mujer.* Ooo—poor belly."

"His wife's downstairs with Martha," the sheriff's son offered. "Maybe she'll say yes for him."

The doc rose heavily.

" 'Cordin' to *mah* understandin', so long as he's still concious, he got to say it hisself. Elts ah'm liable. Ah give him first aid 'n that's all ah kin do within the law."

I remember Wolfe staring down like an idiot trying to remember something important. He watched the seeking fingers falter, until his own eyes faltered. While outside the rain began again and I heard its whispered consent at last.

"*Sí, los pobres, sí.*"

But no one heeded the rain. For the rain came every day at any hour, and forever whispered whatever one wished to hear.

The last I saw of "Fox" Wolfe was in a crowded courtroom about ten o'clock of a windy April night. He seemed to have had the notion that, whatever the jury decided, he and Jesse would, for better or for worse, somehow remain together. But Jesse had been free for hours, and Wolfe had just been sentenced to four years on the pea farm at Huntsville and the sheriff had one hand on the back of his CCC belt and with the other was shoving him past the jury box. He would wait a couple weeks for the wagon to Huntsville and he wanted to cry, I believe, at the prospect of going hungry another two weeks, another four years, another forever. Yet, somehow, he was managing to look Jewish and stubborn, as though assuring himself that he wasn't sorry, even now, about not waiting that extra week to get his letter.

When I got a floater out of the state I planned to ride as far as El Paso. But at the last moment, with the train in sight, I decided to go east instead just to change my luck. I leaned against a water tank in the dark, feeling that getting out of Texas in any direction was a job and that I had my work cut out for me, when I spotted Jesse Gleason leading a little girl by one hand and carrying a full grocery basket in the other. He was still wearing Wolfe's CCC uniform, tucked, at the middle of the calf, into a spanty-new pair of black Spanish boots.

The boots were sharply pointed, high-heeled, and spurred like a fighting cock. I started to call out, then saw he was now a respectable citizen and remembered in time that I was still a bum.

Each of the boots bore a red star in a white circle toward the top. I stood in semidarkness and saw the spurs catch light from the big Western arc lamp at the corner. Under the lamp he put the basket down to shake hands with a well-dressed youth in a college-cut topcoat and he wasn't fifty yards from me then. He'd gotten a barbershop haircut, leaving long Spanish sideburns, and he swept the sombrero off his head and began twirling it, in an off-center spin, about his middle finger. It wasn't till he stopped twirling it that I could tell for sure. Then I could tell all right. It was Portillo's sombrero.

There are still more bad Mexicans than there are good horses in West Texas, the argument runs.

ROBERT LOWELL
1917–1977

One of the preeminent American poets of the twentieth century, Robert Lowell experienced prison at a formative stage of his writing career. In the first year of U.S. participation in World War II, Lowell registered for the draft and attempted unsuccessfully to enlist in the armed forces. But by mid-1943, when he received his draft notice, he had become appalled by the U.S. commitment to unrestrained bombing of civilian pop-

ulations. In his public letter of refusal to be inducted he declared: "Our rulers have promised us unlimited bombings of Germany and Japan. . . . If this program is carried out, it will demonstrate to the world our Machiavellian contempt for the laws of justice and charity between nations."

In October 1943, Lowell was convicted of draft evasion and sentenced to a year in federal prison. While waiting to be transported to serve his sentence in the Federal Correctional Center at Danbury, Connecticut, he was incarcerated for several days in New York City's West Street Jail. In an adjoining cell was gangster boss Louis "Lepke" Buchalter, awaiting execution for his role in Murder Incorporated. According to Ian Hamilton's Robert Lowell: A Biography, *Lepke asked, "I'm in for killing. What are you in for?" and Lowell replied, "Oh, I'm in for refusing to kill."*

Lowell's minor obscurantist poem about the five months he actually served at Danbury, "In the Cage," was published in Lord Weary's Castle *(1946), which received the Pulitzer Prize for 1947. It was not until 1959 that he published his major poem about his prison experience, "Memories of West Street and Lepke," a work now regarded as one of his finest achievements.*

Memories of West Street and Lepke

Only teaching on Tuesdays, book-worming
in pajamas fresh from the washer each morning,
I hog a whole house on Boston's
"hardly passionate Marlborough Street,"
where even the man
scavenging filth in the back alley trash cans,
has two children, a beach wagon, a helpmate,
and is a "young Republican."
I have a nine months' daughter,
young enough to be my granddaughter.
Like the sun she rises in her flame-flamingo infants' wear.

These are the tanquillized *Fifties*,
and I am forty. Ought I to regret my seedtime?
I was a fire-breathing Catholic C.O.,
and made my manic statement,
telling off the state and president, and then
sat waiting sentence in the bull pen
beside a Negro boy with curlicues
of marijuana in his hair.

Given a year,
I walked on the roof of the West Street Jail, a short
enclosure like my school soccer court,
and saw the Hudson River once a day
through sooty clothesline entanglements
and bleaching khaki tenements.
Strolling, I yammered metaphysics with Abramowitz,
a jaundice-yellow ("it's really tan")
and fly-weight pacifist,
so vegetarian,
he wore rope shoes and preferred fallen fruit.
He tried to convert Bioff and Brown,
the Hollywood pimps, to his diet.
Hairy, muscular, suburban,
wearing chocolate double-breasted suits,
they blew their tops and beat him black and blue.
I was so out of things, I'd never heard
of the Jehovah's Witnesses.
"Are you a C.O.?" I asked a fellow jailbird.
"No," he answered, "I'm a J.W."
He taught me the "hospital tuck,"
and pointed out the T shirted back
of *Murder Incorporated's* Czar Lepke,
there piling towels on a rack,
or dawdling off to his little segregated cell full
of things forbidden the common man:
a portable radio, a dresser, two toy American
flags tied together with a ribbon of Easter palm.
Flabby, bald, lobotomized,
he drifted in a sheepish calm,
where no agonizing reappraisal

jarred his concentration on the electric chair—
hanging like an oasis in his air
of lost connections. . . .
as if beseeching voyage. Voyage?
Down and down; the compass needle dead on terror.

1959

THE MOVEMENT
AND THE PRISON

MALCOLM X
1925–1965

When The Autobiography of Malcolm X *appeared in 1965, it was the first published full-length autobiography of an African-American common criminal and convict. It marked the beginning of a new epoch in American prison literature and soon became one of the most influential books in late-twentieth-century American culture.*

The Autobiography *opens with a 1925 scene of hooded, gun-brandishing Ku Klux Klansmen riding around his family's house in Omaha, threatening his mother, who is pregnant with Malcolm. When he is four, white terrorists burn down his family's home in Lansing, Michigan. This is his "earliest vivid memory," a "nightmare night" of "pistol shots and shouting and smoke and flames." When he is six his father, an organizer for Marcus Garvey's Universal Negro Improvement Association, is killed. In 1937, at the age of twelve, Malcolm is taken away from his mother.*

About three years later, Malcolm moves to Boston, gets a job as a shoeshine boy, and drifts into the world of the hipster. One of the famous scenes in the Autobiography *is his description of his first "conk," "my first really big step toward self-degradation: when I endured all of that pain, literally burning my flesh to have it look like a white man's hair." In 1941, at the age of sixteen, he enters the "life" in Harlem, soon becoming a drug addict and a zoot-suited hustler, pimping and pushing dope. Four years later he returns to Boston, sets up a burglary ring, and is eventually caught and sentenced to prison. The most powerful and influential section of the* Autobiography, *excerpted here, describes his transformation in prison.*

When he walked out of the Norfolk Prison Colony in 1952, after almost seven years of imprisonment, Malcolm was a devout Muslim, a formidable intellectual and scholar, and a man destined to become one of the most significant political leaders of modern America. His rise to leadership in the Nation of Islam, his break with Elijah Muhammad, his conversion to the Sunni Muslim faith, his establishment of the Organization of Afro-American Unity (OAAU), his movement toward socialism, and his assassination at the age of thirty-nine—all are familiarly known sequels to his prison experience.

Perhaps less familiar are the consequences for prison literature. After the assassination of Malcolm, prison writers acknowledged him as both their political and spiritual leader; he is conventionally compared to Moses, Jesus, even Allah. Etheridge Knight, who has written several poems about Malcolm, cut through to the essence of his role in "It Was a Funky Deal," a poem about the assassination:

> You rocked too many boats, man.
> Pulled too many coats, man.
> Saw through the jive.
> You reached the wild guys
> Like me.

In a chapter entitled "Initial Reactions on the Assassination of Malcolm X" in Soul on Ice *(1968), ex-convict Eldridge Cleaver argues that Malcolm reinforced the belief of the majority of black prisoners, including himself, that they were not so much "criminals" as "prisoners of war." Bobby Seale begins* Seize the Time *(1970), a book written in jail, with these words: "When Malcolm X was killed in 1965, I ran down the street," threw bricks at a police car, "cried like a baby," and vowed, "I'll make my own self into a motherfucking Malcolm X."* Look for Me in the Whirlwind, *the 1971 collective autobiography of twenty-one Black Panthers prosecuted for criminal conspiracy in New York, has an entire section about how Malcolm changed the thinking and lives of its authors. Among the countless poems about him by convicts, "Black Thoughts '71 (malcolm)" by Insan (Robert Preston) sums up the core of Malcolm's message in the thought "what he was i am / capable of being plus some."*

from *The Autobiography of Malcolm X*

Satan

I GOT TEN YEARS.

The girls got one to five years, in the Women's Reformatory at Framingham, Massachusetts.

This was in February, 1946. I wasn't quite twenty-one. I had not even started shaving.

They took Shorty and me, handcuffed together, to the Charlestown State Prison.

I can't remember any of my prison numbers. That seems surprising, even after the dozen years since I have been out of prison. Because your number in prison became part of you. You never heard your name, only your number. On all of your clothing, every item, was your number, stenciled. It grew stenciled on your brain.

Any person who claims to have deep feeling for other human beings should think a long, long time before he votes to have other men kept behind bars—caged. I am not saying there shouldn't be prisons, but there shouldn't be bars. Behind bars, a man never reforms. He will never forget. He never will get completely over the memory of the bars.

After he gets out, his mind tries to erase the experience, but he can't. I've talked with numerous former convicts. It has been very interesting to me to find that all of our minds had blotted away many details of years in prison. But in every case, he will tell you that he can't forget those bars.

As a "fish" (prison slang for a new inmate) at Charlestown, I was physically miserable and as evil-tempered as a snake, being suddenly without drugs. The cells didn't have running water. The prison had been built in 1805—in Napoleon's day—and was even styled after the Bastille. In the dirty, cramped cell, I could lie on my cot and touch both walls. The toilet was a covered pail; I don't care how strong you are, you can't stand having to smell a whole cell row of defecation.

The prison psychologist interviewed me and he got called every filthy name I could think of, and the prison chaplain got called worse. My first letter, I remember, was from my religious brother Philbert in Detroit, telling me his "holiness" church was going to pray for me. I scrawled him a reply I'm ashamed to think of today.

Ella was my first visitor. I remember seeing her catch herself, then try to smile at me, now in the faded dungarees stenciled with my number. Neither of us could find much to say, until I wished she hadn't come at all. The guards with guns watched about fifty convicts and visitors. I have heard scores of new prisoners swearing back in their cells that when free their first act would be to waylay those visiting-room guards. Hatred often focused on them.

I first got high in Charlestown on nutmeg. My cellmate was among at least a hundred nutmeg men who, for money or cigarettes, bought from kitchen-worker inmates penny matchboxes full of stolen nutmeg. I grabbed a box as though it were a pound of heavy drugs. Stirred into a glass of cold water, a penny matchbox full of nutmeg had the kick of three or four reefers.

With some money sent by Ella, I was finally able to buy stuff for better highs from guards in the prison. I got reefers, Nembutal, and benzedrine. Smuggling to prisoners was the guards' sideline; every prison's inmates know that's how guards make most of their living.

I served a total of seven years in prison. Now, when I try to separate that first year-plus that I spent at Charlestown, it runs all together in a memory of nutmeg and the other semi-drugs, of cursing guards, throwing things out of my cell, balking in the lines, dropping my tray in the dining hall, refusing to answer my number—claiming I forgot it—and things like that.

I preferred the solitary that this behavior brought me. I would pace for hours like a caged leopard, viciously cursing aloud to myself. And my favorite targets were the Bible and God. But there was a legal limit to how much time one could be kept in solitary. Eventually, the men in the cellblock had a name for me: "Satan." . . .

[M]y sister Ella had been steadily working to get me transferred to the Norfolk, Massachusetts, Prison Colony, which was an experimental rehabilitation jail. In other prisons, convicts often said that if you had the right money, or connections, you could get transferred to this Colony whose penal policies sounded almost too good to be true. Somehow, Ella's efforts in my behalf were successful in late 1948, and I was transferred to Norfolk.

'The Colony was, comparatively, a heaven, in many respects. It had flushing toilets; there were no bars, only walls—and within the walls, you had far more freedom. There was plenty of fresh air to breathe; it was not in a city.

There were twenty-four "house" units, fifty men living in each unit, if memory serves me correctly. This would mean that the Colony had a total of around 1200 inmates. Each "house" had three floors and, greatest blessing of all, each inmate had his own room.

About fifteen per cent of the inmates were Negroes, distributed about five to nine Negroes in each house.

Norfolk Prison Colony represented the most enlightened form of prison that I have ever head of. In place of the atmosphere of malicious gossip, perversion, grafting, hateful guards, there was more relative "culture," as "culture" is interpreted in prisons. A high percentage of the Norfolk Prison Colony inmates went in for "intellectual" things, group discussions, debates, and such. Instructors for the educational rehabilitation programs came from Harvard, Boston University, and other educational institutions in the area. The visting rules, far more lenient than other prisons', permitted visitors almost every day, and allowed them to stay two hours. You had your choice of sitting alongside your visitor, or facing each other.

Norfolk Prison Colony's library was one of its outstanding features. A millionaire named Parkhurst had willed his library there; he had probably been interested in the rehabilitation program. History and religions were his special interests. Thousands of his books were on the shelves, and in the back were boxes and crates full, for which there wasn't space on the shelves. At Norfolk, we could actually go into the library, with permission—walk up and down the shelves, pick books. There were hundreds of old volumes, some of them probably quite rare. I read aimlessly, until I learned to read selectively, with a purpose. . . .

Saved

I did write to Elijah Muhammad. He lived in Chicago at that time, at 6116 South Michigan Avenue. At least twenty-five times I must have written that first one-page letter to him, over and over. I was trying to make it both legible and understandable. I practically couldn't read my handwriting myself; it shames even to remember it. My spelling and my grammar were as bad, if not worse. Anyway, as well as I could express it, I said I had been told about him by my brothers and sisters, and I apologized for my poor letter.

Mr. Muhammad sent me a typed reply. It had an all but electrical effect upon me to see the signature of the "Messenger of Allah." After he welcomed me into the "true knowledge," he gave me something to think about. The black prisoner, he said, symbolized white society's crime of keeping black men oppressed and deprived and ignorant, and unable to get decent jobs, turning them into criminals. . . .

I became increasingly frustrated at not being able to express what I wanted to convey in letters that I wrote, especially those to Mr. Elijah Muhammad. In the street, I had been the most articulate hustler out there—I had commanded attention when I said something. But now, trying to write simple English, I not only wasn't articulate, I wasn't even functional. How would I sound writing in slang, the way I would *say* it, something such as, "Look, daddy, let me pull your coat about a cat, Elijah Muhammad—"

Many who today hear me somewhere in person, or on television, or those who read something I've said, will think I went to school far beyond the eighth grade. This impression is due entirely to my prison studies.

It had really begun back in the Charlestown Prison, when Bimbi first made me feel envy of his stock of knowledge. Bimbi had always taken charge of any conversation he was in, and I had tried to emulate him. But every book I picked up had few sentences which didn't contain anywhere from one to nearly all of the words that might as well have been in Chinese. When I just skipped those words, of course, I really ended up with little idea of what the book said. So I had come to the Norfolk Prison Colony still going through only book-reading motions. Pretty soon, I would have quit even these motions, unless I had received the motivation that I did.

I saw that the best thing I could do was get hold of a dictionary—to study, to learn some words. I was lucky enough to reason also that I should try to improve my penmanship. It was sad. I couldn't even write in a straight line. It was both ideas together that moved me to request a dictionary along with some tablets and pencils from the Norfolk Prison Colony school.

I spent two days just riffling uncertainly through the dictionary's pages. I'd never realized so many words existed! I didn't know *which* words I needed to learn. Finally, just to start some kind of action, I began copying.

In my slow, painstaking, ragged handwriting, I copied into my tablet everything printed on that first page, down to the punctuation marks.

I believe it took me a day. Then, aloud, I read back, to myself, everything I'd written on the tablet. Over and over, aloud, to myself, I read my own handwriting.

I woke up the next morning, thinking about those words—immensely proud to realize that not only had I written so much at one time, but I'd written words that I never knew were in the world. Moreover, with a little effort, I also could remember what many of these words meant. I reviewed the words whose meanings I didn't remember. Funny thing, from the dictionary first page right now, that "aardvark" springs to my mind. The dictionary had a picture of it, a long-tailed, long-eared, burrowing African mammal, which lives off termites caught by sticking out its tongue as an anteater does for ants.

I was so fascinated that I went on—I copied the dictionary's next page. And the same experience came when I studied that. With every succeeding page, I also learned of people and places and events from history. Actually the dictionary is like a miniature encyclopedia. Finally the dictionary's A section had filled a whole tablet—and I went on into the B's. That was the way I started copying what eventually became the entire dictionary. It went a lot faster after so much practice helped me to pick up handwriting speed. Between what I wrote in my tablet, and writing letters, during the rest of my time in prison I would guess I wrote a million words.

I suppose it was inevitable that as my word-base broadened, I could for the first time pick up a book and read and now begin to understand what the book was saying. Anyone who has read a great deal can imagine the new world that opened. Let me tell you something: from then until I left that prison, in every free moment I had, if I was not reading in the library, I was reading on my bunk. You couldn't have gotten me out of books with a wedge. Between Mr. Muhammad's teachings, my correspondence, my visitors—

usually Ella and Reginald—and my reading of books, months passed without my even thinking about being imprisoned. In fact, up to then, I never had been so truly free in my life.

The Norfolk Prison Colony's library was in the school building. A variety of classes was taught there by instructors who came from such places as Harvard and Boston universities. The weekly debates between inmate teams were also held in the school building. You would be astonished to know how worked up convict debaters and audiences would get over subjects like "Should Babies Be Fed Milk?"

Available on the prison library's shelves were books on just about every general subject. Much of the big private collection that Parkhurst had willed to the prison was still in crates and boxes in the back of the library—thousands of old books. Some of them looked ancient: covers faded, old-time parchment-looking binding. Parkhurst, I've mentioned, seemed to have been principally interested in history and religion. He had the money and the special interest to have a lot of books that you wouldn't have in general circulation. Any college library would have been lucky to get that collection.

As you can imagine, especially in a prison where there was heavy emphasis on rehabilitation, an inmate was smiled upon if he demonstrated an unusually intense interest in books. There was a sizable number of well-read inmates, especially the popular debaters. Some were said by many to be practically walking encyclopedias. They were almost celebrities. No university would ask any student to devour literature as I did when this new world opened to me, of being able to read and *understand*.

I read more in my room than in the library itself. An inmate who was known to read a lot could check out more than the permitted maximum number of books. I preferred reading in the total isolation of my own room.

When I had progressed to really serious reading, every night at about ten P.M. I would be outraged with the "lights out." It always seemed to catch me right in the middle of something engrossing.

Fortunately, right outside my door was a corridor light that cast a glow into my room. The glow was enough to read by, once my eyes adjusted to it. So when "lights out" came, I would sit on the floor where I could continue reading in that glow.

At one-hour intervals the night guards paced past every room. Each time I heard the approaching footsteps, I jumped into bed and feigned sleep. And as soon as the guard passed, I got back out of bed onto the floor area of that light-glow, where I would read for another fifty-eight minutes—until the guard approached again. That went on until three or four every morning. Three or four hours of sleep a night was enough for me. Often in the years in the streets I had slept less than that.

GEORGE JACKSON
1941–1971

At the age of eighteen, George Jackson was brought to trial for allegedly stealing $70 from a Los Angeles gas station. Although he insisted that he was innocent, he had two prior convictions and his court-appointed lawyer convinced him to plead guilty so that he would get a light sentence in a county jail. Instead, Jackson received an indeterminate sentence of one year to life in state prison. This is where he spent the rest of his life.

During his eleven years in prison, Jackson was in solitary confinement for almost eight years, including a year and a half with the door of his cell welded shut. On January 13, 1970, a white tower guard in California's Soledad prison, where Jackson was incarcerated, shot and killed three black prisoners who were fighting with white prisoners. Three days later a white guard was beaten to death by inmates. The prison administration charged three black militant prisoners with murder: George Jackson, Fleeta Drumgo, and John Clutchette. All three were placed in isolation and prevented from communicating their situation, even to family members, until Clutchette managed to smuggle out a letter to his mother. This brought the case to the attention of noted defense attorney Fay Stender, who soon became a champion of the three "Soledad Brothers." Stender helped to arrange publication of the book Soledad Brother, *a collection of George Jackson's letters, including the one to her reprinted here. Published in October 1970, with a powerful introduction by Jean Genet,* Soledad Brother *quickly sold more than 400,000 copies.*

Meanwhile in August 1970, George's seventeen-year-old brother, Jonathan, staged a raid on the Marin County Courthouse, armed three black San Quentin prisoners being tried there, seized hostages, demanded the immediate release of the three Soledad Brothers, and was killed in the resulting shootout. George dedicated Soledad Brother *to him.*

In February 1972, George Jackson published Blood in My Eye, *a book consisting mainly of political analysis and revolutionary theory. By this time, he was regarded by many as a major revolutionary thinker.*

On August 21, two days before the trial of the three Soledad Brothers was finally to begin, George Jackson was killed during a purported escape attempt from San Quentin. He died in the prison yard from a shot fired by a tower guard from high above while Jackson was supposedly brandishing a pistol and running toward a twenty-foot-high wall. Defying most laws of physics, the fatal bullet entered below his tenth rib and exited the top of his skull. When the trial of the two remaining Soledad Brothers did take place, the state's evidence proved to be exceedingly flimsy and both men were acquitted, casting even more doubt on the story that Jackson had been trying to escape. "No Black person," James Baldwin later wrote, "will ever believe that George Jackson died the way they tell us he did."

When he died at the age of twenty-nine, Jackson was both an internationally acclaimed author and the central figure in the burgeoning resistance movement among American prisoners. Nine days after his death, all the convicts in New York's Attica State Prison memorialized him in a ceremony described by revolutionary inmate Sam Melville in his posthumous Letters from Attica:

At the midday meal (the large meal in prison), not a man ate or spoke—black, white, brown, red. Many wore black armbands. . . . No one can remember anything like it here before. . . . G.J. was beloved by inmates throughout the country.

Ten days after this letter came the Attica uprising, in which Sam Melville was one of the forty-three prisoners and guards killed in the assault by state troopers.

from *Soledad Brother*

April, 1970

DEAR FAY,*

On the occasion of your and Senator Dymally's tour and investigation into the affairs here at Soledad, I detected in the questions posed by your team a desire to isolate some rationale that would explain why racism exists at the prison with "particular prominence." Of course the subject was really too large to be dealt with in one tour and in the short time they allowed you, but it was a brave scene. My small but mighty mouthpiece, and the black establishment senator and his team, invading the state's maximum security row in the worst of its concentration camps. I think you are the first woman to be allowed to inspect these facilities. Thanks from all. The question was too large, however. It's tied into the question of why all these California prisons vary in character and flavor in general. It's tied into the larger question of why racism exists in this whole society with "particular prominence," tied into history. Out of it comes another question. Why do California joints produce more Bunchy Carters and Eldridge Cleavers than those over the rest of the country?

I understand your attempt to isolate the set of localized circumstances that give to this particular prison's problems of race is based on a desire to aid us right now, in the present crisis. There are some changes that could be made right now that would alleviate some of the pressures inside this and other prisons. But to get at the causes, you know, one would be forced to deal with questions at the very center of Amerikan political and economic life, at the core of the

---

* Mrs. Fay Stender, the author's lawyer.

Amerikan historical experience. This prison didn't come to exist where it does just by happenstance. Those who inhabit it and feed off its existence are historical products. The great majority of Soledad pigs are southern migrants who do not want to work in the fields and farms of the area, who couldn't sell cars or insurance, and who couldn't tolerate the discipline of the army. And of course prisons attract sadists. After one concedes that racism is stamped unalterably into the present nature of Amerikan sociopolitical and economic life in general (the definition of fascism is: a police state wherein the political ascendancy is tied into and protects the interests of the upper class—characterized by militarism, *racism*, and imperialism), and concedes further that criminals and crime arise from material, economic, sociopolitical causes, we can then burn *all* of the criminology and penology libraries and direct our attention where it will do some good.

The logical place to begin any investigation into the problems of California prisons is with our "pigs are beautiful" Governor Reagan, radical reformer turned reactionary. For a real understanding of the failure of prison policies, it is senseless to continue to study the criminal. All of those who can afford to be honest know that the real victim, that poor, uneducated, disorganized man who finds himself a convicted criminal, is simply the end result of a long chain of corruption and mismanagement that starts with people like Reagan and his political appointees in Sacramento. After one investigates Reagan's character (what makes a turncoat) the next logical step in the inquiry would be a look into the biggest political prize of the state—the directorship of the Department of Corrections.

All other lines of inquiry would be like walking backward. You'll never see where you're going. You must begin with directors, assistant directors, adult authority boards, roving boards, supervisors, wardens, captains, and guards. You have to examine these people from director down to guard before you can logically examine their product. Add to this some concrete and steel, barbed wire, rifles, pistols, clubs, the tear gas that killed Brother Billingslea in San Quentin in February 1970, while he was locked in his cell, and the pick handles of Folsom, San Quentin, and Soledad.

To determine how men will behave once they enter the prison it is of first importance to know that prison. Men are brutalized by their environment—not the reverse.

I gave you a good example of this when I saw you last. Where

I am presently being held, they never allow us to leave our cell without first handcuffing us and belting or chaining the cuffs to our waists. This is preceded always by a very thorough skin search. A force of a dozen or more pigs can be expected to invade the row at any time searching and destroying personal effects. The attitude of the staff toward the convicts is both defensive and hostile. Until the convict gives in completely it will continue to be so. By giving in, I mean prostrating oneself at their feet. Only then does their attitude alter itself to one of paternalistic condescension. Most convicts don't dig this kind of relationship (though there are some who do love it) with a group of individuals demonstrably inferior to the rest of the society in regard to education, culture, and sensitivity. Our cells are so far from the regular dining area that our food is always cold before we get it. Some days there is only one meal that can be called cooked. We *never* get anything but cold-cut sandwiches for lunch. There is no variety to the menu. The same things week after week. One is confined to his cell 23½ hours a day. Overt racism exists unchecked. It is not a case of the pigs trying to stop the many racist attacks; they actively encourage them.

They are fighting upstairs right now. It's 11:10 A.M., June 11. No black is supposed to be on the tier upstairs with anyone but other blacks but—mistakes take place—and one or two blacks end up on the tier with 9 or 10 white convicts frustrated by the living conditions or openly working with the pigs. The whole ceiling is trembling. In hand-to-hand combat we always win; we lose sometimes if the pigs give them knives or zip guns. Lunch will be delayed today, the tear gas or whatever it is drifts down to sting my nose and eyes. Someone is hurt bad. I hear the meat wagon from the hospital being brought up. Pigs probably gave them some weapons. But I must be fair. Sometimes (not more often than necessary) they'll set up one of the Mexican or white convicts. He'll be one who has not been sufficiently racist in his attitudes. After the brothers (enraged by previous attacks) kick on this white convict whom the officials have set up, he'll fall right into line with the rest.

I was saying that the great majority of the people who live in this area of the state and seek their employment from this institution have overt racism as a *traditional* aspect of their characters. The only stops that regulate how far they will carry this thing come from the fear of losing employment here as a result of the outside pressures to control the violence. That is O Wing, Max (Maximum Security) Row Soledad—in part anyway.

Take an individual who has been in the general prison population for a time. Picture him as an average convict with the average twelve-year-old mentality, the nation's norm. He wants out, he wants a woman and a beer. Let's say this average convict is white and has just been caught attempting to escape. They may put him on Max Row. This is the worst thing that will ever happen to him. In the general population facility there are no chains and cuffs. TVs, radios, record players, civilian sweaters, keys to his own cell for daytime use, serve to keep his mind off his real problems. There is also a recreation yard with all sorts of balls and instruments to strike or thrust at. There is a gym. There are movies and a library well stocked with light fiction. And of course there is work, where for 2 or 3 cents an hour convicts here at Soledad make paper products, furniture, and clothing. Some people actually like this work since it does provide some money for the small things and helps them to get through their day—*without thinking* about their real problems.

Take an innocent con out of this general population setting (because a pig "thought" he may have seen him attempting a lock). Bring him to any part of O Wing (the worst part of the adjustment center of which Max Row is a part). He will be cuffed, chained, belted, pressured by the police who think that every convict should be an informer. He will be pressured by the white cons to join their racist brand of politics (they *all* go under the nickname "Hitler's Helpers"). If he is predisposed to help black he will be pushed away—by black. Three weeks is enough. The strongest hold out no more than a couple of weeks. There has been *one* white man only to go through this O Wing experience without losing his balance, without allowing himself to succumb to the madness of ribald, protrusive racism.

It destroys the logical processes of the mind, a man's thoughts become completely disorganized. The noise, madness streaming from every throat, frustrated sounds from the bars, metallic sounds from the walls, the steel trays, the iron beds bolted to the wall, the hollow sounds from a cast-iron sink or toilet.

The smells, the human waste thrown at us, unwashed bodies, the rotten food. When a white con leaves here he's ruined for life. No black leaves Max Row walking. Either he leaves on the meat wagon or he leaves crawling licking at the pig's feet.

Ironic, because one cannot get a parole to the outside prison directly from O Wing, Max Row. It's positively not done. The parole board won't even consider the Max Row case. So a man licks at the feet of the pig not for a release to the outside world but for the privilege of going upstairs to O Wing adjustment center. There the licking process must continue if a parole is the object. You can count on one hand the number of people who have been paroled to the streets from O Wing proper in all the years that the prison has existed. No one goes from O Wing, Max Row straight to the general prison population. To go from here to the outside world is unthinkable. A man *must* go from Max Row to the regular adjustment center facility upstairs. Then from there to the general prison population. Only then can he entertain throughts of eventual release to the outside world.

One can understand the depression felt by an inmate on Max Row. He's fallen as far as he can into the social trap, relief is so distant that it is very easy for him to lose his holds. In two weeks that little average man who may have ended up on Max Row for *suspicion* of *attempted* escape is so brutalized, so completely without holds, that he will never heal again. It's worse than Vietnam.

He's dodging lead. He may be forced to fight a duel to the death with knives. If he doesn't sound and act more zealous than everyone else he will be challenged for not being loyal to his race and its politics, fascism. Some of these cons support the pigs' racism without shame, the others support it inadvertently by their own racism. The former are white, the latter black. But in here as on the street black racism is a forced *reaction*. A survival adaptation.

The picture that I have painted of Soledad's general population facility may have made it sound not too bad at all. That mistaken impression would result from the absence in my description of one more very important feature of the main line—terrorism. A frightening, petrifying diffusion of violence and intimidation is emitted from the offices of the warden and captain. How else could a small group of armed men be expected to hold and rule another much larger group except through *fear?*

We have a gym (inducement to throw away our energies with a ball instead of revolution). But if you walk into this gym with a

cigarette burning, you're probably in trouble. There is a pig waiting
to trap you. There's a sign "No Smoking." If you miss the sign,
trouble. If you drop the cigarette to comply, trouble. The floor is
regarded as something of a fire hazard (I'm not certain what the
pretext is). There are no receptacles. The pig will pounce. You'll be
told in no uncertain terms to scrape the cigarette from the floor
with your hands. It builds from there. You have a gym but only
certain things may be done and in specified ways. Since the rules
change with the pigs' mood, it is really safer for a man to stay in
his cell.

You have work with emoluments that range from nothing to
three cents an hour! But once you accept the pay job in the prison's
industrial sector you cannot get out without going through the bad
conduct process. When workers are needed, it isn't a case of accepting a job in this area. You take the job or you're automatically
refusing to work, even if you clearly stated that you would cooperate in other employment. The same atmosphere prevails on the
recreation yard where any type of minor mistake could result not
in merely a bad conduct report and placement in adjustment center,
but death. A fistfight, a temporary, trivial loss of temper will bring
a fusillade of bullets down on the darker of the two men fighting.

You can't begin to measure the bad feeling caused by the existence of one TV set shared by 140 men. Think! One TV, 140 men.
If there is more than one channel, what's going to occur? In Soledad's TV rooms there has been murder, mayhem, and destruction
of many TV sets.

The blacks occupy one side of the room and the whites and
Mexicans the other. (Isn't it significant in some way that our numbers in prison are sufficient to justify the claiming of half of all
these facilities?)

We have a side, they have a side. What does your imagination
envisage out of a hypothetical situation where Nina Simone sings,
Angela Davis speaks, and Jim Brown "splits" on one channel, while
Merle Haggard yodels and begs for an ass kicking on another. The
fight will follow immediately after some brother, who is less democratic than he is starved for beauty (we did vote but they're 60 to
our 40), turns the station to see Angela Davis. What lines do you
think the fighting will be along? Won't it be Angela and me against
Merle Haggard?

But this situation is tolerable at least up to a point. It was worse.

When I entered the joint on this offense, they had half and we had half, but our half was in the back.

In a case like the one just mentioned, the white convicts will start passing the word among themselves that all whites should be in the TV room to vote in the "Cadillac cowboy." The two groups polarize out of a situation created by whom? It's just like the outside. Nothing at all complicated about it. When people walk on each other, when disharmony is the norm, when organisms start falling apart it is the fault of these whose responsibility it is to govern. They're doing something wrong. They shouldn't have been trusted with the responsibility. And long-range political activity isn't going to help that man who will die tomorrow or tonight. The apologists recognize that these places are controlled by absolute terror, but they justify the pig's excesses with the argument that we exist outside the practice of any civilized codes of conduct. Since we are convicts rather than men, a bullet through the heart, summary execution for fistfighting or stepping across a line is not extreme or unsound at all. An official is allowed full range in violent means because a convict can be handled no other way.

Fay, have you ever considered what type of man is capable of handling absolute power. I mean how many would not abuse it? Is there any way of isolating or classifying generally who can be trusted with a gun and *absolute* discretion as to who he will kill? I've already mentioned that most of them are KKK types. The rest, all the rest, in general, are so stupid that they shouldn't be allowed to run their own bath. A *responsible* state government would have found a means of weeding out most of the savage types that are drawn to gunslinger jobs long ago. How did all these pigs get through?! Men who can barely read, write, or reason. How did they get through!!? You may as well give a baboon a gun and set him loose on us!! It's the same in here as on the streets out there. *Who* has loosed this thing on an already suffering people? The Reagans, Nixons, the men who have, who own. Investigate them!! There are no qualifications asked, no experience necessary. Any fool who falls in here and can sign his name might shoot me tomorrow from a position 30 feet above my head with an automatic military rifle!! He could be dead drunk. It could really be an accident (a million to one it won't be, however), but he'll be protected still. He won't even miss a day's wages.

The textbooks on criminology like to advance the idea that prisoners are mentally defective. There is only the merest suggestion that the system itself is at fault. Penologists regard prisons as asylums. Most policy is formulated in a bureau that operates under the heading Department of Corrections. But what can we say about these asylums since *none* of the inmates are ever cured. Since in every instance they are sent out of the prison more damaged physically and mentally than when they entered. Because that is the reality. Do you continue to investigate the inmate? Where does administrative responsibility begin? Perhaps the administration of the prison cannot be held accountable for every individual act of their charges, but when things fly apart along racial lines, when the breakdown can be traced so clearly to circumstances even beyond the control of the guards and administration, investigation of anything outside the tenets of the fascist system itself is futile.

Nothing has improved, nothing has changed in the weeks since your team was here. We're on the same course, the blacks are fast losing the last of their restraints. Growing numbers of blacks are openly passed over when paroles are considered. They have become aware that their only hope lies in resistance. They have learned that resistance is actually possible. The holds are beginning to slip away. Very few men imprisoned for economic crimes or even crimes of passion against the oppressor feel that they are really guilty. Most of today's black convicts have come to understand that they are the most abused victims of an unrighteous order. Up until now, the prospect of parole has kept us from confronting our captors with any real determination. But now with the living conditions of these places deteriorating, and with the sure knowledge that we are slated for destruction, we have been transformed into an implacable army of liberation. The shift to the revolutionary antiestablishment position that Huey Newton, Eldridge Cleaver, and Bobby Seale projected as a solution to the problems of Amerika's black colonies has taken firm hold of these brothers' minds. They are now showing great interest in the thoughts of Mao Tse-tung, Nkrumah, Lenin, Marx, and the achievements of men like Che Guevara, Giap, and Uncle Ho.

Some people are going to get killed out of this situation that is growing. That is not a warning (or wishful thinking). I see it as an "unavoidable consequence" of placing and leaving control of our lives in the hands of men like Reagan.

These prisons have always borne a certain resemblance to Dachau and Buchenwald, places for the bad niggers, Mexicans, and poor whites. But the last ten years have brought an increase in the percentage of blacks for crimes that can *clearly* be traced to political-economic causes. There are still some blacks here who consider themselves criminals—but not many. Believe me, my friend, with the time and incentive that these brothers have to read, study, and think, you will find no class or category more aware, more embittered, desperate, or dedicated to the ultimate remedy— revolution. The most dedicated, the best of our kind—you'll find them in the Folsoms, San Quentins, and Soledads. They live like there was no tomorrow. And for most of them there isn't. Some- where along the line they sensed this. Life on the installment plan, three years of prison, three months on parole; then back to start all over again, sometimes in the same cell. Parole officers have sent brothers back to the joint for selling newspapers (the Black Panther paper). Their official reason is "Failure to Maintain Gainful Em- ployment," etc.

We're something like 40 to 42 percent of the prison population. Perhaps more, since I'm relying on material published by the media. The leadership of the black prison population now definitely iden- tifies with Huey, Bobby, Angela, Eldridge, and antifascism. The savage repression of blacks which can be estimated by reading the obituary columns of the nation's dailies, Fred Hampton, etc., has not failed to register on the black inmates. The holds are fast being broken. Men who read Lenin, Fanon, and Che don't riot, "they mass," "they rage," they dig graves.

When John Clutchette was first accused of this murder he was proud, conscious, aware of his own worth but uncommitted to any specific remedial action. Review the process that they are sending this beautiful brother through now. It comes at the end of a long train of similar incidents in his prison life. Add to this all of the things he has witnessed happening to others of our group here. Comrade Fleeta spent eleven months here in O Wing for possessing photography taken from a newsweekly. It is such things that explain why California prisons produce more than their share of Bunchy Carters and Eldridge Cleavers.

Fay, there are only two types of blacks ever released from these places, the Carters and the broken men.

The broken men are so damaged that they will never again be suitable members of any sort of social unit. Everything that was

Prison will affect you [handwritten annotation]

still good when they entered the joint, anything inside of them that may have escaped the ruinous effects of black colonial existence, anything that may have been redeemable when they first entered the joint—is gone when they leave.

This camp brings out the very best in brothers or destroys them entirely. But none are unaffected. None who leave here are normal. If I leave here alive, I'll leave nothing behind. They'll never count me among the broken men, but I can't say that I am normal either. I've been hungry too long. I've gotten angry too often. I've been lied to and insulted too many times. They've pushed me over the line from which there can be no retreat. I *know* that they will not be satisfied until they've pushed me out of this existence altogether. I've been the victim of so many racist attacks that I could never relax again. My reflexes will never be normal again. I'm like a dog that has gone through the K-9 process.

This is not the first attempt the institution (camp) has made to murder me. It is the most determined attempt, but not the first.

I look into myself at the close of every one of these pretrial days for any changes that may have taken place. I can still smile now, after ten years of blocking knife thrusts and pick handles, of faceless sadistic pigs, of anticipating and reacting for ten years, seven of them in Solitary. I can still smile sometimes, but by the time this thing is over I may not be a nice person. And I just lit my seventy-seventh cigarette of this 21-hour day. I'm going to lay down for two or three hours, perhaps I'll sleep . . .

Seize the Time.

ICEBERG SLIM (ROBERT BECK)
1918–1992

Virtually unknown to mainstream reviewers and readers, the writings of Iceberg Slim (Robert Beck) have had astonishing popularity and considerable cultural influence. His subterranean effects on rap music were hinted at when rap singer Ice-T acknowledged that he acquired his name from his youthful recitations of long passages from Iceberg Slim. Dictionaries of slang and works on black English frequently cite

Iceberg Slim as a source. Holloway House, which has published all of his books as well as an entire subgenre of urban black literature, boasts that Iceberg Slim's sales of six million copies rank him as the most widely read African-American author. Yet when he died in 1992, no major newspaper printed an obituary.

Iceberg Slim burst into prominence in African-American culture with the 1967 publication of his first book, Pimp: The Story of My Life. *In the midst of the Depression, Robert Beck had dropped out of Tuskegee Institute to embark on his career in the "life," the distinct world of black pimps. His first clumsy attempt at pimping got him incarcerated at the age of seventeen. As he refined his techniques, he became an embodiment of one of the few kinds of success available for black men within the ghetto, a flamboyant role model ostentatiously parading symbols of wealth and power for other young men. Such success, as Beck later realized in prison, was in reality an illusory and feeble imitation of the authentic wealth and power of the men who ruled society. After conning his way out of prison, being recaptured, and spending ten months in solitary, he decided to find a new path to success: writing. Hence* Pimp.

Iceberg Slim's second book and first novel, Trick Baby: The Story of a White Negro *(1967), was filmed in 1973, the same year as the blaxploitation cult classic* The Mack, *which owed large unacknowledged debts to* Pimp. *His writing became much more overtly political with* Mama Black Widow, *a 1969 novel about the destruction of a black southern family in a northern city, and his 1971 collection of essays,* The Naked Soul of Iceberg Slim. Long White Con *(1977) was a sequel to* Trick Baby, *and* Airtight Willie & Me *(1979) tells the stories of six "players" in the "life." His most impressive fiction is* Death Wish *(1977), a novel in which a battle between organized crime and a multiracial revolutionary organization ultimately leads to a feminist consciousness that momentarily transcends the violence.*

from *The Naked Soul of Iceberg Slim*

I WANT TO SAY at the outset that I have become ill, insane as an inmate of a torture chamber behind America's fake facade of justice and democracy. But I am not as ill as I was, and I am getting better all the time. And also, I want to make clear that my reason for starting these notes at a point of personal anguish and suffering is that these experiences marked the end of a corrupt pimp life and were the prelude to a still mauled, but constructive new life. I am not "playing the con" for sympathy.

In the cold-blooded academy of ghetto streets I was taught early that suffering is inevitable and necessary for an aspiring pimp, pickpocket or con man and even just a nigger compelled to become a four-way whore for the Establishment. I learned also that sympathy is a counterfeit emotion for suckers which is usually offered with a crooked con grin of amused contempt and rejected with a spittled snarl.

Within the moldering walls of Chicago's House of Correction, in one of its ancient cellhouses, is a row of steel punishment cubicles where rule-breaking inmates spend at most several days. In 1960 I was locked in one of the steel boxes for ten months. I owed the joint an unserved part of a sentence from which I had vanished thirteen years before like a wisp of black smoke and without the usual damage to joint fixtures or guards' skulls. And apparently the sweet joker who ordered me stuffed into the steel box to commit suicide or go mad (when I was returned to the joint on escape charges) felt he owed vengeance on me to his long-ago fellow clique of torturers and grafters who must have suffered a shit storm of consternation and rage when nigger me bypassed their booming instant release service and hadn't bought out, but thought out.

But that second mob of debonair demons sure butchered off a hunk of my mental ass. For even now, a new life and a decade later, I will lay odds that until the grave the images and sounds of that violent, gibbering year will stomp and shudder my mind.

One instance, among many: I am in a pleasant mood when I hear through an open window the profane chanting of teenagers playing a merry game of ghetto dozens (*dozens*—the denigration of another's parents or ancestors) that explode in a montage of pain, bright as flame, that shocks my brain. Again for the thousandth time I see and hear the likable little black con in the steel box next to mine, my only buddy, suddenly chanting freaky lyrics of a crazy frightening song about how God is a double-crossing cocksucker, and how he is going to sodomize and murder his crippled bitch mama.

I cry out like a scalded child, leap off my straw mattress and stand on trembly legs peering into Shorty's cubicle through a ragged break in the weld of the sheet steel wall. He's buck naked and his soft black baby face is twisted hard and hideously old as he stands slobbery with his hands flying like frenzied bats up and down his long stiff penis.

I have the vague hope that he's "gaming," playing the con, for the heartless white folks for some personal benefit or advantage. But there's a chilling realism, a perfection about Shorty's awful performance, so I rib him gently.

"Buddy, put your pants on and stop that chump jeffing. (*Jeffing*—playing or employing a low grade of con based on one's blackness and the projection of the contemptible "Sambo" or "Rastus" image.) Instead of a hospital broad tucking you between white sheets, the ass kickers will show any minute now. Dummy up for me, pal. Huh? I like you and I got a weak belly."

Shorty gives me zero response and his walling eyes are like coals of white fire. I feel a jolt of panic in my chest and a terrifying fluttery quaking inside my skull.

And because I know that madness can be catching I get stupid and scream, "You little jive ass, you're suppose to be a player. Remember? What you gonna do, let these dirty white folks crack you up?"

But he's so pitiful I go soft and plead, "Shorty, get your head together. Please pal, listen to me!"

I beg him until I stink of emotion sweat and my voice fades to a squealy whisper. But Shorty doesn't listen for the pathetic reason that he can't hear me or anything else except his private hellish drum beat.

The guards come soon to take Shorty away forever and he yelps and whimpers like a puppy under their fists and feet. I quiver and my teeth slash into my bottom lip with every thud. And as Shorty is dragged away I sink to the concrete floor and roll myself into a fetal ball against a frightening chaos of pulsing green-streaked puffy bladders that whirl madly in terrible near collision on a shuddery screen inside my head. I feel great anguish and terror as if the berserk missiles are really sections of myself facing bloody destruction.

The tragedy of Shorty and its recurring long range misery for me is but one "House" horror among many that haunt my new life.

A day or so before my expected legal release date from the "House," I was taken from my steel box to an interview with a charmer who told me with a choreographed Billy Graham type smile that a new computation of my time served and owed left me in debt to the joint for two additional months. I had spent the two months in County Jail where I had been taken after Captain Churchill, a "House" bloodhound, backed by city police, crashed my pad and cracked me on an ancient fugitive warrant for the escape from the "House."

I had expected the attempt to steal from me the two months served in County Jail. I stood battered but tall before the desk of the head Nazi and bombed the freakish grin off his fat face with the recital of an affidavit I had composed and memorized. Having no legal training, I could only sense its validity intuitively.

My position was that Captain Churchill, a "House" official, had arrested me. I was from the instant of that arrest legally in the custody of the "House," and even in the event that Captain Churchill had somehow managed to jail me on as unlikely a place as the moon for two months, I technically would have been serving "House" time. I closed my argument with a flexing of fake muscle based on the misfortune of a "House" guard who had furnished grist for recent newspaper headlines. He was then under indictment for selling and delivering a hacksaw blade to a group of half corpses in the steel caskets down the way from mine.

So for a dramatic flexing of that personal muscle I hunched my wasted frame forward and arrogantly glued my palms to the mirror-like top of the Nazi's desk. I flinched back from a remarkable likeness of the wolfman staring up at me and switched my eyes to the fat red face before me. I told it in that low, disarming tone of voice used by sneaky cops just before they stomp or kick you into insensibility that the notorious guard under indictment had delivered, to a friend of mine on the outside, several pieces of explosive and embarrassing (for the Nazi and his City Hall bosses) mail.

His face turned from red to white to blue, and I remembered the rumors about his faulty pump. I stood there grinning and watched him choking and gasping for air. I went on to assure him that the letter contained the names of racketeering guards and an exposé of corruption within the joint that perhaps even he was not aware of. And I assured him that my friend would make public the contents of the letters if I did not get my legal release date.

I secretly hoped that convict me and my threats might have triggered a fatal attack. My emotions made of that pulse-leaping moment a monument of vengeance, an event that could not have been excelled except by the exquisite pleasure of blowing out his diseased brains. And for the first time since I'd been caged in the steel box I felt like a human being—like a man.

He seemed to be strangling as I smiled at him and slipped out the door to the escort guard waiting in the corridor for me. I paced the steel box in an agony of suspense: Was the torturer dead? Then panic and despair: I couldn't survive in the box for those extra two months! Wouldn't the muscle of my bluff and my chance for a legal release date die with him?

Later that afternoon the cellhouse vibrated with the sudden thunder of profane raillery and the feet of shop cons going to their cells on the tiers above me. I tuned my ears up high, but no gleeful announcement of the head keeper's death filtered down through the bedlam of voices and epidemic farting.

He had survived and the chances were that I would escape the steel box within forty eight hours. But suddenly I was terrified at the prospect of freedom. Almost immediately I realized why. I was caught in the nightmare bind that an older pimp faces after the age of thirty-five. He is then prone to many setbacks and disasters. Any one of them can put him on his uppers and without the basic gaudy bait, like an out-of-sight car, psychedelic wardrobe, the diamonds necessary to hook and enslave a fresh stable of humping young whores.

I still owned a portion of the mind of a young whore. But my bottom or main whore of many years had delivered my car, jewelry, clothes and other vital pimp flash to an obscure but younger, fresher monster than I. The young mud kicker had written me frequently and she had regularly sent me small money orders. She had left a Montana bordello to run afoul of a spermy gambler who ruined her commercial curves and blew away my heady dreams of mountainous greenbacks by blasting a squealer into her belly.

And now her sobby letters indicated that she was petulantly waiting for me, her favorite field marshall of cunt huckstering, to liberate her from her slum pad and her unwanted motherhood.

But she didn't know I'd had the jolting insight that I had been a sucker, conned by my own velvet bullshit that the whores had bought for a generation, about the magnificence of the pimp game. She didn't know I was determined not to join that contemptible group of aging pimps I had seen through the years and pitied as they went their pathetic way with a wild dream of new glory and a big fast stable of young freak mud kickers.

Young whores give an old pimp down on his luck merciless treatment. They flirt with him, play on him, give the corrupt old dreamer hope and then viciously poke fun at him as they coldly reject him. No, I was not going back to become one of them. And I was just as determined not to become a suicidal stickup artist or other "heavy" hustler.

But how was I going to make it out there in the free world with no training except in the art of pimping? I vowed there in the box to kill myself before I became like "Dandy" Sammy. He had been a boss pimp whom I had idolized as a boy when I was getting street poisoned.

One dazzling summer afternoon in Cleveland at the peak of my pimphood I was confronted on the sidewalk outside my hotel by an old, stooped black man. He clutched a shoeshine box and he stank of the vomit encrusting his ragged shirt front. His pitch was a poem of pathos.

I declined a shine, but the seamed ruin of his face nudged a ghost inside my skull. Almost mechanically I gave him a twenty dollar bill and went past him. His face haunted me across a dozen states and cities.

Six months later I was shooting "H" in a fellow pimp's pad. An old whore got dreamy eyed and cracked about how much bread she had made for Dandy Sammy and what a helluva pimp he had been. And then suddenly I knew who the filthy old bum with the shoeshine box had been.

Now I waited in a steel box with compounded misery, Mama was dying of an incurable disease out in California, and the guilt I felt for my neglect of her through the years was crushing. Mama's friends had sent me more than enough money for the trip to California. I had promised Mama I would come to her upon my release.

I got my legal release date and stood weakly outside the joint blinking in the April sun. I was a confused, wasted shadow of myself—unsure of in what direction lay the Southside. I chose a direction and found freedom from the box so intoxicating that I walked miles before my legs got rubbery. I staggered into a greasy spoon on the Southside and gulped down a bowl of gumbo. Peeping at my gruesome reflection in the chrome napkin holder, I wondered how my cute young whore would react to a face as wrecked as mine.

I went to a barber shop on Forty-third Street and got a shave and mud massage with scalding towels galore. I relaxed beneath the searing steam and tried to piece together exit con for the girl. I had expected the barber to perform a minor miracle, but his mirror told me I looked like my own grandpaw.

I walked toward the El station in my still blurry state of mind and stupidly decided I wouldn't go to the girl's kitchenette pad and display my ruin. Perhaps I was afraid that my sick pimp brain couldn't cope with the certain temptation face to face to peddle her plush pussy. I would catch the first plane or train leaving Chicago and send her a nice creamy letter from Los Angeles.

Then it hit me! The girl's trip to employment in Montana was still within the White Slave statute of limitations. I stopped and leaned weakly against a lamp post. I realized that I would be asking for a bit in the federal joint if I split from the girl in a way to leave her hostile.

I was one of the dozen or so black pimps the F.B.I. kept constant tabs on to nail on a white slave beef. Their deadly method was to swoop down on an angry girl, usually when she was facing a jail term for prostitution, and offer her freedom if she would sign a criminal complaint against the pimp who'd left her raw and vengeful.

I'd been shipped off once to a federal pen because I'd been careless and cut a girl loose in the rough. The greatest fear a seasoned pimp has is that some salty whore he has split from will sign a paper offered by an eager F.B.I. agent stipulating she was sent across state lines to hustle.

It was early afternoon when I went through the foyer of the

tenement building and spotted her at the end of the first floor hall-
way. She was holding the infant in her arms and laughing gaily
with an ebony skeleton who was jiggling inside an orange print
tent and popping her fingers to the music and lyrics of the
"Madison"—a then current dance craze.

I walked to within three feet of them before my girl saw me.
For a moment her tan face was a cool, indifferent blank. And then,
in a series of lightning changes, it twisted with recognition from
wincing shock at my ghastly ruin, to puckered-mouth pity to the
fraud of neon-eyed, squealy-mouthed ecstasy. I felt violence bubbling inside my skull, but I managed a grotesque grin and took the
tiny infant in my arms. I heard the skeleton giggle derisively and
dance away as I lowered my mouth to the curvy lips of my one
and only (and last) whore.

I felt that old hot writhing of her lips and my tongue was instantly flogged by the wet whip lashing forth with its spray of
honey. I began to wonder about how tough the exit from her life
could possibly be.

I followed her into the furnished dungeon and sat in a rickety
rocker beside a half-open, soot-streaked window. I pretended to be
fascinated by the scabrous view of the garbage strewn alley as I
frantically tried to frame exit dialogue that wouldn't get me crossed
into a long bit in a federal joint.

All of the countless whores I have known and those I have controlled revealed a hunger for notoriety and for punishment, psychic
or physical or both. The phony glamour and cruelty of the pimp
fill these needs and are the magnets that attract and hold the whore
to the pimp.

Since I was aware of these things, my strategy to cop a heel
smoothly from the young whore was obvious. I had to convince
her of my inability to handle her affairs and to blaze again in pimp
glory. I was going to ignore her freakish yen for the punishment
ritual of "kiss, kick" that is the pimp's trade.

I had to come on with low voltage, square world dialogue and
saccharine sweetness. I couldn't quit her because of the "white
slave" threat, and I had to be certain that she quit me not in anger,
but in pity.

I held the gambler's squealer and tuned out the girl's rundown
on the yoyo affairs of pimps and whores we knew until twilight.

After we had eaten a soul food supper and the baby was asleep, she lay in my arms and beat me to the nitty gritty by peevishly saying, "You haven't been rapping much, and the little you've rapped sounded 'off the wall' like a chump trick. You salty 'cause I had that sucker's baby?"

I playfully spanked her behind and said, "Sweet puppy, accidents happen to a genius, so how can I be salty with you about the kid? She's beautiful. It's just going to take a little time to come to myself after what the white folks did to me in that steel box. And I'm confused like a sucker fresh from the sticks."

She said icily, "I can dig it. But what the hell about the game and are you going to keep me in this lousy pad forever? I'm the only bitch that stayed in your corner when you went to the joint. Don't forget that."

I kissed the brown skin bomb from belly button to ear lobe and said sweetly, "Baby Angel, I'm hip you're my star, but my head is really bad. I'm ashamed to tell you how bad. I don't see how my foggy head can put together a stable of girls and control it. And besides it wouldn't be right for a beautiful young girl like you to hump her heart out to get the playing front for a washed out old nigger pimp like me. And Angel, what about the poor little kid? She needs her mama all the time and you need a man with ideas or with a job. My brain is dead and I'm too sick to work. Maybe I should split the scene so some fast young stud can come in and take care of your business. It's up to you, Baby Angel, you call the shots. Like I told you, I'm dead upstairs."

She stiffened in my arms and was silent for a long moment.

Finally she raised herself on an elbow and stared into my eyes and said quietly, "For real, I can call the shots?"

I nodded and she sprang to her feet. She slipped into a kimono, went to her purse on the dresser and dashed out the door. I heard a coin clinking into the phone in the hall.

I got up and stuck my ear against the door. I heard her placing a collect long distance call to a whorehouse in northern Michigan. The sudden racket of missile warfare between a shouting couple across the hall blotted out the girl's voice.

I was sitting on the side of the lumpy bed faking my cool when she joyously pranced in and screeched out the numbing news. It was bad, way out bad for me and Mama on her death bed out in California. The establishment in Michigan would have an opening for her three-way talent at the end of the week. She went into a detailed rundown on how to feed, bathe, burp and diaper the gambler's squealer while she was away nobly flatbacking our escape from the kitchenette dungeon.

There was at the time a very deep reason or fear that overrode the obvious ones why I was not aching to help this poor frustrated mother to employment in the Michigan flesh factory. Several years before an over-confident pimp acquaintance of mine had sent his one and only whore to the Michigan spot under consideration directly that she healed from the dropping of twin boys.

I visited mama pimp at his pad and pointed out that the town was crawling with shit-talking, whore-starved young studs, and that a dizzy young hot money tree like his was certain to be chopped down by a new master under the strain of whorehouse boredom and loneliness. He sneered and went into the usual novice pimp monologue about how "tight" he had his woman and the power of his "game."

He was surprised that I wasn't aware of the trump he held in the twins to bind his girl to him forever. He was an arrogant ass, so I made no effort to "pull his coat" to the street-tested truth that while whores simpered their love and loyalty, they were really pressure-shocked robots who prayed for the pimp's destruction and often dumped babies in alleys like garbage.

Within a month the Michigan mud kicker found her new master and the naive young pimp was stuck with a brace of howling crumb crushers. But fortunately for the twins, the pimp's mother found them adorable and took them over.

And now in the funky autumn of my life I was apparently being set up for mamahood. What with the white slave thing still pulsing, it was a treacherous and explosive situation with a five-day fuse. I considered extreme strategy as I lay beside her in midnight misery.

I decided to play the role of rapidly worsening senility. "What is usually most disgustingly flawful about the senile?" I asked myself. "No control of the plumbing, of course," I answered.

I scooted back from the girl's sleeping form and shortly managed a stout stream which momentarily made of her a peninsula. But she slept on, wearing on her lovely face the last beatific (or any other) smile I was to witness. Soon, above the din of erotic rats squeaking their rodent rapture within the dungeon walls, I joined my whore madonna in pungent slumber.

Next morning she was curly-lipped furious and my slack-jaw idiocy augmented by even looser bowels had by nightfall inspired her to masterworks of creative profanity. She roughly diapered me on the greasy couch (my new bed) with a mildewed bath towel and she literally reeled away in disgust when I gurgled like a big black happy baby.

Much later I heard her tiptoe to the hall phone and repeatedly call numbers and ask for "Cat Daddy," an ancient pimp with enormous light gray eyes and a penchant for young whores. I was praying that they made a contract together because a whore almost never sends her exiting pimp to the penitentiary when her new pimp is on the scene to witness her treachery.

The next day when the girl was out with the baby I went to the corner drugstore and talked to Mama in California. We really cried more than talked, but I felt happy that she was still alive as I walked back to the dungeon. I was a hundred yards from the building when I saw the girl with the squealer in arms alight from Cat Daddy's orchid-hued spaceship. I stopped and sat down on a stoop. She stood outside the car and for a minute and a half she dipped and nodded her head toward the gesticulating silhouette inside. I suddenly felt a weird combination of joy and loss for I realized that she was giving Cat Daddy the classic "yes" response a young whore plays out for her new pimp.

I sat on the stoop for over an hour after she had gone in. When I went in she pulled me down beside her on the bed and went into her thing. She told me in a pleasant voice that she felt very sorry that my illness had forced her to get herself and the baby a sponsor. She was moving soon, like within twenty-four hours, into a groovy pad furnished by the sponsor. But she was awfully worried about me, and perhaps I would be smart to run a game for care on one of the County institutions until our luck changed.

I strangled my wild joy (and a pang of loss) behind a blank mask and mumbled, "Baby daughter, I'm going to my Mama. She knows better than anybody how to nurse me back to the pink. And Angel Dumpling, as soon as I get myself and my game together I'll write you at that bar on Forty-seventh Street and send for you and my baby girl."

Later I lay sleepless in the stifling room watching her sleeping. Her magnificent body was nude except for wisps of whorehouse costume that seemed ready to burst against the buxom stress of her honey toned curves and fat jet bush gleaming through the peach gauze.

I remembered the fast stacks of greenbacks, the icy, goose-pimpling, hot-sweet torture of that freak tongue, and the exquisite grab of that incredibly heavy-lipped cunt in the giddy beginning when her sick whore's skull was bewitched by my poisonous pimp charisma. My erection was sucker swift and rock hard, but as I started off the couch toward her, it collapsed. I suddenly realized that I had lost all power over her and therefore in her cold-blooded whore judgment I was just another customer, a chump john. I turned my face to the wall and worried until dawn about my moves and the wisdom of willfully blowing off a young freak whore with mileage galore left to hump away.

I was fully dressed, standing by the side of the bed looking down on her, when she awoke and cringed away. I smiled and flapped good-bye with my fingers like a child. Her lips mutely formed "good luck" and I went quickly away. In the cab on the way to the airport, I felt a stab of regret that I was leaving her forever back there. But then immediately the pain was gone in the great relief of my smooth exit from her and the terrible emptiness of the pimp game. And it was good to realize that no longer would I brutalize and exploit black women.

MSHAKA (WILLIE MONROE)

Dates unknown

When Celes Tisdale included this poem in Betcha Ain't: Poems from Attica, *his wonderful 1974 collection chosen from the workshop he had given at Attica State Correctional Facility, the only information he could give about Mshaka was: "Diminutive, incisive young man who was released from the prison or transferred after two sessions in the workshop."*

The poem refers to the 1971 Attica prison uprising, which ended with an assault by state troopers, ordered by Governor Nelson Rockefeller, that left thirty-two prisoners and eleven guards dead.

Formula for Attica Repeats

. . . and when
the smoke cleared
they came aluminum paid
lovers
from Rock/The/Terrible
refuser
of S.O.S. Collect Calls,
Executioner.

They came tearless
tremblers,
apologetic grin factories
that breathed Kool
smoke-rings
and state-prepared speeches.
They came
like so many unfeeling fingers
groping without touching
the 43 dead men
who listened . . .
threatening to rise
again . . .

PIRI THOMAS
1928–

*One of seven children born to Puerto Rican parents living in
Spanish Harlem, Piri Thomas grew up with even more identity problems than most children. He was punished in school
for speaking Spanish but remained a stranger to his parents'
island home. Frequently called a "negrito" because of his dark
skin, he sometimes considered himself African-American. The*

only world familiar to him was that of the streets, and he plunged into its culture of drugs and crime.

In 1950, Thomas was wounded and arrested in an attempted armed robbery. He spent the next six years in Sing Sing and Comstock prisons, where he began serious writing and completed a book-length autobiographical manuscript. As he said in a 1995 interview, "Creativity was my salvation in prison because it kept me from becoming a vegetable or a psychopath."

After his release, Thomas devoted much of his time to programs aimed at turning young people away from drugs and crime. His work with youth gangs was the subject of Piri & Johnny, *a 1964 award-winning documentary film produced by Time-Life, as well as* The World of Piri Thomas, *a National Educational Television film written and narrated by Thomas and directed by Gordon Parks.*

Just when he finally got an opportunity to secure a major publisher for his autobiography, someone accidentally threw it into an incinerator. It took him five more years to rewrite what turned out to be Down These Mean Streets, *published by Knopf in 1967 with immense popular and critical success. In 1995* The New York Times *listed it as one of "The 10 Best Books About New York" and in 1997 Vintage published a special thirty-year memorial edition.*

Thomas published two more autobiographical works: Savior, Savior, Hold My Hand *(1972) and* Seven Long Times *(1974), which focused directly on his prison experience and displayed a more developed political consciousness than the earlier volumes. In 1983, Thomas moved to the San Francisco Bay Area, where he now makes tapes and CDs such as* Sounds of the Streets *(1994), consisting of "word songs" chanted before a background of blues, jazz, and salsa, while working on a sequel to* Down These Mean Streets.

from Seven Long Times

Is THERE NO WAY OUT? L'il Henry and I were walking up and down the length of the prison yard, chewing the rag about this and that, when suddenly the prison siren split the air with its wail. The sound rose and fell again and again like some unearthly thing in the throes of ear-shattering pain. We stopped walking and looked at each other. All around us, inmates and guards were doing the same.

"It's a break, brother," L'il Henry ventured a guess.

"What makes you think so?" I asked, though I believed he was dead right.

"The way that siren's blasting, it can only be two things—break-out, or we're about to be bombed."

I nodded my head in agreement.

Breakout it was. The hacks were rigid and their heads swung from side to side.

"How the hell did he or they ever get outside the walls?" Henry asked the chilly air. "This damn place is maximum security."

"Maybe he got help from the outside," I answered.

"Well, he better have a fast car waiting, a nearby airport with a private plane, plenty of money, and a passport to some place where extradition is a dirty word."

The trumpet blew. Lockup time had been pushed ahead because someone had taken a thousand-to-one shot and maybe made it. There was no doubt the majority of us were rooting for whoever it was to make it; if this escape from the slams was a success, there was hope for someone else making it. All you needed was to stop being afraid of dying by shucking off the care of living and go for broke. The word came passing through from mouth to mouth. Some con named Red had split.

The guards moved the line at a fast clip and we were herded into our cells. Keys were turned and master locks thrown with an urgency that had an odor of fear mixed with hate. The suspense in the air was shared by hacks and cons alike.

"You think he got away?" a loud voice from way out in A-Block asked. And a voice from my own C-Block yelled back, "I sure fuckin' hope so, man. It's about time one of us got a break."

"Shut your goddamn mouth up there," broke in another voice.

"Who the fuck are you?" came back a reply.

"I'm a guard, goddammit. Now shut up."

"Well, la-de-da, motherfucker. You can kiss my ass."

"Tough guy, eh? I'd like to know where your voice is coming from. Come on. Be a man and let me know."

"From 110th Street, motherfucker."

There was some laughter from us cons, not mirthful, but to let our fellow con know we were with him. A voice with a kidding sound to it yelled out to the angry con, "Hey, you meant that about the hack kissing your ass?"

"Damn right I meant it."

"Well, er, I'd be careful about that shit. There's a lotta cats in here might like to take you up on that."

More laughter . . . drowned out by the blasting escape siren.

"Hey, people, cool it. Hack's on his way up there," a con's voice warned.

Everyone cooled it and the hack found nothing but innocence in every cell. No sooner had his footsteps faded away than our voices became alive again. Some source of information via con blared out, "Hey, Red made the break from outside. The cat worked on the farm!"

I laid on the bed and refused to stare out through the green-painted bars of my cell, contenting myself with checking out the steel ceiling of a damn hole in the wall called C-5-13.

I mused over all the times I had thought about escape. There isn't a convict who doesn't think about it sometimes—or all the time. I was no exception. I used to spend hours in my cell dreaming up ways to break out. I strained my memory to recall books I had read with prison breaks in them, as well as films I'd seen, most of which ended with the escapees being riddled by machine-gun fire and falling like flies from the rope they were climbing to get over the wall. Sometimes they'd make it to a fast get-away car and roar off to a short-lived freedom that ended in a gun battle with the police or some small-town sheriff. The only one I could think of who came close to escaping was Paul Muni in *I Am a Fugitive from a Chain Gang*, and he was last seen being hunted and melting into the shadowy fog-filled night after saying good-bye to his sweetheart, as he mumbled something about, "They've made an animal out of me."

There weren't many success stories about escapes. The legendary Willie Sutton ranked as one of the best escape artists in prisondom and even he was eventually recaptured. The last time he got busted, they handed him what I believe totaled 155 years.

I thought of escaping by hiding under the prison trucks that brought in supplies. I thought of dyeing my prison grays a dark green and brown for summer escape and snow white for a winter walk-away . . . of braiding me a rope out of odds and ends and trying for an anchor shot over the wall. I thought of cutting into one of the huge ventilators that led up to the roof—I'd lower myself down four or five stories to the ground, leap over or dig under a fifteen-foot electrified wire fence, slip invisibly by guards with automatic weapons, and having no outside get-away car waiting for me, nonchalantly hitch me a ride to El Barrio, Nueva York, El Big Apple. *After all, my brown skin shouldn't keep me from getting a ride from some good folks*—whose relatives were probably guards in the prison.

Man, I even thought of learning yoga and copping some kind of mystical power whereby I could slow my heart down to nothing, play dead, and get my corpse shipped home C.O.D., whereupon I would bring myself back to life, free as a bird, even if it meant scaring the living crap out of whoever opened the coffin. Silly fantasies, eh? But I wasn't the only one thinking about freedom.

There was Flaco, who was always a little weird in his moodiness and uptight attitudes. While most of us thought about escape, he talked about it constantly despite our warnings to cool it lest he be busted headfirst into solitary accompanied by some painful injuries played on his head. I ran into him in the prison yard one day and he motioned me over to a spot at the side of the wall not occupied by cons or hacks.

"Hey man, I think I finally hit on how to get the fuck outta here." Flaco tried to talk out of the side of his mouth like a good self-respecting con is supposed to, but his declaration came out as loud and clear as if he were running for some kind of office.

"*Coño*, man, cool it. I don't mind so much getting busted for really escaping, but to get a jive-ass bust for just talking about it— no way."

Flaco shrugged his shoulders, looked at me tolerantly and,

apparently deciding to overlook my nervousness or coolness, went on.

"Ya see this deck of cards?"

I nodded. "You're getting out by doing card tricks?"

"Na, stupid. This is scientific."

"Yeah?" I was getting worried about Flaco.

"Yeah." He went on as if patience was difficult to muster.

"Look. I read in a book that there was this prisoner in a dungeon and he was rotting away with guards beating on him from time to time and rats doing the same."

"So?" I smiled, trying to look interested.

"So, he gets ahold of an ordinary deck of playing cards, some matches, and a small piece of lead pipe with a screw cap on each end."

"Yeah, and . . . ?"

Flaco was really warming up. "And he takes only the cards with the red numbers on them and cuts out the red-painted pieces of all the cards."

"Where'd he get the knife in solitary, let alone matches, playing cards, not to mention a lead pipe with two screw caps on each end?"

"Turkey," Flaco good-humoredly insulted me. "The mother-fucker had good connections."

I nodded and said, "That sounds logical, not to mention fair. Go on."

"Well, he takes all the red pieces of the playing cards and wets them into a soggy mass, then caps one end of the pipe and jams the soggy red mass into the open end, stamping them in good and tight. He fills up the empty space with plain pieces of the deck and closes up the pipe tight. He puts one end of the pipe into his mouth and with the matches sets fire to a piece of wool. . . ."

I looked at Flaco and he added, ". . . that he ripped from his cell stool. Then he begins to heat the pipe."

"So how does that get him out?" I pushed.

"Simple, man. The heat at the one end of the pipe causes some kind of gas buildup from the chemical in the red pieces of playing cards, causing a vacuum. The pressure got so great inside that the pipe did a wan-go—bombs away. It blew up."

"Asshole," I said disgustedly. "How did that help him get away?"

"By blowing his head off. He wanted to commit suicide."

"You believe the crap about the playing cards?"

"Sure do. I'm getting the stuff all together and—"

"You gonna blow your head off?" I asked gently.

"Naw, brother, just the lock at the front gate."

"Oh, I see. Good luck," and I walked away from him, the prison's one and only Puerto Rican anarchist.

Sometime later I ran into Flaco again and out of curiosity asked how he was making out with his bomb. He shook his head sadly and said he had everything but the piece of pipe that had to be specially made with grooves and caps on each end.

"Wish you luck, Flaco." I grinned, then added, "Too bad you don't have the connections that cat had who blew off his head."

"I'll get it yet. Don't worry. It works, I tell you, powerful bomb. There wasn't enough left of that guy in the book to put on a spoon. The cell walls were just dripping with him after the explosion. Shit, with that kind of power, I could bring the whole fuckin' walls down."

Flaco walked away, leaving me thinking about the walls of Jericho. I laughed out loud. Humor is a great safety valve. I stared after Flaco's skinny five-foot-five frame ambling off, walking street-wise hip. Funny how his dark-brown eyes were always shining bright. They seemed to give color to his otherwise pale skin. Caramba, *Flaco should watch his cool. He's looking for a flip trip to a nut factory.* But I wondered if it was really possible to make a bomb out of a deck of cards.

My mind turned to Red, who was a *blanco.* The word on the grapevine was that he may have made it safely outside the prison walls.

He had worked outside the walls on the prison farm, where he drove a tractor. From somewhere out there, he had lifted some civilian clothes, but instead of cutting out, he had come back to the prison, hung his gray convict uniform on the huge steel back gates of the prison, and attached a note damning the whole system. The delay was a bad loss of precious time. His prison clothes and note had been found, and the hunt was on. What he did could only have been an act of defiance and contempt for the prison system.

Red was captured, and according to cons and some guards, he had offered no resistance, but surrendered quietly. That didn't stop the hell that fell on him. He was brought back to the prison and beaten to a pulp, with practically all his teeth smashed out of his mouth. Some said they could not recognize Red after that beating. They smashed him so much his red blood covered his white color. I swore to myself one more time that I was going to survive.

I stepped out into the bright sunshine of the prison yard but didn't enjoy its Sunday warmth. It seemed somehow dulled by the ever-present color of blue hack uniforms and the drab gray of prisoner clothes. I leaned against a railing and caught a blurred reflection of myself in a dirty window. I felt my face with an indifferent hand. There was no doubt about it. It wasn't the same Piri who had come into prison over what seemed a thousand years ago. The reflection that stared back at me was young-old, harder, and prison wise. My days in prison had passed slowly through a hole in time and had become three years.

I stared harder at the dirt-streaked glass and it seemed I could see a montage of past events of my life in this concentration camp of inhuman debasement. I saw the past. I knew the present and was vaguely trying to see if the dirty windowpane would project a future when I was brought back from my reverie by the sound of familiar voices.

Bayamon, Zorro, L'il Henry, and Juan de Jesus were engaged in animated conversation. I studied Juan, who was very well educated and who spoke seldom and only to the point. Juan was holding a prison-worn copy of the *New York Times*. L'il Henry saw me, and as always with anyone he considered a friend, his dark face broke out in a grin and he waved for me to come over. I waved and thought how there wasn't a real evil bone in L'il Henry's body. His was a real honest free spirit who acted without malice, but somehow it always seemed to get him in trouble. The hacks who had no love for any skin that wasn't white seemed determined to wipe out the good-natured feeling in L'il Henry's heart, but to no avail.

I walked slowly toward the group, waving a greeting. *"Hola, hermanos."*

"Hey, brother Piri, come and join us," said Juan. His face was grim though under control. The headlines in our two-week-old *New York Times* read: ASSASSINATION OF TRUMAN FOILED IN GUN FIGHT OUTSIDE BLAIR HOUSE; PUERTO RICAN PLOTTER, GUARD DIE. I let out a soft whistle. The attack had occurred on November 2, 1950. I had known about the Nationalist Party's struggle for independence for Puerto Rico ever since I was a youngster. It always stood for political change through peaceful and legal channels. *Un antipático* broke into my thoughts.

"Cripes, ain't that the stupidest thing in the world to pull. Imagine trying to off the President of the United States. Crazy people, man, gotta be crazy people. Only a fucking fanatic would do a thing like that. Shit, what does Puerto Rico need independence for? Christ sakes, it's got the United States on its side. It don't have a damn thing to worry about. Who's gonna mess with Puerto Rico with such a big gun on its side?"

"Nobody except the people who want to be free," answered Juan. "And to correct you further, the big gun is not on our side. It is pointed at our heads."

"Well, shit, man, if the United States is so damn bad, what the hell are so many Puerto Ricans doing living in the States? That's downright ungrateful," the unfriendly inmate pushed.

"I am for a *Puerto Rico libre,*" Juan continued. "I'm an ingrate. Speaking for myself and for freedom-loving Puerto Ricans, I can say we have nothing to be grateful for. We've been bought by the simple expediency of making us so economically dependent on the United States for our existence that the majority of us are afraid to go it alone as a free country and are content to lean on the security of the United States as one would lean on a crutch."

I turned and walked away, barely hearing the response of the antagonized inmate. In my own way I had to work off the crushing oppressiveness of the prison atmosphere. It was pretty hard hearing about freedom for a country when you yourself were not personally free. Political awareness was not too big a thing with me at that time. Survival was.

JACK HENRY ABBOTT

1944–

Jack Abbott's In the Belly of the Beast, *a collection of letters he had written to Norman Mailer while in prison, became an overnight literary sensation when it appeared in early 1981, going through five printings in a few months and winning frequent comparisons to the writings of Jean Genet and Albert Camus. In June, Abbott was paroled. Still a prisoner of the U.S. government, he was dumped into a sleazy halfway house in the Bowery section of Manhattan. A month later, he killed a man. Disillusion immediately spread among many of those who admired his writing, and his name was used to anathematize prison literature in general.*

But did Abbott's actions on that fatal July night invalidate—or dramatize—the message of his book? First, the circumstances of the killing are by no means clear. Abbott gives his version of the case in a play included in his 1987 collection My Return. *The uncontested evidence is that he became involved in an altercation with the night manager of a café near the halfway house, which ended with Abbott stabbing the man once in the heart. The manager may have threatened or even assaulted Abbott, who in any event believed that he was being assaulted and contended that he acted in self-defense. Although the media had already convicted him of murder, the jury acquitted him of that charge and found him guilty only of manslaughter.*

Whatever happened that night certainly does not negate In the Belly of the Beast. *For in that book Abbott was trying to communicate to his relatively affluent readers what kind of people they are creating in their system of "corrections."*

First incarcerated when he was nine years old, Abbott was sent to a juvenile penal institution at the age of twelve for the crime of "failure to adjust to foster homes." There he was imprisoned, except for sixty days, until he was eighteen. After being free for five months, he was next given an indeterminate sentence of up to five years in the Utah State Penitentiary for the crime of "issuing a check for insufficient funds." Three years later, he killed another convict in a fight. Between the ages of twelve and thirty-seven, when In the Belly of the Beast *was published, he had been free for a total of less than one year's time.*

Abbott's revelations about his decades of torture—beatings, starvation, forced injections of dangerous drugs, and a total of more than fourteen years spent in solitary confinement, sometimes in total darkness, almost always in cells awash in feces and urine—demonstrate how our penal institutions force each prisoner to become either a broken, cringing animal, fawning before all authority and power, or a rebel, clinging to human dignity through defiance and violence.

Abbott was given a sentence of fifteen years to life imprisonment for the manslaughter conviction. As of 1997 he was back in solitary confinement, this time in Attica.

from *In the Belly of the Beast*

State-Raised Convict

I'VE WANTED somehow to convey to you the sensations—the atmospheric pressure, you might say—of what it is to be seriously a long-term prisoner in an American prison. That sentence does not adequately say what I mean. I've wanted to convey to you what it means to be in prison after a childhood spent in penal institutions. To be in prison so long, it's difficult to remember exactly what you did to get there. So long, your fantasies of the free world are no longer easily distinguishable from what you "know" the free world is really like. So long, that being free is exactly identical to a free man's dreams of heaven. To die and go to the free world . . .

I was born January 21, 1944, on a military base in Oscoda, Michigan. I was in and out of foster homes almost from the moment of my birth. My formal education: I never completed the sixth grade. At age nine I began serving long stints in juvenile detention quarters. At age twelve I was sent to the Utah State Industrial School for Boys. I was "paroled" once for about sixty days, then returned there. At age eighteen I was released as an adult. Five or six months later I was sent to the Utah State Penitentiary for the crime of "issuing a check against insufficient funds." I went in with an indeterminate sentence of up to five years. About three years later, having never been released, I killed one inmate and wounded another in a fight in the center hall. I was tried for the capital offense under the old convict statute that requires either *mandatory* death if malice *aforethought* is found, or a sentence of from three to

No sense of actual freedom

twenty years. I received the latter sentence. An "indeterminate term" is what justifies the concept of *parole*. Your good behavior determines how long you stay in prison. The law merely sets a minimum and a maximum—the underlying assumption being that *no one* serves the maximum. A wrong assumption in my case. At age twenty-six I escaped for about six weeks.

I am at this moment thirty-seven years old. Since age twelve I have been free the sum total of nine and a half months. I have served many terms in solitary. In only three terms I have served over ten years there. I would estimate that I have served a good fourteen or fifteen years in solitary. The only serious crime I have ever committed in free society was bank robbery during the time I was a fugitive.

It was a big red-brick building with two wings. It stood about four stories high. It was constructed by the U.S. Army back when the state was still a territory. It was one of several buildings that had served as disciplinary barracks for the military. These barracks had long ago passed into the hands of the state and were part of a juvenile penal institution.

In the basement of the big red-brick building were rows of solitary confinement cells. The basement was entered from outside the building only.

I am about twelve or thirteen years old. It is winter. I am marching in a long double-file of boys. We are marching to the mess hall. There is a guard watching as we march toward him. There is a guard walking behind us as we march.

My testes shrink and the blood is rushing and my eyes burn, ache. My heart is pounding and I am trying hard to breathe slowly, to control myself.

I keep glancing at the guards: in front and behind the line.

The fields beyond are plowed and covered with an icy blanket of snow. I do not know how far beyond those fields my freedom lies.

Suddenly my confederate at the front of the line whirls and slugs the boy behind him. The front guard, like an attack dog, is on them both—beating them into submission. Seconds later the guard at the back rushes forward, brushing me as he passes.

I break away from the line, and run *for my life*. I stretch my legs as far as I can, and as quickly as I can, but the legs of a boy four feet six inches tall cannot stretch very far.

The fields are before me, a still flatland of ice and snow, and the huge clods of frozen, plowed earth are to me formidable obstacles. The sky is baby-blue, almost white. The air is clear.

I haven't covered fifty yards when I hear the pursuit begin: "You! Stop!" I immediately know I will be caught, but I continue to run.

I do not feel the blow of his fist. I'm in midair for a moment, and then I'm rolling in frozen clods of soil. I am pulled to my feet; one of my arms is twisted behind my back; my lungs are burning with the cold air; my nostrils are flared. I am already trying to steel myself for the punishment to come.

The other inmates stand in a long straight line, flanked by guards, and I am dragged past them. I do not respect them, because they will not run—will not try to escape. My legs are too short to keep up with the guard, who is effortlessly holding my arm twisted high up behind my back, so I stumble along, humiliated. I try hard to be dignified.

I see the door to the basement of the red-brick building, and we are approaching it in good time. A snowflake hits my eye and melts. It is beginning, softly, to snow.

At the top of the stairs to the basement, I am flung down against a high black-steel door. I stand beside it at attention as the guard takes out a huge ring of keys and bangs on the door. We are seen through a window. The door yawns open and an old guard appears, gazing at me maliciously.

We enter. We are standing at the top of a number of wide concrete steps that descend to the floor of the basement. I am thrown down the stairs, and I lie on the floor, waiting. My nose is bleeding and my ears are ringing from blows to my skull.

"Get up!"

Immediately I am knocked down again.

"Strip!"

I stand, shakily, and shed my clothing. His hands are pulling my hair, but I dare not move.

"Turn around!"

I turn.

"Bend over!"

I bend over. He inspects my anus and my private parts, and I watch, anxiously, hoping with all my might he does not hurt me there.

He orders me to follow him.

We enter a passageway between rows of heavy steel doors. The passage is narrow; it is only four or five feet wide and is dimly lighted. As soon as we enter, I can smell nervous sweat and feel body warmth in the air.

We stop at one of the doors. He unlocks it. I enter. Nothing is said. He closes and locks the door, and I can hear his steps as he walks down the dark passageway.

In the cell, there is a barred window with an ancient, heavy mesh-steel screen. It is level with the ground outside. The existing windowpanes are caked with decades of soil, and the screen prevents cleaning them. Through the broken ones I peer, running free again in my mind across the fields.

A sheet of thick plywood, on iron legs bolted to the floor, is my bed. An old-fashioned toilet bowl is in the corner, beside a sink with cold running water. A dim light burns in a dull yellow glow behind the thick iron screening attached to the wall.

The walls are covered with names and dates—some of the dates go back twenty years. They were scratched into the wall. There are ragged hearts pierced with arrows and *pachuco* crosses everywhere. Everywhere are the words: "mom," "love," "god"—the walls sweat and are clammy and cold.

Because I am allowed only my undershorts, I move about to keep warm.

When my light was turned out at night, I would weep uncontrollably. Sixty days in solitary was a long, long time in those days for me.

When the guard's key would hit the lock on my door to signal the serving of a "meal," if I were not standing at attention in the far corner of the cell, facing it, the guard would attack me with a ring of keys on a heavy chain.

I was fed one-third of a regular meal three times a day. Only one day a week I was taken from my cell and ordered to shower while the guard stood in the shower-room doorway and timed me for three minutes.

Locked in our cells, we could not see one another, and if we were caught shouting cell-to-cell, we were beaten. We tapped out messages, but if they heard our taps, we were beaten—the entire row of cells, one child at a time.

I served five years in the big red-brick building, and altogether, two or three in solitary confinement. When I walked out, I was considered an adult, subject to adult laws.

I served so long because I could not adjust to the institution and tried to escape over twenty times. I had been there for the juvenile "crime" of "failure to adjust to foster homes." *Nobody tried to help*

. . . He who is state-raised—reared by the state from an early age after he is taken from what the state calls a "broken home"—learns over and over and all the days of his life that people in society can do anything to him and not be punished by the law. Do anything to him with the full force of the state behind them.

As a child, he must march in lock-step to his meals in a huge mess hall. He can own only three shirts and two pair of trousers and one pair of shoes.

People in society come to him through the state and injure him. Everyone in society he comes in contact with is in some capacity employed by the state. He learns to avoid people in society. He evades them at every step.

crazy In *any* state in America someone who is state-raised can be shot down and killed like a dog by anyone, who has no "criminal record," with full impunity. I do not exaggerate this at all. It is a fact so ordinary in the minds of state-raised prisoners that it is a matter of common sense. If a prisoner were to show a skeptical attitude toward things of this nature, the rest of us would conclude that he is losing his mind. He is questioning what is self-evident to us: a practical fact of life.

. . . My mind keeps turning toward one of the main aspects of prison that separates ordinary prisoners who, at some point in their lives, serve a few years and get out never to return—or if they do, it is for another short period and never again—and the convict who is "state-raised," i.e., the prisoner who grows up from boyhood to manhood in penal institutions.

I have referred to it as a form of instability (mental, emotional, etc.). There is no doubt (let us say there is *little* doubt) that this instability is *caused* by a lifetime of incarceration. Long stretches of, say, from ages ten to seventeen or eighteen, and then from seventeen or eighteen to ages thirty and forty.

You hear a lot about "arrested adolescence" nowadays, and I believe this concept touches the nub of the instability in prisoners like myself.

Every society gives its men and women the prerogatives of men and women, of *adults*. Men are given their dues. After a certain age you are regarded as a man by society. You are referred to as "sir"; no one interferes in your affairs, slaps your hands or ignores you. Society is solicitous in general and serves you. You are shown respect. Gradually your judgment is tempered because gradually you see that it has real effects; it impinges on the society, the world. Your experience mellows your emotions because you are free to move about anywhere, work and play at anything. You can pursue any object of love, pleasure, danger, profit, etc. You are taught by the very terms of your social existence, by the objects that come and go from your intentions, the nature of your own emotions— and you learn about yourself, your tastes, your strengths and weaknesses. You, in other words, mature emotionally.

It is not so for the state-raised convict. As a boy in reform school, he is punished for being a little boy. In prison, he is punished for trying to be a man in the sense described above. He is treated as an adolescent in prison. Just as an adolescent is denied the keys to the family car for *any* disobedience, *any* mischief, I am subjected to the hole for *any* disobedience, *any* mischief. I will go to the hole for murder as well as for stealing a packet of sugar. I will get out of the hole in either case, and the length of time I serve for either offense is no different. My object is *solely* to avoid leaving evidence that will leave me open to prosecution out there in the world beyond these walls where a semblance of democracy is practiced.

Prison regimes have prisoners making extreme decisions regarding moderate questions, decisions that only fit the logical choice of either-or. No contradiction is allowed openly. You are not allowed to change. You are only allowed to submit; "agreement" does not exist (it implies equality). You are the rebellious adolescent who must obey and submit to the judgment of "grownups"—"*tyrants*" they are called when we speak of men.

A prisoner who is not state-raised tolerates the situation because of his social maturity prior to incarceration. He knows things are different outside prison. But the state-raised convict has no conception of any difference. He lacks experience and, hence, maturity. His judgment is untempered, rash; his emotions are impulsive, raw, unmellowed.

There are emotions—a whole spectrum of them—that I know of only through words, through reading and my immature imagination. I can *imagine* I feel those emotions (know, therefore, what they are), but *I do not.* At age thirty-seven I am barely a precocious child. My passions are those of a boy.

This thing I related above about emotions is the hidden, dark side of state-raised convicts. The foul underbelly everyone hides from everyone else. There is something else. It is the other half— which concerns *judgment, reason* (moral, ethical, cultural). It is the mantle of pride, integrity, honor. It is the high esteem we naturally have for violence, force. It is what makes us *effective,* men whose judgment impinges on others, on the world: Dangerous killers who act alone and *without* emotion, who act with calculation and principles, to avenge themselves, establish and defend their principles with acts of murder that usually evade prosecution by law: this is the state-raised convicts' conception of manhood, in the highest sense.

The model we emulate is a fanatically defiant and alienated individual who cannot imagine what forgiveness is, or mercy or tolerance, because he has no *experience* of such values. His emotions do not know what such values are, but he *imagines* them as so many "weaknesses" precisely because the unprincipled offender appears to escape punishment through such "weaknesses" on the part of society.

But if you behave like a man (a man such as yourself) you are doomed; you are feared and hated. You are "crazy" by the standards of the authorities—by their prejudices against prison-behavior.

Can you imagine how I feel—to be treated as a little boy and not as a man? And when I was a little boy, I was treated as a man— and can you imagine what that does to a boy? (I keep waiting for the years to give me a sense of humor, but so far that has evaded me completely.)

So. A guard frowns at me and says: "Why are you not at work?"

Or: "Tuck in your shirttail!" Do this and do that. The way a little boy is spoken to. This is something I have had to deal with not for a year or two—nor even ten years—but for, so far, eighteen years. And when I explode, then I have burnt myself by behaving like a contrite and unruly little boy. So I have, in order to avoid that deeper humiliation, developed a method of reversing the whole situation—and I become the man chastising the little boy. (Poor kid!) It has cost me dearly, and not just in terms of years in prison or in the hole.

I cannot adjust to daily life in prison. For almost twenty years this has been true. I have never gone a month in prison without incurring disciplinary action for violating "rules." Not in all these years.

Does this mean I must die in prison? Does this mean I cannot "adjust" to society outside prison?

The government answers *yes*—but I *remember* society, and it is not like prison. I feel that if I ever did *adjust to prison,* I could by that alone never adjust to society. I would be back in prison within months.

Now, I care about myself and I cannot let it happen that I cannot adjust to freedom. Even if it means spending my life in prison—because to me prison is nothing but mutiny and revolt.

. . . A round peg will not fit into a square slot. I don't think they'll ever let me out of prison so long as my release depends upon my "good adjustment to prison." . . .

I have never accepted that I did this to myself. I have never been successfully indoctrinated with that belief. That is the only reason I have been in prison this long.

Indoctrination begins the moment someone is arrested. It becomes more thorough every step of the way, from the moment of arrest to incarceration. In prison, it finds its most profound expression.

Every minute for years you are forced to believe that your suffering is a result of your "ill behavior," that it is self-inflicted. You are indoctrinated to blindly accept *anything* done to you. But if a guard knocks me to the floor, only by indoctrination can I be brought to believe I did it to myself. If I am thrown in the prison hole for having violated a prison rule—for having, for example, shown insolence to a pig—I can only believe I brought this upon myself through *indoctrination.*

. . . I might have become indoctrinated were it not for the evil and ignorant quality of the men who are employed in prisons.

A prisoner is taught that what is required of him is to *never* resist, *never* contradict. A prisoner is taught to *plead* with the pigs and accept guilt for things he never did.

I have had guards I have never seen before report me for making threats and arguing with them. I have been taken before disciplinary committees of guards for things I have never done, things they all knew I never did. And I have been ordered to the hole for things *they knew* I never did.

My prison record has in it more violence reported by guards than that of any of the 25,000 federal prisoners behind bars today, and I am not guilty of nine-tenths of the charges. Yet there is nothing at all I can do about it.

If I were beaten to death tomorrow, my record would go before the coroner's jury—before anyone who had the power to investigate—and my "past record of violence" would vindicate my murderers. In fact, the prison regime can commit any atrocity against me, and my "record" will acquit them.

The government shows that record to judges if I get into court on a civil suit against the prison or on a petition for writ of habeas corpus. It is designed to prejudice the judge—a man who relishes any opportunity to prejudice himself against prisoners.

. . . Responsibility? I am not responsible for what the government—its system of justice, its prisons—has done to me. I did not do this to myself.

This is not easy to say; it is not an easy *point of view* to hold. Why? Because it has cost me, so far, almost two decades of imprisonment. This I hold is the *greater* responsibility: I did not do this to myself.

I do not share in the sins of this guilty country; we are not "all in this together"! Who in America today would *dare* take the responsibility for himself and others that I and countless other prisoners like me have taken?

. . . I know you aren't mean enough to think I'm trying to shift the responsibility for my own "corrupt self." Indeed I am not. I have only tried to indicate the opposite: that I demand responsibility for myself. . . . It has been not only my personal observation but the experience of all prison authorities: the most dangerous prisoners—and I mean that also in the "physical" sense—are "readers and writers."

In Maximum Security, I served *years* barefooted, with only my books and my balls and a punishment set of white standard (five sizes too large) coveralls. Novels and dictionaries. And then philosophy, until it came out of my eyes and ears—and finally, on occasion, my mouth: nine-tenths of my vocabulary I have never *heard* spoken. I remember the words "college" and "rhetoric." Small incidents of embarrassment when I discovered I had been pronouncing them wrong all my life. The word "guru" also—and "a priori." I fell into all the sciences at one time or another—so naïve in my grasp that I grasped things only someone like Bohr had. With me, I cannot learn practical things until I've studied the subject in the purest theoretical form. I did not really understand the first things about calculus until I studied Hertz and—of all people—Hegel on the subject. A child's primer would *mystify* me. Theoretical physics is simple to me, but applied physics leaves me stunned with a gross feeling. I can understand symbolic logic —Frege, Russell, Whitehead, Carnap, Quine, etc.—better than schoolboy arithmetic. It all found expression—and came together in the most elegant sense—in the findings of Marx. And that is a *world* of science and literature which the world you and I live in conceals from us. It took *great* effort and imagination on my part to seek out and obtain truly great advancements in our culture that the world we live in in the West tries so hard to suppress. Having contacted that world and communicated to a degree, to that degree I have become free.

Books are dangerous where there is injustice.

I've served time for just *requesting* books. I've been subjected to frame-ups and prejudice and the worst forms of discrimination because of the title of books I read. (Even a book with the word *Plato* on the cover can get you in trouble.)

No federal penitentiary (and there are only six top-level penitentiaries; the rest are ordinary prisons) has a prison library. The authorities say we "misuse" our knowledge if allowed to educate ourselves according to our natural impulses. They say we use the *Britannica* encyclopedias to make bombs, guns, acids, etc., etc., from the information they impart. They say Marx lies to us about our condition and makes us immoral and craven and desperate.

That is why they now have "education programs" in prison, i.e., so we learn *only* what they want us to learn. *I pride myself on the fact that I've never been in a prison school.*

Ironic

You stumbled across the biggest sore-spot in the prison system when you asked why books are such touchy subjects to prison regimes. You have a problem understanding this because you are free and living in New York. But oppressed men know the value of books, because if they ever become enamored of, or even curious about, a *single* idea—and pursue it—they are on the road to rebellion. I mean by "rebellion" the bloodiest violence, the most ruthless murder and deterioration you can imagine. A taste of freedom in prison is not unlike a taste of heroin—a taste that obsesses you: a "taste" that addicts you—you'd *kill* for it in a literal sense. They go for your mind in prison today—where before, it was all physical suffering. The stakes are much, much greater today. The most dangerous convicts in American prison history are behind bars today. They kill quicker, more efficiently, are more liable to die for *beliefs*—more sophisticated in every way. I think you keep thinking of prison in terms of a military barracks. There is no comparison. It compares much more with a gladiator prison ("school") in ancient Rome during the suppression of slaves and Christians. We are naturally pitted against each other by degrees of stoicism (a kind of "class" system) through prison manipulation.

The *books* we have we hold almost by force of arms—literally. We have no legal rights *as prisoners,* only as citizens. The only "rights" we have are those left to their "discretion." So we assert our rights the only way we can. It is a compromise, and in the end I greatly fear we as prisoners will lose—but the loss will be society's loss. We are only a few steps removed from society. After us, comes you.

ASSATA SHAKUR
(JoANNE CHESIMARD)
1947–

In 1972 and early 1973, the FBI orchestrated a media campaign to brand Black Liberation Army member JoAnne Chesimard (Assata Shakur) as a bank robber, kidnapper, and cop killer. On the night of May 2, 1973, New Jersey State Trooper James Harper spotted Assata Shakur, Zayd Malik Shakur (John Costan), and Sundiata Acoli (Clark Squire) driving on the New Jersey State Turnpike, stopped their car on the pretext of a faulty taillight, and hurriedly called in reinforcements. In an ensuing shootout, Zayd Shakur and one trooper were killed, and Harper and Shakur were wounded.

Despite her serious wound, Shakur was kept in conditions that attorney Lennox Hinds described as "barbarous" while she was prosecuted for the six crimes she had allegedly committed to get on the FBI's Most Wanted list. Three separate cases were eventually dismissed for lack of evidence: an armed robbery of the New York Hilton hotel, the murder of a drug dealer, and an attempted murder of a New York policeman. In three separate trials between 1973 and 1976, she was acquitted of a bank robbery in Queens, a bank robbery in the Bronx, and the kidnapping of a New York drug dealer. The only remaining charges came from the May 1973 shootout.

Because she had become pregnant by her codefendant in the Bronx bank robbery trial, her New Jersey trial was postponed until after the birth of her daughter. Despite considerable medical and forensic evidence that, contrary to the police account, she could not have fired any weapon and that she was shot while her hands were raised in surrender, Shakur was convicted in 1977 by an all-white jury of premeditated murder and attempted murder of the New Jersey troopers, as well as all other charges, and she was sentenced to life imprisonment plus a minimum of twenty-six additional years.

Shuttled from prison to prison, she was shipped in February 1979 from the federal maximum security unit in Alderson, West Virginia, to the Clinton Correctional Institution for

Women in New Jersey. The following November, three black men and a white woman rescued her from Clinton in a daring armed foray. For years thereafter, federal and state police conducted numerous raids on predominantly African-American homes and housing projects, sometimes sealing off whole neighborhoods, in their hunt for the fugitive. In 1984, Shakur managed to flee to Cuba, which promptly granted her political asylum.

In 1987, Shakur publicly announced her presence, along with that of her thirteen-year-old daughter, in Cuba and gave her own account of her life in Assata: An Autobiography. *To circumvent U.S. laws against her receiving royalties, the book was technically published by a British company, which licensed printing and distribution rights back to its U.S. publisher. Despite efforts to prevent its sale, ten thousand copies of* Assata *were bought in the first month alone.*

The two passages reprinted here bracket her prison experience. The first describes her removal from hospital to prison in 1973. The second, the final passage of her book, tells of her condition just before her escape.

from *Assata*

IT SEEMED LIKE the middle of the night. Someone was calling me. Waking me up. What did they want? Suddenly i was aware of all kinds of activity. Police, the crackling of walkie-talkies. The place was buzzing.

"Here, put this on," one of them said, handing me a bathrobe.

"What's going on?" i asked.

"You're being moved."

"Where am i being moved to?"

"You'll find out when you get there."

A wheelchair was waiting. I figured they were taking me to jail. There was a caravan of police cars outside the hospital. It looked like i was gonna be in a parade again.

The ride was pleasant. Just looking at houses and trees and people passing by in cars was good. We arrived at the prison at sunrise, in the middle of nowhere. It was an ugly, two-story brick building. They pushed me up the stairs to the second floor.

I was put in a cell with two doors. A door of bars was on the inside, and directly outside of that was a heavy metal door with a tiny peephole that i could barely see through. The cell contained a cot with a rough green blanket on it and a dirty white wooden bench with a hundred names scratched on it. Adjacent to the cell was the bathroom, with a sink, a toilet, and a shower. Hanging above the sink was the bottom of a pot or pan. It was supposed to serve as a mirror, but i could barely see myself in it. There was one window covered by three thick metal screens facing a parking lot, a field, and, in the distance, a wooded area.

I walked around the cell, to the bath, to the window, to the door. Back and forth until i had tired myself out. I was still pretty weak. Then i lay down on the cot and wondered what this place was going to be like. Here i was, my first day in prison.

In about an hour, a guard unlocked the outside door and asked me if i wanted breakfast. I said, "Yes," and in a few minutes she came back with eggs and bread in a plastic bowl and a metal cup containing something that was supposed to be coffee.

The eggs didn't taste too bad. "Maybe prison food isn't as bad as they say it is," i remember thinking.

I heard voices and it was clear they weren't police voices. Then the radio came on. Black music. It sounded so good. I looked through the peephole and saw faces, weird and distorted because of the concave glass, but Black faces to match the Black voices i had heard.

"How y'all doin'?" i asked.

No response. Then i realized how thick the metal door was, so i shouted this time: "How y'all doin'?" A chorus of muffled "Fine"'s came back. I was feeling good. Real people were just on the other side of the wall.

The guard opened the metal door and handed me some uniforms, maid's uniforms—royal blue, white buttons, collars, and cuffs.

I kept trying them on until two of them fit. Then she gave me a huge cotton slip that looked like a tent dress and a nightgown that looked exactly like the slip.

"You are entitled to a clean uniform once a week."

"Once a week?" i nearly screeched. They had to be crazy. Behind the guard, through the open door, i could see some of the women standing around. They were all, it seemed, Black. They smiled and waved at me. It was so good to see them, it was like a piece of home.

"When are you going to unlock me and let me go out there?" i asked, motioning to the other women. The guard looked surprised.

"I don't know. You'll have to ask the warden."

"Well, when can i see the warden?" i pushed.

"I don't know."

"Well, why am i being locked in here? Why can't i go out there with the other women?"

"I don't know."

"Then why can't you let me out?"

"We were told you were to remain in your room."

"Well, how long am i supposed to stay in here locked up like this?"

"I don't know."

I saw it was useless. "Would you please tell the warden or the sheriff that i would like to see him?" i requested.

The guard locked the door and was gone.

The metal door was unlocked again. An ugly, shriveled white woman stood in front of the bars. "My name is Mrs. Butterworth and I am the warden of the women's section of the workhouse." She reminded me of a dilapidated horse. "Well, JoAnne, is there something I can do for you?"

I didn't like her looks or her tone of voice, but i decided to ignore that for the moment and get to the business at hand.

"When can i be unlocked from this cell and go outside in the big room with the other women?"

"Well, I don't know, JoAnne. Why do you want to go out there?"

"Well, i don't want to stay in here all day, locked up by myself."

"Why, JoAnne, don't you like your room? It's a very nice room. We had it painted just for you."

"That's not the point," i said. "I would like to know when i will be able to be with the other women."

"Well, JoAnne, I don't know when you'll be able to come out. You see, we have to keep you in here for your own safety because

Blk of rapy minds

there are threats on your life. You know, JoAnne," she said, lowering her voice like she was speaking confidentially, "cop killers are not very popular in correctional institutions."

"Have any of the women here made threats against me?"

"Well, I don't know, but I'm sure they have."

"I'll bet," i said to myself. "Nobody has threatened my life. They just don't want to let me outta here."

"Well, JoAnne, the important thing is for you to behave and to cooperate with us so that we'll be able to send a good report to the judge. It's important for our girls to behave like ladies."

This woman was making me sick. Did she think i was fool enough to believe that either she or the judge was gonna help me in any way? But it was the superior-sounding tinge to her voice that really ticked me off.

"Butterworth, is it?" i asked. "What's your first name?"

"Why, I never tell my girls my first name."

"I'm not one of your girls. I'm a grown woman. Why don't you tell people your first name? Are you ashamed of it?"

"No, JoAnne, I'm not ashamed of my name. It's a matter of respect. I am the warden here. My girls call me Mrs. Butterworth and I call them by their first names."

LOL

"Well, you haven't done anything for me to respect you for. I give people respect only when they earn it. Since you won't tell me your first name, then i want you to call me by my last name. You can either call me Ms. Shakur or Ms. Chesimard."

"I'm not going to call you by your last name. I'm going to continue calling you JoAnne."

"Well, that's okay by me, if you can stand me calling you Miss Bitch whenever i see you. I don't give anybody respect when they don't respect me."

"Lock the door," she told the guard and walked away.

Days passed. Evelyn called the sheriff, the warden (there were two wardens in that jail: Butterworth and a man named Cahill. Cahill had all the power, though. Butterworth was only a figurehead) and everybody else. Nothing more could be done outside of going to kourt.

I had little or no feeling in my right arm. I knew i needed physical therapy if i was ever to use it again. I had learned to write with my left hand, but that was no substitute. I needed a more specific diagnosis of exactly what had been damaged before i would know whether or not i would ever use it again, even with physical therapy.

Isolation was driving me up the walls. I needed materials to write and to draw, paint, or sketch. All my requests went unheeded. I was permitted nothing, including peanut oil and a small ball to aid movement in my arm.

When the jail doctor examined me i asked him about my arm.

"Why, we doctors aren't gods, you know. There's nothing anyone can do when someone is paralyzed."

"But they said i might get better," I protested. "Oh, yes, and the physical therapist at Roosevelt Hospital said that some peanut oil might help."

"Peanut oil?" he asked, laughing. "That's a good one. I can't write a prescription for that now, can I? My advice to you is to forget about all of that stuff. You don't need any of it. Sometimes in life we just have to accept things that are unpleasant. You still have one good arm."

I kept talking but i could see i was wasting my time. He had no intention of even trying to help me. "Well, would you at least prescribe some vitamin B?"

"All right, but you really don't need it."

Every time they called me to see the doctor after that, i went reluctantly. He would take my arm out of the sling and move it back and forth about two inches. "Oh, yes, you're getting better," he would say. I always asked about physical therapy and he always said there was nothing he could do.

Finally, Evelyn went to court. Some of the items we petitioned for were ridiculous. In addition to physical therapy and nerve tests, we asked for peanut oil, a rubber ball, a rubber grip, books, and stuff to draw or paint with. The kourt finally granted a physical therapist if we would find one and pay the bill, but i never got one. It seems that no physical therapist in Middlesex County was willing to come to the prison to treat me, and only a physical therapist from Middlesex County was permitted.

But i did get the peanut oil and the grip. And in a short time i had a whole physical therapy program worked out.

I was receiving a lot of mail from all over the country. Most of it came from people i didn't know, mostly militant Black people, either in the streets or in prison. I got some hate mail, though, and some letters from religious people who were trying to save my soul.

I wasn't able to answer all of those letters because the prison permitted us to write only two letters a week, subject to inspection
and censorship by the prison authorities. It was hard for me to
write anyway. I was also very paranoid about letters. I could not
bear the thought of the police, FBI, guards, whoever, reading my
letters and getting daily insight on how i was feeling and thinking.
But i would like to offer my sincerest apology to those who were
kind enough to write to me over the years and who received no
answer.

I spent my first month at the Middlesex County workhouse
writing. Evelyn had brought some newspaper clippings and it was
obvious the press was trying to railroad me, to make me seem like
a monster. According to them i was a common criminal, just going
around shooting down cops for the hell of it. I had to make a
statement. I had to talk to my people and let them know what i
was about, where i was really coming from. The statement seemed
to take forever to write. I wanted to make a tape of it and enlisted
Evelyn's help. As my lawyer, she was dead set against it and advised
me not to make the tape. But as a Black woman living in amerika,
Evelyn understood why it was important and necessary. When the
prosecutor found out about the tape he tried to get her thrown off
the case. She was ordered by the court never to bring a tape re-
corder again when she visited me.

I made the tape of "To My People" on July 4, 1973, and it was
broadcast on many radio stations. Here is what I said:

> Black brothers, Black sisters, i want you to know that i love
> you and i hope that somewhere in your hearts you have love
> for me. My name is Assata Shakur (slave name joanne chesi-
> mard), and i am a revolutionary. A Black revolutionary. By
> that i mean that i have declared war on all forces that have
> raped our women, castrated our men, and kept our babies
> empty-bellied.
>
> I have declared war on the rich who prosper on our
> poverty, the politicians who lie to us with smiling faces, and
> all the mindless, heartless robots who protect them and their
> property.
>
> I am a Black revolutionary, and, as such, i am a victim of
> all the wrath, hatred, and slander that amerika is capable

of. Like all other Black revolutionaries, amerika is trying to lynch me.

I am a Black revolutionary woman, and because of this i have been charged with and accused of every alleged crime in which a woman was believed to have participated. The alleged crimes in which only men were supposedly involved, i have been accused of planning. They have plastered pictures alleged to be me in post offices, airports, hotels, police cars, subways, banks, television, and newspapers. They have offered over fifty thousand dollars in rewards for my capture and they have issued orders to shoot on sight and shoot to kill.

I am a Black revolutionary, and, by definition, that makes me a part of the Black Liberation Army. The pigs have used their newspapers and TVs to paint the Black Liberation Army as vicious, brutal, mad-dog criminals. They have called us gangsters and gun molls and have compared us to such characters as john dillinger and ma barker. It should be clear, it must be clear to anyone who can think, see, or hear, that we are the victims. The victims and not the criminals.

It should also be clear to us by now who the real criminals are. Nixon and his crime partners have murdered hundreds of Third World brothers and sisters in Vietnam, Cambodia, Mozambique, Angola, and South Africa. As was proved by Watergate, the top law enforcement officials in this country are a lying bunch of criminals. The president, two attorney generals, the head of the fbi, the head of the cia, and half the white house staff have been implicated in the Watergate crimes.

They call us murderers, but we did not murder over two hundred fifty unarmed Black men, women, and children, or wound thousands of others in the riots they provoked during the sixties. The rulers of this country have always considered their property more important than our lives. They call us murderers, but we were not responsible for the twenty-eight brother inmates and nine hostages murdered at attica. They call us murderers, but we did not murder and wound over thirty unarmed Black students at Jackson State—or Southern State, either.

They call us murderers, but we did not murder Martin

Luther King, Jr., Emmett Till, Medgar Evers, Malcolm X, George Jackson, Nat Turner, James Chaney, and countless others. We did not murder, by shooting in the back, sixteen-year-old Rita Lloyd, eleven-year-old Rickie Bodden, or ten-year-old Clifford Glover. They call us murderers, but we do not control or enforce a system of racism and oppression that systematically murders Black and Third World people. Although Black people supposedly comprise about fifteen percent of the total amerikkkan population, at least sixty percent of murder victims are Black. For every pig that is killed in the so-called line of duty, there are at least fifty Black people murdered by the police.

Black life expectancy is much lower than white and they do their best to kill us before we are even born. We are burned alive in fire-trap tenements. Our brothers and sisters OD daily from heroin and methadone. Our babies die from lead poisoning. Millions of Black people have died as a result of indecent medical care. This is murder. But they have got the gall to call us murderers.

They call us kidnappers, yet Brother Clark Squire (who is accused, along with me, of murdering a new jersey state trooper) was kidnapped on April 2, 1969, from our Black community and held on one million dollars' ransom in the New York Panther 21 conspiracy case. He was acquitted on May 13, 1971, along with all the others, of 156 counts of conspiracy by a jury that took less than two hours to deliberate. Brother Squire was innocent. Yet he was kidnapped from his community and family. Over two years of his life was stolen, but they call us kidnappers. We did not kidnap the thousands of Brothers and Sisters held captive in amerika's concentration camps. Ninety percent of the prison population in this country are Black and Third World people who can afford neither bail nor lawyers.

They call us thieves and bandits. They say we steal. But it was not we who stole millions of Black people from the continent of Africa. We were robbed of our language, of our Gods, of our culture, of our human dignity, of our labor, and of our lives. They call us thieves, yet it is not we who rip off billions of dollars every year through tax evasions, illegal price fixing, embezzlement, consumer fraud, bribes, kickbacks, and swindles. They call us bandits, yet every time most Black people pick up our paychecks we are being robbed. Every time we walk into a store in our neighborhood we are being held up. And every time we pay our rent the landlord sticks a gun into our ribs.

They call us thieves, but we did not rob and murder millions of Indians by ripping off their homeland, then call ourselves pioneers. They call us bandits, but it is not we who are robbing Africa, Asia, and Latin America of their natural resources and freedom while the people who live there are sick and starving. The rulers of this country and their flunkies have committed some of the most brutal, vicious crimes in history. They are the bandits. They are the murderers. And they should be treated as such. These maniacs are not fit to judge me, Clark, or any other Black person on trial in amerika. Black people should and, inevitably, must determine our destinies.

Every revolution in history has been accomplished by actions, although words are necessary. We must create shields that protect us and spears that penetrate our enemies. Black people must learn how to struggle by struggling. We must learn by our mistakes.

I want to apologize to you, my Black brothers and sisters, for being on the new jersey turnpike. I should have known better. The turnpike is a checkpoint where Black people are stopped, searched, harassed, and assaulted. Revolutionaries must never be in too much of a hurry or make careless decisions. He who runs when the sun is sleeping will stumble many times.

Every time a Black Freedom Fighter is murdered or captured, the pigs try to create the impression that they have quashed the movement, destroyed our forces, and put down the Black Revolution. The pigs also try to give the impression that five or ten guerrillas are responsible for every revolutionary action carried out in amerika. That is nonsense. That is absurd. Black revolutionaries do not drop from the moon. We are created by our conditions. Shaped by our oppression. We are being manufactured in droves in the ghetto streets, places like attica, san quentin, bedford hills, leavenworth, and sing sing. They are turning out thousands of us. Many jobless

Black veterans and welfare mothers are joining our ranks. Brothers and sisters from all walks of life, who are tired of suffering passively, make up the BLA.

There is, and always will be, until every Black man, woman, and child is free, a Black Liberation Army. The main function of the Black Liberation Army at this time is to create good examples, to struggle for Black freedom, and to prepare for the future. We must defend ourselves and let no one disrespect us. We must gain our liberation by any means necessary.

> *It is our duty to fight for our freedom.*
> *It is our duty to win.*
> *We must love each other and support each other.*
> *We have nothing to lose but our chains:*

In the spirit of:

Ronald Carter
William Christmas
Mark Clark
Mark Essex
Frank "Heavy" Fields
Woodie Changa Olugbala Green
Fred Hampton
Lil' Bobby Hutton
George Jackson
Jonathan Jackson
James McClain
Harold Russell
Zayd Malik Shakur
Anthony Kumu Olugbala White

We must fight on.

The workhouse had a whole heap of rules, most of them stupid. No newspapers or magazines were permitted. When i asked why we couldn't read newspapers, they told me that newspapers were "inflammatory." Obviously, if a person read in the paper that his or her sister had been raped, he would wait until the rapist came to jail and then do him bodily harm.

"But," i protested, "the other inmates watch television and listen to the radio (i wasn't allowed either). They could receive the same information that way or from a visit from home."

"In that case," the warden told me, "we don't let you read newspapers because they are a fire hazard."

One of the saddest rules prohibited children from visiting their mothers in jail. I could see the children waiting outside, looking up at that ugly old building with sad, frustrated faces. Their mothers would run to the only window that faced the parking lot just to get a glimpse of their children. Yelling out of the window was a no-no, but once in a while somebody would get carried away. Sometimes their frantic screams went unheard.

Gradually, i began to know the women. They were all very kind to me and treated me like a sister. They laughed like hell when i told them that i was supposedly being protected from them. Those first days, before i had really learned to maneuver with one hand, they did whatever they could to make things easier for me. They volunteered to iron my uniforms and sneak them into the laundry to be washed more than once a week. When they told me their charges and the time they were doing, i couldn't believe it. Quite a few of them were doing time for the numbers, either six months or a year. In New York, doing time for number running was practically unheard of, and it certainly didn't get six months or a year. Everybody in the world knows that the numbers business keeps the cops fat. These women hadn't hurt anybody or stolen anything, yet they were sitting in jail, probably busted by the same cops that they paid off. Their only crime was competing with the state lottery. Most of them had already been sentenced. If the sentence was less than a year, time was served in the county jail rather than in the state penitentiary.

If i had expected to find so-called hardened criminals or bigtime female gangsters or gun molls in the workhouse, i would have been sadly disappointed. The rest of the women who weren't doing time for the numbers were in for some form of petty theft, like shoplifting or passing bad checks. Most of those sisters were on welfare and all of them had been barely able to make ends meet. The courts had shown them no mercy. They brought in this sister shortly after i arrived who was eight months pregnant and had been sentenced to a month for shoplifting something that cost less than twenty dollars.

Later a middle-aged sister began coming to the workhouse on

weekends. She worked during the week and served her six-month sentence for drunken driving on weekends. Knowing that white women with the same charges would never have received such a sentence, i thought it was harsh. But i didn't realize how harsh until she told me that she had been arrested for drunken driving in the driveway of her own house. She hadn't even been on a public road. She also told me that the cops had arrested her because they didn't like the way she talked to them.

In that jail it was nothing to see a woman brought in all beat up. In some cases, the only charge was "resisting arrest." A Puerto Rican sister was brought in one night. She had been so badly beaten by the police that the matron on duty didn't want to admit her. "I don't want her dying on my shift," she kept saying. It was days before this sister was able to get out of bed.

In spite of it all, those sisters kept the place jumping. They told all kinds of funny stories about their lives, things they had seen and experienced. Some had a natural knack for comedy. What amazed me was the way they told the saddest stories in the world and made everybody laugh about them.

Girl, that nigga was always in my pocketbook stealing my money. And all he did with it was blow it at the racetracks. Girl, that man spent so much money on the racetracks, he made me wish i was a horse. One day i fixed his ass, though. I was sick and tired of his mess. Betcha he won't go in no-body's pocketbook no time soon. I put a mousetrap in that sucker. Girl, you should have heard that nigga howl.

My husband and me, we used to fight like cats and dogs. And he was jealous as the day is long. Chile, we went to the bar this night and the nigga got all high, and started thinkin' i was messing around with some dude at the bar. As soon as we got outside, boy, he jumped on me like a gorilla jumps on a banana. Don't you know that man hit me so hard he knocked my teeth straight out of my mouth. "Now, hold on a minute!" i told that fool. "We can fight later. I ain't got no 'nother four hundred dollars to spend on no false teeth." Chile, we was drunk as skunks, down on our knees for 'bout an hour looking for those teeth. And when that fool found them, he said the teeth jumped up and tried to bite him. Lord, chile, that man is a fool.

I could listen to these stories only when the outside door was open. During the day they had a female "sheriff's officer" posted outside my cell. When she was there, the door usually stayed open.

The whole time i was at that jail i saw very few white women. The few who did come were there only a few hours or a day or so before they were bailed out. There was one white woman who was busted on the turnpike with fifty pounds of reefer. Everyone waited to see what her bail would be. Then we found out she had been released on her own recognizance (that is, without bond). To be released on recognizance in the state of new jersey, one of the requirements is jersey residence. The woman lived in Vermont. But nobody was really shocked. She was white. . . .

My mother brings my daughter to see me at the clinton correctional facility for women in new jersey, where i had been sent from alderson. I am delirious. She looks so tall. I run up to kiss her. She barely responds. She is distant and stand-offish. Pangs of guilt and sorrow fill my chest. I can see that my child is suffering. It is stupid to ask what is wrong. She is four years old, and except for these pitiful little visits—although my mother has brought her to see me every week, wherever i am, with the exception of the time i was in alderson—she has never been with her mother. I can feel something welling up in my baby. I look at my mother, my face a question mark. My mother is suffering too. I try to play. I make my arms into an elephant's trunk stalking around the visiting room jungle. It does not work. My daughter refuses to play baby elephant, or tiger, or anything. She looks at me like i am the buffoon i must look like. I try the choo-choo train routine and the la, la, la song, but she is not amused. I try talking to her, but she is puffed up and sullen.

I go over and try to hug her. In a hot second she is all over me. All i can feel are these little four-year-old fists banging away at me. Every bit of her force is in those punches, they really hurt. I let her hit me until she is tired. "It's all right," i tell her. "Let it all out." She is standing in front of me, her face contorted with anger, looking spent. She backs away and leans against the wall. "It's okay," i tell her. "Mommy understands." "You're not my mother," she screams, the tears rolling down her face. "You're not my mother and I hate you." I feel like crying too. I know she is confused about who i am. She calls me Mommy Assata and she calls my mother Mommy.

I try to pick her up. She knocks my hand away. "You can get out of here, if you want to," she screams. "You just don't want to." "No, i can't," i say, weakly. "Yes you can," she accuses. "You just don't want to."

I look helplessly at my mother. Her face is choked with pain. "Tell her to try to open the bars," she says in a whisper.

"I can't open the door," i tell my daughter. "I can't get through the bars. You try and open the bars."

My daughter goes over to the barred door that leads to the visiting room. She pulls and she pushes. She yanks and she hits and she kicks the bars until she falls on the floor, a heap of exhaustion. I go over and pick her up. I hold and rock and kiss her. There is a look of resignation on her face that i can't stand. We spend the rest of the visit talking and playing quietly on the floor. When the guard says the visit is over, i cling to her for dear life. She holds her head high, and her back straight as she walks out of the prison. She waves good-bye to me, her face clouded and worried, looking like a little adult. I go back to my cage and cry until i vomit. I decide that it is time to leave.

This whole story sucked (emotionally)

THE LITERARY
RENAISSANCE

MALCOLM BRALY
1925–1980

When Malcolm Braly died in an automobile crash in 1980, he had been out of prison for fifteen years. This was the only extended period of freedom in his adult life. It was also the time when he was beginning to attain recognition as one of the finest novelists to emerge from America's prisons.

First incarcerated in 1942 at the age of seventeen, Braly spent most of the next quarter of a century doing four terms for burglary and armed robbery. He began writing fiction during his third stretch in San Quentin, and his first three published novels were written behind bars: Felony Tank *(1961),* Shake Him Till He Rattles *(1963), and* It's Cold out There *(1966). When the California prison authorities threatened to revoke Braly's parole because he was working on a manuscript based on his prison experience, he had to finish it surreptitiously and delay publication until he was off parole. Published in 1967 as* On the Yard, *it was labeled by Kurt Vonnegut as "the great American prison novel"—a judgment echoed by many. Braly's 1976 autobiography,* False Starts: A Memoir of San Quentin and Other Prisons, *was immediately recognized as a work of major importance and led to the reprinting of his four novels.*

On the Yard *brilliantly dramatizes the deadening sameness and implacable power of prison, the convict fantasies that vitalize some lives and destroy others, the ways in which inmates replicate the exploitative relationships of the society that has entrapped them, and the diversity and potential of the lives concealed inside prison uniforms. The pivotal figure is Chilly Willy, a ruthless manipulator whose downfall comes when his icy shell is cracked by a passion—the closest he can come to love—for a convict queen.*

from *On the Yard*

"THINK OF all them fools out there bustin their asses so them bitches can sit under those hair dryers," Chilly Willy said idly.

It was six-thirty by his watch. He knew the sun was probably shining already out there in the free world, but it hadn't yet crested the high walls of the big yard. Chilly was cold but he was trying not to show it. He had read somewhere that if you relaxed when you were cold, rather than hunching and shivering, it was easier to bear. It seemed to be true. He wasn't comfortable, but neither was he giving anyone the satisfaction of appearing uncomfortable.

"Sure," Society Red was saying, "but look at all the bedtime action those fools are getting." Red jumped up, spun around and shouted "Hot cock!" like a street vendor.

"That's a trick's notion," Chilly Willy said, amused scorn playing in his eyes. "I don't know, Red, I'm trying to educate the fool out of you, but sometimes I wonder if it isn't buried too deep."

"I ain't real swift," Red acknowledged slyly. "If I was I wouldn't be beating this yard morning after morning."

Chilly smiled at the shaft. Red was the type of stud that just when you were sure he was a fool and a clown came up with something half sharp. The two men were watching the other inmates straggling from the mess hall. It was a hungry morning. There were three such mornings and today's was French toast, an offering so distorted in mass production that it was often referred to as fried linoleum. Another hungry morning featured a stack of thick and sodden hot cakes cooked hours before. The third and most dreaded was a notorious concoction known as the square egg, prepared from powdered eggs and fatback, baked into rubbery sheets, which were cut into square servings. The square egg was universally regarded as inedible.

Hungry mornings meant little to Chilly Willy. He seldom ate mainline chow. At the moment he was looking for someone who owed him, who could be pressured into standing in the canteen line for rolls and coffee, sometimes an hour's wait, and a job so humble he wouldn't even ask Red to do it unless it were important.

"And here he comes," Red said, "just like he never left."

Chilly turned to watch Nunn walking towards them through the clusters of shivering cons sheltered under the rain shed. He moved as if he were seriously ill and there was nothing in his drained and leaden face to contradict this impression except the brittle light of his flat gray eyes.

"You come back to die?" Chilly asked.

"No, to build myself up. Those streets tear up your health."

The two men shook hands.

"Well, what'd you bring this time?" Chilly asked.

"Nothing much. A one to five for Receiving."

"Receiving?" Chilly was incredulous.

"They set me up, Chilly. They flat set me up. In court they claimed I'd turned out Jimmy Brown—you remember him?"

"The freak they used to call Frosty?"

"That's the one. They claimed I put him to boosting for his fixes."

"Did you?"

"More or less."

"That's you then, isn't it?"

"One stinking suit. That's what they nailed me on."

"It was good enough, wasn't it?"

"I guess it was. We're not holding this conversation in the lobby of the St. Francis."

"And how many times have you stood right here and said no one but a fool would steal anything but money?"

"Okay, Chilly."

"I hope you looked real clean in that hot suit."

"It didn't fit."

Red started laughing and Nunn turned to ask, "You still putting out them withered backs of yours?"

"I ain't puttin out nothing 'cept'n old people's eyeballs."

"Well." Chilly ignored the byplay. "You had your vacation. How long? Seven months?"

"That's no record, but you're whipping around pretty fast. Well, it's only a nickel, even if they stick it all to you, you can still see the end of it."

"Chilly, you going to score?" Red wanted to know.

"Just hang tough until I find a horse to put in the line."

Nunn slapped his hollow stomach. "Good. Long as I've been looking at that slop, I still can't eat it. You'd think I'd get used to it."

"It's not really food," Chilly said in the solemn mocking tone he thought of as his educational voice. "It's more like fuel. Like Presto logs. It'll keep you moving around if you don't want to move too fast, and they're not keen to have you move too fast anyway."

"This time I'd like to make some of those variety shows they put on for the free people. They scoff them good steaks."

"What're you going to do on the variety show," Red wanted to know. "Perform on the meat whistle?"

"Hit it, punk," Nunn said. "I wouldn't move in on your specialty."

"Your mammy's specialty," Red countered.

But Nunn had turned back to Chilly. "How about it, Chilly, couldn't you get us on the show as stagehands, or some other light-weight shuck. We could lay up and eyeball them fine broads, then fix on free-world food."

"Maybe," Chilly said.

"You want to get in some righteous eyeballing?" Red asked, beginning to clamor for attention. "Make it to church. Some of them Christer broads are all right."

"All right for your mammy," Nunn said. "Adenoidal, pinch-breasted, dry-crotched, nowhere bunch of hymn-singing pigs."

"Your mammy's a pig."

Chilly Willy sighed. "Sometimes I wonder why I stand out here year after year listening to you two swapping mammies."

"Because you got nothing better to do and nowhere else to do it," Nunn said in a much different tone from the one he used for banter with Red.

Chilly smiled an acknowledgment, but made no answer. He had continued to monitor the men who were still filtering from the mess hall, and now he stepped forward to call, *"Larson!"* Then he hooked his thumbs in his back pockets while he waited for Larson to come to him. Chilly Willy wasn't corny. He created an impression of taut, finely drawn, but elastic strength, and with it there was a contrary suggestion of denseness as if he would be difficult to move from any spot where he had chosen to stand. His eyes were habitually mocking, elaborately insincere, but they also conveyed a sense of still, cold bottoms.

"You owe me?" Chilly asked when Larson was shuffling unhappily in front of him. Larson nodded. "And you've been owing me for some time?"

Nunn and Society Red watched, but without any pose of menace. Menace wasn't their game. Each of them in his own way was interested in the discomfort Larson was so obviously experiencing. Society Red inserted his left index finger in his right nostril and his eyes grew somber as he mined this lode. He removed something, examined it, then wiped it on his pants leg.

Chilly was nodding thoughtfully. "I may have to sell your debt to Gasolino for collection. You've heard of Gasolino?"

Larson had. Everyone had. Nunn and Society Red were smiling now watching the dismay on Larson's face. They were Gasolino's buddies and this was their share of his power. Nunn had come up in the same four-square blocks with Gasolino, the lapland between a poor white neighborhood and an even poorer Mexican neighborhood, and they had smoked their first pot together, tea they had called it then, or gage, and banged their first bitches and gone on heavy together. Now they all knew Gasolino had flipped—the evidence was clear in his round mad eyes. For years he had been sniffing the carbon tet from the joint fire extinguishers. The Mexican boys had named him Gasolino because he drank gasoline mixed with milk.

He was an excellent collector of bad debts not because he was the most dangerous man in the prison, though he was dangerous enough, but because he didn't seem to be afraid of anything. He was always laughing even when he was sticking shoe leather to someone's head.

"I'll get it up, Chilly," Larson was saying. "Everything's been going sour on me, but I got stuff coming. You'll get paid."

"I better. And for now, suppose you jump in that canteen line and get me a package of rolls and three jars of coffee."

"Sure, Chilly," Larson said already moving. "Glad to."

Nunn watched Larson take his place at the end of the line. "Fear's an awful thing to see," he said lightly.

"Yeah," Chilly agreed. "We'll brood about it while we scoff them rolls."

The big yard was beginning to clear. The last men had moved reluctantly from the warmth of the mess hall and now the sluggish traffic was shifting through the big gate at the head of the yard. The guards stood with their hands in their pockets, neither looking nor not looking. Occasionally they said "Move along" to no one in particular. Assigned men were supposed to be going to work, but since out of the five thousand there were over fifteen hundred unassigned it was impossible in most instances to know who was supposed to be heading towards their jobs and who didn't have to—or didn't get to, depending upon their individual attitude. The guards watched the blue figures moving along with denim collars turned up and long-billed caps pulled down and they quickly became a shuffling blur. "The bastards all look the same," the guards said. They were like cowboys riding the edge of a vast herd—only the exceptional or troublesome animal ever became fixed in their minds as an individual.

By seven-thirty Chilly's horse was fifty men from the head of the canteen line, and the sun they still couldn't see was beginning to glow on the breasts of the seagulls drifting restlessly from wall to wall. The domino games were starting, and a quartet of Negroes were loud-talking each other, their voices clearly audible a hundred feet away.

"Sucker, you bes' be keerful. I stick big-six to yore ass."

"Now, you jus' signifying, fool. I got big-six myself."

"Maybe you eat it too."

"Get on! You can't play no dominos, you jus' play mouf." They slammed the dominos at the wooden table with furious energy.

The yard crew, all outpatient psych cases, came sweeping down with street brooms. They moved in a line like beaters attempting to flush a tiger. They flushed orange peels, apple cores and empty cigarette packs.

Chilly was beginning to take a few bets. He was currently booking football. In the winter he booked basketball and in the spring and summer baseball. When the tracks were running he booked horses. He was prepared to make some bet on any fight, national or local, or any other sports event except marble tournaments and frog jumping contests. He felt he did well.

By convict standards he was a millionaire. In various places throughout the institution he had approximately three hundred cartons of cigarettes. Several men who had reputations for holding big stuff were little more than the managers of one of Chilly's ware-houses. He never exposed their floor shows. They took heat off him and when occasionally they were busted and the cigarettes lost to confiscation, Chilly accepted it as a business reverse. If he cornered every butt in the joint and a year of futures he still wouldn't have anything, but the slower and more difficult accumulation of soft money could some day mean something. In the hollow handle of the broom leaning carelessly in the corner of his cell he had a roll of bills totaling close to a thousand dollars. If the Classification Committee became careless he might get a chance to use it.

This was money he had made handling nasal inhalers. The economics of this trade were fierce and the profits, by anyone's standards, enormous.

Chilly had hit the big yard broke at twenty-three. He had borrowed enough to subscribe to a national sports sheet, and by consistently following the picks of the experts, rather than betting by signs, hunches and hometown prejudice, he had won far more than he had lost. A steady flow of cigarettes had moved into his hands, but they had proved an inconvenience and he had decided to put them to work. He needed an important horse, a free man horse, and he had finally settled on a clerk in the mail office, a small man with meager eyes and a sad fringe of soft hair. His name was Harmon and he was partially crippled. Chilly had made friends with Harmon and had spent hours telling Harmon how different kinds of girls were, thinking with some bitterness that he probably knew even less from actual experience than the small brown man who listened to him so avidly. On Harmon's birthday Chilly had given him a hand-tooled wallet he had taken in lieu of a debt from an inmate hobby worker. In the secret compartment he had placed a twenty-dollar bill. Harmon hadn't returned the bill to Chilly, and he hadn't reported it to custody either. He's ready, Chilly had decided. *Gaining trust*

But it had been another month before Harmon would start packing. He had been scared, but he had been greedy too, and he had wavered, and once had almost cried. But Chilly had continued to press him until Harmon agreed to smuggle the nasal inhalers in his lunch. Then, of course, he hadn't been able to stop. Chilly paid him well.

These inhalers of various brands were packed with an average of three hundred milligrams of amphetamine sulphate or some similar drug with the same properties, and retailed in any drugstore for approximately seventy-five cents. Harmon was paid two dollars for each tube he smuggled in, and Chilly, without ever touching them, turned them over to his front man in the gym.

At this point the inhalers were cracked open and the cottons in which the active drug was suspended were removed. It was tacitly understood that if a tube were cut into thirds, the thirds were sold for halves, and if it were cut into fourths, the fourths were sold for thirds, on down to tenths which were actually fifteenths. Such a fifteenth, wrapped in wax paper, was sold for either three dollars soft money or a carton of cigarettes. The profit was approximately thirty-five dollars on a single inhaler.

The wads of charged cotton were known as leapers because of the energy and optimism they released in the men who choked them down, but except for those just below Chilly no mainline user ever managed to secure enough of the drug to do more than mildly stimulate himself, and having already paid high for this, he promptly paid a second time with a sleepless night where he lay up listening to the faint jingle and creak of the guards moving through the darkness, and continued to pay through the memories of the women he had once known, more vivid now and swelling until they seemed almost tangible in the feel of his hot crumpled pillow and the lonely dream of his hand. And pay finally watching the bars emerge against the dawn of another prison day.

"No more," they said. It was better to build time as a vegetable than to suffer as a man. But a week would pass and this powerful antidote for monotony would begin to seem attractive again, and they would find themselves thinking, "If I could just score enough to really get on." And they would start scheming on the money that would further enrich Chilly Willy.

The money came in over the visiting table. Their women brought it—the mothers, daughters, girl friends, aunts, grandmothers, sisters and wives. Custody was aware of this, and procedures had been established to prevent it, but there was a major flaw in their routine. It had long been observed that officers conducting shakedowns were skittish around the crotch. They slapped vigorously and thoroughly up the legs until instinct warned them that their next upward reach would encounter the mechanism hanging there and they stopped suddenly and shifted their attention to another part of the body. Some inmates had small pockets sewn in the crotches of their shorts, others carried a piece of adhesive tape to fix the bill to their scrotum.

Money flowed in steadily, saved out of the women's small salaries, saved out of their pension and welfare checks, not only as a further gift of life to their fathers, sons, husbands and brothers, but because the women almost always hated the system of bars, locks and badges more than their men.

The edge of the sun was beginning to show over the east block before the rolls and coffee were delivered to Chilly. The yard began to warm, the sky was clear. They unbuttoned their jackets. During the fall and winter any day it didn't rain was a good day.

Chilly opened the rolls and squeezed one of them. He smiled wryly. These rolls sat in a supermarket until it came time to rotate them, then they were sold without reduction in price on the inmate canteen. That this practice differed in no essential from selling a third of a tube for a half was an irony that wasn't lost on Chilly Willy.

"Want some of this hardtack?" he asked Nunn.

"Try me," Society Red said, already reaching for a roll.

"I would," Chilly said, "if only you weren't so godawful ugly."

"Put him face to the wall," Nunn suggested.

"It don't help. His backs are like a bramble patch."

"I got your bramble patch hanging," Red countered.

"Don't trip over it."

Red scowled in confusion. He was obviously trying to come up with something sharp.

"And don't start in on my mammy," Chilly said quietly.

"I wouldn't do that, Chilly."

"Just don't. Sometime I'd like to see one morning go by without dragging our mothers into it."

Society Red nodded respectfully while Nunn watched with a faint smile. They squatted down on their heels like Yaquis, the open package of rolls in the center. There were eight rolls, two apiece and two left over. This arithmetic was of vital interest to Red. He wasn't able to enjoy the roll he was eating because he was afraid he was going to have to settle for two rolls while the others ate three apiece. It wasn't just his hunger, and he was hungry, but each time he was sloughed off with the short end of the goodies his place in the group was clearly defined for that moment—a mascot, or a pet. Under this pressure he remembered an entertainment he had planned, and he took a coverless magazine from his pocket. The edge was frayed and soiled. Opening it to a photograph he passed the magazine to Chilly.

"How'd you like to stick this fine freak bitch?"

Chilly glanced at a woman posed in a brief costume of feathers and rhinestones. He was automatically suspicious of any leading question and in addition there was something odd about the woman, something indefinable; it was sufficient to cause him to flip back to the masthead of the magazine. It was titled *Gay*. He handed the magazine back to Red.

"You were right about the freak part."

Red looked put down. "How'd you figure it was a freak, Chilly?"

"A man in trick pants is still a man."

Nunn said, "I've seen them when you couldn't tell them from broads. Real freaks."

"If I couldn't tell a sissy from a broad, I'd begin to worry about myself," Chilly said.

Red replaced the magazine in his back pocket. "As far as I'm concerned there ain't no difference. Action's action."

Nunn rocked on his heels, sipping his coffee. He held out his hand to watch his fingers tremble. "I'm whipped," he said. "I had an oil burner going. The nut was a bill a day."

"I told you," Chilly said.

"That's easy to do."

"I still told you."

"What do you want? A medal or some kind of a certificate?"

"I want you to stay in shape to take care of business—now that playtime's over."

"Shit, I might just jump up and file my nut hand."

"You already did that when you went out there and strapped that habit on your ass."

"Ahhh, I don't know, Chilly, sometimes it was like part of me was dead, and it was worth anything to be able to forget it for a while."

"By hiding?"

"Why not?"

"Well, there's nothing to hide in here. The joint's clean of heavy."

Nunn shrugged. Talk faltered and they sat in silence. Red was starting on his second roll.

"¡Ese!"

They all looked up to see Gasolino standing over them. Short, massive, heavy-headed, his hair chopped off short and smoothed down over his forehead with a thick pomade. His eyes seemed mostly iris and they held no true focus. He might be looking straight at you, and he might not. No one could tell, and few wanted to ask.

"What's happening, maniáco?" Nunn asked.

Gasolino stared at him. "Hey, what you doing back?"

"I didn't go out. I was in the hospital."

"¿Verdad?"

"Righteous. How you making it?"

"I'm straight," Gasolino boasted. His eyes glittered and his hand sketched a slow dreamy oval in the air.

"What're you straight on?" Chilly asked. "Lighter fluid?"

"No, man, good stuff."

"Glue from the furniture factory," Nunn said.

Chilly kicked the package of rolls. There were two left. "Eat these damn things," he told Gasolino.

Gasolino squatted down between Nunn and Society Red, and pulled the package towards him with one hand, scooping the remaining cellophane free with a bearish swipe of his other hand. He took half a roll in one bite, and chewing, unable to talk, he motioned for Red's coffee. Red handed it over and quickly folded his arms. He turned to find Nunn smiling at him.

"What's funny, you tuberculosis-looking mother fucker?"

"Red, you're a side show."

Society Red started to say Your mammy's a side show, but he remembered Chilly's warning and kept silent.

Gasolino cleared his mouth and leaned towards Chilly. "You got any action for me?"

"Nothing right now."

"I get restless. Then these bulls start looking easy to me." Gasolino grinned. "Maybe I fire on one of them."

"That's a good way to get your ass gang stomped," Red said. "They work on you in shifts."

"It's a form of group insurance they've devised," Nunn added.

But Gasolino only stared at them, grinning his contempt for anything bulls might find to do.

A young guard walked up to them. His face was stern, probably because he was afraid no one was going to take him seriously. "If any of you men are assigned, you'd better move out."

They didn't move or answer.

"Oberholster, I know you've got a job."

Chilly stood up slowly. It was closely timed. Twice the young guard opened his mouth to say something, then hesitated, uncertain. Then Gasolino started hissing through his teeth.

"Knock that off!"

"¿Qué?" Gasolino asked blandly, his eyes opaque and dim.

The guard made a shooing motion like a farmwife hustling chickens. "All right, break it up. Move along. Oberholster, you better get to work."

Chilly moved off, Red at his side. After a few steps he started whistling "When They Ring Out Those Golden Bells," a hymn he had heard his mother singing many times. He didn't remember the words or even that it was a hymn, but he whistled forcefully down the scale where his mother had once sung: "A glor-ee hal-a-lu-ya ju-ba-lee!"

"I think I'll hit the gym," Red said.

"Okay, I'll see you up there."

As they were passing the long stucco building that housed the education department, someone hailed Chilly, and he turned to find a man he knew as Juleson coming towards him. Juleson was a notorious state man. He had a yellow pencil behind his ear, and a bunch of keys hooked to his belt.

"Oberholster, can I borrow a box at three-for-two?"

"Maybe. Which draw will you pay on?"

"The second draw in December. That's about a month."

"That's right. Did you learn lightning calculation in there?" Chilly indicated the ed building.

Juleson smiled. "How about it?"

"Sure, three-for-two's my game. What kind you want?"

"Camels."

"Come on up to the gym, I'll get them for you."

The gym was reached by crossing a narrow footbridge that spanned the industrial alley and then climbing three flights of metal stairs that zigzagged up the outside of the building. On the stairs, Chilly touched the keys at Juleson's belt.

"You must be a wheel," he said.

"Half of them don't open anything."

"Then you might say they were decorative?"

"They were on the ring when they gave it to me. They don't give me a feeling of mastery, if that's what you're getting at."

Chilly smiled. "Curiosity's my vice, and you're a stud who provokes curiosity."

They were entering the gym with its stench of sweat and liniment. "Not intentionally," Juleson said. Their shoes rang hollowly on the splintered planks.

"That makes a difference."

He went up to the wire cage from which the athletic equipment was issued, and asked the inmate on duty, "Caterpillar around?"

"Caterpillar!"

The stuttering rhythm of a speed bag was audible from the boxing section, and from the opposite side in the weight lifting section came the thump and ring of iron. A young blond man, over two hundred pounds, stepped through a door in back of the equipment cage.

"What's happening, Chilly?"

"Give this stud a box of Camels."

"Three-for-two?"

"Yeah, but—" He turned to Juleson. "You pay me. That'll put it on a more personal basis."

Juleson appeared vaguely uneasy, but he accepted the carton of cigarettes Caterpillar brought from the back room, and told Chilly, "Thanks."

"No thanks needed. It's just business."

Chilly watched Juleson walk away and start back down the steps. He turned to Red. "That's one box I hope I get beat for."

"You're jiving."

"What's a box?" Chilly asked.

"It's the idea of it—no one burns you."

"That's right."

Chilly started off, then turned back. Red was already headed for the boxing section. "Hey, Red, let me look at that freak book."

ETHERIDGE KNIGHT
1931–1991

Raised as one of a poor black family's seven children in a rural Mississippi town, Etheridge Knight dropped out of school in the ninth grade, worked as a shoeshine boy, hung out in bars and poolrooms, served four years in the army after enlisting at the age of sixteen, was wounded in the Korean War, became a drug addict and street hustler, and in 1960 was sentenced to serve ten to twenty-five years in the Indiana State Prison for snatching a purse.

In 1973, Knight was nominated for both the Pulitzer Prize and the National Book Award, and he soon won the American Book Award for Poetry, the Shelley Memorial Prize for Poetry, a Guggenheim Fellowship, teaching positions at several universities, and wide recognition as a major American poet. He explained what had transformed his life on the cover of his stunning first volume, Poems from Prison, *published in 1968, the year he was paroled: "I died in Korea from a shrapnel wound and narcotics resurrected me. I died in 1960 from a prison sentence and poetry brought me back to life."*

But Knight was already a poet before his incarceration— an oral poet in an Afro-American art form that has played a major role not only in Afro-American culture but in American culture and hence global culture. Drifting through the bars and poolrooms of the urban ghettos, Knight had become a master of "toasts," memorized and improvised long narrative poems, usually in rhymed couplets, often celebrating the sexual and fighting prowess of either the poet or some folk hero. During his six years in prison, he continued to develop the art of the toast and simultaneously began to transmute it into written forms of poetry. One can still hear the tones and cadences of the toast within some of his subsequently most anthologized poems, especially if one listens to the 1968 recording of Knight reading Poems from Prison *to a jazz-band accompaniment in Indiana State Prison (the tape was issued by Broadside Press when it published that first volume). One can also hear in Knight's poetry the continuity from slave songs to toasts to modern-day rap.*

The Warden Said to Me the Other Day

The warden said to me the other day
(innocently, I think), "Say, etheridge,
why come the black boys don't run off
like the white boys do?"
I lowered my jaw and scratched my head
and said (innocently, I think), "Well, suh,
I ain't for sure, but I reckon it's 'cause
we ain't got nowheres to run to."

Hard Rock Returns to Prison from the Hospital for the Criminal Insane

Hard Rock / was / "known not to take no shit
From nobody," and he had the scars to prove it:
Split purple lips, lumped ears, welts above
His yellow eyes, and one long scar that cut
Across his temple and plowed through a thick
Canopy of kinky hair.

The WORD / was / that Hard Rock wasn't a mean nigger
Anymore, that the doctors had bored a hole in his head,
Cut out part of his brain, and shot electricity
Through the rest. When they brought Hard Rock back,
Handcuffed and chained, he was turned loose,
Like a freshly gelded stallion, to try his new status.
And we all waited and watched, like a herd of sheep,
To see if the WORD was true.

As we waited we wrapped ourselves in the cloak
Of his exploits: "Man, the last time, it took eight
Screws to put him in the Hole." "Yeah, remember when he
Smacked the captain with his dinner tray?" "He set

The record for time in the Hole—67 straight days!"
"Ol Hard Rock! man, that's one crazy nigger."
And then the jewel of a myth that Hard Rock had once bit
A screw on the thumb and poisoned him with syphilitic spit.

The testing came, to see if Hard Rock was really tame.
A hillbilly called him a black son of a bitch
And didn't lose his teeth, a screw who knew Hard Rock
From before shook him down and barked in his face.
And Hard Rock did *nothing.* Just grinned and looked silly,
His eyes empty like knot holes in a fence.

And even after we discovered that it took Hard Rock
Exactly 3 minutes to tell you his first name,
We told ourselves that he had just wised up,
Was being cool; but we could not fool ourselves for long,
And we turned away, our eyes on the ground. Crushed.
He had been our Destroyer, the doer of things
We dreamed of doing but could not bring ourselves to do,
The fears of years, like a biting whip,
Had cut deep bloody grooves
Across our backs.

For Freckle-Faced Gerald

Now you take ol Rufus. He beat drums,
was free and funky under the arms,
fucked white girls, jumped off a bridge
(and thought nothing of the sacrilege),
he copped out—and he was over twenty-one.

Take Gerald. Sixteen years hadn't even done
a good job on his voice. He didn't even know
how to talk tough, or how to hide the glow
of life before he was thrown in as "pigmeat"
for the buzzards to eat.

Gerald, who had no memory or hope of copper hot lips—
of firm upthrusting thighs
to reinforce his flow,
let tall walls and buzzards change the course
of his river from south to north.

(No safety in numbers, like back on the block:
two's aplenty. three? definitely not.
four? "you're all muslims."
five? "you were planning a race riot."
plus, Gerald could never quite win
with his precise speech and innocent grin
the trust and fists of the young black cats.)

Gerald, sun-kissed ten thousand times on the nose
and cheeks, didn't stand a chance,
didn't even know that the loss of his balls
had been plotted years in advance
by wiser and bigger buzzards than those
who now hover above his track
and at night light upon his back.

PAUL MARIAH

1937–1996

*Soon after Paul Mariah arrived in the San Francisco Bay Area
from an Illinois prison in 1966, he became a leading figure in
gay literature. In 1969, he founded* ManRoot *magazine and
ManRoot Books, which discovered and published dozens of
authors. By 1974, one reviewer noted that Mariah himself has
had "over 500 poems published in 120 magazines in four
countries in the last seven years."*

*Before the end of the 1960s, Mariah had been an editor of
three magazines besides his own; personal secretary to Robert
Duncan and Kay Boyle; one of the main researchers for the
Kinsey Report; a creative writing instructor at San Francisco*

State College; and an organizer of COSMEP (Conference of Small Magazine Editors and Publishers). In his writings, lectures, and poetry readings, Mariah continually struggled for recognition of the rights of both gays and prisoners.

"Shakedown & More," reprinted here, encapsulates a main theme of his volume The Spoon Ring *and much of his other writing: the protean nature of human beings that can turn almost any object into either an instrument of death or a symbol of love.*

Quarry/Rock: A Reality Poem in the Tradition of Genet

I.

O, Seeger, the night you tied the cabbie
to the tree
        and shot him, did you know
the shadow of the chair was waiting for you?
You, murderer, guillotined one,
You of the severed head,
You on death row for seven years,
You six feet seven taker of life,
you with the death shrouded head.

One night you walking in line
to your cell, swung and touched
hands with your love, Stevie.
You two walking in line
to your cells, swung and touched
hands. Swung hands and touched
the only way you could say good-night
swung hands and touched.

later, that same night Stevie
lying in his 6 by 9 cell

in the quiet one-man cell
in the quiet of his only home
his desires became rampant
wanting you wanting
wanting you touching him wanting

(O Seeger, what have they done to Stevie?
What have they done to Stevie?)

(The County had said his voyeur eyes
were too blue and should be
put away until the color changed to grey)

Wanting you wanting
wanting you touching him wanting

the broom became you
the broom became the strength of you
the broom became the anal worship of you
the broom became the regular stroke of you
the broom became the reality of you

until he fell off the bed
and broke
            the broom off, inside where
you were in the quiet of his night
he was visited by red horror
he was visited by red horror
not withstanding, not waking

II

O, Seeger, the night you tied the cabbie
to the tree
            and shot him, did you know . . .

that you would wait seven years
to be strapped in a chair?

that they would kill your love
in isolation, in lonely isolation?

that in the cubicle of a cell you
would want him, would want to love him?

It was the evening after you knew
Stevie had died that I heard

green tears whimper from your cell
and knew that in that severed head

you still had human tears.

(O, Seeger, what have they done to Stevie?
What have they done to Stevie?)

Later, when Stevie was taken
to pauper's field where dandelions
grow in reverence to the sun.

When his parents refused his body,
refused their son. It was then
I heard you rage like a wild tiger.

In the cold antigone of your dreams
I saw you in defiance go out
and bury the body. And in revenge
you took to the fields
looking for his parents
hiding in the forest of your dreams
in cabbie clothing.

O, Seeger, the night you tied the cabbie
to the tree
            and shot him, did you know
you still had green tears?

Always We Watch Them

They watch us always. You
And I
See their thugs drag

Blond Patrick out and down
The walk
Way to the shock room.

We know the routine. In
Weeks
Patrick will reappear

On the yard, in the circle
Walking
Walking off their casts

Muttering inconsequential
Nothings
Loudly, very loudly for all

His days to come. He is now
Among
Their number. His ears

Numbed to darkness, ache
Sput
Sputterings of electric circuit

Tangle his mind. He is engaged
To marry
The Electric Holding Company.

Shakedown & More

Silver is missing
From the messhall;
All

Prisoners suspect.
Cells torn open
Like wounds

Setting out
In search of
The germ,

The spoon stolen,
Each frisked
As he returns

To his cell.
Shakedown for
Contraband.

All known hands
Are checked
For shivs.

One lives in
Terror that it's
Not marked

For him. Still
It may be found
As a ring on

Newly wedded hand
Or as a worse attack
A knife in the back.

NORMA STAFFORD
1932–

*The youngest of ten children born to a poor farm family in
the Tennessee hills, Norma Stafford managed to get into
nurse's training at the age of nineteen. But when the school
discovered that she was a lesbian, she was forced to leave.
After a brief marriage, she began a ten-year relationship with
a woman, often running from and falling into the hands of
the law. Mainly on bad-check charges, she did time in countless local jails and spent five and a half years in Alabama and
California state prisons, where, she says, "I earned my Ph.D.
from Hell."*

*In 1972, during her second term in the California Institu-
tion for Women, she enrolled in the first college-credit class to
be offered to women in California prisons, a course on women
in society. Here she discovered a passion for the written word
and began writing whenever she could, first prose and then
poetry. Ms. magazine published some of her poems in February 1973, and in 1975 Dear Somebody, her first volume of
poetry, was published.*

*Since her parole in 1973, Norma Stafford has been living
in a rural area in Mendocino County, California. Her most
recent work is She Stands: The Daisy Benson Story, a one-
woman stage presentation in poetry and prose of the case of a
woman who was tried and sentenced to life while helpless from
the effect of massive forced doses of psychotropic drugs. Set to
music, She Stands was performed in Philadelphia in 1996.*

In Santa Cruz

Sitting warming her back in the spring sun
that dared to force its way through the cafe blinds
an ivory-handled walking cane leaned against her thigh.

The beauty of all her ages was upon her.
Seven face lines bore a hard east to west direction,
made a sharp right turn at her ear
then disappeared into the north.
Nibbling toast past her old woman's black whiskers,
hands lined like two roadmaps
gave a delicate tremble, then
lifted her cup of Sanka
and sent it chasing after the toast.
I said to her, "My sister, the growth rings of a tree
know many secrets of this life,
but the tree does not speak.
These lines that you wear
are your growth rings, hiding the
knowledge you have gained while
traveling this life for almost a century.
Tell me what you know."

She carefully wiped her almost invisible lips,
took her cane and walked away from me
leaving on her empty seat
bits of bark and one oak leaf.

The Gone One

"Count Time! Count Time!"

One hundred twenty feet
scuttling toward respective cells,
outlined with goodnight embraces and kisses
(called "queer actions" by our keepers).
Instant silence as the whole shuts its mouth
for what, behind locked cell doors?
To pee, flush toilets, to masturbate its body and life
searching for the brightness of come
trying to burn out the shadows of bars
transmitted on nosey moonbeams.

No voices now.

In crepe-soled hush puppy oxfords
the Guard (she calls herself a W.C.S. I or II or III)
clomps ninety-seven steps
peeking in cells along the way
making a mark for each head she sees.
Totaling her marks she seeks a count
of sixty marks to equal sixty heads.

Furious pencil frightened guard
her count refuses to be but fifty-nine.

       "Frozen Count."

Fifty-nine hearts speed up to jolt
Fifty-nine bodies erect listening in the dark.

       "Frozen Count."

The whole freezes.

Count again you female St. Peter!

Face red, steps angry
Pencil still furious unable to make sixty
Out of the true total fifty-nine.

A Sister Is Gone.

Gritty bitch, traitor to us cowards — *She did something they couldn't*
Run gone one, run, while I sleep
with a smile just for you.

WILLIAM WANTLING
1933–1974

Called by Walter Lowenfels "the best poet of his age," William Wantling is better known in England, Australia, and New Zealand than in his native United States. Enlisting in the marines at the age of seventeen, Wantling was severely wounded in the Korean War. After ten days in a coma and eight weeks of hospitalization, he returned home with the rank of sergeant, an assortment of medals, and a drug addiction. As he put it: "When I was in Korea they gave me my first shot of morphine. It killed the pain. It was beautiful. Five years later I was in San Quentin on narcotics."

Arrested for possession of heroin in Los Angeles, Wantling pleaded guilty, assuming that he would get probation for this first offense. Instead, he was sentenced to one to fourteen years in San Quentin, where he served from 1958 to 1964. In the decade after his release, as Wantling's volumes of poetry attracted a small but enthusiastic international following, he cycled through periods of creativity and self-destruction. A final binge with drugs led to a fatal heart attack at the age of forty-one.

from *Sestina to San Quentin*

FOR KEN WHELAN

Do you remember now?
How the grey and green walls rose invincible about us?
How we raised our eyes to the sheer heights climbing to a final
    pinnacle perspective
Until high, high off over our heads we saw the
Sun-stricken gun-towers, the archer-turrets of ancient castles?
And how, scudding by the turrets, scudding through the child-
    blue sky

Great puffed balls of popcorn clouds went tumbling by, the
Chaste being chased by reflected crimson from a dying sun?

Do you remember how the gulls went wheeling and crying their
    shrill plaintive cries?
How they spun down in tightened spirals to spy upon us and
    climb again?
How their wings pounded the air until, catching a rising
Current of warmth they spread their wings wide and were free,
    free and still, serene, hanging
Poised and then swiftly gliding as the chance quick current
Drifted them off over the deep blue waters of the bay?

Poetry

I've got to be honest, I can
make good word music and rhyme

at the right times and fit words
together to give people pleasure

and even sometimes take their
breath away—but it always

somehow turns out kind of phoney.
Consonance and assonance and inner

rhyme won't make up for the fact
that I can't figure out how to get

down on paper the real or the true
which we call life. Like the other

day. The other day I was walking
in the lower exercise yard here

———

at San Quentin and this cat called
Turk came up to a friend of mine

and said Ernie, I hear You're
shooting on my kid. And Ernie

told him So what, Punk? And Turk
pulled out his stuff and shanked

Ernie in the gut only Ernie had a
metal tray in his shirt. Turk's

shank bounced off Ernie and
Ernie pulled his stuff out and of

course Turk didn't have a tray and
he caught it dead in the chest, a bad

one, and the blood that came to his
lips was a bright pink, lung blood,

and he just laid down in the grass
and said Shit. Fuck it. Sheeit.

Fuck it. And he laughed a soft long
laugh, 5 minutes, then died. Now

what could consonance or assonance or
even rhyme do with something like that?

Who's Bitter?

when judge Lynch
denied probation
& crammed that 1-14
up my ass
for a First offence
I giggled

when Dr God
stuck 7 shocktreatments
to me
for giving my chick
in Camarillo
2 joints
I laughed aloud

now
when the State of Illness
caught me bending over
2 jugs of Codeine
cough medicine
& charged me w/Possession
and Conspiracy
I shrieked
in idiot joy

a bit worried
they all inquired
— What are you Wantling?
—A goddam Masochist?
I, between hilarious gasps
O howled—No,
—I'm a Poet!
—Fuck me again!

MICHAEL HOGAN
1943–

*Ever since his first two books of poems were published in 1975,
while he was in his eighth year in the maximum security Arizona State Prison, Michael Hogan has been a prominent and
admired figure in prison literature. His poem "Spring" won
first prize in the 1975 PEN Writing Awards for Prisoners and
the following year he received the Joseph Fels Award, the*

Pushcart Prize for poetry, and a National Endowment for the Arts Fellowship.

Cofounder with poet Richard Shelton of the influential Arizona State Prison Writers Workshop, Hogan, after his own release in 1976, has traveled to dozens of prisons around the country to teach creative writing. He has now published nine books of poetry, edited three others, and been widely anthologized.

In 1997, Hogan published The Irish Soldiers of Mexico, *the first major study of the Irish soldiers who fought on the Mexican side in the Mexican–American War. He is currently head of the Department of Letters and Humanities at the American School in Guadalajara, Mexico.*

Spring

Ice has been cracking all day
and small boys on the shore
pretending it is the booming of artillery
lie prone clutching imaginary carbines.

Inside the compound returning birds
peck at bread scraps from the mess hall.

Old cons shiver in cloth jackets
as they cross the naked quadrangle.
They know the inside perimeter is exactly
two thousand eighty-four steps
and they can walk it five more times
before a steam whistle blows for count.

Above them a tower guard dips his rifle
then raises it again dreamily.
He imagines a speckled trout
coming up shining and raging with life.

[handwritten margin note: Contrasts between imagination & reality]

Confessions of a Jailhouse Lawyer

I grow old
Searching through dog-eared tomes
For the one case, the clincher,
Which will set me free.
In vain I search
Through the veins and arteries
Of the corpus juris,
Plumb the depths of the Pacific Reporter
In vain.
There is no such case, no such law
Because such laws were never written.

I grow musty, my spine
An old edition of Blackstone
Bent with time;
My brain a collection of loose-leaf
Law Week memories.

I grow weary of helping others
To the light
At the end of the tunnel
Frightened and self-conscious in the light
Myself.

I am perhaps destined to be here
Meant to ride Rosinante through the pages
Of reported cases
And watch the bubbling lead
In the cauldron of my own absurdity.

CAROLYN BAXTER
1953–

Carolyn Baxter's extraordinary poetry first drew attention when she participated in the Free Space Writing Project while serving time in the New York City Correctional Institution for Women. Her poems have been anthologized in Songs from a Free Space: Writings by Women in Prison *(the chapbook from that project),* Joseph Bruchac's collection The Light from Another Country: Poetry from American Prisons, *and Judith Scheffler's* Wall Tappings: An Anthology of Writings by Women Prisoners. *Her own collection was published in 1979 as* Prison Solitary and Other Free Government Services: Poems by Carolyn Baxter.

Born in Harlem, Baxter has studied at New York City Community College and Bard College, and she has been a playwright, actress, and professional musician.

Lower Court

She opens her mouth, a switchblade falls out, along
with a .22 automatic, a few shells, crumpled one
dollar bills, some change in attitude (she's uncomfortable)
now.
Her pimp steps in,   slaps her,   see jugular
vein separate from neck muscle.

She opens her mouth wider, crumpled one dollar bills
fall out, along with prophylactics, 10¢ perfume, lipstick,
a newspaper clipping for a pair of $30 boots, a whip,
an explanation for the forged driver's license/a
picture of her favorite group, "The Shantells."

She closes her mouth,   The lights dim
in the courtroom.   As her pimp turns her left ear

She's a prostitute

with his fist, activating last night's streetreel of how
hot it was on the hoe stroll, projected out her eyeballs,
/smell of tricks.

> Legal Aid Lawyer says: Cop Out!
> She does.

Another nite.
Trapped between gavel/wood.   Making it possible for
her to hit the streets.
Sound of her heels cut grey morning air,
/recite her life back, (in the) same order.

35 Years a Correctional Officer

Ms. Goodall does not drink, swear, or masturbate.
"It's against God's will," she says.

Ms. Goodall does not gamble, gets paid to be slick
an' creep around after 1:00 AM to listen for
creaking beds, so she can give out incident reports
to anyone she catches by the creaks
of their bed "Masturbating!"
"It's against God's will," she says.

So I lay naked on floor, along with cold
tile, I feel like a private under the bunk,
hiding from the enemy.

/as her Sears/Roebuck crepe soles creep by the door—
I wanted to ask, what's the difference between a
creaking bed/a manic breathing heavy under the door.

On Being Counted

Standing next to the radiator, watching the room,
Do my tarot cards for the 1000th time.
I hear the radiator whispering, how stupid I was to
trade your warmth for his.
And I brood over you not letting me steal your hands.
To dry up my pains.

I smell lemon powder, thinking of my name.
Trying to remember femininity.
I can't sleep until I pay my personal digits to
Washington.

2

It's lights out,
yawns, coughs, and dreams from different realities.
Pack up the day, and seek refuge in the night.
Traveling down dark invisible roads.
Hoping to tap a stranger on the back.
Only to find it's their old friend.
Freedom.

I lay down, thinking thoughts that
were one time real,
But are now like houses that have been torn down,
and families that have moved away.

3

I smell the questioning flashlights,
walking down the hall, closing the storage doors
on dead lives,

demanding I recite the patented number, stamped on
my ass,
which is presently subletting the space
my soul used to own.
I'm also asked where I got my map of the justice system.

I say the judge traded it for my birth certificate.
The interrogator smiles, saying he'd never trade his,
and that I'm getting prettier with age.
Not mentioning ugly with time. *Time as in Jail time*

4

The dark highlights my barren existence,
that's gushed from me so far.
And I wonder, how there's even a corpuscle of patience
left.
The closing door joins the lock in the key
of finality, in three years from today time.

5

Spotlight invades my public privacy.
Like a peeping tom, inspiring me to sleep insomnia.
I turn to the radiator for some warmth, as I mumble
I feel like I gotta vomit.
The cold radiator yells, not on me bitch.
I have to live here too.

Joining the moon singing do you know the way to
San Jose.
In two part cruelty.

Asking do I know the words to nobody knows da
trouble I seen.

6

So I hum, off key thoughts, that were one time,
real.
But are now like houses that have been torn down
and families that have moved away.

JIMMY SANTIAGO BACA
1952–

Although at the age of twenty he could not read or write, Jimmy Santiago Baca has achieved international recognition as a major American poet, has taught in universities, and has won a Wallace Stevens Yale Poetry Fellowship, a Pushcart Prize, and the 1988 American Book Award for Poetry.

Half Chicano and half "detribalized Apache," Baca was committed when he was five years old to a New Mexico orphanage, from which he fled at the age of eleven to live a precarious life in the streets. When he was twenty, he was sentenced to a long term in an Arizona maximum security prison, where he spent four years in solitary and was subjected to electric shock treatments. While in the hole, Baca taught himself to read and write, discovered freedom in language, and began to compose poetry.

Although at one point the warden tore up his poems, Baca persisted. He submitted three poems to Mother Jones *magazine, whose poetry editor then happened to be Denise Levertov. Immediately recognizing the tremendous power of Baca's poetry, Levertov not only accepted it but encouraged him and eventually helped find a publisher for his first volume,* Immigrants in Our Own Land *(Louisiana State University Press, 1979), which received wide and enthusiastic reviews. Even greater praise greeted Baca's award-winning fifth volume,* Martín and Meditations on the South Valley, *published in 1987 by New Directions with an introduction by Levertov.*

In recent years, Baca has branched into fiction and scriptwriting. He reads and lectures at prestigious international forums, in universities, and to convicts in many of the nation's jails and prisons.

The New Warden

He sat in the cool morning.
He had a handful of seeds in his palm.
He sat there contemplating
Where he would plant them.
A month later he tore the kitchen down
and planted apple seeds there.
Some of the convicts asked him why:
"Apples," he said, "is one of America's
great traditional prides. Remember
the famous ballad Johnny Apple Seed?"
Nobody had heard of it, so he set up
A poetry workshop where the death house had been.
The chair was burned in a great ceremony.
Some of the Indian convicts performed
Ancient rituals for the souls of those executed in the past.
He sold most of the bricks and built
Little ovens in the earth with the rest.
The hospital was destroyed except for one new wing
To keep the especially infirm aged ones.
And funny thing, no one was ever sick.
The warden said something about freedom being the greatest cure
For any and all ailments. He was right.
The cellblocks were razed to the ground.
Some of the steel was kept and a blacksmith shop went up.
With the extra bricks the warden purchased
Tents, farming implements and bought a big yellow bus.
The adjoining fields flowed rich with tomatoes, pumpkins,
Potatoes, corn, chili, alfalfa, cucumbers.
From the nearby town of Florence, and as far away as Las
    Cruces,
People came to buy up loads and loads of vegetables.
In one section of the compound the artists painted
Easter and Christmas and other holiday cards, on paper
previously used for disciplinary reports.
The government even commissioned some of the convicts
To design patriotic emblems.

A little group of engineers, plumbers, electricians
Began building solar heating systems and sold them
To elementary schools way under cost. Then,
Some citizens grew interested. Some high school kids
Were invited to learn about it, and soon,
Solar systems were being installed in the community.
An agricultural program opened up.
Unruly convicts were shipped out to another prison.
After the first year, the new warden installed ballot boxes.
A radio and TV shop opened. Some of the convicts' sons
And daughters came into prison to learn from their fathers'
trades and talking with them about life.
This led to several groups opening up sessions dealing with
Language, logic, and delving into past myths and customs.
Blacks, Mejicanos, Whites, all had so much to offer.
They were invited to speak at the nearby university
Discussing what they found to be untouched by past historians.
Each day six groups of convicts went into the community,
Working for the aged and infirmed.
One old convict ended up marrying the governor's mother.

The County Jail

Men late at night cook coffee in rusty cans,
just like in the hills, like in their childhoods,
without rules or guidance or authority, their fathers
dead or wild as gypsies,
their mothers going down for five dollars.
These are the men who surface at night,
The sons of faceless parents,
the sons of brutal days dripping blood,
the men whose faces emerge from shadows,
from bars,
and they join in circles and squat on haunches,
share smokes, and talk of who knows who,
what towns they passed through;
while flames jump under the coffee can,

you see new faces and old ones,
the young eyes scared and the old eyes
tarnished like peeling boat hulls,
like wild creatures they meet,
with a sixth sense inside of them, to tell them
who's real and who's the game;
and their thoughts are hard as wisdom teeth,
biting into each new eye,
that shows itself around the fire.

The coffee is poured steaming hot into cups,
and the men slowly sip.
Shower stalls drip bleakly in the dark,
and the smell of dumb metal is inflamed
with the acrid silence, and once in a while,
a car horn will sound from outside the windows,
and the man with only a cheek illuminated by the fire,
the rest of his face drenched in shadows,
will get up and leave the circle,
return to his bunk.

I Applied for the Board

. . . a flight of fancy and breath of fresh air
Is worth all the declines in the world.
It was funny though when I strode into the Board
And presented myself before the Council
With my shaggy-haired satchel, awiry
With ends of shoestrings and guitar strings
Holding it together, brimming with poems.

I was ready for my first grand, eloquent,
Booming reading of a few of my poems—
When the soft, surprised eyes
Of the chairman looked at me and said no.

And his two colleagues sitting on each side of him,
Peered at me through bluemetal eyes like rifle scopes,

And I like a deer in the forest heard the fresh,
Crisp twig break under my cautious feet,
As they surrounded me with quiet questions,
Closing in with grim sour looks, until I heard
The final shot burst from their mouths
That I had not made it, and felt the warm blood
Gush forth in my breast, partly from the wound,
And partly from the joy that it was over.

JACKIE RUZAS
1942–

*Born to an Irish-American mother and Lithuanian-American
father in the Queens borough of New York City, Jackie Ruzas
attended Catholic parochial school and seemed destined for a
conventional working-class life, even after dropping out of
Aviation Trades High School to take a job at the shoe factory
where his mother had worked for sixteen years. But meanwhile, he had begun snorting heroin. When he was eighteen,
his father got him an apprenticeship in the Carpenters' Union,
and after a brief fling in California, he worked from 1961 for
three years doing construction for the New York World's Fair
that opened in 1964. His heroin habit led to his first arrest in
1965, for auto theft and drug possession. Nine months in a
hospital program for addicts merely put him in contact with
other men further down the slippery slope. He began sticking
up stores with a starter's pistol, got caught at the age of
twenty-five, and emerged from his first prison sentence at the
age of thirty.*

*He went back to construction and managed to stay off
drugs for a little over a year. But in 1974, a jewelry store heist
that he pulled with two other men led to a blundering highway shootout in which he killed a state trooper. He was spared
the death penalty by the jury's decision that he did not intend
to kill. Convicted of second-degree murder, he has been serving a life sentence in Sing Sing, Attica, and presently in New
York's Wallkill State Prison.*

In 1988, he married a woman who had been in love with

him since her teens, and they have four children from her previous marriage. His short story "The Day the Kept Lost Their Keeper" won first prize in the 1982 PEN Writing Awards for Prisoners, and his poems have been published in the Irish American Voice, Saiorge U-Eihrearin, *the* American Poetry Review, *and the anthology* Candles Burn in Memory Town.

Easy to Kill

The door.
I can see its molding if I scrunch in the
  left corner of my cell
  and peer through the bars to my right.
Each morning I awake
  one day closer to death.

The prison priest, a sometime visitor,
  his manner warm, asks,
  "How are you today? Anything I can do for you, son?"
"Is it just that I'm so easy to kill, Father?"
  His face a blank, he walks away.

Play my life back on this death cell wall,
  I wish to see my first wrong step.
To those who want to take my life,
  show me where I first started to lose it.

Reflects where he went wrong

Madison County, 1975

The Bus Ride

The bus travels the thruway from past to future,
I sit by a window somewhere in between
Another trip, another transfer, another prison
At day's end.

Summer's lush green mantle covers the landscape
From roadside to mountains far away.
I didn't know I loved green.
Green, the color of life, so hard to be in winter,
Praises summer for its chance to be.
She had green eyes and black hair.
I had green eyes and black hair.
She wore my ankle bracelet.
I wore her name, Camille, on my garrison belt.
We shared an eclair on a bench in Linden Park.
She took a bite. I took a bite. We kissed in
The middle, so long ago.

The billboard shows a Budweiser face, "America's
    Favorite Beer."
I didn't know I loved beer.
An eleven year abstinence from the me who helped
Construct the Big Apple from scaffolds in the sky.
My throat recalls the taste of malt & barley.
Two adolescent fingers flashed outside the Tumble Inn
Bar, signaled two quart containers.
A climb over the fence, a dollar passed through
The back window to Tony's trembling old hand, clinched it.
An hour later the fence was a trap that brought six stitches.

A rabbit! Was it a rabbit I saw scamper through the woods?
I didn't know I loved rabbits.
His name was Bugs, and I got him from Ol' Farmer Steve
Who now presses grapes to wine in heaven.
My uncle Jim didn't want rabbit shit in the cellar,
So Bugs froze to death in the battered doghouse,
While I slept snug in my child's cocoon.

I didn't know I loved bus rides.

Attica/Sing Sing '83

EDWARD BUNKER
1933–

Deserted by his mother, Edward Bunker was made a ward of a California court at the age of four. By age ten, he was in reform school. At seventeen, he became the youngest convict at San Quentin. He served time at Folsom, Marion, and Leavenworth, and he even made the FBI's Ten Most Wanted list.

A prison psychologist noted in Bunker's file that a prime manifestation of his immature fantasies was his announced decision to teach himself to become a writer. In San Quentin and Folsom, Bunker typed by day and wrote at night on yellow tablets by flashlight under blankets. During three terms in prison over eighteen years, he wrote six novels and more than one hundred short stories, all unpublished. Many of his manuscripts were confiscated by prison administrators. Then, on the same day that he received a letter from Harper's *accepting his essay "War Behind Walls,"* Norton *accepted his novel* No Beast So Fierce, *which was published in 1972.*

Paroled in 1975, Bunker has built a successful career as a significant novelist, freelance journalist, and screenwriter. His 1977 wrenching prison novel The Animal Factory *was followed in 1981 by* Little Boy Blue, *perhaps the finest dramatization of how society turns troubled children into professional criminals. When* No Beast So Fierce *was filmed as the 1978 movie* Straight Time *starring Dustin Hoffman, Bunker co-wrote the screenplay. He was the main screenwriter who turned an old script by Akira Kurosawa into Andrei Konchalkovsky's 1985 existential film* Runaway Train, *in which Bunker had a role as a longtime convict. The authenticity of his fiction is matched by his acting, as he demonstrated in the role of Mr. Blue in* Reservoir Dogs *(the 1992 directorial debut of Quentin Tarantino).*

Bunker's 1996 novel Dog Eat Dog *has won a wide audience, in England as well as in America, despite its uncompromisingly bleak vision. Its doomed protagonists emerge from long terms in prison to find themselves in a decaying California, sinking ever deeper into a self-sustaining vortex of personal and societal crime and vengeance.*

from *Little Boy Blue*

ALEX HAMMOND spent the next six weeks in Juvenile Hall while the wheels of the unseen bureaucracy turned, processing his commitment to the California Youth Authority. This time he got along better because he'd learned how to fight. Rather, he'd learned how to *cop a Sunday*—strike a sneak, full-force punch and follow the advantage with a volley of feet and fists. The black monitor had kicked him in the rump for whispering while in line en route to supper. It was his second day back. The counselor was watching so Alex took it silently, though his brain reddened with fury and he could barely choke his food down. After the meal, the company went outdoors for recreation. The huge yard had an area for each company; mixing wasn't allowed. This company had the basketball court.

During the meal and the march out, Alex's eyes had met the black monitor's several times. When the company was dismissed, Alex met the eyes again. The black was slender and tall, with a grace of movement indicating muscular coordination. He had to be a good fighter to be a monitor. Alex's stomach mixed anger and apprehensiveness. He couldn't let the kick pass, but he didn't know exactly what to do.

The decision was taken from him. The black youth sidled over, his manner tense and ready. "Say, suckah," the black said. "You cuttin' yo' eyes at me like you got somepin' on your mind. You wanna get it on or somepin'?" He was leaning forward, hands partly up, coiled to fight.

"Man, I don't want no trouble," Alex said, spreading his hands with the palms up.

The tension went out of the black. Alex could see it ooze away, the eyes becoming milder. That was the moment Alex swung as hard as he could punch—left and right, using his shoulders and body weight the way First Choice Floyd had taught him. Both blows landed full-force, making loud "splat, splat" sounds, and Alex could feel the shock run up his arms.

The black dropped instantly, flat on his back, blood gushing from his mouth where his teeth were driven through his lip. He was out cold. It was the first time Alex had ever knocked someone unconscious. And from the encounter he learned the value of surprise. He was certain the black could whip him in a fair fight.

The fight cost him five days in "seclusion." He didn't mind because a prior occupant had stashed half a dozen books under the bunk. Two were Zane Grey Westerns, which he always enjoyed, and three were from the Hardy Boys series, which he'd once loved but now found too simple. Still, he read them. The last book didn't have a title that meant anything to him—*Native Son*—and he put it aside until nothing else remained. It was a little hard to read at first, but soon he forgot the words he sometimes missed and was lost in its world of ghettos and blackness and *life*. He was too young to know why it was affecting him so much, why it was so different from everything else he'd read. It was as if the brutalized and hate-filled young Negro reflected an unbelievable amount of what Alex had seen and experienced and felt. Alex still had the last few chapters to read when a counselor told him to get ready for the main population. He wasn't supposed to have books in seclusion, so he couldn't carry it out. Feeling a pang of guilt, he nevertheless tore out the remaining chapters and stuffed them down the front of his denims. He *had* to finish this book. He did so that night seated on a toilet in the small dormitory restroom under a wan light after the regular lights were turned off.

The black monitor still had strands of catgut jutting from his drooping lower lip. But when his glance met Alex's, the black looked away, and the white boy recognized his own victory. He'd expected another challenge and was ready to fight without bothering to talk. The monitor's nickname was T-Bone, and whenever the counselor brought out the boxing gloves, T-Bone put them on with anyone who dared. After seeing T-Bone, Alex was even more certain that the black could beat him up. But T-Bone didn't know it, nor did anyone else in the company. Thereafter Alex had far less trouble than during the first sojourn in Juvenile Hall. On Sunday afternoons, following the visiting hours, the boys got the packages of candy and magazines brought by their families. Alex got no visitors, but he always was offered lots of candy and the first chance at the magazines. He had gained status in a pecking order built entirely on violence. He was too young to question its values, where a cretin could be the most highly respected if he was the toughest, but nonetheless his intelligence gave him an advantage. He had beaten the black by thinking fast, and now he had an upper hand because he'd been smarter.

During the weeks of waiting for delivery to reform school, Alex kept pretty much to himself, his demeanor aloof, discouraging any attempts at friendship. Even the fact that he was going to reform school, the worst punishment the state possessed, gave him added status in Juvenile Hall.

During a long rainstorm, the worst to strike southern California since 1933, a counselor came to the classroom to fetch him. If it had been someone in Juvenile Hall calling him for an interview, a monitor would have come with the pass; the counselor meant that transportation to Whittier was waiting.

A pair of men in cheap business suits were waiting for him and two others. The men were from Whittier. The other two boys were Chicano; they were brothers who had inflicted multiple slices on a youth from a different street gang. These two brothers were from "White Fence," a barrio with a block-long white fence in it. They were also afraid of Whittier; White Fence was a gang at war with nearly all other Chicano gangs. It was without allies. And its members, unless unusually tough, were given a rough time in the youth institutions. They'd been pointed out to Alex by another Chicano, a friend of Lulu's from Temple Street. Lulu was already in Whittier.

The Chicano brothers were already in civilian clothes and being handcuffed together when Alex entered; one of them was holding a shoebox of letters and snapshots. A rain-pelted tree was wind-lashed so it scratched a window; it was the loudest sound as Alex changed into his own clothes, now musty from hanging unwashed for so long. The men from the reform school watched him, and when he was through one of them patted him down and brought out another pair of handcuffs.

"Should we put this one in the middle?" he asked his partner. "He's the jackrabbit in the bunch."

"Naw, he'll be okay on the outside."

The steel was fastened around Alex's right wrist, binding it to the left wrist of one Chicano. The trio was shepherded through the electronically controlled doors and hurried with heads down through the rain gusts—one man leading, the other following—to a station wagon with State of California on its side.

The drive took an hour. Whittier was a suburban community east of Los Angeles, and at first Alex had a terrifying thought that they were really going back to Pacific Colony, which was also east. Whittier, however, was ten miles to the south.

Elsewhere the storm was hitting the southern California coast with wicked backhand slaps, and causing canyon houses to slide off their perches; but here it was merely shivering trees and overflowing gutters and empty sidewalks. Once the driver had to slam a heel into the brake pedal to avoid plowing into a stalled car. Everyone in the station wagon lurched forward. Alex was shot through with a moment's fear as the car slid on the wet street, but as it straightened out and they gained momentum, he wished that they'd been wrecked—a bad wreck in which the prisoners had a chance to run. In later years, whenever he was transported anywhere he would beg fate for such an accident. This was just the first time.

The tires hissed on the wet asphalt as they passed beyond the barrios of East Los Angeles to the stucco suburbs and citrus groves. Trees leaned and writhed. The few vehicles moving around traveled slowly, their headlights turned on.

Whittier State School had its name on the front gate. The gate was open and no fence ran along the front. It faced a busy boulevard. The rear, however, had tall fences with rolled concertina. The buildings spread out were brick Tudor. The grounds were twenty acres of manicured lawns and trim lodges. It looked more like a small college than a reform school. It took close inspection to see the chains welded across the windowframes, making sure they wouldn't open wide enough for a body.

Receiving Company was what its name indicated, a place where newcomers were processed and indoctrinated. The first day was spent at the institution hospital; he was examined, vaccinated, inoculated, and, because of his history, interviewed by a psychologist. Half of the next day was spent with a social worker, who had the court records but wanted to know what schools and institutions he'd been in, what social service agencies had handled him. Whittier would write for more information about him. Such things were immaterial to Alex; he was concerned solely with learning the reform school routine, the mores and styles, in learning his role and being accepted. The routine was basically military school discipline, enforced by civilians. The main civilian in each company was called a housefather; he and his wife lived in the cottage with the boys. Two other men worked the morning and graveyard shifts; they were counselors. Aiding the civilians were "officers," three boys, one of each race; they called the cadence, gave orders, and were quick to kick the slow-witted in the buttocks for dozens of infractions.

Mr. Morris, the Receiving Company housefather, still had traces of an English accent. In his fifties, he was a balding physical-fitness zealot. So was his petite-framed wife. In addition to the perforated paddle ("Bend over and grab your ankles"), Mr. Morris enforced discipline by liberal calisthenics. Minor infractions, such as audibly cutting wind in the dayroom or whispering in line, brought thirty-five situps or twenty pushups. Serious matters could bring an ear-ringing cuff on the head, a kick in the rump, or swats with the paddle, depending on circumstances and mood. Then, in the evening, the miscreants (there were several every day) did one hundred pushups in five sets of twenty, fifty deep knee bends, and fifty situps, which Mr. Morris did with them. Often his wife did them too. Despite being forty years old, she'd kept a taut figure, and the boys watched her brown legs and tried to sneak glances up her dress. The most adventuresome attached tiny bits of mirror to their shoes, then stood close to her, swearing later that they saw hair via the mirror.

Three hours a day were spent learning how to march. Alex already knew how from his sojourns in military schools, but he was a rarity. For the first three days, a newcomer was taught by a boy officer away from the rest of the company. After that, he was put with the others to learn or suffer. Being out of step brought a boot in the butt, as did any other drilling error. At the end of each drill period, the company did half an hour of strenuous exercises; they also did them before breakfast. When they went to a regular company they were in top condition, the thin arms of boyhood growing a ridge of muscle at the tricep, an unusual thing in young boys; and instead of boyhood's usual tummy, they developed rippling stomach muscles. Mr. Morris worked hard to create healthy bodies; he didn't think they had minds, so he didn't bother with that. In weeks they marched like a military drill team.

Because Alex knew how to march and had had the experience of other institutions, he avoided conflict with the officers. But he had a small, hard nugget of resentment for what they did, meanwhile recognizing that any of them could make mincemeat of him. Nevertheless, he knew that any kick or punch on the shoulder would make him fight whoever did it. He must have radiated his preparedness, for he wasn't kicked when he whispered during silent periods. The officers just signaled him to be quiet. They were obviously picked first because they were among the toughest in the company, and secondly because they would do so for extra prerogatives; few thirteen- and fourteen-year-olds understood the underworld "code" to the extent where this behavior violated it. They did know that outright "snitching" was *wrong,* but doing the Man's work of enforcing order was different. Alex seemed to be the only one who had misgivings when an officer beat up another boy for breaking the rules. A big, tough white officer (he weighed one seventy and shaved regularly at fifteen) nicknamed Skull kicked a smaller Mexican for horseplay in the shower line. The Mexican was snatching a towel from the waist of another Mexican in front of him. When kicked, he turned and punched—and the fight was on. The Mexican lost, but it was a hard, vicious brawl where the two boys stood toe to toe and the much larger Skull had a black eye and bumps on his face. When the Mexican officer went to a regular company, the fighting Mexican was promoted to the vacated position. He began kicking those who started the horseplay in line, those who talked, those who did anything, and joyfully pummelled any who fought back. A few boys were immune from the officers because they were too tough; they, themselves, would have been promoted except that they were just too much trouble—too rebellious. Mr. Morris took care of them. Another category received kicks, but "pulled," delivered at half-force with the flat side of the shoe; the culprit could arch his back and take it painlessly. The majority, however, learned to march and follow the rules by bruising kicks. They learned quickly, too; and any sign of protest brought a fist in the mouth.

Receiving Company was especially strict. Everything was done in silence. Every process, from wakeup, through washup, breakfast, drill and even showers, was done by the numbers. For example, they filed into their narrow lockers preparatory to showers. The officer gave them a left face, so they stood at attention facing each locker. At the command of "one" they put their hands on the locker; at "two" they opened it; at "three" they took out the towel and put their shoes inside. . . .

So it went for months and months. Alex knew he'd been marked as a troublemaker from things Mr. Morris said. Word had come from the front office, based on the files. "We'll break you," Mr. Morris said once. "You're not so tough," he said another time. But Alex didn't get into any trouble; the extreme discipline somehow made him patient and watchful. It was a challenge. He didn't know anyone in this company, which was newcomers from the whole state of California. Receiving wasn't allowed to mingle with other companies, but Alex saw faces he knew in church. Everyone had to attend either Catholic Mass or Protestant services. He went for the Mass because many boys wore the rosary as jewelry; he liked how it looked, and he got one from the priest. At Mass he saw Lulu, who grinned and nodded a greeting. It made Alex warm inside. He also saw Max Dembo, who waved a greeting. A few others from Juvenile Hall waved recognition and greeting. Some newcomers knew nobody, but others, especially blacks and Chicanos, saw a score or more of friends from their neighborhoods. It was old-home week to them.

The youngest boys at Whittier, from eight to ten years old, were in Wrigley Cottage; their "dress" clothes were Cub Scout uniforms. Wrigley Cottage was famous for its marches. Wrigley not only won close-order drill competition from the rest of Whittier, it had also beaten the U.S. Marine drill team from Camp Pendleton. Hoover Cottage was for slightly older boys, eleven or even twelve. Then came Scouts and Washington. The oldest and toughest boys were in Roosevelt and Lincoln. Most were fifteen and some were sixteen.

Alex was later transferred to Scouts, and he had mixed feelings about it. By comparison to the other cottages, Scouts was less regimented. It was the only cottage with private rooms instead of dormitories. On Sundays, it provided escorts for visitors from the front gate to the picnic area or auditorium; the weather dictated which. The boys thus had a chance to ask the visitors for cigarettes, the most valuable commodity in the institution. Running a distant second was Dixie Peach hair pomade; it was also contraband, as were all pomade and hair oil, because the boys drenched themselves and grossly stained the bedding. Their intricate hairdos, all with fancy ducktails, required lots of grease to stay in place. Access to the visitors allowed boys from Scouts to smuggle in cigarettes and pomade for others. The boys were searched, but the escorts could hide things in bushes en route here and there. They were too young, at least in this era, for marijuana, though a few had experience with it, and many claimed experience.

Scouts Cottage also went on more "town trips" than the others: the Boy Scout jamborees, parades, and an occasional movie. Such things were all to the good. To the bad—what caused Alex's misgivings—was that boys too soft for Washington, Lincoln, or Roosevelt were also sent to Scouts. Not all were thus. Most were average delinquents and a few were "crazier" than average. But the twenty percent in Scouts because of being weak gave a stigma to the others; the question was always raised if a newcomer was assigned there—until he proved himself, anyway. So, despite the comparatively easier living—and it was entirely by comparison— it rankled Alex that anyone might assume him too weak for a different cottage. He was ready to fight a grizzly to prove himself.

Scouts had faces that Alex recalled from Juvenile Hall, but he couldn't put names to them and didn't know them. The white boy officer got him bedding and linen and showed him the room he was assigned on the second floor. All the rooms were there, down two hallways at right angles. Where the hallways joined was the stairwell and a heavy door, the only exit. Here sat the night man's desk, too.

The room was nicer than any Alex had had in a foster home or military school. The small space was used efficiently. The bunk was built in against a wall, and its bottom had large drawers for extra clothes and property. A tiny wardrobe cabinet was fitted at the foot of the bed to the wall beside the door. The room door was never locked because the showers, washroom, and toilets were down the corridor. Writing desk and chair faced the room's small window, which had curtains and no bars. But he couldn't climb out because a short chain had been welded to the windowframe so it wouldn't open far enough.

Alex noted these things while making the bed. The white boy with the English-style officer's bars on his collar waited in the doorway.

"Tomorrow's Saturday," the officer said. "We have a room inspection before lunch. You gotta get the dust even from the corners of the bedframe *under* the mattress, for example."

Alex wanted to reply sarcastically but held back. He didn't resent the information but how it was given. The tone wasn't friendly advice; it was an order with an implicit threat. Moreover, Alex had previously noted this boy and disliked him. His last name was Constantine (everyone used last names almost exclusively, as in the army), and he conveyed (at least to Alex) a snobbish, superior attitude, as if he thought himself better than the others. Where nearly all the boys, including Alex, combed their hair in ducktails, Constantine parted his and had a small pompadour. Where the style was to pull pants far down and roll them up at the bottom (this was the "hep" look), Constantine wore his conventionally. The man often used him as an example. He was the housefather's pet, and yet he had to be able to fight or he wouldn't have been an officer.

Thinking about Constantine occupied Alex while he "squared" the corners of the bed in the neatest manner.

"Do the rest later," Constantine said, meaning the rest of the cleaning of the room. Somehow this simple instruction likewise grated on Alex. Saying nothing, he knew that he and Constantine would eventually collide. Alex doubted that he could whip Constantine in a fair fight; he would have to obtain, and maintain, some kind of an advantage. . . .

Whittier's youngest boys, those in Wrigley and Hoover cottages, attended school all day. Their classrooms were in the cottages. They were kept away from the corrupting influence of the older boys, who attended school for half a day in the education building, then worked the other half. Some were assigned to vocational shoe shop, print shop, paint shop, sheet metal, and so forth; they learned to put heels on institutional brogans and slop whitewash on institutional dayrooms. Others took care of the hundreds of chickens and the herd of milk cows, or irrigated the alfalfa. A handful were on the Extra Squad, a crew that labored wherever needed. Sometimes they raked leaves or swept a road—but a broken pipe beneath the road had them digging through asphalt, dirt, and clay. Alex found himself doing the work of a grown man. For the first week his back and legs ached in the morning, but his body adjusted and toughened. Although he vilified the assignment and listened to boys ridiculing it (a shovel was one of the "idiot sticks" of the world), deep inside he derived pleasure from the work. It validated him as a man, and he got a gut pleasure from the bite of the shovel into the earth and the bunching of his shoulder muscles as he hoisted it. He didn't drive himself to special effort, but he did enough to avoid yells from the man, usually a relief counselor from one of the cottages who had nothing to do while the boys were at school. The housemother, the wife of the housefather, who had the afternoon and evening shift, kept a few boys for "housecats." They cleaned and polished the cottage. But the day counselor had other duties, supervising a work crew or helping to watch Jefferson Cottage, the disciplinary company. Jefferson really worked hard.

Alex had been on the Extra Squad for two weeks (he attended afternoon school) when the regular man called in sick. The day counselor from Lincoln filled in. He was younger than most, barely thirty, and he was nicknamed "Topo" (Gopher) because of his protuberant front teeth. Nobody called him Topo to his face, but disguised voices often called to his back: *"Topo es puto,"* or "Topo sucks dicks." He reacted with rage. His real name was Mr. Lavalino, and the boys thought he was tough. They respected toughness but not cruelty. Mr. Lavalino was also cruel occasionally; he used the boys under his control to vent a variety of frustrations. Alex knew him only by sight when he took the Extra Squad one bleak, rain-threatened morning. The dozen boys were digging up a leaky pipe near the front of the institution. They'd reached the pipe the day before, but the actual leak wasn't precisely where they'd excavated. They were enlarging the ditch by following the pipe. The earth was soft, but the work was sloppy. It had rained during the night and turned things to mud.

The boys had divided themselves into shifts because everyone couldn't work simultaneously. Some loosened the earth with mattocks; others shoveled out what had been loosened. Alex was half-leaning on his shovel, watching the other shift do their stint, when the dirt clod hit him behind the ear and shattered. It didn't hurt, but it stunned him momentarily, the surprise of it. When he turned, confused with shock, his face commencing to draw up in anger, he expected to see another boy. Whether it was a joke or an insult, he was ready to issue a challenge.

No boys were looking at him. But Mr. Lavalino was. The man was standing beside a fifty-gallon drum with a fire in it. He wasn't warming his hands. He was glaring at Alex.

"Get your ass in gear," he said. "Quit lollygagging and leaning on that shovel with your finger up your ass."

Every word was like an unexpected slap. He didn't even want to explain how the work was divided; he was trying to fight the redness growing in his eyes and brain; it made any long, explanatory sentence impossible. "Did you . . . throw that?" he choked out; even those few words were difficult.

"Yeah, yeah," Mr. Lavalino said, nodding his head for emphasis, voice rising, "I threw it. You don't like it or something . . . punk?"

Alex couldn't reply, not in words. "Punk" was the ultimate insult. He was beginning to pant, his breathing loud and strained, the excessive oxygen further dizzying his brain. All peripheral sights disappeared. In the reddening world he could only see the grotesque face of Mr. Lavalino grinning with malicious challenge.

The fury that erases thought took over. With a gasping scream he raised the shovel like a baseball bat and ran at the man—he meant to erase the grin with gore. He would bash in *that* face. . . .

But Mr. Lavalino no longer grinned. In seconds he blanched, seeing the truth. He flinched back one step and then turned and ran, yelling out, "Help! Help!"

The original distance between them was fifteen feet, but it was across the ditch and the mound of soft, damp earth. Alex stumbled, nearly falling, but found his balance and veered around the ditch.

Within moments the violent drama turned to comedy. Mr. Lavalino ran around the ditch, keeping it between himself and the enraged youth. The boy chased him around it once, sinking into the soft dirt, unable to get close enough to swing the shovel.

The other boys on the crew had stood dumfounded. Boys fought boys, not the Man, especially not a man such as Topo, who was notorious for kicking around anyone who showed the slightest rebelliousness. And this newcomer brandishing the shovel while sobbing in rage was obviously crazy. Nobody but a crazy kid would do this.

After the second time around the ditch, both of them panting, Alex stopped. So did Mr. Lavalino, keeping the ditch between them like a moat. Using a shred of reason, Alex feinted continuation of the chase, and then he started to charge directly over the ditch. He could leap it and cut off his prey. But first he had to go over the pile of soft dirt dug from the ditch. It was too soft. He sank in, stumbled, and fell to his knees, the shovel out of control.

At that instant, a fat black boy, compelled by a loathing of violence he would never admit (scarcely even to himself), took three quick steps and tackled Alex from behind. It was a high tackle, the black boy's shoulder slamming into Alex's back. The shovel jumped from Alex's hands, and he went face-down into the dirt, the weight of the heavy boy pinning him.

"Motherfucker!" Alex yelled reflexively, keeping his mouth from the earth and trying to struggle.

Other boys saw the madman disarmed and came forward to subdue him. The front office, and maybe the parole board, would look favorably on this humanitarian behavior. Young they were; naïve they were not. "Settle down, settle down," one of them said, meanwhile putting a headlock on Alex.

Alex twisted his head away from the soft dirt so he could breathe. Struggle was useless, but he muttered curses, for now into his mind jumped the certainty of punishment. To threaten their power was the worst behavior imaginable. They went half crazy over being attacked. And the worst part was that the punishment would come without his having had the satisfaction of smacking Topo with the shovel.

"Lemme up," he said.

"Take it easy, pal," the fat black said. "You'll just get in bad trouble."

Mr. Lavalino came around the trench as the fat black and two others helped Alex rise, meanwhile still holding him securely. Two hands pinned each arm, and resistance was useless. Alex watched the man approach, anticipating blows and planning to duck his head as much as possible, the memory of the terrible beating in Pacific Colony flashing into clear focus. Maybe he could tuck his chin next to his shoulder and take the punishment on the forehead. That was better than taking fists in the mouth and nose. It might even hurt the motherfucker. Hands often broke on foreheads.

Mr. Lavalino was pale with fright, not florid with rage. His hands were raised with open palms. "Easy, Hammond, easy." Every other time he'd asserted his authority—these were tough punks who only understood and respected force—it ended there. It never got to the administration building about a kick or a cuff. This one would go to the disciplinary company for the attempted assault, no matter what the provocation, but throwing the dirt clod could cause repercussions—at least a reprimand in the personnel file; it would be seen during promotion hearings.

Alex was still being held by two boys, and Mr. Lavalino was still frowning his indecision, when the institution patrol car pulled up. The supervising counselor, who cruised the reformatory check-ing on things, had seen the boys standing around instead of work-ing. He didn't get out of the automobile, merely rolled down the window as Lavalino came over.

"Anything wrong?" the supervisor asked.

"Naw, not really. Just some bullshit friction I can handle okay."

The supervisor looked at Alex; he had been told about him in a staff meeting just last week, as were many newcomers over the course of time. "That's Hammond, isn't it? He's supposed to be wild . . . borderline psychopath with real problems about authority. So keep your eye on him."

"Oh, I can handle him," Lavalino said, smiling in a way that added to the claim.

"I know you can."

"What's on the menu? It's almost lunch."

"Boys' mess hall or staff's?"

"Both. I eat where it's best."

"Chili mac for the gunsels. Salisbury steak for us."

"Both lousy. But the chili's free."

The supervisor chuckled, said good-bye, and drove off. Lavalino clenched his teeth and turned to deal with Alex. The man's shoul-ders were round in unconscious body language supplication, and his hands were extended palms up, showing he was hiding nothing. "Easy does it, young'un. You don't have to be upset."

The tone more than the words jolted Alex, surprising him, for he'd expected a raging adult who would curse and threaten at the very least, and very possibly might lose control. The conciliatory tone stopped Alex cold, yet he sensed that this wasn't the man's real nature. The man who'd thrown the dirt clod was the true Lav-alino, not this phony with a soothing voice.

The adrenaline was gone from Alex, so instead of continued rage there was thought, and even a moment's reflection said that paci-fying the situation was the right thing to do. He had *won;* the man with power was now calming him. How different from three minutes go—the dirt clod and the arrogant challenge.

"Let him go," Lavalino said, having made sure the shovel was at a safe distance. "Are you cooled off?"

"Yes, I'm okay." Actually, he was trembling from nervous exhaustion.

"C'mon," Lavalino said, then glanced at the dozen boys standing around, all of them watching intently. "Take a break," he said to them.

Warily, Alex followed the man's beckoning gesture and fell in beside him.

"I'm not going to report this. If I did, you'd be in the disciplinary company for at least thirty days . . . and that's no picnic. And it'd probably mean an extra few months before parole, too. But it's partly my fault. I didn't mean to hit you in the head with that chunk of dirt. Bounce it off a leg or something . . . just get your attention so you'd work."

"I *was* working . . . hard as anybody. The mattocks were loosening it up for the shovels to dig."

"Okay, okay, let's not argue about it. Anyway, you're not getting a disciplinary report . . . but keep it quiet, 'cause my Italian ass would be in a sling, too, for not reporting something this serious."

"Don't worry. I'm not a fink."

"And lemme give you some advice, kid . . . rein in that temper. It's gonna bring you lots of misery if you don't." Lavalino punctuated the advice with a big brotherly squeeze of Alex's shoulder. The man's solicitude, real or faked, short-circuited the undercurrent of anger still in Alex. The lonely boy within washed over the tough kid. Momentarily his eyes were wet, and he turned his face away, stifling the telltale sniffle. Lavalino was still talking, but Alex didn't hear. He was asking inwardly: Why do I always have to fight? Why is it so ugly? God, I'd just like to be like everyone else.

From the institution power plant came the blast of the noon whistle, signaling it was time to return to the detail grounds for lunch. The whistle also exploded flocks of sparrows from roofs and trees. After lunch Alex went to school. He and Lavalino turned back to where the youths were gathering the tools and lining up. The incident of violence was over.

But not forgotten. The boys on the crew were from various cottages, and by evening all had told the story of "some crazy motherfucker in Scouts, a white guy named Hammond, tried to knock Topo in the head with a shovel . . . had the dirty bastard running with his tail between his legs." Boys fought each other without thought, but what Alex had done was the ultimate "craziness." During the next couple of days he was pointed out on the detail grounds, and the storytellers embellished what they'd seen so that some boys thought Alex was a "maniac," which wasn't a pejorative, and some boys thought him a "ding," which was definitely pejorative.

Distorted word of the assault got to most of the counselors, too, despite the lack of a report. A boy officer in Roosevelt Cottage gossiped to the night man (who smuggled cigarettes in at a dollar a pack when they cost fifteen cents), and the night man told his morning relief, who told others at lunch. When Lavalino was approached, he disparaged the seriousness; he couldn't admit running scared from a twelve-year-old. The counselors never got the whole story, but they got enough to recognize that Alex, although certainly no match in a fight against many of Whittier's youths, was one of the more unpredictably explosive. Some men would simply watch him closer, others would be cautious, and a few would take it as a personal challenge and decide to come down hard if he showed any temper toward them.

Thus, within a few weeks of leaving the receiving cottage, Alex Hammond had gained high visibility—was known by the majority of the boys and counselors. He noticed it on the detail grounds. The cottages marched there at work call twice a day. They were dismissed to go to specified areas according to their assignment. For a few minutes all could mingle. The only other time it was allowed was at church. Otherwise the inhabitants of one cottage were kept away from those in different cottages. After the shovel chase, Alex got occasional nods of recognition at work call. Boys he didn't know would nod or wink on meeting his eyes and say, "All right, Hammond." Or, "Easy does it, Hammond." It happened four times in two weeks. It made him feel good.

It also got him in a brief fight. While joining the school line one afternoon (the largest single group, some hundred and fifty boys), the officer ordered: "Right dress!" The arm that came up didn't just extend for spacing; it shoved him violently.

"Hey, man!" he said, regaining balance, looking at the boy who had shoved him. He was smaller than Alex but he was in Lincoln, the toughest cottage, where his size made him stand out. Alex had noticed him before. His name was Fargo.

"You don't like it?" The challenge was thrown.

"Naw, I don't like it from a fuck. Don't shove."

"Aww, you might tell Topo what to do, but you're just another punk from Scouts, so don't tell me nuthin'."

Punk! Punk! The word of words in the reform-school lexicon. A fight was inevitable. That thought was in Alex's mind when Fargo kicked him in the ankle; a hard kick with steel-capped toes. While the pain shot through Alex, his fist shot out into Fargo's nose. Blood poured instantly and profusely. Alex stepped back and out of line to get room to fight. The ranks broke up for the combatants.

Fargo, however, was leaning forward, holding his head extended so the blood wouldn't drip on his clothes. He was muttering obscenities.

The teacher supervising the march to classes saw the bleeding boy and called a halt. He ordered Fargo aside and had them form into ranks. Alex watched Fargo being led toward the hospital by a counselor, and then he was marching on to school. Throughout the afternoon, Alex couldn't concentrate—not that anyone else even tried to concentrate, or any teacher cared. Reform-school youths have no concern about education, and teachers who wanted to teach resigned to work elsewhere. Whittier had school classes because the state law required it. Everyone did what they wanted short of rebellion and riot. But where most others drew pictures, played games, or leafed through magazines and cut out lingerie ads, Alex tried to learn some things because they interested him: history, geography, social studies. He refused even to try to learn mathematics or science, but the teacher was happy to have a boy desirous of learning anything—most couldn't read and didn't care to learn how—so she let him decide, helping him. It really came down to reading; he liked what he could learn simply by reading.

This afternoon, however, the printed pages became sheets of squiggles. At evening recall on the detail grounds he would have to continue the fight. He wasn't afraid. Rather, the fear was controlled and he was ready to fight—but the wait had his mind running repeatedly over the situation. His brain was stuck like a gramophone record. Once more he wondered why he had to fight continually. Other people didn't have to; he knew that from books. Momentarily, he considered "turning the other cheek," but it made him chuckle. If he turned the other cheek they'd have him bent over spreading *both* cheeks of his ass while making a toy-girl of him—a punk. . . .

Alex was quickly out of the classroom door when the whistle sounded. He waited on the walk while the line of classrooms emptied. He knew an aggressive demeanor might give him an advantage, especially if he started swinging first.

Fargo wasn't at school. He hadn't returned following the bloody nose.

When the school formation marched onto the detail grounds and was dismissed, Alex didn't go to the area where Scouts formed. Instead he stayed in the center, visible and available, while work crews and shop crews arrived and dispersed to the various cottage formation areas.

Fargo was still absent. Was it fear? That was hard to believe, both from how he'd acted and because he lived in Lincoln, the toughest cottage. The smallest guy in Lincoln, too. Yet where was he?

Alex could wait no longer. Cottages were forming ranks. He started toward his own and saw Lulu Cisneros, his first acquaintance in Juvenile Hall, coming toward him. Weeks before, when Alex had gotten out of Receiving, Lulu had given him half a pack of Camels. (Lulu's visitors made him reform-school rich by smuggling him two packs every Sunday; Alex carried them in from the visiting grounds for five cigarettes.) Later, from the shoe shop, Alex pilfered him a pair of capped-toe brogans, a shoe much favored by the boys. Having a pair was a status symbol.

"I was lookin' for you—where you line up?" Lulu said.

"I've been waitin' here for another guy."

"Little Fargo?"

The surprise on Alex's face was sufficient reply.

"He's at the cottage," Lulu continued, "and maybe has a broken nose. It's swollen up and both eyes are black. That's why I'm here. Do you wanna forget it?"

"He fucked with me. I didn't fuck with him."

"Man, man, fuck all that. We ain't got all day. We gotta line up . . . remember."

"Yeah, okay. What's happenin'?"

"I talked to Fargo and he copped out that he started it. He's salty about his nose, but he can laugh at it, too. He didn't expect it. Somebody told him you were a punk or something. But he'll let it drop if you will . . . unless you start talking shit and bragging."

"Afraid of getting his ass kicked." Alex said it without reflection;

it was the standard conclusion by the routine values of the reformatory. Anyone who avoided any fight by so much as "excuse me" or one step backward was deemed afraid.

"Naw, uh-uh, that little cat ain't afraid of a grizzly bear. He's a fightin' motherfucker . . . an' probably can kick your ass. In fact, 'cause he is a tough little cat and everybody knows it, he can let it slide without anybody thinkin' he punked out. He knows he was dead wrong and respects you for having guts."

The detail grounds was now virtually empty. A few stragglers were running toward their formations. Cottages were straightening ranks while a counselor took a head count.

A supervising counselor was bearing down on Alex and Lulu, waving an arm for them to move on. They started to move, angling away from each other while going in the same general direction.

"So what'll I tell him?" Lulu called from ten feet away.

"It's over as far as I'm concerned. I'll shake his hand when I see him."

"Man, don't get fuckin' sickening." Lulu turned and began sprinting for Lincoln, which was the farthest formation. Alex half-walked, half-trotted toward where he belonged, a sudden elation filling him. He'd been ready to fight but was happy that it was unnecessary. It was the sudden removal of the tension, however, that made him glow inwardly.

"Where the fuck have you been?" Constantine snapped when Alex reached the cottage and slipped into his position.

"Just late, man, just late." The smile went, the elation died. As he marched in step, able to do so without thinking about it, he rankled at the way Constantine had spoken. Sooner or later I'm gonna have trouble with him, Alex thought. Then he remembered the cigarette hidden in his pants cuff. The cottage would fall out at the recreation area for half an hour, then wash up and march to supper. It was summer, with long evenings, so after supper there'd be a softball game. He would be the center of three or four boys because of the cigarette. He'd have to share it to get a match, but he didn't mind. He liked sharing. They would lie on the grass as far away from the counselor as possible and pass the butt around surreptitiously. He felt good looking forward to it. . . .

The houseparents were a couple in their early fifties named Hoffman. They had twin daughters who were married, and a third in

278 | Edward Bunker

the WACs. Although one counselor worked from midnight to eight a.m., and a second counselor worked from eight a.m. to five p.m., the Hoffmans were in charge. Living in a small apartment in the cottage, they were nearly as available as real parents. Any boy could knock on their door except, infrequently, when a DO NOT DISTURB sign dangled from the doorknob. When it was there the boys speculated on what was happening within. Roosevelt and Lincoln cottages, with older boys, didn't have housemothers, but all the others had the same staff setup as Scouts. The Hoffmans, however, were more involved with their boys, and did all they could to make institutional living as homelike as possible. They used their own money for a record player, and to have ice-cream-and-cake birthday parties once a week for every boy having a birthday in that period. The Hoffmans tried to break down the "codes" of the underworld that these teenagers were making their personal ethics. When it became obvious that a boy was no longer malleable, he was transferred to another cottage, unless he was under the care of the institution psychiatrist, who was also the only physician. Scouts Cottage was deliberately more lax than the other cottages. Alex sometimes felt that he didn't belong there, but he was nonetheless grateful—except for Constantine.

Two boys were assigned to the cottage as a work assignment. Called "housecats," they cleaned and did light maintenance. Every boy had some small cleanup duty in addition to his own room, for Mrs. Hoffman kept the cottage immaculate, despite fifty delinquents, many of whom knew nothing except slovenliness and dirt, which go with poverty.

The Hoffmans showed a special interest in Alex. They were interested in all the boys, but even real parents have favorites, albeit secretly, and the Hoffmans were more interested in some boys than others. When a housecat went home, Mrs. Hoffman offered Alex the job. It was better than digging ditches, raking leaves, or pushing a lawnmower, and Alex had no desire to learn a trade—shoe shop, paint shop, sheet metal. . . .

Constantine, without doubt, was Mr. Hoffman's most favored boy. Tall, well-built, and good-looking, with curly black hair and a seductive smile, it was easy to see why he was a monitor, especially when so many others were unattractive—unattractive in both looks and manner. Many were grossly ignorant and angry, illiterate black boys from the rural South, brought to Watts as sharecropping diminished in favor of mechanized farming; their parents searched for factory work and they took to the streets of the city. The Chicanos, many of them, had similar stories, except that their parents came across the border. And Okie accents were common among the whites, children of the Dust Bowl—or of broken homes and alcoholics. Youths of all races unable to respond to affection except with suspicion, unable to handle any problem except with rage, children disturbed by an endless list of family and social ills. Scouts Cottage had more boys with severe emotional problems than did the other cottages. Though the Hoffmans were fair, or tried to be, it was impossible not to prefer one who seemed near the All-American ideal. Constantine knew the value of his handsomeness. He hid his rage better than the others, and he also hid his background; his mother was a call girl, and he was a mistake. *Nobody* knew who his father was.

From the beginning Constantine saw Alex as a potential rival with the Hoffmans. The newcomer's education also rankled Constantine, for Alex occasionally, and unintentionally, used some word that the ill-educated boys didn't know. The second day that Alex was in the cottage, Constantine chalked an announcement on the bulletin board. Without thinking, Alex spoke up to correct a misspelling. The correction flushed Constantine's cheeks and planted the seed of hostility.

Many of the authority-hating boys disliked Constantine, whispering, "He's just a kiss-ass snitch." But they were also afraid of him. When they saw how he felt about Alex, they kept their distance from the latter. It wasn't "silence," and he could always find someone to help him smoke the cigarettes Lulu gave him, but he couldn't make any close friendships, and oftentimes he ached with loneliness, although he didn't see anyone in Scouts whom he really liked and wanted for a buddy. He doubted that he could whip Constantine, though he wasn't afraid to try—except he knew that it would turn Mr. Hoffman against him. He was careful to give Constantine no excuse to start anything. Getting out of step, making a marching mistake, or talking in ranks would bring a foot in the ass, the standard summary punishment approved by Mr. Hoffman and the superintendent. Alex was among those, and they were many, who never accepted a kick without a fight. That would bring Mr. Hoffman down on him, win or lose. Ergo, he made no mistakes. His quarters were immaculate. The anxiety would have been too great, and he would have gone at Constantine no matter what, except that he could relax completely in the mornings when he worked for Mrs. Hoffman. All the boys were gone in the mornings except for the other housecat, a thin Chicano nicknamed Hava. They usually worked for an hour or two, waxing the dayroom, pruning weeds from the shrubbery outside the cottage, washing windows. . . . Even then his mind could relax. Then, invariably, Mrs. Hoffman would call them into the apartment for donuts or cake or some other sweet delicacy. Whenever he thought of Mrs. Hoffman in the later years, he always thought of brownies; she gave him the first one he could ever remember. He dreaded noon when he and Hava joined the rest of the cottage on the grounds detail. Even though he didn't see Constantine at school in the afternoon, he had to stay ready. Seldom did an afternoon pass without at least one fist fight.

NATHAN C. HEARD
1936–

Nathan Heard grew up in a Newark ghetto and spent fifteen years in New Jersey reformatories and jails. While serving a sentence for armed robbery in Trenton State Prison from 1961 to 1966, he became a voracious reader of literature and history. One day, after reading a sex novel borrowed from his cellmate, Heard said, "I could write a better book than that," and so began a new career. Before his release he had finished two novels, including Howard Street, *a searing naturalistic work set in his old neighborhood, published by Dial Press in 1968 to enthusiastic reviews and selling more than a million copies.*

In the 1970s, Heard published three more novels, all with major publishers: To Reach a Dream, A Cold Fire Burning, *and* When Shadows Fall. *He also taught creative writing at Fresno State College, where he won the Most Distinguished Teacher Award, and at Rutgers University. It was not until 1983, however, with the publication of* House of Slammers, *that Heard focused his creative gaze directly on his prison experience.*

House of Slammers *is the most penetrating novel yet published about the late-twentieth-century American prison. It centers on the ethical dilemma of "Beans" Butler, who has transformed himself from a small-time armed robber in the Newark ghetto to a deeply committed humanist thinker and aspiring activist, as he is thrust into leadership of a convict movement for some modest reforms in Trenton State Prison.*

In the scene reprinted here, Butler emerges from a confrontation with the most implacable prison authority to face intractable contradictions among the convicts themselves, embodied by the leaders of a white supremacist group (Casey), the prison's Muslims (Mustafa), the black nationalists (Wally), the Puerto Ricans (Chino and Paco), as well as Joe Valli, whose minor role in organized crime makes him a big shot among the convicts, and Pittsburgh Pete, the pen's most dangerous black wheeler-dealer.

from *House of Slammers*

THEY SEEMED TO APPROACH each other with the cautious stealth of guerrilla fighters. Casey Ryan and Joe Valli headed up a six-man delegation of white inmates. Wally Allen, Mustafa, and Pittsburgh Pete Jones were fronting a loosely formed group of eight inmates including two Puerto Ricans representing the Hispanic prisoners. Beans had been the last one to reach the big yard. He watched the two groups and became filled with a feeling of irony that could not match the near-nauseous pain that overlay his acutely tuned sensibilities.

The clouds were sparse and high, and the sun painted the expanse in between a delicate blue that in the near distance thinned into an off white, framing a crescent-shaped sliver of moon that looked like it could have been an opening to eternity. The winds were relatively mild for a change; the temperature was in the high forties, but it felt much warmer. Beans watched the groups moving toward each other from opposite sides of the yard, and the revolutionary maxim, "The enemy of my enemy is my friend," seemed to become not only less absolute, but less applicable as well. The deeper he got involved, the more he despaired to trust his comrades.

Almost the first thing one learned in prison was to believe in paradoxes, to believe everything and believe nothing. The devastation that accrues to any man's or woman's mind because of the faith one must maintain each day in absurdities (merely in order to continue lying down and getting up) is perhaps the least of everyone's concerns. Yet life in an institution is sustained by the heavy dose of illusions that helps offset the course one takes to make a friend of time for another day. Beans watched them. . . . They watched each other. It seemed he could still hear Chief Deputy Rangler's hard voice warning, *"You've got a big problem, Butler. You have eyes but you refuse to see. Look around you. Look at what you might be giving away. Look at who you're giving up your future opportunities for."* Rangler had pointed in the general direction of the prison's wings. *"You don't even have very much in common with the great majority of these jokers, so why are you willing to lose everything you've worked for just for them?"*

Beans' wry smile was the least indicator of the great distance that separated them across the small extent of Rangler's desk, and he had replied, *"I know what you mean, Chief—really, but I don't see that as my biggest problem. I think my biggest problem is your inability to understand that I am them—like it or not, I am them."*

The two groups of prisoners met out in right field, about two hundred and fifty feet from home plate. They scrutinized each other across a ten-foot-square grate that covered a pit near the wall where mysterious underground isolation cells left over from the last century were supposed to be hidden, according to the jailhouse know-alls. All Beans had ever seen whenever he'd looked down into the black depth was a crisscross series of pipes. Like others he had at one time or another speculated upon whether he could escape under the wall, if he could somehow without being seen secret himself in the blackness that the grate covered. To his knowledge, no one had even tried to escape via that method, and it seemed to suggest to everyone that that way did not provide a way out. So the grate got most of its attention from the right fielders of the softball teams who knew that a false step could provide them with the kind of escape nobody wanted—via the hospital.

Beans watched as the two groups immediately engaged themselves in the only kind of political act that had ever worked for them: They thrust with their silent manhood stances at the others' macho postures, without wondering how far they would have to carry the pretense—which so often went beyond itself, becoming senseless acts of pure instinctive defiance. The desperation was the same particular attitude they showed to the administration, indeed toward all the vague officialdom that ruled their desperate lives. Each man worried at how far into the pit of violence he might have to go, but most were prepared, however reluctantly, to go a little farther than was needed. No one could say where fear began and desperation ended. And it was always better to be thought cold or crazy than be thought a punk. A dude's attitude was often his only security. Most prisoners agreed on that. But on the other hand most prisoners were not sophisticated enough, or never got far enough removed from their particular straits, to show a different or deceptive face to their adversaries. Thus for the most part they were constrained to appear as they were.

As he came up to them, Beans knew that they were, first of all, each other's adversaries. Of the three identifiable emotions he felt —frustration, anger, despair—it was despair that held sway. He could not shake himself of the feeling that seemed to get stronger each day—that the people he felt needed change the most would resist change the most—not that they themselves didn't want changes, but simply that they weren't quite ready to trust a different kind of uncertainty—one of their own making.

Casey Ryan stood in front of the white inmates with his hands thrust into his waist jacket. He stiffly faced Mustafa and Wally Allen and Chino Morales as if his fists would automatically attack them if he allowed them to escape his pockets. Pittsburgh Pete and a Puerto Rican, Paco (a newcomer to prison but a leader by virtue of his "successful" street reputation as a small-time drug supplier), were talking to each other.

When Beans got close enough, he heard Wally Allen's voice tensely warning Casey:

". . . you ain't got nuthin' to do with tellin' my men *nuthin*', man! These prison officials is the same kinda fascist you is—they just bigger, and deal less in personal racism than ordinary white trash do."

Casey leaned forward on the balls of his feet. He was like a deadly predator about to strike. "You callin' me white trash?" he asked in low, even tones.

Wally, while alert for an attack, shrouded himself in calm, playing possum, halfheartedly deceiving the enemy. To him the preeminent adversary engagement was dictated by the principles of the Cool School all oppressed minorities attended. For only the weak had to be cool—until they learned that, either directly or indirectly, they had the least to lose. And they never really surprised each other, for they knew each other's game so well.

Wally's long lashes dropped enough to make him appear tired, bored, and sleepy—none of which he was. "Well, let me tell you what I think white trash is," he said to Casey. "And you can tell me whether you is or not. Now what I calls white trash is them whites who ain't got no more'n black people: they in the jails like black folks, they in the unemployment lines like the black folks, they on the welfare roles just like the blacks, they ain't got no more economic or political power than black folks, but somehow they still remain dumb enough to think they better than black folks. That's what I calls white trash," Wally ended in a voice that matched his placid facade.

"That ain't callin' *me* white trash," Casey retorted, satisfied that he was giving the distinct impression that Wally wasn't being personal. Casey's own deception was, of course, just as blinding as Wally's, except his adversary engagement (due to the great symbolism of his skin) directed him to blustering and bluff instead of Cool School tactics. The paradox of their mutual powerlessness, however, incensed them both to such a disastrous degree that their words to each other were like blows that gave terrible pain; words so true that at the snap of a finger each man would kill to silence them.

Beans hurried to step between the two tensed figures. He heard Rangler's laughter ringing in his head. It made him angrier than he'd been in a long time. He didn't want to see his sacrifice wasted by the pettiness of a hatred that was first of all ill-directed.

"What the hell're you guys arguin' for?" he demanded. "Can't you see what it does? If you don't stop all this dumb shit, then we might as well call this whole thing off."

"I ain't arg'in'!" Wally snapped. "I'm just lettin' a few things be known up front, that's all."

"Well, we'd better all deal up front, 'cause the chief is out for blood," Beans said. "We don't even have a proper set of grievances yet—can't you guys see what's happenin' here?"

Like a true egomaniac Wally resented being thought petty, and grew angrier at the implication that he was being stupid as well. He stood with his fists tightly balled against his thighs, where they involuntarily beat a tattoo that punctuated his words. "I just don't want no fascist cracker tryin' t'be no boss. I ain't goin' for it!"

Casey pointed a thick finger at Wally. "Well, you're a goddam communist, ain't ya? Ya think I'd take orders from you—I'd take y'r fuckin' head off, that's how I'd follow a commie-nigger like you!" His clear emphasis exempted the other blacks from the insult, and they seemed to understand it.

The two contesters, however, were obliged by the vague rules of manhood to advance—to attack. Or to invite attack, which was only less admirable because the loser always had the option of claiming that the element of surprise, rather than his opponent's ability, was what defeated him. An unworthy excuse. In such a place as this, where one's purest triumphs were still not clean enough to suit the world (even on the outside), nobody wanted sullied victories. To their world a convict was the lowest piece of shit that God had ever shat upon the earth. And the only ones to whom the judgment really mattered were the convicts. So they would fight off the image by fighting each other and only later perhaps understand how they had helped make the judgment come true.

Beans struggled to keep his voice from trembling with the anger he felt. "I want this stuff to stop! We got real problems to deal with—"

Wally turned on him. "You ain't no goddam boss either, man!"

Beans kept himself calm, though he was burning to respond to Wally in kind. It was clear that the black nationalist leader was in a rumbling mood—and he was hotheaded enough to try anyone. Like so many men who wind up in prison, he had lived life on intimate terms with his temper. Its flare-ups gave off sparks that sought to prove there was plenty of life behind dull, dark eyes, and the sudden flashes always provided a safe shelter for self-righteous reasoning.

"Look, Wally," Beans finally said. "I'm not tryin' to be anybody's boss. But I don't intend to allow you guys' personalities, politics, or religion to get me messed up f'nuthin'."

"Well I just want it known here that *I'm a man,* man. And I don't need no white folks to lead me *nowhere,*" Wally ended strongly. He had made his position known and it immediately mollified him.

Mustafa spoke more softly than usual. "The brotha-man wants his pride. I can understand that."

"So can I," Beans replied. "But if we keep on reactin' to jive situations out of some fucked-up pride-filled notion—one-sided more than anything—we'll always be actin' against our own best interests, whether in politics, economics, or to see what nigga can run the hundred-yard dash the fastest. Pride becomes counterproductive if it's the goddam basis for action. Pride is real, but it's only an intangible commodity in a real world, man."

"I don't agree with that," Wally said. "Pride is the essence of everything we's about." He paused, then recited: "It's the wellspring from which everything that aspires to human nobility must come."

Beans could not remember where he'd heard or read that philosophical axiom before, but he was sure that he had. It sounded trite enough to last forever.

Wally looked quite pleased with himself, as if he'd said the penultimate word. The realm of pride was dear to him, and to Mustafa as well. It was the area where they most resembled each other.

"Listen, you guys," Casey broke in. "Like I been sayin', me and my men're ready to work with anybody to get what we want outta this. We ain't makin' no heavy demands on nobody; we ain't just tryin' t'be friends with nobody; we're only tryin' t'make it better in here for everybody, since we all gotta be here. We're organized, but you guys obviously need to think it over. We'll wait over by the wall for a while till all this pride stuff settles—" He left it hanging and motioned to Joe Valli and the other white inmates to follow him.

Beans' smile was steady, but his heart was beating like jazz drummers Elvin Jones and Tony Williams were playing simultaneous solos inside his chest. He had already committed himself deeply, and Chief Deputy Rangler was going to be hot on his case; and now these hot-headed dudes were on the verge of throwing all of it out the window for the sake of a definition of pride.

He spoke calmly—felt calm, too—as he looked from Mustafa to Wally and back again. Morales seemed caught between staying with the blacks or following the whites. He settled for joining Pittsburgh and Paco, both of whom hadn't really tuned in to what had been happening.

"You know, in order to deal with a problem, you gotta first admit that one exists. And many of them exist beyond our definitions—if not beyond our control. Patience and hard work become supremely important because we gotta use them both to turn our anguish into tactics and strategies that address the real issue, instead of soothing our fuckin' pride. Man, don't waste what we can do here. We can't afford to waste anything."

"I agree wid that." Wally nodded vigorously. "And I consider myself a producer in the interests of my brothas and sistuhs. I mean, ain't no tellin' how many-a these young bloods me and my Simbas—and the Muslim brothas, too—done kept from bein' turned into fags. And goddamit, I don't care how much me and the Muslims disagree about religion, we both start from the same point of black pride; pride in self breeds pride in one's people. And I just wanna say that, far's I'm concerned, anybody, *anybody* who says different is a traitor to black people."

Beans didn't have to look at Mustafa to know that he was in heavy accord with Wally's sentiments, at least on this particular point. He was himself, up to a point—a limited point.

"I don't know how I can make you see that we have no real disagreement, Wally," Beans said, trying to send out waves of sincerity toward Wally and Mustafa. Between the two, he was most in tune with Mustafa, who by virtue of his belief was acutely constrained—he could not go to the ultimate degree, for his actions would have to be directed from a metaphysical source, as it was "written." The enemy had no such constraints upon them, but the Ranglers of the world easily matched the Muslims' righteousness with a greater self-righteousness only conquerors can feel.

"All I'm sayin' is that pride is relative, man," Beans explained. "But it's irrelevant to the facts as we gotta deal with 'em. I'm sayin' that your pride, like anybody else's, is mostly a matter of opinion, unless you have the power to be the opinion-maker. Do y'all wanna argue opinions? Y'wanna debate the degree of *manhood* a man's gotta have in order to be a man—*in your opinions?* I don't care how many guys you've kept from becomin' fags. I know they could prevent it from happenin' themselves if they'd really wanted to." Beans looked directly at Mustafa and almost as an afterthought said,

"And if any fags wanna join in the demonstration for the good of everybody, I ain't gon' deny 'em a proper place."

Mustafa stiffened. "I won't allow the Fruit to be corrupted by sexual degenerates, brother Butler. We've gotta draw the line somewhere."

"The lines are already evident," Beans said. "They're also voluntary—made so by your different choices in life-styles. Those guys' assholes belong to them, man, and they can haul red-hot coals inside of 'em if they wanna, as long as it doesn't burn me."

Wally was unwrapping a stick of chewing gum. He carefully balled the wrapper and launched it toward the grate, where it disappeared down into the darkness. He looked directly at Beans. "I ain't got nuthin' personal against fags, man. But be for real about this thing—Them sissies is after pleasure for themselves first and foremost. A revolutionary attitude comes by fightin', not fuckin' —Shit, man, that's one of the ways the Panthers got castrated: Too many-a them niggas had empty heads and loaded dicks 'steada the other way around."

Beans was getting really weary of trying to penetrate both Wally and Mustafa's socio-politico-religious opinions. Over the years he had found out (in some very dangerous ways, too) how futile it could be to argue against a person's beliefs, no matter how ridiculous those beliefs and opinions might seem. No facts can move a rationale that is inspired by the heavy tandem forces of selfishness and willful ignorance that concerns itself primarily with eternal mysteries as seen through the burning eyes of utterly mundane messengers.

His need was for an increasing reality. Somehow he had grown into a practicality that they, for their particular reasons, could never seem to accept. They had been hurt and perhaps successfully frightened off by a system that allowed them only the bare minimum means to survive, not to mention cope. But only they at least could best describe where they hurt—and that was what was important to him, for then some kind of remedy could be devised for that area. But he saw that these guys wanted an immediate and total relief, which is why they chose to argue against or for the qualifications of physicians—though they weren't even near-qualified to test any of the ones they chose.

Beans looked over at Casey's group, where Joe Valli had everyone's attention as he talked, gesticulated, and paced a few steps in front of them. He was a very hairy man. Some of the hair on his arms appeared to be an inch long. Hair bristled up and over the front of his shirt; it shot out of his ears like porcupine quills. His chin maintained a five o'clock shadow—even five minutes after he'd shaved—and he was forever reaching stubby fingers inside his nostrils in order to snatch out the stiff strands that grew there like crabgrass. It gave added ammunition to his enemies among the prisoners who behind his back called him a bugger-eater. It showed a much greater contempt than did Wop, Guinea, or spaghetti-bender—and it was much more enjoyable to the name-callers because he was unaware of his habit (which no one ever dared mention to him) or of the contempt-material it provided to those who needed it.

Beans turned to face Mustafa—as if to avoid more of Wally's rhetorical outburst. "We'd better examine the basic question here, Mustafa," he said solemnly. "I'm only gon' say this one time, so everybody'd better pay attention or count me out of this shit right now—"

He called to Casey to bring the others over, then announced, "You guys are gettin' nowhere because you can't even agree where the hell it is you wanna go. Y'all don't want full participation by this, that, or the other guy or group for the dumbest reasons: somebody's color or because they choose to take or give a dick to somebody else. I haven't heard any real concrete thoughts come out of all the runnin' off at the mouth you been doin', 'cause you dudes only deal in abstracts—social mores, religious opinions, moral truths, which in the end all the forces rallied against us don't even give a shit about. Now either you guys git your shit together or I'm goin' back to my cell and finish out my bit—like I'm beginnin' to think I shoulda done in the first place. Y'all make up y'minds, man." He walked away leaving the dozen or so men still loosely gathered looking at each other and for a way to break the ensuing silence.

Joe Valli spoke. "Hey, listen, we gotta have unity here. I seen the value of unity on the docks of Port Newark and the New York harbor. I seen guys who didn't want each odda to live another minute longer suddenly come togedda because they had common interests—"

"And that's all we got t'do!" Casey put in. "We're workin' on bigger things here than our personal differences, which I'm willin' t'lay aside."

"Well, bully f'you," Wally cracked.

"You damn right, bully f'me," Casey returned. "It's also lucky—"

Wally braced: "Fa-*who*, cracker?"

"For *you*, nigger!" Casey said.

Joe Valli and Mustafa quickly got between them. And suddenly Pittsburgh Pete was back in the picture. "*Hey, ol' dudes!* Where y'all think y'all at? This the yard, man, and fightin' costs ten days in the hole—"

Casey's face was a swarthy mass of anger as he stared at the smirking Wally. He allowed Joe Valli to pull him away, but not without effort. He was mumbling under his breath, but everyone could clearly hear several "nigger bastard" epithets span the hatred between them.

Beans was back to watching them from across the big yard. Anger and frustration had put a tiny hole in his spirit. Now the futile attempt at organizing people who had never known organization before threatened to make that hole as large as the one in the ground in right field. He wondered why so-called sexual purism, religion, and deeply penetrating hatred always seemed to hang together in the affairs of people who needed to be about other things.

CHARLES CULHANE
1944–

One of seven children of Irish-American working-class parents, Charles Culhane grew up in the east Bronx, went to Catholic parochial school, dropped out of high school, worked in a department store, and then, in his late teens, stuck up a taxicab driver with a toy gun. After serving more than two years in prison and while still on parole, he held up a gas station with a real gun, getting shot twice in the process. His criminal career came to an end in a bizarre episode two years later.

In September 1968, Culhane was being transported to court with two other prisoners in a sheriff's car. One of the other prisoners grabbed a gun from one of the two deputy sheriffs and demanded the key to his handcuffs. The other deputy drew his gun, shot the would-be escapee, who then shot him and one of the other prisoners. Culhane crossed his handcuffed hands in front of his head just before the dying deputy fired a final shot that went through both his hands and lodged in his skull.

Culhane was tried for felony murder, that is, participating in a felony (the attempted escape) during which someone is killed. His first trial ended in a hung jury. In a second trial he was convicted and sentenced to death in 1971. He was spared execution when the Supreme Court ruled in 1972 (in Furman v. Georgia) that existing capital punishment laws were unconstitutional, but he remained on death row through 1973, when both the death sentence and the conviction itself were overturned on appeal. Meanwhile, a defense committee, headed by Allen Ginsberg, Pete Seeger, and William Buckley, was active on his behalf. Turning down an offer to plead guilty to manslaughter, Culhane was convicted in a third trial and sentenced to twenty-five years to life. When he was paroled in 1992, he had been imprisoned for twenty-six of his forty-eight years.

While in prison, Culhane was inspired by a biography of Arthur Rimbaud to write poetry as "my way out of the sense-lessness and pain that had become my life." His chapbook An Argument for Life *appeared in 1973, and his poems have been published in numerous journals and anthologies, including* Time Capsule, Candles Burn in Memory Town, *and* The Light from Another Country. *He now holds the rank of lecturer and regularly teaches criminal justice courses in the American Studies Department of the State University of New York at Buffalo and devotes much of his life to combating the death penalty and the prison-building frenzy.*

Of Cold Places

FOR ANNE WATKINS

I used to keep a list of foreign prisons:
Lubyanka in Moscow, Portolova in Spain,
California's Terminal Island,
exotic names of cold places.

And I thought: one day I'll make a poem
listing all the names
and conjure from their histories
hard memories
of humans among stone.

I'm older now, the lists grow
the edges of paper curl up, turn brown.
The names still cry out
without voice
without ear to hear them
and I can't remember what it was
I was supposed to do
except live nearer the fire.

Sing Sing, 1984

Autumn Yard

I sit bundled in the peaceful sun.

To my right, a slip of colored sail
     goes downriver
       behind the old death house.

Two prisoners circle a dirt path
     bordering a green field

double-fenced and walled
with liberal layers of barbed wire.

Buck, a Lifer, works on the bars
doing chins and dips
building his house trim and strong
against the long years.

"House" is his body

George, hands scrunched in wordless pockets
walks with recent loss
of his young brother.
We nod hello, and faded pennants
snap in the wind along the fencetop.

Sing Sing, 1985

First Day of Hanukkah

Old Doc, my neighbor
in his dark wrinkled prison clothes
in the dim tier-light of evening
put out his cell light
put on an electric blue yarmulke
over wild shocks of white hair.

Inseparable from weighty congested traffic
of bodies each with its own language
mumbling along the edges of concrete confusion
bracketed by cries of steel & silent histories
moving through daunting time, somber, calm
guilt and expiation emblazoned along neon walls
as clear as unseen galaxies, as uncertain.

Just a man in his cell praying amidst the chaos of prison.

Amidst the bustle & the boredom
of maximum security life
he lit three candles on the bars
& sat on the end of his bed w/prayerbook.
He prayed in the small light

in his sixty-ninth year
neither murderer nor holy man
just a bit of bone & spirit
remembering the song beyond the ruins.

Sing Sing, 1986

PATRICIA McCONNEL
1931–

Before she was sixteen, Patricia McConnel had ridden freights, hitchhiked across the country, and spent her first time in jail. After a brief stint in the U.S. Army and several jobs as a B-girl, waitress, and machine-shop worker, she describes her life like this: "She turned to a life of crime, which seemed to offer high wages for people like herself, that is, with no particular skills. After failing at that as well, eventually ending up in a federal prison, she tried marriage, the worst disaster of all. When you've failed at everything you ever tried, what's left? To become a writer, of course."

Thanks to income from her first book—The Woman's Work-at-Home Handbook: Income and Independence with a Computer—*and two writing fellowships from the National Endowment for the Arts, McConnel was able to work on serious fiction.* Sing Soft, Sing Loud, *a volume of interconnected stories based on her prison experience, was published in 1989 by Atheneum, received significant critical acclaim, and soon appeared in a French translation. The title story reprinted here is taken from the revised edition of that book, currently available from Logoría, her own publishing house in Flagstaff, Arizona, which has also issued her* Guidebook for Artists Working in Prison.

"Having accepted once and for all that she is unemployable," McConnel says, she makes her living at home doing editing and programming. She also spends considerable time reading to prisoners and working for prison reform.

Sing Soft, Sing Loud

YOU GOTTA UNDERSTAND what it's like in here at night. We can start with black. Here, when they say "Lights out!" they mean lights fuckin' *out*. They don't leave *nothin'* on. There's no windows, so light can't even filter in from the street, and when they throw that switch, you're just lost in a black hole. The first guy who said "You can't see your hand in front of your face" was talking about this here jail. That's why when they come in here in the middle of the night and throw the lights on, you're so blinded you can't see nothin' for a couple of minutes, and you feel like somebody threw a spotlight on you.

The reason all this is going on is this is the receiving tank where I'm at, 'cause I ain't been to trial yet and I can't get out on bail 'cause Arnie's holding all the money and he won't go my bail 'cause it's a felony this time. I'm gonna do some real time behind this one and he figures I'm just a lost cause, even though I got busted on accounta him, holding his shit, me that never yet stuck a needle in my arm. So here you are trying to sleep and a bunch of things happen all at once: you hear the creak and groan of this giant metal door opening, blinding lights go on in your eyes, some woman is screaming all kinds of bad shit 'cause she's drunk and they're dragging her in here, and the metal door gets slammed shut hard 'cause the screw is pissed off with the drunk giving her a bad time, and if you happen to be deep asleep when all this goes off you wake up thinking the world blowed up in your face.

But I ain't through yet. When they bring the drunks in they're hollering and cussing, mad to be busted if they even know what the hell is going on. But more than likely they got busted 'cause they been wrecking some joint or beating up on their ol' man or their kids, and they was mad to begin with. So they raise hell for about a half a hour before they conk out. Then along towards three in the morning some of 'em start with the throwing up and the d.t.'s. Them that's sober enough to think of it tries to find the toilet to throw up in, but it's so dark they can never find it, and in the morning you wouldn't believe the smell and the mess. Some of them has fell down and bruised themselves. Anyway, when they start with the throwing up and the d.t.'s you'd be glad to go back to the lights and the cussing. These women are snake-pit crazy. They think someone's trying to kill 'em, or they think they're eating poison food, or someone's coming at 'em with a knife, or they're being thrown in a pit of fire, or there's rats and snakes coming out of the walls—that's a favorite around here. Weekends are the worst of course. When five or six of 'em get to going at once it's like being in a insane asylum in hell.

One night all this stuff is going on and I'm just laying there trying to be cool and stay sane through the night, and I hear this one woman with a strong clear voice and she ain't seeing rats or nothin', what she's seeing is flying saucers full of enemy aliens, and they're landing in her backyard and eating up her children, and she's taking charge of everything and she's telling someone to put on his radiation-proof suit and get the ray gun. And then I guess they're going out there to save the kids, 'cause she's shouting, "Watch out for that radioactive puddle!" and shit like that.

There's something about that voice that gets to me. I feel like crying, I feel like I know that person, and after a while I realize I *do* know that person. That's Millie's voice. I sit straight up on my bunk and listen hard. Maybe it's somebody sounds like Millie, but it's not, it's Millie; she's got just this certain combination of small-town Western accent and cigarette husky in her voice that ain't like nobody else's.

Jeezuz god on a fuckin' bicycle, I never been here when Millie come in before. I never knew she got that crazy drunk. After I'm sure who it is, I can't even lie down again I'm so freaked out and miserable. First I try not to listen and then I *have* to listen; this is *Millie* talking crazy here. I feel embarrassed, like I'm someplace I ain't supposed to be, like I walked in on somebody masturbating or something, but worse. But I can't help listening, this is *Millie* for chrissake, like I never knowed her. Fuckin' bonkers, jeezuz.

So I'm sitting bolt upright on my bunk, staring out into the black, when the lights go on again and the tank door whocks open. In a few seconds I hear the screws stomping up the steel stairs to the upper ramp. They must be full up on the first tier. And in another few seconds they go by my cell with a black chick who looks like she can't hardly walk, like her legs are gonna buckle under her any second, and there's two screws with her instead of one like usually, and they're holding her up and pushing her along by her arms. I only see her for a couple of seconds, but you know

how it is when something's knocked you for a loop; all your cir-
cuits is blowed wide open and it don't take you long to take in a
whole lot, and that's how I am when they go by with this chick. I
get a good look at her face, and in the condition I'm in, all upset
about Millie, this chick's face hits me hard. She's got a look people
only get when they been down and out a long time, usually they
been in and out of jails a lot, and so that's why I call this look
jailface.

Partly, jailface just happens when you been under everybody's
heel too long, but after a while you learn to do it on purpose so
you never let on that you're scared or feeling pain or worry or
sickness. What you do is, you freeze your face so nothin' moves.
Your eyebrows don't scrunch together in a frown, your mouth
don't twitch or smile or sneer. Freeze ain't exactly the right word
'cause it makes it sound like the face goes hard, when actually it
goes limp and you don't let it tighten up over nothin' at all, ever.
The real mark of jailface, though, is the eyes. They don't never look
straight at nobody and they don't even focus half the time. You
can't look into the eyes of somebody with jailface 'cause your look
bounces off a glassy surface of eyeball that's so hard it would
bounce bullets.

Jailface ain't necessarily a bad thing to have, 'cause the minute a
screw knows you're scared or weak she's got the upper hand, and
she jumps on you with both feet and don't let up 'til she's had her
satisfaction, which in most cases is to see your spirit dead. But if
you're walking around with jailface she can't tell if something is
still stirring in there or not. Most likely she thinks by your look
that you're already dead, so there's no challenge, nothin' in there
to kill, see. But people ain't really dead 'til they're really dead, if
you know what I mean. Maybe you've given up, maybe you're a
fuckin' zombie, but just about anybody got a little life left in 'em
that can spark up the minute they latch on to a little piece of hope,
and if you got jailface you can keep that hid from the screws so
they can't stomp it out of you.

Well, anyway, in this second or two while this chick is passing
my cell I decide she's a junkie, 'cause a junkie going to jail is about
the most given-up person you ever seen, and 'cause she's black,
'cause funny thing is, black chicks don't get jailface as a general
rule. I mean they *can*, but not usually. I get in trouble saying stuff
like this 'cause you ain't supposed to say Black is like this and

White is like that, but I can't help it, it's the truth. Black women just seem to do their time different. They sing more, goof around more. They don't zombie out like the rest of us. They even get mad more, fight more, and when they turn funny in here, they fall in love harder. I figure the singing and the goofing around is how black chicks cover up, something they use instead of jailface. I don't know for sure—I never been black. But all I know is, when a black chick has jailface it's gotta be something very very bad that's going on, like being a sick junkie.

So anyway I figure this girl is a sick hype and when the screws put her in the cell next to mine I think, Oh great, now I'm gonna have a sick junkie screaming right next door, on top of everything else. As the screws leave, ol' Blodgett sees me sitting up on my bunk and she says, with this nasty grin on what she has the nerve to call a face, "What's the matter, Iva, can't you sleep?" "Ha ha ha," I says, but they already gone by.

There's a lull in the alkie olympics downstairs. Maybe they was shocked silent by the lights. I'm glad I can't hear Millie no more. But in the quiet I can hear the chick next door moaning, "Oh sweet Jesus, I'm sick, I'm sick."

"Don't you start too," I says. "It's bad enough around here. I don't need nobody moaning and groaning right next door." She don't answer and I don't hear another peep outa her. Millie seems to be quiet now too. In fact, they all quieted down now, finally wore out and passed out, I guess. But I'm too shook up about Millie to go to sleep. I just sit there staring into the dark for a while, and then I start hearing the junkie next door breathing. She's breathing funny, not regular like you're supposed to, catching her breath and trying not to cry or something. I start to feel bad about yelling at her. "You want a cigarette?" I says.

She says, "Girl, I'm too sick to smoke."

So I just sit there staring in the dark, and I wonder what Millie's gonna be like in the morning, and then I don't want to think about it so I don't think about nothin'; I just sit there staring. It's about twenty minutes later when the junkie begins to sing. Real soft, real tender her voice is, and I like listening to a sweet voice singing soft like that. She sings sad dreamy songs, like "Me and My Shadow" and "Down in the Valley." She's gonna sing herself to sleep and me with her. It don't feel so much like being buried alive in the dark with her singing sweet like that. What a relief from all that screaming and crying.

But in a while her songs start getting more upbeat, 'til finally she's singing stuff like "I Can't Get No Satisfaction," and some Aretha Franklin and Tina Turner and Janis Joplin—jeez, I didn't think nobody even remembered ol' Janis no more. She's singing a whole lot of stuff I'm really into, and I just can't help singing with her. When she hears me chiming in she starts clapping her hands, and so I clap too, and when the pace wears us out we go back to old funkies like "Frankie and Johnny" and "Bye Bye Blackbird." Finally somebody hollers, "For chrissake shut up!"

We stop singing and I ask her, "How you feeling?"

"I think I better sing some more. It helps to sing."

"Don't they give you nothin' to help you through it?"

"Girl, they don't know I'm sick. I got busted for s'liciting and they never checked me for no marks. If I can keep them from finding out I'm sick, maybe I'll get thirty days for s'liciting 'stead of having to take the cure. What's your name?"

"Iva. What's yours?"

"Angora. What you in for?"

I do some fast thinking. I don't want to tell her I'm here for possession for sale. Too much to explain. The stuff wasn't even mine—everybody says that. So I says, "Same as you—soliciting."

"And you don't got a habit?"

"No."

"Good for you, girl. Does your old man treat you good?"

"He's all right."

"Uh-huh. I hear you ain't saying he treat you real fine. Listen, don't let him give you no habit. They like you to get hooked so they can control you. You stay clean. There ain't nothin' worth this misery."

"I managed so far. Listen, you said you want to sing some more. Do you know the slow version of 'Cocaine Blues'?"

"How do it go?"

I sing, "Early one morning while a-making the rounds/ Took a shot of cocaine and I shot my woman down/ Shot her down 'cause she made me sore/ I thought I was her daddy but she had five more."

"Naw, I don't know that one. I never heard it."

So I teach her all the words I can remember, then she says, "Do you know the peaches song?"

"No."

She sings, "If you don't like my peaches/ Why do you shake my tree?/ If you don't like my peaches/ Why do you shake my tree?/ Get out of my orchard/ And leave my fruit tree be.

"Let me be your little dog/ 'til the big dog come./ Let me be your little dog/ 'Til your big dog come./ When the big dog come/ Just tell him what the little dog done."

We giggle over that one, and then I think of "C. C. Rider," and she knows it too, so we sing it together, and then she asks me if I know "Gloomy Sunday," and I says, "Yeah. You know, when that song first come out thousands of people committed suicide all over the country, and they tried to outlaw the song."

"Yeah, I heard that too."

So we sing "Gloomy Sunday" and "I Shall Be Released." These are all songs you learn if you spend a lot of time sitting around in jails, and she's pretty impressed that I know all that stuff. We're having a real party considering the circumstances. Then we hear the tank door clang open and heels clunking on the concrete floor. That can only be Blodgett. She's built like a buffalo and wears size-thirty shoes with lead in the heels. The footsteps stop somewhere under us and Blodgett yells, "Cut out that singing up there or I'll throw you in flatbottom." Then she stomps out and I tell Angora, "A screw can't stand to think there's ever ten minutes you ain't doing real hard time. If we was crying or moaning with pain or screaming with the d.t.'s she wouldn'ta said nothin'."

"I need a cigarette now."

We have to grope in the dark for each other's hands and when her hand touches mine it's ice cold and she's shaking. I pass her a book of matches and when she's lit up she says, "What's flatbottom?"

"It ain't a nice place. Ain't you been in jail before?"

"Not this one."

"I thought all jails had flatbottoms. Anyway, it's a cell on the first tier with nothin' in it. No toilet, no cot, no water, no nothin'. If you piss, you piss on the floor. If you shit, you shit on the floor. Then you sleep in it 'til they let you out to clean it up. They ain't supposed to leave you in there more than twenty-four hours but they keep you there long as they want. It ain't supposed to be for punishment but that's what they use it for."

"What's it for, then?"

"Protective custody, they call it. Somebody's crazy, trying to commit suicide or something, they put 'em in there 'til they cool off. Sort of like a padded cell without the padding."

"I don't see what good it do to make a person shit on the floor."

"I seen people try to stuff their heads down the toilet. Anyway, the screws use it mostly to keep people in line, and it works pretty good that way. So we better not sing no more."

But Angora says, "Girl, if I don't sing, I'll scream. Now I don't mind if I have to go to flatbottom, but I don't want to start screaming 'cause once I start I won't be able to stop." And so she starts off again. At first I keep quiet, but after a while I think, Oh, what the hell, I strung along with her this far, I can go to the end. So I sing with her, but softly now. And pretty soon the screw comes back and this time the lights all go on and she comes upstairs and marches straight to Angora's cell. I hear the cell door open and then shut, and then she pushes Angora past my cell and Angora is singing "Won't You Come Home Bill Bailey" and she's doing a little dance step as the screw drags her along the ramp to the stairs. This time I notice how skinny she is.

I hear the door to flatbottom open and then slam shut. Even though I know I was singing too soft for Blodgett to hear me this time, I wait for the sound of her boots coming back up the stairs to get me. Instead, the lights go out and the tank door clongs shut and it's deep pit black again.

At first I feel relieved, but in a few minutes I feel bad. I know this chick is really hurting now, and lying on a cold cement floor. So I start singing a Dinah Washington song, and in a couple of minutes Angora chimes in and away we go again. But when we sing a couple of songs she calls up to me, "You better cool it, girl, or you gonna be down here with me."

"Hell, I don't care. I got a lotta time ahead of me anyway. I might as well do something."

"You ain't gonna do a lot of time for s'liciting."

I forgot I tole her that. I think fast. "I been busted a bunch of times before. They're gonna give me a habitual this time."

"That's too bad, and maybe you don't care 'bout coming down

here, but I do. Think how it gonna smell in here in the morning with two of us in here."

"You got a point there."

I don't sing no more, but she keeps right on. I never knew one person could know so many songs. Blodgett pokes her head back in once to tell her to shut up, but the kid is already in flatbottom, what more can they do to her? So she don't pay no attention and keeps right on singing. I lie down at last and I'm almost sung to sleep when I hear the tank door open again. This time the lights don't go on. Angora keeps on singing like she don't even hear the screw coming, but over the song I can hear the heels clunk-clunking and they don't stop 'til it sounds like she's all the way to the back of the tank. I sit up on my bunk and listen close 'cause I can't figure out what she could be doing in the dark. Then the faucet goes on and I can hear water filling up a bucket and I think, Oh shit, she's gonna douse her, and then I think, Christ, she's gonna have to sit in water all night and her sick as a dog already. I'm gonna call out to tell her to shut up but what's the use? She's gonna get it now anyway, and right then I hear the splash.

Angora screams like someone knifed her in the gut, a awful wail that bounces off the walls and breaks over me from all sides and I think for a second that she's shattered the walls and the jail is gonna cave in on us. I'm so scared I can't move, and then the scream dies away and it's quiet except for the women whimpering, scared out of their gourds, and I can hear Margarita praying. Then I hear the clunk-clunks working their way back to the door and the clang and the click that mean we're locked up tight again.

From flatbottom I hear Angora moaning and crying, and the whole damn thing is finally too much for me, Arnie and Millie and Angora and this fuckin' snake pit, and I scream, OH JESUS LET ME OUT OF HERE! and I cry loud enough for myself to drown out the sobs of the sick hype in flatbottom and the chorus of women crying and praying and after a while I just give out and go to sleep.

In the morning I wake up when they bring the breakfast cart in, but I don't want to get up. I must not've slept more than a hour or so, but mainly I don't want to go down and see Angora. I don't want to see Millie. But we don't get enough to eat around here and if I skip breakfast I'm gonna be awful hungry the rest of the day, and besides, I remember that I got floor-scrubbing detail after breakfast. I got to get up anyway. So I go down and look in flatbottom but Angora ain't there, just a puddle of water. She ain't in any of the other cells either, but Millie's asleep in number 8. She smells awful and she looks sick. And old. Millie's about forty, but today she looks sixty. Just smelling her makes me feel sick too, and I think of all the mornings Millie and me has moved our card game upstairs to avoid the stinking alkies and I wonder, Don't Millie know she smells like that when she comes in? I wonder should I wake her up for breakfast but I decide she's not gonna feel like eating, just the smell of food will prolly make her sicker, so I leave her there sleeping.

I ask Elsie, the trusty who comes with the breakfast cart, if she knows what happened to the chick in flatbottom. "They moved her to the other tank," she says. "What happened, anyway? Her face and arms are all blistered, like she got burned."

"They throwed a bucket of water on her."

"It musta been boiling, then. They brought her over there at five in the morning, and it woke me up, is how I happened to see her."

"I never knowed tap water could be hot enough to blister you."

"Well, I guess it must be."

I'm depressed and ain't had enough sleep and all I feel like doing is hiding in my bunk, but if I don't do my floor I'll get hassled by the screws and maybe go to flatbottom myself, so I figure I better get to it. After I eat I go to fill my bucket and I can't find the box of lye we use for scrubbing the cement, and it only takes a second for it to hit me what become of it. *Oh jeezuz.* I sit down on the floor against the wall and hold my knees and put my head down on my arms and cry, but when I hear the tank door open for the screw to let Elsie out with the cart I jump to my feet and start working.

All morning I keep checking Millie's cell, waiting for her to wake up, but she's totally zonked. I want to talk to her, even though I know when she wakes up she ain't gonna be in no shape to talk to. But I want to talk to her anyway; I never been so depressed in here like I am today.

When the lunch wagon comes, Elsie hands me a kite. She says, "The spade chick you were asking about give it to me." I stick the kite in my pocket 'til the screw that comes with the food cart is gone and the tank is shut up tight. Then I go to my bunk and read it:

Dear Barbera Strysand,

They took me out of flatbottom cause they was afraid I'd catch cold and give there nice hotel a bad name. I got some frends gonna come bring me some loot today and i'll send you the cigs I owe you. Hang in there, girl. I'll sing loud enuf tonight so you can hear me over there.

Very truly yours,
Angora

I feel a whole lot better after I read this, and I write her a note back saying I hope she's feeling better and she better not sing if she knows what's good for her, and maybe I'll see her after I been to court and get transferred out of the holding tank. I gotta hold the kite until suppertime and give it to a trusty, so I stick it in my pocket and go on downstairs.

Millie is up at last, sitting on a bench just staring, and I see now she has a big black eye and bruises on her arms. But when I walk up to her she busts into this big happy grin, and I see right away why she looks so old. She got no teeth in her mouth. She looks so pitiful I just about cry to look at her, but she says, "Iva! Fancy meeting you here!" And she laughs.

"Millie, if I wasn't so sorry to see you all beat up I'd be glad to see you. What happened to you?"

"Oh well. I fell down, I guess." Millie looks down at her feet, 'cause she's lying, of course. I shouldn'ta asked. I know perfectly well that her ol' man beats up on her when they get to drinking. Jeezuz. What the hell else is gonna happen around here? But I know he didn't knock every one of her teeth out. She musta had false ones. So I says, "What happened to your teeth?"

Millie puts her hand over her mouth, all embarrassed, like she just now realized she don't have 'em. She says, "Well, to tell the truth, I don't know. I mighta lost 'em somewhere along the line, but sometimes when I come in they take 'em away from me so's I won't break 'em or something. If they got 'em, I'll get 'em back later. You got a cigarette?"

I hand Millie a cig and when I go to light it her hand is shaking so bad I can hardly connect. The stench coming off her is sickening, and I'm having trouble with the fact that my friend Millie looks and smells just like all them alkie hags I bitch to her about all the time.

Millie says, "What day is this?"

"Sunday."

"Well, we don't go to court 'til tomorrow then."

"I got no trial date yet, Millie."

"What do you mean?"

I sit down and tell Millie what happened, about holding for Arnie, about not having bail money, about for sure I'm gonna go to the joint since I got all these priors for hustling. She listens to all this just sitting there shaking her head and looking real sad. I want to talk to her about Angora too, about how I lied to Angora about being busted for possession for sale, like somehow it was my fault she's a junkie, and about everything that happened last night, but somehow I just can't get myself to say nothin'. So I just tell her about my own gig, and when I get through she says, "It's a little late to say this, Iva, but I don't think you should have anything to do with that Arnie when you get out. I shoulda said that to you a long time ago maybe."

"Millie, you don't always have a choice about who you got to do with."

"Yeah, I'm a fine one to talk, huh? Me with my Merv. Listen, I gotta take me a nap."

"You want me to wake you up for supper?"

"Naw. I won't be able to keep anything down 'til tomorrow prolly."

I figure I got a nap coming myself, and so I go upstairs to my cell and zonk out.

I don't know the trusty that comes with the dinner cart, and you gotta be careful about trusties around here since half the time they only get to be trusties 'cause they're the screws' little stoolies, so I hang on to my kite and wait 'til the next morning to ask Elsie about Angora.

"Christ, she's a mess," she says. "They won't let her go on sick call 'cause of the way it happened, and she's got a fever and stuff running out of her ear."

Like a dope I ask, "Is she singing?"

"Singing? Have you flipped out? What's she got to be singing about? She don't even sit up or eat."

At lunchtime Elsie tells me they let Angora loose, just like that. Just turned her loose. No court, no bail, no nothin'.

I try not to think about her after that, and I got plenty of my own miseries to keep me busy for a while. But after I go to the state joint, sometimes I sit up at the window after lights out and sometimes someone is singing out a window across the mall in one of the other dormitories and my heart gets a catch in it and I think for a second it's Angora. Or sometimes there's not even any singing and she just comes into my mind and I start singing for her again, only this time I sing as loud as I can. But I never keep it up very long 'cause I know it don't matter how much I sing, I can never sing loud enough or long enough to change what happened to her back there. It was singing that got her in that fix in the first place, anyway. I just wish I had sang louder at the time, that's all, even though it wouldn'ta done no good then either. Or maybe I coulda got all the women in the tank to sing with us. Just suppose I coulda got 'em to do it. Feature this: all them alkies and junkies and hookers and boosters raising the jailhouse roof with song, and Angora singing lead. Wouldn't that be something? What could the screws do—throw scalding lye on all of us? Of course I know not even all of us singing at the top of our lungs woulda changed a goddam thing in that goddam jail, but it tickles me to think of it. Them screws—it woulda blown their friggin' minds.

KIM WOZENCRAFT
1954–

Growing up in a Dallas, Texas, suburb, Kim Wozencraft seemed to be on a successful all-American path, even when she dropped out of college at twenty-one to become a police officer. Rather than allowing her to attend the police academy, her department assigned her to work as an undercover narcotics agent. Like many narcs, Wozencraft herself became an addict while conducting a long-term investigation in the drug underworld. Barely escaping with her life, she ended up serving a prison sentence in the Federal Correctional Institution in Lexington, Kentucky.

Released in 1983, she moved to New York to become a writer, soon earned a master of fine arts degree from Colum-

bia University, and had an early work published in Best American Essays *of 1988. Her first novel,* Rush *(1990), which drew heavily on her own experience as a narc, was made into a major motion picture starring Jennifer Jason Leigh. The selection reprinted here is from her second novel,* Notes from the Country Club *(1993). She is currently working on her third novel while living with her husband, Richard Stratton, and their two sons.*

Wozencraft and Stratton, himself an ex-convict and author of the 1990 novel Smack Goddess, *were editors of* Prison Life *magazine, and both have been laboring for years to promote prison reform and encourage prison writing.*

from *Notes from the Country Club*

NINA SAYS THE SECRET to being a lady is to keep your knees slightly bent.

"Even when you walk," she says, "never straighten them completely." She drops next to me on the couch in the dayroom, running one hand through freshly dyed blond hair. "Advice from my mother," she says. "Smartest thing she ever told me."

She is doing five years for paperhanging, Nina, and when she finishes her federal time, she'll have bench warrants waiting for her in nine different states. Two of them have already put holds on her. The authorities will have to fight over who gets her first.

She told me the day I came in that her only offense was partying her way across the United States. "But just as we drove into Reno," she said, "lightning hit the proverbial outhouse." Nina is, or was, a master at passing bad checks, and sees Dr. Hoffman twice a week in forty-minute sessions behind the cloudy glass door of his office.

"Remember," she says now, "you heard it from me. How long did you say your sentence was, anyway?"

I notice that Harold is only pretending to read the newspaper. He sits in the corner of the room, his corner, with his ears pricked in our direction. Harold is a hack; that is what they call guards in this place. He said inmates must call him Mr. Kojak, but none of them do, so I don't either.

"Nina," I say, "I've told you. I'm only here for an evaluation. I'm here to prove my competence. They said six weeks."

"And what, it's been three already? Good luck, girlfriend. Where'd you catch your case?" This as though it were something contagious.

"Right here in Texas."

"Six weeks, eh?" Her laugh is a honey-sweet drawl that starts in Georgia and winds its way to somewhere around Trenton, New Jersey, ending with a choking, coughing ack-ack-ack. I'm not certain why the Feds have her here instead of in the main compound, but I do know that she often has days when she does nothing but eat, smoke and cry.

"So where'd you leave your accent?" she asks. "You don't talk like any Texan I've heard in recent history."

I tell her I spent most of my twenties living at Riverside and Eighty-eighth, which seems to please her.

"Ah, the Apple." She smiles. Then, in a lilting, reasonably good mimic of a southern Black accent: "New York City. Jest like I pictured it. Skyscrapers an' everything."

I remain in place, staring at something on the TV screen while Nina scuffs toward the stairs, pulling a cigarette from the pocket of her fluffy blue chenille bathrobe. Size eight. I have an eye for these things.

"What time is it?" she yawns. "When is my appointment? And where's Herlinda hiding?" She hangs the cigarette between her lips and leans her way through the yellow doors to the stairwell, looking as though she is being led by her unlit smoke.

Only hacks and nurses carry matches, though sometimes one of the Cuban women, usually Herlinda, will have a pack. She has them smuggled in from the main population for her religious ceremonies, furtive occurrences that fall somewhere between voodoo and American Catholicism.

"Not quite one, sweetheart; you see him at three o'clock." Herlinda's voice floats through the stairwell doors, and I hear Nina's reply banging off the yellow-painted cinder block walls.

"Two entire hours," she moans. "Eternity. What am I going to do for two whole, complete, entire, unmitigated motherfucking hours. And why's he wasting time with Three Sheets, anyway? Got a match?"

If it is not quite one, I should go downstairs, back to work, but I don't move. Dr. Hoffman has reserved his one o'clock slot on Tuesdays and Thursdays for Three Sheets, a fortyish matron who's in for bludgeoning her husband. She's doing a life sentence and has been here for as long as anyone can remember, longer even than Glenda, who's been here nearly four years. Nina swore to me early on that Three Sheets had used a GE steam iron. "His head must have looked like road pizza," she said, "but, hey, they bring good things to life."

Three Sheets stays in 301, the room three doors down from mine on the third floor. She spends exactly four hours each day hand-polishing to radiance a nine-square-foot section of the floor outside her room, using tiny wads of toilet tissue to shine each individual linoleum tile. Dr. Hoffman has her doing the Thorazine shuffle, slow-dancing through the minutes. Perhaps that is why we call her Three Sheets.

Nina and I have agreed that, unlike Three Sheets, we are not prone to hallucinations. We have seen for ourselves that the doctor really does wear his wristwatch on his right ankle. Neither of us has yet asked him why, but we have decided that we appreciate his attempt to keep time off our minds. The flourishing grapevine that winds through the halls has it that Dr. H works here because he was arrested in Saint Louis for being too liberal with prescriptions.

I hear Nina coming back up the stairs now, the slow sandpaper sound of her slippers against the safety treads on each step. Her cigarette is finally lit and she glides, bent-kneed, around the day-room looking for something to use as an ashtray. She settles for a gum wrapper, which she folds into a careful square, foil side up, before sitting down next to me. Chewing gum, like matches, is contraband, which makes it something worth coveting.

She is doing this to try to make Harold angry, but he ignores her, instead taking a cigarette from his own pocket and making a big show of using his plastic lighter. After adjusting the flame to the size of a small blowtorch he touches it to his cigarette and takes a long serious drag before pocketing the lighter and pretending to return to his paper. Nina ignores him.

"You know," she says, "the fucking *federales* got me in the Apple, though no place nearly so cool as Riverside Drive. The Southern District of New York, that was the end for me. While I was staying with this guy who had this really tiny apartment. His view was incredible, though; it looked right out at a big healthy chunk of the city. Did you like it there?"

"Loved it," I say.

"Yeah. Drag. It was weird, though, with this guy. He wasn't exactly in tune with how the cow ate the cabbage, don't you know. Every evening, just at dusk, he would put on Boz Scaggs singing 'Somebody Loan Me a Dime' and get down on his knees and arms on this old blue sort of oriental rug he had, and stare out the window at the Chrysler Building." She flips an ash in the general direction of the gum wrapper. "When I asked him what he was praying for," she says, "he told me it wasn't what you prayed *for* that was important, it was who you prayed *to*. Said any truly good prayer is always two things. Gracious and simple." She raises a blond eyebrow at me, smirks. Then, with a sigh, "I don't know." She says, "All I ever heard him say was 'Thank you, Lee.' "

She stops talking long enough to blow an oval smoke ring and watch it float toward the insulated ceiling as Three Sheets baby-steps her way across the dayroom to the hall. Then she closes her eyes and lets her head rest on the back of the couch.

"Yeah," she says, "he was a real trip."

"What happened to him?"

"Who knows? Not me. I haven't seen him or heard from him since the Feds grabbed my ass."

I tell her I'm late for work.

"Cynthia," Harold says, listening in as usual and momentarily roused from his stupor, "get your butt downstairs."

"Lace those bags," Nina drawls. "Work for the Uncle. I love it."

I pull myself up from the couch, wondering how to part company. "What are you doing for dinner?" I ask. She sighs again and gets up to change the channel. At least I got her to smile. I always feel better when the others smile.

The air in the stairwell is humid and warm. I push my way through the gymnasium smell to the first floor. The windows in the workroom reach almost from floor to ceiling. We have a view of the courtyard.

I work because Dr. Hoffman feels it is essential if he is to evaluate me properly. So, along with five other women, including Herlinda, I report each day to the small room at the end of A Hall on the first floor. We are employed by Federal Prison Industries, Inc. (trade name UNICOR) a "wholly owned, self-supporting Government corporation" that "maintains 80 industrial operations in 37 institutions, providing goods and services for sale to Federal Agencies." Monday through Friday, from nine to eleven A.M. and again from noon to four P.M., I think of myself not as a prisoner or a lunatic, but as an employee of the United States Postal Service. I imagine the Lonely Letter Carrier, trudging through rain, macing vicious suburban German shepherds, dropping envelopes decorated with the even-teethed smile of Ed McMahon into mailboxes across the land. Those envelopes, perhaps even one with the winning numbers enclosed, at some point in their journey may have been bundled into a maroon canvas bag that I had a hand in finishing. I wonder at the sense of pride this gives me, the sense that I am, though locked away, still somehow contributing.

The job itself requires no concentration. I remove a stack of stiff canvas bags from the trolley wheeled into the room each day by ancient Officer Svejk, an alarmingly thin hack with a glass eye who stands watch over us as we lace the bags. When I asked him how he wound up assigned here, he said, "Why, girlie, I'm just riding the old gravy train toward the retirement home. I'd rather spin it out in a basement full of loonies than over in the main compound. Ain't nearly so much conniving in here." Another day he told me that the thing he likes best about crazies is their honesty. I feel duty bound to lie to him.

I remove the bags in stacks of twenty, lug them to my place at the long table against the wall and seat myself on a stool between Herlinda and Lu Ng, a Vietnamese woman who cheated the Welfare Department. Dr. Hoffman says that Lulu has a neurological problem, not a mental one, because she was struck in the head by the butt of a rifle, courtesy of the 25th Infantry Division. Although I'm convinced that the neurological problem is real (headaches of six years' duration, occasional vertigo, weakness of the right limbs and blurred vision for the same period of time), I don't think it precludes mental-emotional disturbance.

On the table are ropes of clothesline, already cut and bundled, also in twenties. Next to that is a pile of metal clamps and next to that a pile of what look like metal shavings. These are made of something that weighs like aluminum but smells like nickel.

I pick up a length of rope and push it through the holes at the top of the mailbag—in one hole, out the other, in one hole, out the other—pull the ends of the rope even and thread them through the openings on a clamp before using a special kind of pliers to crimp the bits of metal onto the looped ends of the rope. And then I do it again.

Dr. Hoffman feels that a work routine will benefit Lulu; otherwise he would leave her free to wander the unit each day, as do Glenda, Nina and Three Sheets. I'm not at all certain that I agree with this course of therapy, though I know in my own case it is just what I need. Lulu, however, frequently misses a hole or two in the threading process; many of her bags are defective.

The stools they provide us with are too tall for the table, and by the time I've done eight or ten bags I feel my spine complaining, ranting about assembly line workers, Detroit, Chinese women in lower Manhattan, piecework, meat cutters, eight hours a day screwing bolt after bolt into barbecue grill after barbecue grill, about the massive backbreaking, all the sweat that pours so we can have the latest, newest, most improved antiperspirant, about the millions who leave work at five to go home and check the mailbox for a letter from Ed that says, *You may already be a winner.*

But I don't let minor physical discomforts or occasional attitude lapses interfere. I sit up straight and make one dollar and fourteen cents for every hundred bags I finish. My average is a hundred and eighty a day—a little more than two dollars and five cents for my labors. The money goes directly into my commissary account, and I am permitted to make purchases against my earnings. At present, because my status is "confined to unit," I deliver a list to whoever's on duty each Thursday and my shopping is done for me. Some of the women are allowed to walk, single file, under guard, down the wide corridor that leads to the main compound and the commissary, where they shop in person. Though Nina says it's almost as much fun as going to the mall, I don't mind having to stay inside. I've been told that if there is a balance in my account on the date of my release, I may expect a government check within six to eight weeks of my discharge back into the real world. I have vowed to keep my purchases to a minimum, not to squander my earnings on candy bars and ice cream.

It isn't the money, obviously, that drives me to work so quickly and efficiently. Most of the women who work here on One finish around a hundred bags a day. I am productive beyond the Bureau of Prisons' wildest dreams. I do this to prove that I am stable, employable, reliable and earnest. If only the doctor would endorse my claim of sanity, I could take my case to a jury and once again become a contributing member of society. Of course, there's the possibility the jury might find me guilty. But I'm getting ahead of myself.

Doing the bags has become almost automatic, even though I've been less than a month on the job. When I wish to, I can sit here and let my hands work and think about other things. Often I choose to concentrate on what my hands are doing. Though I'm relatively new and almost certainly temporary, I have decided already that the Federal Bureau of Prisons does an admirable job of dealing with closed systems by assigning numbers, even here in the women's psychiatric unit. They have tempered the institutional nature of the place by naming it Veritas. It is a beautiful name, I think, subtly appropriate, best heard as a whisper.

Within the walls of my room are a stainless steel locker, a stainless steel sink-toilet combination and two beds. All of these are numbered. The gray metal stand next to my bed has an engraved aluminum plate attached to its left rear leg. Government issue, therefore numbered and periodically accounted for. There is crisscross green wire over the window, which looks out onto a courtyard formed on three sides by the red brick walls of this hospital. The fourth is a thick wall of the same brick topped off with chain link and concertina wire. Nina is fond of saying that it looks like a goddam war zone around here. She is 00926–086, I am 00917–088. Nina fights it, reversing or inserting digits whenever she must put her number on a form, I haven't yet told her how much I cherish mine. *Why would she cherish it?*

I do not know my roommate's number; we are not that well acquainted. Her name is Emma, and before Dr. Hoffman assigned me to 304, he took me aside and asked me to keep a close eye on her, to call for help if I thought she might be about to make an attempt. I was reluctant at first to share a room with someone who was suicidal, but realized that doing so might help me prove myself to the doctor. I must move carefully, for if I make myself too valuable to him, he may attempt to keep me here regardless of whether I convince him I am competent. That is one of my most recently acquired fears.

It was during the so-called intake interview that Dr. Hoffman first put the idea in my mind. He was efficient that day; I was still in a state of shock, or something close to it, having been just delivered to this place by the marshals who took me from the courtroom. I was put in a room. I was left alone in the room for what seemed a long time, although I'm not sure, in clock time, exactly how long it was. I remember that it was cold; I remember feeling alone, feeling myself the only living presence in that room. And feeling precisely how cold it was, though it was April in Texas, and certainly warm outside. Outside there were clouds, and I was alert, aware of my body being in that place, that room, as though I were standing in a corner looking at myself perched on the edge of the chair, alone and frightened. After however long it was, Dr. Hoffman walked in and put a briefcase on the table between us. There was one other chair. Otherwise, the room was bare. He opened the case, removed some files, looked through them, pulled one out and spread its contents on the table. He took a pen from inside his navy sportcoat. It wasn't so much that I disliked him as that I thought it would be impossible for me to like anyone who occupied his position.

"Why did you do it?" he asked. "Did you think you were God?"

I was taken aback, more than taken aback. I was astonished. Afraid of my own anger. I said nothing. He stared at me.

"Name?"

"Cynthia Mitchell."

"Date of birth?"

"August 9, 1954."

"Place?"

"Fort Worth, Texas."

"You lived here then," he said. "Before. You lived here?"

"In Rancho Milagro. North of here."

Did I think I was God?

"Doctor," I ventured, "don't you already have all this information? I mean, I've given it to the police, the federal officers, the court, the marshals. I've told each of them. Is this interview necessary?"

"Not very much is," he said. "But if it makes you uncomfortable I can have my secretary take care of it. I sometimes find, though, that it helps, shall we say, to break the ice."

"I'm sorry," I said. "I am trying to be cooperative, but I am exhausted. I cannot tell you how tired I am. I don't remember the last time I slept."

"Understandable," he said. "Were you employed?"

"When? I've been employed all my life."

"Prior to the—immediately prior to the incident."

"I was freelancing for a public relations firm."

"What did that involve?"

"I conducted focus groups. I ghost-wrote or edited articles for doctors who couldn't."

"Couldn't what?"

"Write."

"Foreign nationals, you mean."

"Most of them were Americans."

"What kind of papers?"

"Journal articles, mostly. In praise of some new drug or another."

"I can't say I read them. I find them tedious."

"As do I."

"Mrs. Mitchell, do you know why you're here?"

"I am here so that you can find me competent to stand trial. Is there any doubt in your mind, doctor, that I am competent?"

He began putting folders back in his briefcase.

"There is a great deal of doubt," he replied. "But that's why I'm here. To determine if you should be."

"Here? I don't think so."

"Well, then," he said, "at least one of us is certain. Actually, you should be glad you're here and not in some hellish state prison somewhere. It was smart of you to do him in on federal property. You're fortunate to have landed here. They say it's a country club, compared to most. Have you ever been in treatment? Any therapy?"

"No."

"Wonderful," he said.

I wasn't sure how to take his reaction. I wasn't sure of anything, except that I needed to close my eyes. I answered his questions the best I could.

"Yes," I responded. "No," I responded. "I don't know," I responded. It seemed to take hours. "Not lapsed, doctor," I responded. "Failed. I am a failed Catholic."

"Why such negativity?"

"That's a matter of opinion," I said.

———

I haven't learned much more about him in these intervening weeks, days, hours, minutes, et cetera. I've not learned much about anything. A little of this and a little of that about the women with whom I'm locked up. Et cetera. That time is passing is the only thing of which I'm certain.

Though I don't yet know Emma, my roommate, I have learned her routine. Every night, except Sundays, she sits cross-legged in the middle of her bed and makes paddling motions with her arms. "We are floating," she says always, "on the Sea of Compliance. Start rowing." She doesn't seem to mind when I pull the covers over my head.

On Sunday evenings she goes to the dayroom on Two and listens to Coffee recite. Coffee is in for armed robbery, and this is reflected in her poems. She is sometimes hostile. Dr. Hoffman has placed a video camera in the dayroom and given her permission to use it. So, once a week, while most of the inmate-patients are in the dayroom on Three watching something, Emma sits in a corner of the dayroom on Two while Coffee reads her poems into the vacant grayblack eye of the camera. Dr. Hoffman views the videos at his convenience. I hope one day to ask him if I may try my hand. He has not yet scheduled me for any tests. He is, he says, simply observing.

I am trying hard to adjust to my environment. Lights out is at ten, and Harold, looking more simian each time I see him, lopes in precisely on the hour to chase us from the dayroom. On Sundays, Coffee stands up to him quietly, removing her tape from the camera and handing it over with a dignity that forces him into a silent acknowledgment of her oppression.

Nights are difficult, tonight more than most. Beneath the blanket, I smell the saltiness of my own tepid breath and press my eyelids to keep the spiders out.

Today while I was at work, Coffee stole my wedding band. I'm sure of this. I thought I had it sufficiently hidden, tucked away in a bottle of moisturizer in the metal nightstand next to my bed.

I saw her eyeing it the first night I was in Veritas, when she stood in the doorway of 304 telling me she was afraid to come in because I had wicked-evil eyes. I assured her that was only because I'd seen some things. I sensed immediately that she would steal the ring, and forgave her instantly, before she was even fully aware of her decision to thieve from me. She left my watch, as I knew she would, and this reassures me. When I try to sleep, I hold my watch tightly in my left hand. The manufacturer has guaranteed that it is accurate to within three one-hundredths of a second per year.

Though I find it difficult to admit, I had grown fond of my wedding band. It was heavy, and of hammered gold, as was the afternoon of the ceremony. I will miss it even though my marriage was less than successful. My husband has been dead for just over a month now.

But I am sincere when I hope that the wedding band will bring Coffee some kind of pleasure. This should help me fall asleep, though tomorrow I will have to make a complaint. I don't want to; the idea of involving the authorities is wretched. Yet Coffee expects it of me; I must do it for her. She longs to lean against the wall with a smile on her lips and my wedding band up her ass while the hacks tear her room apart. Her gleeful anticipation demands that I report the theft. I know that it will be inconvenient for the rest of the inmates, including me, because the hacks will destroy our rooms when they conduct the search. Emma will be distraught when they rip the bedclothes from her personal *Narren-schiff*, her very own Ship of Fools, and toss them onto the floor. I will have to stand next to her, in the place just to the left of the green-painted doorframe where we are required to stand each afternoon for the four o'clock count, and assure her that she is not drowning. The count is important. We must all be here. I try to pay close attention. I urge myself to *Be Here Now*, to witness the event fully, even to the point of witnessing my own participation. I have learned to be both within myself and outside myself in these moments, but no one could tell just by looking.

Every day at four, weekends included, every single federal prisoner in every single federal prison is counted and accounted for. Down to the last. One by one the prisons call in their counts to the bureau headquarters in Washington. Only after each and every prisoner here and all of those out on the main compound are known to be present is the institutional all clear sounded. Then, unit by unit, we are released for evening chow. Unless, like those of us here in Veritas, we happen to be in a special unit, where only the few who have been declared semifit by Dr. Hoffman are permitted onto the compound for meals. Most of us will stay locked

where we are. Emma and I will stay. And Coffee and Nina and
Three Sheets. Herlinda and her minions. Most of us.

Perhaps, while the hacks are counting, I should stand close to
Emma and whisper to her that she must keep her knees slightly
bent. Although Nina thinks it's only the secret to being a lady, I
know better. Locked knees interfere with the circulation of the
blood, trapping it in the lower extremities. By keeping the knees
slightly bent, one may avoid fainting.

JEROME WASHINGTON
1939–

*When Jerome Washington was twelve, an aunt gave him four
hundred books, and he vowed to read them all. By the late
1950s, he was reading poetry in the beat coffeehouses of
Greenwich Village. After graduating from college, he enlisted
in the army and served as a medic in Vietnam, returning in
1962. Going back to New York, Washington earned a master's
degree in journalism from Columbia and became a civil rights
activist, registering voters in the South as a member of the
Student Nonviolent Coordinating Committee (SNCC) and
the Congress of Racial Equality (CORE). He then helped organize one of the first groups of veterans opposed to the
Vietnam War.*

*Washington was arrested in 1972 for the murder of a man
whose body was found in the back room of an after-hours
club, confined for fourteen months in New York City's Tombs
prison, and finally tried in late 1973. Convicted in an out-
landish trial that some observers compared to a scene out of
either Kafka or Lewis Carroll, Washington was sentenced to
fifteen years to life.*

In Auburn prison, he founded and edited The Auburn Collective, *the first New York State inmate newspaper to achieve
national recognition (it received fifteen awards) and also established courses in newswriting and creative writing. He was
transferred to Attica in 1978, explicitly because his writings
criticized the prison system. While at Attica, many of his man-*

uscripts were destroyed and his typewriter confiscated but he continued writing. His short stories and essays began to receive publication and considerable critical acclaim, and five of his plays were staged in various venues, including the Swedish Embassy in New York City. The first collection of his prison writings, A Bright Spot in the Yard, was published in 1981.

Released in 1989 after seventeen years of imprisonment, Washington moved to the San Francisco Bay Area, where he lectured about African-American literature, read poetry, taught creative writing, and edited the Tenderloin Times. In 1994 he published another collection, the award-winning Iron House: Stories from the Yard, from which the following selections were taken. Washington presently lives on the Mendocino coast of California.

Diamond Bob

TWO DAYS AFTER Diamond Bob came to Sing Sing he was called in to meet with the Program Committee—three civilian officials who assign prisoners to work stations or educational programs.

The Committee's chairperson picked Diamond Bob's file from the pile of folders on the long wooden table and thumbed through it. After moments of indecision, he frowned at what he saw and put the folder aside.

"Do you have a trade?" the chairperson asked Diamond Bob.

Diamond Bob slouched in his seat. He paid more attention to his fingernails than he did to the chairperson, projecting an attitude that let everybody know he'd been through this procedure many times before, and that he was bored.

"Do you have any skills?" the chairperson went on. "Plumbing, bricklaying, cutting hair? Anything at all?"

"Sure," Diamond Bob said, "I'm skilled. I'm highly trained." And then without the slightest hesitation, he added, "I've got a Ph.D. in G."

The chairperson's face screwed up as he looked to the other committee members for understanding, but they were no help. One was engrossed in furious note-taking, while the other sat like a dunce with confusion stamped on his face. "You have a Ph.D. in *what?*" The chairperson leaned forward with elbows on the table, trying to unravel the riddle.

" 'G.' " Diamond Bob was indignant. "Don't you know what 'G' is?"

The three Committee members all confessed their ignorance.

" 'G' stands for 'Game,' " Diamond Bob proclaimed with a casual flip of his fingertips, "and Game is what we pimps, players and fast-life hustlers do for a living. Game is older than the pyramids and faster than lightning. We play it in the streets, in bars, with fast women and fancy cars. Our Game is called 'G' for short."

"I see," the chairperson said, exchanging snide smiles with the two other committee members. "And you have a Ph.D. in this Game of yours. Is that correct?"

"Sure do. I'm a grandmaster." Diamond Bob, tuned in to his own hype, puffed with pride. "Women sell their product, and I manage their affairs."

"What product?" the committee member who looked like a dunce asked.

"Flesh!" Diamond Bob said, "Body flesh. What other product does a woman have?"

Everybody except Diamond Bob fidgeted in his chair. "Your Game is not what I had in mind," the chairperson said. "I'm asking about work skills."

Bob was annoyed, but maintained his cool. "Game is work. Ain't no work more skilled," he said, "and on top of my skill, I gotta be cold-blooded to do what I do for a living."

"I don't doubt that," the chairperson interrupted. Bob shoved the comment aside and went on rappin'. "I'm the guy who'll hang a rope and drown a glass of water." He snapped his fingers to an unheard beat. "It's 'hoe money, or no money. That's my code."

"What you're talking about is a curse," the chairperson snapped. "That's not an honest living; that's pandering."

Diamond Bob was undaunted. He held his ground. "You asked my profession, and I told the truth." He offered a proposition. "Now, if you got any women in this prison who want to peddle their ass, then call on me—because I'm a qualified pimp. Otherwise," he sneered, "don't offer me none of your plantation gigs. I don't get my fingernails dirty for nobody. Can you dig *that?*"

The chairperson was livid. He balled his fist until the knuckles turned white and stamped a foot on the floor. The two other committee members tried to calm him, reminding him about his high blood pressure. The chairperson shook them off and shouted in Diamond Bob's face. "Get out!" he boomed and jabbed a finger toward the door.

The next morning, even before the sun could knock the night's chill off the exercise yard, Diamond Bob was on his way to see the prison shrink.

"I ain't insane," Diamond Bob repeated as a phalanx of guards escorted him through the prison corridors, "I got a Ph.D. in 'G.' I'm a businessman, an entrepreneur. I'm living the American Dream."

The Blues Merchant

L ONG TONGUE, The Blues Merchant, strolls on stage. His guitar rides sidesaddle against his hip. The drummer slides onto the tripod seat behind the drums, adjusts the high-hat cymbal, and runs a quick, off-beat tattoo on the tom-tom, then relaxes. The bass player plugs into the amplifier, checks the settings on the control panel and nods his okay. Three horn players stand off to one side, clustered, lurking like brilliant sorcerer-wizards waiting to do magic with their musical instruments.

The auditorium is packed. A thousand inmates face the stage; all anticipate a few minutes of musical escape. The tear gas canisters recessed in the ceiling remind us that everything is for real.

The house lights go down and the stage lights come up. Reds and greens and blues slide into pinks and ambers and yellows and play over the six poised musicians.

The Blues Merchant leans forward and mumbles, "Listen. Listen here, you all," into the microphone. "I want to tell you about Fancy Foxy Brown and Mean Lean Green. They is the slickest couple in the East Coast scene."

Thump. Thump. The drummer plays. Boom-chicka-chicka-boom. He slams his tubs. The show is on. Toes tap. Hands clap. Fingers pop. The audience vibrates. Long Tongue finds his groove.

He leans back. He moans. He shouts. His message is picked up, translated and understood. With his soul he releases us from bondage, puts us in tune with tomorrow, and the memories of the cold steel cells—our iron houses—evaporate.

Off to one side, a blue coated guard nods to the rhythm. On the up-beat his eyes meet the guard sergeant's frown. The message is clear: "You are not supposed to enjoy the blues. You get paid to watch, not be human." The message is instantaneously received. The guard jerks himself still and looks meaner than ever.

Long Tongue, The Blues Merchant, wails on. He gets funky. He gets rough. He gets raunchy. His blues are primeval. He takes everybody, except the guards, on a trip. The guards remain trapped behind the prison's walls while, if only for a short time, we are free.

The blues is our antidote, and Long Tongue, The Blues Merchant, is our doctor.

Nobody's Hoss

BO GREEN came to Attica in a snowstorm. Everybody else was chained together in teams of two, but Bo Green was chained to himself. His hands were cuffed and the steel cuffs were padlocked to a heavy link chain locked around his waist. His ankles were shackled like hobbles on a horse, and the ankle chain dragged as he climbed down from the prison bus and shuffled in through the door to the reception hall.

Bo Green's hair was wild and napped in kinks; he had a head cold and his temperature was running high. His eyes were red from the cold and the handcuffs locked to the chain around his waist prevented him from wiping his dripping nose. Snot caked his bushy mustache and was dried in streaks down the front of his prison coat. He was tired and hungry from riding the bus all day and he wasn't in the mood to be friendly.

A beefy-faced hack named Wilson made the mistake of singling out Bo as an example. "Pick the meanest looking one in the bunch," Wilson said, instructing the new-jack rookie guards on how to establish authority when receiving new prisoners. "Get right in his face," he said, "and lean on him. Hard!"

To demonstrate his technique, Wilson slapped his nightstick against the palm of his hand and barked in Bo's face. "This here is Attica prison, boy. This is the last stop before your grave. You're my hoss, and I'm your boss. What *I* say is law. Got that, boy?"

Wilson stood by grinning, self-satisfied, assured, while another guard removed Bo Green's handcuffs and shackles. Then to prove that his authority was absolute, Wilson slapped his stick against the palm of his hand again, and leaned forward to bark into Bo's face once more.

But leaning forward was as far as Wilson ever got. Bo Green's hands were free and his thick body was square as a concrete block. His left jab jammed the words back down into Wilson's throat. Wilson's lips twisted out of shape, his head snapped back, his eyes as wide with surprise as a mugger mugged on his own home turf. He raised his nightstick to make a feeble defense, and looked around for room to run. Bo Green's lashing right cross smashed Wilson's nose, splitting open his upper lip. A short left hook broke Wilson's jaw and drove his out-of-shape body to the floor. "This hoss can kick!" Bo Green shouted over and over as he stomped Wilson's chest.

Four guards pounced on Bo, two more dragged Wilson away. Bo Green fought until his back was to the wall, where they beat him bloody and clubbed him to the floor.

Years later when Bo Green was let out of solitary, he was blind in one eye and walked with a limp. His brace of beautiful white teeth had been broken from the gums, and nerve damage caused his right hand to twitch. The guards' revenge had weakened his body and aged him before his time.

Now he just wanders sort of aimlessly around the yard, and sometimes he sits in the sun. Once in a while he mutters, "I ain't nobody's hoss. Ain't never been, and ain't never will." But he never says much of anything else.

The guards give him plenty of room, and for a while a few of the older prisoners who still remembered would point Bo out. But mostly everyone else has forgotten about the fight, and some of the younger men, new to Attica, refuse to believe it happened at all.

Barracuda and Sheryl

"**Y**OU CAN'T HAVE this package," the guard in charge of the mail-room told Barracuda. "You'll have to mail it back to the sender." The guard held up a life-size, inflatable rubber doll. The doll was named Sheryl and had the shape of a young woman.

Barracuda had ordered the doll from a hard core porno magazine. The advertisement promised: *"All working parts. Detailed, tight fitting and satisfying. Orifices just like a real woman."* Sheryl was guaranteed to thrill or money back.

"There's no way I can let you have this," the guard said. "Toys are not allowed in this prison, especially not a toy like this doll."

Barracuda persisted, claiming a legal and constitutional right to the doll, to the pursuit of happiness.

"The law is one thing," the guard snapped, "but your perversion is another."

"Perversion?"

"Yes," the guard insisted.

"You got me all wrong." Barracuda made a last ditch effort to get the doll. "I don't want it for myself," he said with a straight face. "I just want to take it out in the Main Yard and pimp it to other guys."

The guard listened with keen ears for a deal, but when Barracuda failed to make him an offer, the guard confiscated the doll as contraband and ordered Barracuda locked in an observation cell.

The next day, the guard gave Sheryl to Leon Green-Eyes, another pimp, who promised to cut him in on the profits.

Shing-a-Ling and China

AT ONE TIME in the joint, there was Shing-a-Ling. As prison slick kids go, Shing-a-Ling was a minor leaguer, but you could never tell him that. We both worked in the prison's maintenance shop. He was in charge of tools; he'd issue them, receive them, clean and put them away. I handled the inventories, the typing and the filing. There was never much work and plenty of time to talk.

One summer day, while working and listening to Sam Cooke sing "You Send Me" over the shop's radio, Shing-a-Ling said to me: "Man, I'm in love. In love like a mudderfucker."

"Beautiful," I said as I went on with my work. "Solid on that. Who's the lucky broad?"

"The new queen."

"The new what?" I put my work aside and looked at him.

"The new queen. Name is China 'cause of that mellow, high yellow shine, and them slanted eyes."

"Wait one minute," I said. "Give me a replay. Slow-drag that past me again."

"She digs me."

"She? That's a man." I emphasized the words: "A man. Spelled M-A-N. Man."

"I know." He lit a cigarette and blew a cloud of smoke. "But the dude is fine. Super fine."

"You crazy?"

"No jive."

"Shit."

"No bull. I'm serious."

He pushed himself up from the chair and bopped around the room. "I laid my heaviest game down, and China went for it. Fact is, she ain't have no choice 'cept to go for it. Couldn't resist." He laughed and slapped his thighs. "Man, when Shing-a-Ling plays the tune, everybody dances."

"You better cool your role." I sipped my coffee and went back to filing the morning maintenance reports. "Next," I said, "you'll be strutting and swishing and carrying on around here like a go-go dancer."

"I'm a thoroughbred player." He poured himself a cup of my coffee, mixed in cream and sugar, took a sip and said, "I'm a pimp, not a simp. I can con a swan. My game is playing game, not being lame."

"Don't pad your part," I cautioned him. "If you deal, you'll shuffle; if you pitch, you'll catch. So, dig yourself."

Another routine week of prison life passed. The matter was out of mind until Shing-a-Ling said, "Dig it. I got that broad uptight. The chick really digs me."

"Who?" I was busy typing the monthly inventory.

"China. My queen. Remember?"

I continued to hunt 'n' peck on the typewriter and asked, "What makes you figure 'it' digs you?"

"Keep this under your hat, Jay." He grinned and his face radiated pride. "Read this bulletin the broad laid on me."

Shing-a-Ling handed me the note which I unfolded with caution. It was a plainly printed message and I almost died choking back my laughter.

"Hey good buddy," I smiled up at him. "Are you sure this is the right note?"

"Damn is."

"Then what makes you think that your game is on target?"

"Says so right there." He pointed to the note in my hand. "Says she loves me."

"Man," I asked as discreetly as possible, "can you read?"

The smile drained from his face.

"What do it say?" His voice went a whisper.

"Here." I held the note out to him. "Read it again."

Shing-a-Ling hesitated. "Jay," he said, "I can't read."

"Man, spare me the dumb shit."

"Really, I can't."

"Don't pull that I-can't-read game on me," I laughed.

He stood fallen-shouldered and looking at the floor.

"Jay," his voice was humble, "not more than three people in this here joint know the truth, but man, I really can't read."

The humor was gone.

I looked up at him, and looked at the note, and remembered the many times I had watched Shing-a-Ling lug his tome of sport facts and records through the Control Gate and into the maintenance shop—coming like Moses down the mountain to settle an angry argument. How many times had I laughed as he defiantly hurled the volumes down and spat out the challenge: "There, you jive turkey. Read page 634. Read and weep." He'd shout, "Read out loud, so everybody can hear how dumb you really are."

And too, how many times had I played the sucker and lunged for the greasy pig by going for his letter-from-home game—always starting with him moping around in a blue mood and ending with me being hustled into reading his mail aloud.

And in the Main Yard, when dealing with the smut merchants,

Shing-a-Ling would say, "Dig it. I read slow, so just mark off the pages where the action is heavy; where they is gettin' down to the real funky stuff. Mark the pages and I'll take it from there." Then later that evening in the cell block after we were all locked in and settled for the night, Shing-a-Ling would break the quiet with loud guffaws and bumps against his neighbors' wall until one of them would holler over to him, "Hey man, what the fuck is with you?" And Shing-a-Ling would reply, "Homeboy, this book is a mudderfucker. These people is gettin' down to some real freaky mess." That was the lure. As soon as the guy would say, "Turn me on to it," Shing-a-Ling would say, "All right. Here." He'd pass the book through the bars and over to the next cell. "Read those pages where it's marked," Shing-a-Ling would say. "Read it out loud. Read it so that I can hear, too."

And that's the way it always went.

Now he was standing in front of me saying, "Please read the note. Jay, what do China say?"

I was embarrassed for him. Still, he insisted I read the note.

"*You jive-time sonofabitch,*" I read China's message aloud. "*You ain't man enough for me. Furthermore that thing between your legs ain't nothing but a handle for me to turn you over with. So, if you ever try your popcorn-pimp shit with me, you will soon find out who the real whore is.*" The note was signed, "*China,*" with a postscript: "*Don't fuck with anything you can't handle.*"

When I had finished reading, Shing-a-Ling was devastated. He said nothing. He just took the note from my hand and folded it into his shirt pocket and walked from the shop.

He didn't return to work that day. And when he didn't show up the next morning, I went looking for him. On my way across the yard I ran into Nifty Green, one of Shing-a-Ling's slick sidekicks.

"You seen Shing-a-Ling?" I asked.

"Him's a changed dude," Nifty said, flicking his hands, making sure I saw his newly manicured fingernails. "Him's done changed overnight."

"What's he done?"

"Him's done gone over to the other side. Done squared-up on me and the fellows." Nifty frowned as if the words left a nasty taste on his tongue. "Him's acting like a pedigree, middle-class square."

"Where is he?"

"In the school." Nifty frowned again.

I left Nifty in the middle of the yard, still flashing his fingernails and looking pseudo-slick.

When I got to the school the class period had just ended and the halls were jammed with men, but I didn't see Shing-a-Ling anyplace.

"You seen Shing-a-Ling?" I asked Cleanhead, the inmate clerk in the school's office.

"Yeah," Cleanhead said, looking up from his work, "Shing-a-Ling is in the Learning Lab."

I turned the corner and stepped into the room.

Shing-a-Ling was sitting at the study table, his head bent forward into the learning booths. He was wearing earphones and didn't hear me walk over. For a few seconds I stood behind him reading over his shoulder and watching him flip the pages of the book and mouth the words he heard through the earphones.

"SEE DICK RUN. SEE JANE RUN. SEE DICK AND JANE RUN."

He sensed my presence, shut off the tape player, removed the earphones and looked up as he turned to me.

"Hey now Jay," he said. "What is it?"

"You tell me."

"Gettin' this reading thing together." He smiled.

"That's hip," I said.

"That homo done checked my game. Turned me 'round. Did a number on me." His voice was glum, but he managed to keep a smile. "But all that's cool. I done learned a big lesson," he told me. "If a player ain't got an end game, he ain't got no game at all."

"True."

"But you can't play the game at all, 'less you can read the bulletins when they come."

"I can dig it."

"So," he said, "I'm gettin' it together."

"Solid," I said and started to leave.

"One favor?" he asked.

"Name it."

"Don't call me Shing-a-Ling anymore."

I was blank.

"Call me my real name. It's nicer."

"Sure," I said. "What is it?"

"Vernon Alonzo Bowen. It sounds square, but it's me."

I smiled for him.

He said, "Excuse my back," and put on the earphones again. He turned on the tape player and went back to reading and mouthing the words as he listened. "See Dick run. See Jane run. See Dick and Jane run."

KATHY BOUDIN
1943–

Kathy Boudin was organizing for disarmament and civil rights while still a teenager. The daughter of political activists— famed civil liberties lawyer Leonard Boudin and poet Jean Boudin—Boudin became a leader of the campus Students for a Democratic Society (SDS) at Bryn Mawr College. She was briefly jailed during her junior year in 1963 for demonstrating against conditions in a local black school. After graduation, she spent four years living and working with welfare mothers and other impoverished tenants in a Cleveland slum.

This was 1964 to 1968, when the Vietnam War was inciting an unprecedented antiwar movement in the United States while urban rebellions kept erupting in the nation's ghettos and barrios. Boudin helped organize militant protests at the 1968 Democratic Party national convention in Chicago, and the following year co-authored The Bust Book: What to Do until the Lawyer Comes, *a self-published how-to-do-it legal self-defense guide for the many tens of thousands of protestors being arrested each year (there was so much demand for the book that Grove Press soon reissued it as a popular paperback).*

Boudin was one of the leaders of the organization known as the Weathermen, which emerged from the split of SDS at their 1969 national convention in Chicago to promote battles in the streets and elsewhere against those controlling U.S. society. At the end of 1969, the organization declared its commitment to armed struggle and became the Weather Underground. In March 1970, Kathy Boudin was one of the two women who escaped from a New York City town house that blew up when a bomb being assembled by her comrades exploded prematurely, killing three well-known members of the group.

For eleven years, Boudin lived underground. Her one public appearance during this period was as one of five leading Weatherpeople interviewed in the 1976 documentary Underground, *filmed by Emile de Antonio, Mary Lampson, and Haskell Wexler in a Los Angeles safe house. In 1980, she gave birth to her son Chesa, to whom one of the following poems is written.*

Then in 1981, $1.6 million was stolen in a Rockland County, New York, ambush of a Brink's armored car that left one guard dead and two wounded. The money was switched to a U-Haul van later stopped at a roadblock. In the passenger seat was an unarmed Kathy Boudin, who surrendered to police. Then several men burst out of the van, firing automatic weapons and killing two Nyack police officers before being apprehended.

Two years later, Boudin was married in the Rockland County Jail to Chesa's father, David Gilbert, on the day he was convicted for his participation in the Brink's robbery. In 1984, after three years of incarceration, Boudin pleaded guilty to one count of felony murder (being involved in a felony during which someone is killed) and received a sentence of twenty years to life, which she is currently serving in the maximum security prison for women at Bedford Hills, New York.

Our Skirt

You were forty-five and I was fourteen
when you gave me the skirt.
"It's from Paris!" you said
as if that would impress me
who at best had mixed feelings
about skirts.

But I was drawn by that summer cotton
with splashes of black and white—like paint
dabbed by an eager artist.
I borrowed your skirt
and it moved like waves
as I danced at a ninth grade party.
Wearing it date after date
including my first dinner with a college man.
I never was much for buying new clothes,
once I liked something it stayed with me for years.

I remember the day I tried
ironing your skirt,
so wide it seemed to go on and on
like a western sky.
Then I smelled the burning
and, crushed, saw that I had left a red-brown scorch
on that painting.

But you, Mother, you understood
because ironing was not your thing either.
And over the years your skirt became my skirt
until I left it and other parts of home with you.

Now you are eighty and I almost fifty.
We sit across from each other
in the prison visiting room.
Your soft gray-thin hair twirls into style.
I follow the lines on your face, paths lit by your eyes
until my gaze comes to rest
on the black and white,
on the years
that our skirt has endured.

The Call

You might not be at the other end
of eight cells,
one garlic-coated cooking area
vibrating with the clatter of popcorn on
aluminum pot covers
two guards peering through blurry plexiglas,
the TV room echoing with
Jeopardy sing-song music and competing yells for
answers—
all lying between
my solitude and the telephone.

Or
you might answer
with a flat "hello,"
and I will hear your fingers
poking at plastic computer buttons,
your concentration focused on
the green and blue invaders and defenders.
My words only background
to your triumphs and defeats.

But I long for your voice.
Even the sound of your clicking fingers.
I journey past
eight cells submerged
in rap, salsa, heavy metal and soul
careening along the green metal corridor,
the guards perched on their raised platform,
dominoes clacking on plastic tabletops.
Past the line of roaches weaving
to the scent of overflowing garbage pails
voices shouting down the corridors,
legs halted by the line
that cannot be crossed.

Finally I sit on the floor
of the chairless smoky butt-filled room
to call you
who answers with an ever-deepening voice,
who barely sounds like my son.

"Hi, what are you doing?"
"I'm lying down, burning incense, listening to music.
    Do you want to hear it?"
With such relief
I barely utter "Yes," pushing my ear into the telephone,
my nose into the air.
Your flutes and organs become a soft carpet I walk along
in the musty sweetness and fruit smells
of orange peels and raspberries.
You begin to describe your new room
One wall   the dream catcher   a set of hatchets
    and white feathers wrapped with beads
        of turquoise sky and sunset.
Your bed opposite a full length mirror
Perfect, you say, to view yourself,
a new body, six and half inches in one year.

Then you invite me
into your special boxes,
gifts from your father
made behind bars.
"I keep all my treasures."

I nod breathlessly
My son has taken my voice.
His words fill me in
A naming ceremony.
Slowly his hand lifts
    a coffee brown belt
name carved across,
a menu of favorite food
    shared on the overnight visit.
Father-love.

The QEII ticket stub from
  the final ocean trip with Grandma.
"Eat breakfast, pack your clothes, then you can watch TV,"
his grandfather's voice echoes
  from a note left by his bed.
He moves to the Christmas calendar
  of shared favorite books
Tales of Peter Rabbit to *Huck Finn*
  the story of fourteen years.
A birthday card
  A photo
My son and I stand back to back.
His head inches past mine.

Then you dangle one sandstone earring
  the other in a box in my cell,
"We'll put them together when you get out."
  Your words hang like a glider.
Mother-love.

Then guitar notes rise and fall,
and I say, as always "I love you,"
and you say, as always, "I love you,"
and the phone clicks off.

THE AMERICAN GULAG TODAY

DANNIE MARTIN ("RED HOG")
1939–

Dannie Martin's career as a writer began at the age of forty-six, when the first of his trenchant essays about prison appeared in the "Sunday Punch" section of the San Francisco Chronicle. *By then he had been in and out of reformatories and prisons for more than three decades, doing a total of twenty-one years, including time on a chain gang, and he was six years into a thirty-three-year federal term for bank robbery.*

Martin's essay—"AIDS: The View from a Prison Cell"—began to win him a wide audience and swiftly brought down upon him punitive sanctions authorized by Title 28 of the Code of Federal Regulations Section 540.20(b): "The inmate may not receive compensation or anything of value for correspondence with the news media. The inmate may not act as reporter or publish under a byline." For continuing to violate this federal regulation, Martin was thrown in the hole, deprived of his writing materials, and then transferred to a remote prison in the Arizona desert. When the Chronicle *and Martin jointly sued to protect the rights of the author, the newspaper, and its readers, court proceedings revealed that Section 540.20(b) had been drafted in the 1970s specifically to ensure that federal prisoners with "anti-establishment" views "did not have access to the media."*

Martin's essays became a regular feature of the Chronicle. *In 1993 he and Peter Y. Sussman, his editor at the newspaper, co-authored* Committing Journalism: The Prison Writings of Red Hog. *The book, which includes fifty essays Martin published in the* Chronicle, *takes its title from one of Martin's characteristically pithy observations: "I committed bank robbery and they put me in prison, and that was right. Then I committed journalism and they put me in the hole. And that was wrong."*

Writing as one of the "dinosaurs" left over from an earlier penal epoch, Martin reports how "the concept of rehabilita-tion" has become "a thing of the past" in the modern-day American Gulag devoted purely to "warehousing, punish-ment, and retribution." He sketches from inside the hideous features of this penal system ruled by "awesome, tyrannical power" and filled by new sentencing laws to twice its capacity with people bearing "nightmarish terms of incarceration." In perhaps his most terrifying piece, "A Prescription for Torture," he describes appalling scenes legitimized by the 1990 Supreme Court decision that stripped prisoners of any right to resist the forcible administration of psychotropic drugs.

Martin finally won parole in 1994 at the age of fifty-five. The following year Norton published his powerful naturalistic novel The Dishwasher.

AIDS: The View from a Prison Cell

LOMPOC, CALIF. (Aug. 3, 1986)—In the latter months of 1985, one of the most voracious homosexuals in the federal prison system violated parole in Florida and was returned to the men's maximum-security prison at Lompoc to finish his sentence.

This one was so predatory that the cons had long ago nicknamed him "Honey Bear." Honey Bear was known to shoot a load of "crank" and go walking down a tier advertising favors at every cell he passed; he would enter at the beck and call of anyone who was interested. If there happened to be two men in the cell, appropriate adjustments could be made. The Honey Bear was an accommodating soul.

No one seemed to notice the little sores on the back of Honey Bear's neck, although quite a few of his "clients" had an intimate view of them. Early in 1986, the sores got out of hand, and he was having other health problems. Honey Bear went to the doctor and was soon diagnosed as having AIDS. He was immediately trans-ferred to the medical facility at Springfield, Missouri, and isolated from contact with other prisoners.

Honey Bear liked to do a lot of drugs, especially crank, a stim-ulant he injected by hypodermic needle, or "outfit," as it is called in prison. Outfits are hard to come by in here, and there were only three in the 130-man cellblock where Honey Bear lived.

The men who own these outfits loan them to others in return for a "fix" of the drugs. Sometimes a loaned "rig" will be used by eight or ten people before it is returned to the owner.

After Honey Bear left, a few worried drug users approached the men who owned the outfits, seeking reassurance that Honey Bear had not used them. The news was bad. Honey Bear had not only used them but used all of them several times. This news had a most chilling effect on the future dreams of some of these cons.

The exchange of bodily fluids through sex and the sharing of contaminated needles are the two primary ways that AIDS is spread through a population. In prison or jail, the user of illegal drugs "sterilizes" needles by squirting a little cold water through the needle after using it and before handing it to the next in line. All types of alcohol are contraband.

Some of the cons were relieved when Honey Bear was quarantined in Springfield. The Bureau of Prisons has not yet formulated a firm policy concerning those diagnosed as having or carrying the AIDS virus. Everyone assumed after Honey Bear left that the government intended to at least isolate everyone they determined to have been exposed. Then "The Greek" died here at Lompoc on Father's Day, and that fond assumption became just another shattered illusion.

The Greek was a homosexual, a likable soul with a sunny disposition and an inclination for a quantity and variety of men. He had been serving time at Lompoc for about five years, and if chronicled and illustrated, The Greek's sexual shenanigans would go a good ways toward filling a book the size of a Sears Roebuck catalog.

The Greek got involved in a pickup game of basketball in the gym on Father's Day and, after playing awhile, became exhausted, went to the sideline, began throwing up, and fell out. After prison authorities got him to the hospital, he was said to have choked to death on his own vomit.

When the prison doctor arrived, he told everyone working around The Greek to put on long rubber gloves, since The Greek was a known HIV carrier. Even the officer who was sent to The Greek's cell to pack his personal belongings was told to wear long rubber gloves.

If The Greek was indeed a "known" HIV carrier, it was a fact known only by the medical staff and/or the administration. None of the convicts, including The Greek's sex partners, and none of the mainline prison guards knew anything about it.

Now the convicts wonder if those diagnosed as having the AIDS virus are going to be allowed to roam the yard with everyone else. The Bureau of Prisons has made no public policy statement on the subject. It looks now as if officials intend to treat AIDS just as they do the common cold, except in obviously terminal stages.

It isn't likely that the canteen will soon be selling condoms for safe sex or alcohol to sterilize needles. The only safe sex and drugs in prison will be no sex and no drugs, and so far no one who indulges in either is considering that option. The attitude in here seems to be that life goes on for the living and that the chances of contracting AIDS are about the same as being hit by gunfire during the commission of a felony or dying of an overdose. So what?

Then there are those who rationalize in lieu of curtailing their behavior. One man who had shared an outfit with Honey Bear on several occasions said he wasn't worried about it at all because he is immune to AIDS in any case. When prompted to explain how he is immune to AIDS, he said that the AIDS virus is similar to the hepatitis virus and that he had shared needles for years outside with people who were infected with hepatitis and he had never caught it.

Therefore, by this man's reasoning, he must also be immune to AIDS. He sounds so sure of himself that he makes one wonder if there has been a study done on the correlation between hepatitis and AIDS.

There are married men in here who have had sex with Honey Bear and The Greek while their wives anxiously wait for the day they are freed. They aren't likely to disclose these potentially volatile indiscretions; most of these long-distance marriages are strained and fragile already.

Those of us who don't indulge in drugs or sex in prison stand around like so many buzzards waiting and watching for the next to fall. These days we speculate about the lovers of Honey Bear and The Greek and which among them is likely to go down.

In a world where all the lies have been told and all the jokes have been heard, it does give us something new to talk about. One thing about AIDS is very reliable: About the time you exhaust the talk and speculation about the latest victim, another is sure to bite the dust. Sometimes it is someone we would never have suspected.

A Prescription for Torture

PHOENIX, ARIZ. (March 18, 1990)—On Tuesday, February 27, the U.S. Supreme Court rekindled the convict's worst nightmare.

The court, by a vote of six to three, gave prison officials sweeping power to force convicts to take psychotropic drugs against their will. The ruling may have played well on the street, but it cast a dread pall over the feelings of many of us convicts.

To those of us who have watched convicts being plied with drugs that made them total zombies, the decision was maddening. It's true that some convicts need to be medicated, but we have seen others who don't need the drugs being forced to take them by incompetent and tyrannical bureaucrats.

Justice Anthony M. Kennedy, writing for the majority, said: "Given the requirements of a prison environment, the state may treat a prison inmate who has a serious mental illness with anti-psychotic drugs against his will if the inmate is dangerous to himself or others and the treatment is in the inmate's best medical interest."

Justice John Paul Stevens said in dissent that a mock trial before a prison tribunal doesn't satisfy due process and that a competent individual has a constitutional right to refuse antipsychotic medication.

Many citizens will no doubt agree that medication should be forced on violent or mentally ill convicts. But there's much more at stake. It is our observation that psychotropic drugs are also used to quell what prison officials view as "troublesome" prisoners.

I'll let prison officials give their side of the story independently—they don't give official comments to convict-writers anyhow—but prisoners have simply too many credible stories of psychotropic drug abuse in the prisons to discount them all. Here's the way it looks to many convicts:

The drugs we are talking about are sometimes used in here as exquisite forms of long-term torture. Some of these mind- and body-paralyzing chemicals are Prolixin, Haldol, and Thorazine. They are brand names for a class of major tranquilizers based on the drug phenothiazine, which is widely prescribed for schizophrenia and other severe mental illnesses.

Such is the power of these drugs that I have seen men do things under their influence that almost defy description. One man on an antipsychotic drug at Lompoc penitentiary climbed a roll of deadly-sharp razor wire, oblivious to the danger, and got hung up in the wire about halfway up. A guard fired a warning shot. The convict was then hauled off the wire by other guards.

It's no secret that federal and state prison officials have for years been forcing convicts to take these drugs. But knowing we had recourse to the courts, the officials used discretion about whom they forced them on. Now that we are stripped of access to outside courts, things look grim for our future.

In the mid-1980s, the director of the Bureau of Prisons, Norman Carlson, came to Lompoc for a tour of the prison. About the time he showed up, a friend of mine disappeared from the yard.

I heard a rumor that he had been locked up because a staff member overheard him threaten Carlson. When he showed up on the yard some eighteen months later, he told me about a most chilling journey.

He said he had been taken to the basement of the isolation unit in Lompoc, where the dark cells have solid iron doors and rings on the floor. He said he was chained to the floor and pumped full of Prolixin, and he remained there until he was bundled onto a plane for a trip to the dreaded 10 Building, the psych ward at the Springfield, Missouri, prison hospital.

When he arrived at 10 Building, he told me, he was chained to his bunk in a cell and given more Prolixin. He said of the experience:

"Man, it was pure torture. My eyes would pop open sometimes at midnight, and I'd be wide awake until morning. My mind would be racing, but my body wouldn't function. It was like when you dream you're trying to run and can't move.

"When I defecated on myself, the orderlies would sometimes wait two days to clean me up. It wasn't long before I begged them for some relief, and once I began begging, the staff began to lighten up some.

"I stayed in 10 Building for nearly eighteen months and was kept on heavy doses of Prolixin the whole time."

Other convicts have disappeared into the maw of 10 Building at Springfield and not been heard from for five years or more. I don't know if they remain there, but no one I know has seen them at other prisons. There's a persistent rumor that a member of Detroit's infamous Purple Gang spent thirty years in 10 Building.

Every federal prison has men shuffling around hallways and cellblocks as if they are walking in slow motion. There are some here at Phoenix. It's common practice in federal prisons to heavily medicate those who are perceived as a threat to staff.

But, as I and other prisoners can attest, there are even more violent men who regularly kill fellow convicts. These types are transferred to another prison after they kill someone, and they often do it again. Many of them aren't ever medicated with psychotropic drugs. As long as they are no threat to staff, they continue their murderous sprees. This sends us convicts a pretty clear message.

The people who are medicated become defenseless in the convict community and are often seriously abused by predatory fellow convicts. They are physically unable to defend themselves, and that fact increases their paranoia manyfold.

A little-acknowledged aspect of chemical straitjackets is the direct threat they pose to law-abiding society.

A violent man at Lompoc who was nearing the end of a ten-year sentence was kept heavily dosed with antipsychotic drugs. He'd done every day of his sentence because of lost good time. I used to watch him trying to run the track. He ran as if he were under water. It took him fifteen minutes to complete a lap that I ran in three minutes, and I'm no speed demon.

He was so disagreeable, paranoid, and violent that no one wanted to approach him. When his sentence was finished, the guards walked him to the front gate and shoved him out into the free world—no halfway house, no parole—and I doubt he went off to a psychiatrist and got a prescription to continue on psychotropic drugs. I've often wondered what happened when he regained his physical momentum after ten years of suppression by disabling chemicals.

Another convict who comes to mind is murderer Gary Gilmore, the subject of Norman Mailer's book *The Executioner's Song*. Gilmore was once strapped to a bunk in the Oregon State Prison for five weeks during the early 1970s and injected with massive doses of Prolixin, according to another convict. A man who was there at the time told me that after the ordeal Gilmore completely lost his sense of humor and became "extremely morbid." All this was several years before the savage murders for which he was ultimately executed.

It's apparent that Gilmore had insufficient, if any, follow-up treatment after his release, and what he did and how he did it are more than obvious.

Federal parole was recently abolished. Most of the men who are forced to take psychotropic drugs will one day be released on their own. Meeting and greeting one of them will be like dealing with a pit viper.

Prison guards now have the power to force drugs on them and chemically sedate them, but they will be pulled off those drugs before release, and their rebound—not to mention their hatred and lust for revenge—will be acted out in the arena of unsuspecting citizens. One can only hope they don't get their hands on a weapon before entering a convenience store late at night.

A man here at Phoenix who takes antipsychotic drugs can be seen around the yard jerking like a puppet. He can't be still, either sitting or standing. I once watched him in a TV room, and he stood up and sat back down in his chair twelve times in three minutes.

He moved into a cell here with a man who didn't know he was on psychotropics. At 3:00 A.M. on his first night there, the drugged man awoke and began pacing the cell. His cellmate woke up and watched him with some concern until breakfast at 6:30.

The following night, when the drugged convict fell asleep, his cellie used a roll of tape to secure him in the top bunk. He accomplished that by winding the tape around the man's legs and chest and bringing it all the way around the mattress. The convict woke up again at 3:00 A.M. and, finding himself bound, began screaming so loud he woke up the entire cellblock.

The same man was also forced to take antipsychotic drugs at the Oregon State Prison. He robbed a bank in Portland two weeks after his release while still wearing the dress-out clothes he left prison in.

Another problem with administering psychotropic drugs in here is that dosages are mixed and dispensed by physician's assistants who convicts seriously doubt are qualified to do that. Looking at some of their patients reinforces that doubt.

There's an extraordinary amount of grumbling and disgust in here about the Supreme Court ruling. A man I talked with today pretty well summed up our feelings when he said:

"They already had permission to put on rubber gloves and dig around in our bodies lookin' for drugs. Now they have the power to dig around in our brains as well."

A Mount Everest of Time

PHOENIX, ARIZ. (Oct. 7, 1990)—The big prison story these days is the story of Patrick Grady and Gordon Brownlee and Kevin Sweeney and Curtis Bristow. They all made serious mistakes, and they will all have decades to brood over those mistakes.

Grady, forty-two, has been a close acquaintance of mine over the past two years. He's a Vietnam veteran who wears a mustache because a Vietcong fragment grenade slightly disfigured his upper lip and part of his cheek.

He was also wounded in the leg by gunfire and decorated repeatedly for valor in combat. Along with his wounds in Vietnam, Grady picked up a drug habit. When he returned to his hometown, Seattle, he began selling drugs to support it.

In 1988, he was convicted of numerous counts of conspiracy to possess and sell cocaine. It was his first felony charge. A federal judge in Tacoma, Washington, sentenced him to thirty-six years in prison. He will have to serve thirty-one years before he can be released.

Grady has a wife and a four-year-old daughter and professes shock over the severity of his sentence. "I can't believe that the system of government that I put my life on the line for could do this to me," he says.

"I may be naive, but I've always thought a person could recover from one mistake. I grew up on the old cliché about a 'three-time loser.' Now I've made a mistake, and my wife will be seventy when

I get out and my daughter will be thirty-four. That's the end of my family. I can't ask them to wait that long."

Grady doesn't say much about his sentence, but I can see in his eyes a form of terror and despair akin to what was probably there when he saw a fragment grenade land nearby. A few days ago, he asked me a question.

"How is it that I get thirty-six years in prison for selling cocaine when people who rape a woman, bash her head in with a rusty pipe, and leave her for dead only get ten years? Am I supposed to be four times more evil than them?"

The bitterness and numb disbelief of Patrick Grady are mirrored in the minds of thousands of men and women in the federal prisons, and the numbers are increasing at an alarming rate.

In 1989, there were 44,891 criminal cases filed in federal courts, according to a U.S. judicial report. That was almost triple the 15,135 cases filed in 1980. Those numbers, more than anything, represent the escalation of the drug war in the past decade. More than one-fourth of all criminal cases filed in district courts are drug cases, according to the same report.

But there's a darker side to those statistics, because many people sentenced under new federal drug laws aren't ever getting out of prison. Some who will get out may be so old that they won't remember coming in.

Even prisons such as the one here at Phoenix that are designed for medium-security prisoners are experiencing a large influx of men who have been sentenced to nightmarish terms of incarceration.

Since 1987, federal sentences have been nonparolable. The maximum good time that can be earned is fifty-four days a year. Thus, a person with a twenty-year sentence will serve about seventeen years if he or she is a model prisoner. It used to be that a twenty-year sentence would result in seven to twelve years of "real time."

Many people outside applaud the big numbers and harsh sentences. But those I see in here who are weighed down by the years are not gun-slinging stereotypes; they are real, hurting people, and they have families outside whose lives, like their own, are devastated. The people who support those new sentences should at least look at their effect on the people I meet in here.

A former college professor from the Bay Area whom I met here at Phoenix got life without parole for possession of seven kilos of cocaine. A Sacramento man who is forty-five years old received twenty-seven years for conspiring to manufacture methamphetamines. They both have wives and children who hope they will get out someday.

Now that most of the power is in the hands of prosecutors, long sentences are no longer oddities—they have become the norm.

Gordon Brownlee, a San Francisco native who lives down the tier from me, tells about the pressure a San Francisco prosecutor put on him.

"I was arrested in 1989 with one gram over five kilos of cocaine and charged with possession with intent to sell. Had it been under five kilos, the sentence range would have been five to forty years. But the extra gram made it ten years to life," he says.

"The only criminal record I had was a charge in 1982 for trying to buy marijuana from an FBI agent. The prosecutor told me that if I would become an informer I could get off lightly, but if I didn't he would use the 'prior' to enhance my sentence to twenty years to life."

Brownlee is forty-two years old and has a wife and baby daughter. On July 28, 1989, after a plea of guilty, he was sentenced to twenty years in prison. His release date is in 2006.

Few people in here, including those who were apprehended for drug violations, believe they should get a slap on the wrist or be let off lightly. But convicts believe that this country has entered an era of criminal justice when the punishment for drug offenses heavily outweighs the crimes, and the result in human terms is disastrous.

Bob Gomez, an elderly man who helps fellow convicts with legal work, contends that an oversight by Congress created most of the problem.

"A few years ago," he says, "Congress designed some harsh new sentences for drug offenses. Those terms were drafted with the thought in mind that offenders could be paroled in one-third or do the entire sentence in two-thirds of the total amount.

"When the new nonparolable sentences were approved, they simply grafted the big numbers onto the new sentencing code. No politician had the temerity to jump up and say: 'Hey, we're giving these guys too much time.'"

The problem goes beyond the sheer number of years people get under the new drug laws. Enforcement agents outside, spurred on by the public's drug hysteria, at times seem to be coercing crime as much as they are fighting it.

Kevin Sweeney, thirty-three, and Curtis Bristow, thirty-two, are both former residents of San Diego. They received twenty and fourteen years respectively for conspiracy to make methamphetamines. Their cases raise troubling questions about the "war" against drugs.

Sweeney and Bristow were jailed along with a hundred other defendants arrested in a four-year Drug Enforcement Administration sting operation in San Diego. One defendant was sentenced to thirty years. But the police operation itself had some ugly aspects.

A chemical store had been set up in 1985 by a man who was working with the DEA, according to a DEA agent. He began selling chemicals and glassware to would-be methamphetamine makers and turning their names and addresses over to the DEA, the agent testified. In the ensuing four years, according to trial testimony, he sold hundreds of pounds of ephedrine over the counter. Ephedrine is the key ingredient in illicit meth. It's illegal to sell in the state of California.

One of his customers was a fifteen-year-old boy. At the time, a DEA agent was also directly involved in the store's operation.

At the culmination of the sting operation in 1989, the store owner testified that he cleared $900,000 in one year from the sale of ephedrine that the DEA allowed him to keep in addition to money they paid him.

He also testified that he taught novices how to make the drug using the chemicals and glassware he sold them. A rough estimate of the amount of drugs he put on the street under the auspices of the DEA is mind-boggling.

Attorneys have appealed the charges as "outrageous government conduct," but given the political nature of drugs today, no one holds out much hope for relief.

Bristow, who worked for the government as a sandblaster, had no criminal record other than traffic violations. He was sentenced to 163 months for possession of the chemicals he bought from the chemical store.

Sweeney, with one prior felony on his record, got 240 months in federal prison.

It's easy for a judge to say "twenty years" or "thirty years." It takes only a few seconds to declare. It's also easy for the person in the street to say: "Well, this criminal has harmed society and should be locked up for a long time."

The public is unable to imagine what the added time does to a convict and what it does to his family.

Two years is a lot of time. Twenty or thirty years is a Mount Everest of time, and very few can climb it. And what happens to them on the way up makes one not want to be around if and when they return.

The first thing a convict feels when he receives an inconceivably long sentence is shock. The shock usually wears off after about two years, when all his appeals have been denied. He then enters a period of self-hatred because of what he's done to himself and his family.

If he survives that emotion—and some don't—he begins to swim the rapids of rage, frustration, and alienation. When he passes through the rapids, he finds himself in the calm waters of impotence, futility, and resignation. It's not a life one can look forward to living. The future is totally devoid of hope, and people without any hope are dangerous—either to themselves or others.

These long-timers will also have to serve their time in increasingly overcrowded and violent prisons. As I write this, authorities are building a prefab unit next door to my cellblock that will hold three hundred new convicts. Some two-man cells here already hold three people. There are twelve hundred of us in a prison that was designed and built for five hundred.

A more sinister phenomenon is the growing length of the chemical pill line daily at the prison hospital, the place where convicts go for daily doses of tranquilizers and psychotropic drugs such as Prolixin and Haldol. The need for these medications is a sign of the turmoil inside these long-timers.

Indeed, it is ironic that men who are spending decades incarcerated for illicit drug activities are now doped up by government doctors to help them bear the agony of their sentences.

Two years ago, the chemical pill line was very short. Now it snakes along for a good distance. Society is creating a class of men with nothing else to lose but their minds.

MUMIA ABU-JAMAL
1954–

In late 1968, in the wake of the assassinations of Martin Luther King, Jr., and Robert Kennedy, rebellions in 125 U.S. cities, and the other tumultuous events of that year, fourteen-year-old Mumia Abu-Jamal (then named Wesley Cook) co-founded the Philadelphia chapter of the Black Panther Party. From then through 1981, he was the object of continual police and FBI monitoring. Since 1981 he has been in prison, and on death row since mid-1982.

Between 1970 and 1981, Abu-Jamal was a journalist; his daily show on Philadelphia's WUHY (now WHYY) had attracted a wide audience on National Public Radio, Mutual Black Network, and National Black Network. Known as "the voice of the voiceless," he was especially noted for his searing attacks on police brutality and his association with MOVE (the organization aerial bombed by the Philadelphia police in 1985, incinerating sixty-two homes and eleven people in a predominantly African-American neighborhood).

On a December night in 1981, a Philadelphia policeman stopped Abu-Jamal's brother for a traffic violation and was forcibly subduing him. Abu-Jamal, moonlighting as a cab-driver, arrived on the scene and went to his brother's aid, bearing a lawfully carried revolver. Within minutes, the arresting officer was fatally shot several times and Abu-Jamal was critically wounded from a gunshot to the chest. What actually happened that night has become the subject of national and international controversy, partly because Abu-Jamal's subsequent trial for first-degree murder was grossly and blatantly unfair.

The trial judge (a former Philadelphia undersheriff) ruled that Abu-Jamal could not continue as his own counsel and had to be replaced by a court-appointed attorney, who continued to insist that he was unprepared and unwilling to take the assignment. Abu-Jamal was removed from the courtroom during most of the trial and not allowed access to any audio or written record of the proceedings. Exculpatory evidence was suppressed, witnesses were intimidated by the police into changing their testimony, the defense was denied access to evidence and potential witnesses, and the argument for the death penalty was based largely on Abu-Jamal's political beliefs and affiliations.

After a death warrant was signed for his execution in August 1995, a major effort was launched to secure a new trial for Abu-Jamal. At the time of this writing, his fate is still being decided in the courts.

During his many years on death row, Abu-Jamal has continued writing. His essays have appeared in periodicals such as The Nation *and the* Yale Law Journal, *and two volumes of his writings have been published:* Live from Death Row *(1995) and* Death Blossoms *(1997). When* Live from Death Row *came out, he was put in solitary as punishment for violating Pennsylvania's law against prisoners conducting a "business."*

B-Block Days and Nightmares

> *For whence did Dante take the materials of his hell but from our actual world? And yet he made a very proper hell of it.*
>
> —ARTHUR SCHOPENHAUER,
> "HOMO HOMINI LUPUS"*

A SHOVE, A slur, a flurry of punches, and an inmate is cuffed and hustled to the restricted housing unit (RHU), where a beating commences. Wrapped in the sweet, false escape of dreams, I hear the unmistakable sounds of meat being beaten by blackjack, of bootfalls, yells, curses; and it merges into the mind's moviemaking machine, evoking distant memories of some of the Philadelphia Police Department's greatest hits—on me.

---

* From *The World as Will and Representation* by Arthur Schopenhauer, translated by E. F. Payne; Dover Press, 1966.

"Get off that man, you fat, greasy, racist, redneck pig bitch muthafucka!"

My tired eyes snap open; the cracks, thuds, "oofs!" come in all too clear. Damn. No dream.

Anger simmers at this abrupt intrusion into one of life's last pleasures on B block—"home" of the state's largest death row—the all-too-brief respite of dreams.

Another dawn, another beating, another shackled inmate pummeled into the concrete by a squadron of guards.

This was late October 1989, the beginning of furious days and nights when prisoners throughout the state erupted in rage. The scene had been replayed a thousand gruesome times, leading to the modest demand that Huntingdon's administrators put an end to beatings of handcuffed prisoners in B block. The conflict it prompted was ultimately crushed by club and boot, by fire hose and taser electric stun gun.

As walls fall in the Eastern bloc, and as demonstrators rejoice over an end to state police brutality, walls climb ever higher in the West. Prisons in America jeer at the rhetoric of liberty espoused by those who now applaud Eastern Europe's glasnost. The U.S. Supreme Court has welded prison doors shut. It has cut off the rights of free press, religion, or civil rights. (See *Shabazz v. O'Lone** and *Thornburgh v. Abbott*† for examples.) Indeed, in the late 1980s the term "prisoners' rights" became oxymoronic.

The riots that rocked Pennsylvania prisons were flickering reminders of this reality: they were not riots of aggression but of desperation, of men pushed beyond fear, beyond reason, by the clang not only of prison gates but of the slamming of doors to the courthouse, their only legal recourse.

At Huntingdon's A block, fistfights between guard and prisoner evolved into a full-scale riot.

"Walk, you fuckin' nigger! I'm not gonna carry your black ass!"

"You black nigger motherfucker!" Grunts, thuds, groans, and curses assailed the ear as a bloody promenade of cuffed prisoners, many of them the A-block rebels, were dragged, flogged, and flayed down the dirty gray corridors of B block's death row en route to outdoor cages, man-sized dog pens of chain-link fence.

---

* *Estate of Shabazz v. O'Lone* 482 U.S. 342, 107 S.Ct. 2400 (1987).
† *Thornburgh v. Abbott* 490 U.S. 401, 109 S.Ct. 1874 (1989).

"Officer," a visiting guard barked to a Huntingdon regular, "stop dragging that man!"

"Captain," the local guard answered, her voice pitched higher by rage, "this fuckin' nigger don't wanna walk!"

The prisoners were herded into cages—most bloody, some in underwear, all wet, all exposed to the night air for hours.

Days later, Camp Hill in central Pennsylvania erupted, with prisoners taking hostages, assaulting some, and putting much of the forty-eight-year-old facility to the torch. For two nights the state's most overcrowded prison stole the public's attention. It took a battery of guards and state troopers to wrest back some semblance of control.

"Say 'I'm a nigger!' Say it!" the baton-wielders taunted black prisoners, beating those who refused, according to MOVE political prisoner and eyewitness Chuck Africa, who, although not a participant in the rebellion, was nonetheless beaten by guards.

Days after the fires of Camp Hill cooled, while convicts stood shackled together in the soot-covered yard, Philadelphia's Holmesburg burst into its worst riot in almost twenty years. At its peak, prisoners yelled, "Camp Hill! Camp Hill!"

Now, as costs for "Camp Hell"'s reconstruction soar (latest estimate: $21 million), and bills are introduced to cover county costs for riot prosecutions (to the tune of $1.25 million), one must question the predictably conventional wisdom attributing the days and nights of rage to simple overcrowding. To be sure, the system's "jam and cram" policy was a factor, but only one among many.

In 1987 the Governor's Interdepartmental Task Force on Corrections, composed of eight cabinet-level secretaries, issued a comprehensive report calling for changes in the state's prisons: reform of the misconduct system, institution of earnest (known as "good") time, liberalization of visiting procedures, release of death row prisoners from the RHU, and introduction of substantial education programs. The report, despite its pedigree, died a pauper's death, its biggest promises unfulfilled.

The naming of David Owens, Jr., as prison commissioner in 1987, the first black in the top post, may have heightened expectations, especially among blacks, who make up 56 percent of the prison population, but it also deepened frustrations. Prisoners saw no change in rule by predominantly rural whites over predominantly urban Afros and Latinos. Was it mere coincidence that rebellion burned hottest at Camp Hill, within sight of the commissioner's office?

Owens's tenure proved as short-lived as it was historic. Politicians protested when he proposed nominal compensation for prisoners who lost their property in the state's shakedown after the riots. Mindful of looming gubernatorial elections and of politicians angling to make Owens and the prisons an issue, Pennsylvania's first-term, socially conservative governor, Robert Casey, accepted Owens's resignation. With the state's captive population breaking twenty-one thousand, prisons overcrowded by 50 percent, and more than seven hundred convicts in the federal system, it's not surprising that there are now no takers for Owens's politically sensitive job.

Perhaps there is a certain symmetry in the circumstance of a prison system in crisis in the very state where the world's first true penitentiary arose, under Quaker influence. Two hundred years after initiation of this grim experiment, it is clear that it has failed.*

One state representative (since criticized by her colleagues for making "irresponsible" statements) boldly told United Press International the simple hidden truth. Unless serious change is forthcoming, she predicted, "we are going to continue to have riots."

Repression is not change; it's the same old stuff.

The Nation, April 1990

Skeleton Bay

> *Distrust anyone in whom the desire to punish is powerful.*
>
> —FRIEDRICH NIETZSCHE

As OF 1993, according to U.S. Bureau of Justice statistics, there were 119,951 people including parolees imprisoned in California.† At last count, California had over twenty-eight prisons and spends over $1 billion annually ($1,000,000,000!) on prisons. One

---

* Quaker prison experiment, Walnut St. Penitentiary, 1790, Philadelphia, Pennsylvania.

† A recent *New York Times* poll shows that more than one million people are now in U.S. state and federal prisons.

billion! And then there's Pelican Bay prison, a hellish home for thirty-seven hundred prisoners, located in an isolated rural area called Crescent City, California. If Pelican Bay prison is a hell,* then its special housing unit (SHU), commonly called SHOE, is the lower depths, where nearly thirteen hundred men are consigned to a state program of torture and governmental terrorism, so much so that major news agencies, such as CBS's *60 Minutes*, have reported on the unit.

Prisoners there haven't taken the abusive treatment lying down, as evidenced by a civil suit filed in federal court, charging the state with "lawless" activity. "The law stops at the gates of Pelican Bay," attorney Susan Creighton told the court in her opening argument late September in San Francisco. At the SHU, men are beaten, burned, and isolated by state officers. Prisoners spend twenty-two and a half hours a day in windowless eight-by-ten cells, with no human contact or educational opportunities.

One defense psychologist, Dr. Craig Haney, found "chronic depression, hallucinations and thought disorders" at levels existing at no other prison in the United States. The symptoms were comparable only to findings from a psychiatric prison in the former East Germany, known for torture and solitary confinement, Haney testified. Indeed, the conditions are so horrendous that a former warden of the infamous hellhole Marion, Illinois, openly criticized Pelican, tracing a record of numerous injuries and deaths to guards' routine use of excessive force.

Charles E. Fenton, ex-warden of Marion Federal Penitentiary testified in the suit, "There seems to be an attitude . . . that it's proper for staff to shoot at inmates" (*San Francisco Chronicle*, September 29, 1993).

"They either absolutely don't know what they're doing or they're deliberately inflicting pain," said Fenton.

Marion Federal Penitentiary, known as Son of Alcatraz, was itself condemned as violative of fundamental human rights by Amnesty International. Pelican Bay (called Skeleton Bay by prisoners) is Son of Marion, taken to such an inhumane degree that even Mar-

---

* In January 1995 the U.S. District Court held the state could continue operating Pelican Bay, and while the U.S. District Judge Thelton Henderson was critical of the unit, he declined to declare it unconstitutional, despite evidence that guards inflicted unjustified beatings upon and hog-tying of prisoners.

ion's old warden gasps in shock at the ugliness that is his spawn. Five years from now, will we be moaning about the Son of Pelican?

If we don't rumble now, against *all* fascistic control units, such as Pelican, Pennsylvania's SMU, Shawnee Unit at Marianna, Florida, and Colorado State Penitentiary, you may not be able to rumble later.

The solution is not in the courts but in an awake, aware people.

OCTOBER 1993

Already Out of the Game

THE NEWEST POLITICAL FEVER sweeping the nation, the "three strikes, you're out" rage, will, barring any last-minute changes, become law in the United States, thereby opening the door to a state-by-state march to an unprecedented prison building boom. What most politicians know, however, is what most people do not—that "three strikes, you're out" will do next to nothing to eradicate crime, and will not create the illusive dream of public safety.

They also know that it will be years before the bills come due, but when they do, they'll be real doozies; by then, they reason, they'll be out of office, and it'll be another politician's problem. That's because the actual impact of "three strikes" will not be felt for at least ten to twenty years from now, simply because that's the range someone arrested today would face already (under the current laws), and the additional time, not to mention additional costs, will kick in then.

It seems a tad superfluous to state that already some thirty-four states have habitual offender (so-called career criminal) laws, which call for additional penalties on the second, not the third, felony, in addition to the actual crime. As with every law, taxpayers will have to "pay the cost to be the boss." Pennsylvanians are paying over $600 million this fiscal year for their prisons; Californians, over $2.7 billion this year, with costs for next year expected to top costs for higher education.

As prisons become increasingly geriatric, with populations hitting their fifties and sixties, those already atmospheric costs will balloon exponentially for expected health costs, so that although many Americans, an estimated thirty-seven million, don't have guaranteed health care, prisoners will, although of doubtful quality.

Frankly, it's always amazing to see politicians sell their "We-gotta-get-tough-on-crime" schtick to a country that is already the world's leading incarcerator, and perhaps more amazing to see the country buy it. One state has already trod that tough ground, back in the 1970s; California "led" the nation in 1977 with their tough "determinate sentencing" law, and their prison population exploded over 500 percent, from 22,486 in 1973 to 119,000 in 1993, now boasting the largest prison system in the Western world—50 percent larger than the entire federal prison system. Do Californians—rushing to pass the "three strikes, you're out" ballot initiative—feel safer?

A more cynical soul, viewing this prison-boom bill through the lens of economic interest, might suppose that elements of the correctional industry, builders, guards' unions, and the like are fueling the boom, at least in part.

Another element is the economy itself, where America enters the postindustrial age, when Japan produces the world's computer chips; Germany produces high performance autos; and America produces . . . prisons. Prisons are where America's jobs programs, housing programs, and social control programs merge into a dark whole; and where those already outside of the game can be exploited and utilized to keep the game going.

MARCH 1994

JIMMY SANTIAGO BACA

For biographical material on Baca see page 252.

Jimmy Santiago Baca was the principal screenwriter for Bound by Honor, *a major Hollywood movie directed by Taylor Hackford about Chicano life in the barrio and prison. When Hackford got permission to shoot most of the film in San Quentin, Baca also became a key adviser and participant in the staging. He describes the traumatic effects of this experience in the following piece.*

Past Present

W HEN I FINISHED my last prison term twelve years ago, I never dreamed I would go back. But not long ago I found myself looking up at the famous San Quentin tower as I followed an escort guard through the main gates. I should have been overjoyed since this time I was a free man, the writer of a film which required a month of location-shooting there. But being there had a disquieting effect on me. I was confused. I knew that I would be able to leave every night after filming, but the enclosing walls, the barbed wire, and the guards in the towers shouldering their carbines made old feelings erupt in me. While my mind told me I was free, my spirit snarled as if I were a prisoner again, and I couldn't shake the feeling. Emotionally, I could not convince myself that I was not going to be subjected once more to horrible indignities, that I would not have to live through it all again. Each morning when the guards checked my shoulder bag and clanked shut the iron door behind me, the old convict in me rose up full of hatred and rage for the guards, the walls, the terrible indecency of the place. I was still the same man who had entered there freely, a man full of love for his family and his life. But another self from the past reawakened, an imprisoned self, seething with the desire for vengeance on all things not imprisoned.

As I followed the guard, passing with the crew and the actors from one compound to another, a hollow feeling of disbelief possessed me and I was struck dumb. The grounds were impeccably planted and groomed, serene as a cemetery. Streamlined circles of flowers and swatches of smooth lawn rolled to trimmed green margins of pruned shrubbery, perfectly laid out against the limestone and red brick cellblocks. But I knew that when you penetrated beyond this pretty landscaping, past the offices, also with their bouquets of flowers, past the cellblock's thick walls, there thrived America's worst nightmare. There the green, concealing surface lifted from the bubbling swamp, a monster about to rise from its dark depths. There writhed scaly demons, their claws and fangs primed for secret and unspeakable brutalities.

Even within those walls, the free man that I am eventually found himself able to forgive the sufferings of the past. But the convict in me was inflamed by everything I saw. It was all so familiar, so full of bitter memory: the milk-paned windows and linoleum tiles of the offices, the flyers thumbtacked to cork boards on the walls; the vast lower yard, and the great upper yard with its corrugated shed pocked with light-pierced, jagged bullet holes; the looming limestone cellblocks. The thought of the thousands of human beings whose souls were murdered here in the last hundred years made my blood run cold. The faintly humming body energy of six thousand imprisoned human beings bored a smoking hole in my brain. And through that hole, as if through a prison-door peephole, I saw all the free people going about their lives on the other side, while my place was again with the convicts. Anyone opening that door from the other side must die, or be taken hostage and forced to understand our hatred, made to experience the insane brutality that is the convict's daily lot, and that makes him, in turn, brutal and insane.

Since I was acting in the film, I had to dress out daily in banaroos, prison-issue blue denims. I was made up to look younger than I am, as I might have looked in 1973. After this outer transformation, I seemed more and more to become the person I had left behind twelve years ago, until finally that former self began to consume the poet and husband and father who had taken his place. I didn't know what was happening to me.

Dragged back into dangerous backwaters, I encountered my old demons. The crew seemed to sense this and gave me a wide berth. The familiar despair and rage of the prisoners was like a current sucking me down into the sadness of their wasted lives. The guards who paced the cellblocks now were no different from the guards who had leered and spit at me, beaten and insulted me. Even though I knew that now I wouldn't have to take their shit and that now I could speak up for the cons who had to hold their tongues, part of me was still caught in this time warp of displacement.

When we went to the recreational building, where I was to choose some of the convicts to act as extras, I was surprised by how young they were. I realized I was now the old man among them. In my prison days, the convicts had always seemed to be grizzled older guys, but now, for the most part, they were young kids in their twenties. After I selected the group of extras, I explained to them that the movie was about three kids from East L.A., one of whom goes to prison. As I spoke, my convict stance and manners came back to me, and the old slang rolled off my tongue as if I had never left. Memories of my own imprisonment assailed me, dissolving the barrier between us.

Although technically I was free, that first week I used my freedom in a strange way, venting hatred on anyone who looked at me, the cons included, because they, too, in the prison world, are joined in their own hierarchy of brutality.

One day a documentary crew came to where we were filming in the weight pit and asked to interview me. Prisoners of every race were present. I looked around me and was filled with contempt for every living soul there. After repeatedly refusing to speak, while microphones were shoved in my face, I suddenly decided to answer their questions.

How did I feel about returning to a prison to help film and act in this movie I had written? Was I proud and pleased? I sat on a bench-press seat curling about thirty pounds as I spoke.

I said I hated being back and that no movie could begin to show the injustices practiced here. I said that fame was nothing weighed against the suffering and brutality of prison life. I told them that these cons should tear the fucking walls down and allow no one to dehumanize them in this way. What were my feelings about being here?

I said that I hated everyone and just wanted to be left alone, and fuck them all. Just leave me alone!

I got up and walked away. There was a terrible tearing wound in my heart that I thought no one could see. But Gina, the associate producer, came up to me weeping, pleading for me to come back to myself, to be again the man she knew. She hugged me. One of the actors also approached and talked to me quietly. In spite of their attempts to comfort me, I felt helplessly encaged by powers I couldn't vanquish or control. I was ensnared in a net of memories. When the few convicts who had been hanging with me started to put some distance between us, I felt as if no one could see me or hear me. I was disoriented, as if I had smashed full force into some invisible barrier.

After a couple of days, I came out of it, dazed and bewildered, shocked and weak as if after major surgery. People I previously couldn't bring myself to speak to, I spoke with now. I felt that sense of wonder one feels after a narrow escape from death.

As I continued to live my double life, I became a keen observer of both worlds. On the streets people could cry freely, but in prison tears led to challenges and deep, embittered stares. In prison no one shakes hands, that common gesture of friendship and trust. The talk never varies from the subjects of freedom and imprisonment, the stories and the laughs are about con jobs and scams. Outside everything is always changing, there are surprises, and you talk about that. But in prison the only news is old news. It is a dead land, filled with threat, where there is no appeal from the death sentence meted out for infractions of the convict code. Imagine being hunted through the jungles of Nam day after day for twenty years, and that will tell you a little of what prison is about.

The days went by. When we finished filming, late in the evenings, I would go back to my trailer, change into my street clothes, and walk alone across the lower yard. The dead exercise pit, where many of the men spend a lot of time buffing themselves out, looked forlorn. It was very late as I crossed the lower yard to a waiting van, but the lights around the lower yard, huge, looming, twenty-eyed klieg lights, made it seem like daytime. Everything about prison life distorts reality, starting with the basic assumption that imprisonment can alter criminal behavior, when the truth is that it entrenches it more firmly. Confinement perverts and destroys every skill a man needs to live productively in society.

As I walked on, my mind full of these thoughts, buses from all over California pulled up in the eerie yellow light, disgorging new inmates who were lined up to get their prison clothes before being marched off to the cellblocks. A van was waiting to take me back to my corporate-paid condo, where there was fresh food waiting for me, where I could relax and phone my wife, turn on some soft music and write a little, read a little, in the silence; walk to the window and smell the cool night air and look across the bay to the Golden Gate Bridge and beyond to San Francisco, a city as angelic at night as any heavenly sanctum conjured up in medieval tapestries.

But all of these anticipated pleasures only intensified my anguish for those I was leaving behind, for those imprisoned who have—nothing. The cells in San Quentin's Carson block are so small that a man cannot bend or stretch without bruising himself against some obstacle. And two men share each cell. The cellblocks stink of mildew and drying feces. The noise is a dull, constant, numbing beating against the brain. Had I really inhabited such a cell for seven

years? It didn't happen, it couldn't have happened. How did I survive? Who was that kid that lived through this horror? It was me.
Since that time I had grown, changed; but I was still afraid to touch
that reality with my mind, that unspeakable pain.

On those lonely night walks into freedom, the tremendous grief
and iron rage of the convict revived in me. The empty yard, with
its watchful glare, mercilessly mirrored the cold, soul-eaten barren-
ness of those confined within. In the world outside, convicts have
mothers and wives and children, but here, in this world, they have
nothing but the speed of their fists. They have only this one weapon
of protest against the oppression of brain-dead keepers who represent a society whose judicial standards are so disparate for rich
and poor.

When a man leaves prison, he cannot look into the mirror for
fear of seeing what he has become. In the truest sense, he no longer
knows himself. Treated like a child by the guards, forced to relin-
quish every vestige of dignity, searched at whim, cursed, beaten,
stripped, deprived of all privacy, he has lived for years in fear; and
this takes a terrible toll. The saddest and most unforgivable thing
of all is that most first-time felons could be rehabilitated, if anyone
cared or tried. But society opts for the quickest and least expensive
alternative—stark confinement, with no attempt at help—that in
the future will come to haunt it.

Each day that we filmed at San Quentin, where I was surrounded
by men whose sensibilities were being progressively eroded by
prison society, the urge grew in me to foment a revolt: tear down
the walls, herd the guards into the bay, burn down everything until
nothing was left but a smoldering heap of blackened bricks and
molten iron. And I was filled with a yearning to escape, to go home
and live the new life I had fought so hard to make. The two worlds
I inhabited then were so far apart I could find no bridge between
them, no balance in myself. My disorientation was radical.

My days were spent in this prison, among men who had been
stripped of everything, who had no future; and of an evening I
might find myself in the affluence of Mill Valley, attending a ballet
with my visiting wife and two sons, my wife's cousin's daughter
dancing on stage in a mist of soft lights. . . .

As the weeks passed, I realized I had gone through changes that
left me incapable of recognizing my own life. What was most
shocking to me was not that I had survived prison, but that the

prisons still stood, that the cruelty of that life was still going on; that in San Quentin six thousand men endured it daily, and that the system was growing stronger day by day. I realized that America is two countries: a country of the poor and deprived, and a country of those who had a chance to make something of their lives. Two societies, two ways of living, going on side by side every hour of every day. And in every aspect of life, from opportunities to manners and morals, the two societies stand in absolute opposition. Most Americans remain ignorant of this, of the fact that they live in a country that holds hostage behind bars another populous country of their fellow citizens.

I do not advocate the liberation of murderers, rapists, and sociopaths. But what of the vast majority of convicts, imprisoned for petty crimes that have more to do with wrong judgment than serious criminal intent or character defect? They are not yet confirmed in criminality, but the system makes them criminals. Society must protect itself against those who are truly dangerous. But they comprise only a small proportion of our prison population.

One day, late in the afternoon after we had shot a riot scene, the cellblock was in disarray: burning mattresses, men screaming, hundreds of cons shaking the bars with such force that the whole concrete and iron cellblock groaned and creaked with their rage. The cons were not acting. The scene had triggered an outrage waiting to be expressed. Finally, all that was left were a few wisps of black smoke, the tiers dripped water, and hundreds of pounds of soaked, charred newspapers were heaped on the concrete. Clothing and bed sheets, shredded to rags, dangled from the concertina wire surrounding the catwalks.

Quiet fell, the kind of dead quiet that comes after hundreds of men have been venting their wrath for hours, cursing and flailing and threatening. The smoldering trash on the cellblock floor testified to a fury that now withdrew, expressing itself only in their eyes. One of the convicts walked over to me through the silence. He told me that another convict wanted to speak with me, and led me to a cell that was in total darkness, where he spoke my name. A voice from the top bunk replied. I heard the man jump from the bunk to the floor and come to the bars. He was a tall, young Chicano with a crew cut, whose eyes were white orbs. He lived in the absolute darkness of the blind, in this small cell no bigger than a phone booth. In a soft voice he told me he had a story to tell, and asked my advice. He wanted his story to go out into the world, in print or on film.

Never has a man evoked from me such sympathy and tenderness as this blind warrior. It was plain to me that he had suffered terribly in this man-made hell, and that, somehow, his spirit had survived. I knew that his courage and his heart were mountains compared to the sand grains of my heart and courage. From behind the bars, this tall, lean brown kid with blind eyes told me how, after the guards had fired random warning shots into a group of convicts, he found himself blinded for life. I looked at him and saw the beautiful face of a young Spanish aristocrat who might be standing on a white balcony overlooking a garden of roses and lilies at dawn. I could also see in him the warrior. How softly he spoke and how he listened, so attentive to the currents of sound.

Blind Chicano brother of mine, these words are for you, and my work must henceforth be a frail attempt to translate your heart for the world, your courage and *carnalismo*. While the world blindly grabs at and gorges on cheap titillations, you go on in your darkness, in your dark cell, year after year, groping in your imagination for illumination that will help you make sense of your life and your terrible fate. I couldn't understand you. I could only look at you humbly, young Chicano warrior. You spoke to me, spoke to me with the words and in the spirit in which I have written my poems. Looking at you, I reaffirmed my vow to never give up struggling for my people's right to live with dignity. From you I take the power to go on fighting until my last breath for our right to live in freedom, secure from the brutality in which you are imprisoned. From your blind eyes, I reimagined my vision and my quest to find words that can cut through steel. You asked me to tell your story. I promised I would.

Today, as I was writing these words, a sociologist consulting on the movie led me to a viewing screen to see the eclipse: July 11th, 1991, 11:00 A.M. I looked through the shade glass and saw the sun and moon meet. I thought of you, my blind brother, and how our eyes met, yours and mine, dark moons and white suns that touched for a moment in our own eclipse, exchanging light and lives before we parted: I to tell my people's stories as truly as I can, you to live on in your vision-illuminated darkness. And I thought how the

Mayans, at the time of eclipse, would rekindle with their torches the altar flame, bringing the temples to new light; how their great cities and pyramids came out of darkness and they journeyed to the sun in their hearts, prepared to live for another age with new hope and love, forgiveness and courage. The darkness again gave way to the light, and I thought of you in your darkness, and of myself, living in what light I can make or find; and of our meeting each in our own eclipse and lighting the altar flame in each other's hearts, before passing on in our journeys to give light to our people's future.

Copies of my books that I had ordered from New York arrived in San Quentin on the last day of filming. I signed them and handed them out to the convicts who had helped us. As they accepted these books of my poems, I saw respect in their eyes. To me, I was still one of them; for them, I was someone who had made it into a free and successful life. This sojourn in prison had confused me, re-awakening the old consuming dragons of hatred and fear. But I had faced them, finally, and perhaps I will be a better poet for it. Time will tell.

The next morning, I woke up early and packed my bags. Then I went back to San Quentin for the last time. The production company vans and trailers, the mountains of gear, the crew and the actors, were gone. I made my way across the sad and vacant yard to make my last farewells. This final visit was a purposeful one: I would probably never set foot in a prison again. I was struck with pity for those who had to stay, and with simple compassion, too, for myself: for the pain I had endured in this month, and for that eighteen-year-old kid I once was, who had been confined behind walls like these and had survived, but who would never entirely be free of the demons he met behind bars. This last pilgrimage was for him, who is the better part of me and the foundation for the man I am today, still working in the dark to create for my people our own unique light.

PERMISSIONS

Shakur, Assata, from *Assata* by Assata Shakur. Copyright © 1987 by Zed Books, Ltd. Published by Lawrence Hill Books, an imprint of Chicago Review Press, Inc., 814 N. Franklin Street, Chicago, IL 60610. Reprinted by permission of Chicago Review Press.

Stafford, Norma, "In Santa Cruz" and "The Gone One" from *Dear Somebody: The Prison Poetry of Norma Stafford* (Santa Cruz, Calif.: Privately Printed, 1975). Copyright © 1975 by Norma Stafford. Reprinted by permission of the author.

Thomas, Piri, from *Seven Long Times* by Piri Thomas. Copyright © 1974 by Praeger Publishers. Copyright © 1994 by Piri Thomas. Reprinted with permission from the publisher (Houston: Arte Público Press—University of Houston, 1994).

Wantling, William, from "Sestina to San Quentin," "Poetry," and "Who's Bitter?" Copyright © 1979 by William Wantling. Reprinted by permission of Ruth Wantling.

Washington, Jerome, "Diamond Bob," "The Blues Merchant," "Nobody's Hoss," "Barracuda and Sheryl," and "Shing-a-Ling and China" from *Iron House: Stories from the Yard* by Jerome Washington. Copyright © 1992 by Jerome Washington. Reprinted by permission of QED Press.

Wozencraft, Kim, from *Notes from the Country Club* by Kim Wozencraft. Copyright © 1993 by Code 3 Communications, Inc. Reprinted by permission of Houghton Mifflin Co. All rights reserved.